"Arrest? On what charge?" Gerrard hissed.

Takara spoke once more to the soldier, who replied with an imperious air.

She translated, "The charges include—but are not limited to—invasion, illegal migration, arms smuggling, trafficking with the enemies of Mercadia, refusal to speak High Mercadian—"

Gerrard raked his sword from its scabbard. "Better damned well add resisting arrest! Attack!"

MAGIC: The Gathering®

A World Of Magic

MERCADIAN MASQUES

MASQUERADE CYCLE · BOOK I

Francis Lebaron

Mercadian Masques
©1999 Wizards of the Coast, Inc.
All Rights Reserved.

Cover art by Kev Walker
First Printing: September 1999
Library of Congress Catalog Card Number: 98-88151

9 8 7 6 5 4 3 2 1

ISBN: 0-7869-1188-3
T8733-620

U.S., CANADA, ASIA,
PACIFIC, & LATIN AMERICA
Wizards of the Coast, Inc.
P.O. Box 707
Renton, WA 98057-0707
+1-800-324-6496

EUROPEAN HEADQUARTERS
Wizards of the Coast, Belgium
P.B. 2031
2600 Berchem
Belgium
+32-70-23-32-77

Visit our website at **www.wizards.com**

ACKNOWLEDGMENTS

No writer ever works entirely alone, and no book is truly written by a single person. This book owes a great deal to many people who generously contributed to its pages.

I owe a great debt to the people who edited the book in its various incarnations: Mary Kirchoff, Peter Archer, Pat McGilligan, and Jess Lebow. Lucky is the writer who finds a good editor, and each of mine brought new layers of complexity to the story. The Magic continuity team, led by Scott McGough and Daneen McDermott, made sure I remained true to the spirit and letter of Dominarian history, while conceptual artists Chippy, Don Hazeltine, Dana Knutson, Ron Spears, Mark Tedin, and Tony Waters brought the city of Mercadia and its environs alive for me.

My wife and daughter were far more tolerant of this project than I had any right to expect, and my wife in particular was a disciplined taskmaster, urging me, when I was lounging in front of the television set, to "get into the study and finish the damn book!"

Finally, I want to thank a man who has been both a fine editor, a superior writer, and a good friend. Rob King, this book belongs to you as much as to me. Thank you.

DEDICATION

For Francis L. Archer
(1919 – 1995)

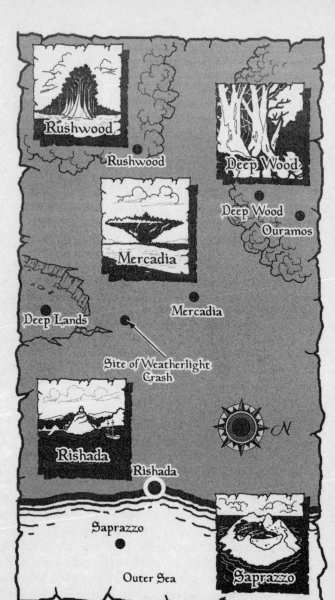

CHAPTER 1

Years later, Atalla could remember every moment of the night he saw the ship that flew.

It was early, at least two hours before morningsinging. The sky still held the pale yellow of dawn, though darker streaks showed where the deeper orange of full daylight was beginning to break through. Atalla had risen before sunrise because Father had promised he might ride his first jhovall, and the ten-year-old boy had been far too excited to sleep. All through the dark hours, he lay on his pallet, staring into the blackness, listening to the soft breathing of Mother and Father asleep in the adjoining bed. In the stillness of the country night, he could hear the mournful cries of mating qomallen to the south, and when the hour was latest he heard the distant booming vibrations of nightsinging from the city.

As the walls of the cottage slowly lightened, Atalla rose. Carefully, to avoid waking his parents, he slipped out the door.

Before him the plains of the west stretched to a horizon that was still only a dim line between sky and earth. Atalla stood still, drinking in the rich, heady smells of the air; the faint odor of human habitation mixed with the scents of farm animals and the wild creatures of the plains. Breezes tousled his black hair and riffled through his nightshirt. His heart thumped in his chest, and he felt deeply, warmly alive.

He passed along the side of the house to the jhovall stable. The six-legged tiger-creatures patiently purred in their stalls. Father had said Atalla might ride the smallest one, Skotcha. The boy stood by her head, gently stroking her wet nose for several minutes. Even a small jhovall could tear across the plain like a dust devil, could kill a red wolf, could carry a farm boy on plenty of adventures. Atalla fondly patted her shaggy gray flank and left the stables.

The air felt dry, even for this early in the day. It would be at least two more turnings of the moon before the rains came, filling the riverbed and pond with water. Now, as the boy watched, distant eddies and clouds of brown dust moved across the endless plain under the brightening sky. The air to the south seemed to shimmer. Predawn light bent and played about the boy, caressing him.

Atalla felt a sudden pressure in the air. Something invisible violently struck his chest. The world before him exploded in a silent sound.

Atalla staggered backward, tripped, and fell. He rolled to his feet in time to see the air divide and slip away from the sides of a ship, which burst across the screaming sky. A flying ship? Atalla had seen oceangoing galleys last year in Rishada, but a flying ship? It hurtled through the air as if shot from one of the great cannons that guarded the city. A flying warship—more than that, a comet, a sign from the heavens. . . .

What was that old myth Father spoke of? The Uniter?

A sudden gale threw Atalla down. Rocks dug into his knees. The grass thrashed like flames. The barn's thatch was ripped free. Jhovalls shrieked in their stalls. Every window in the house shattered. The ship screamed so low overhead that lines trailing from its side slapped the roof. For one frozen moment, a bull's head stared at him over the rail. With a great whoosh, the ship disappeared behind the house.

There was a heart-stopping crash. Wood rent and splintered. Screams came with the sound. Earth flew outward in a pelting hail. The ground shook. There was a loud crack, a thud of some heavy body, and then silence.

The ship had crashed in the plowed field to the north of Atalla's home.

He sprinted around the cottage, meeting his mother and father. A confused babble of voices rose ahead. Charging out to the brow of the low rise, they gazed down. Atalla's jaw dropped as the scene opened before him.

Two deep furrows had been dug right through the heart of the simsass plants. Broken stalks drooped forlornly, sap oozing from their sides. At the end of the furrows was the strange ship. One sail—were they sails? Atalla wondered— had caught against the tartoo tree, the only tree for miles around, and had snapped clean off. So had the top of the tree. The ship lay below, near the dry riverbed.

In unison, Mother and Father muttered, "I'll be damned."

* * * * *

Gerrard Capashen wiped a trickle of blood from his close-cropped beard. The once-healed cut on his left cheek had opened again, but if that was his worst injury, he was lucky. Ribs ached beneath his red waistcoat. He would have fallen if not for the helm, but it had paid him back with a blow that drove the air from his lungs. Clutching the wheel in strong hands, he managed a shuddering sigh.

"I shouldn't have taken the wheel from Hanna." Gerrard released the helm and staggered across the bridge of *Weatherlight*. "Hanna!" he gasped out, approaching the navigator. She slumped across the cartographer's desk. Gerrard tenderly embraced her. "Are you all right?"

Hanna lifted her head, breathing in short, panting gasps. She raked blonde hair back from her face and said breathlessly, "Yes . . . but what of the ship?"

"Ship be damned. What of the crew?" Gerrard said gravely.

The only other crew member on the bridge had been the cabin boy. The goblin had been hurled against the wall and was now a mere bundle of whimpering limbs.

"Are you hurt, Squee?" Gerrard asked, moving toward him.

The green-skinned creature struggled to his feet. There was no sign of serious injury. "Squee's head got cutted off!"

Gerrard smiled. "Not cut off, but I'm not sure it's on straight." As Squee cracked his neck and every other joint, Gerrard strode to the bridge window.

Beyond, the minotaur first mate helped injured crew members. Strong and surehoofed, Tahngarth himself had escaped the crash relatively unscathed.

Hanna was already heading out onto the upper deck. She gave a faint yelp of dismay and ran aft along the slanting planks to view the damage done to the ship's sails.

Gerrard joined the minotaur. "How bad is he?" he asked, gesturing at a young sailor who gingerly cradled his arm.

Tahngarth's eyes blazed yellow beneath twisted horns. There was blood in the minotaur's flaring nostrils. "This one's not bad. Some broken bones, cuts, bruises. Orim's sickbay will be overflowing." He motioned to two crewmen, who helped the injured sailor to his feet and conducted him toward a hatch.

Gerrard nodded gravely. "At least we got out of Rath—"

"Most of us," Tahngarth said. Gerrard had only recently gained the minotaur's trust, and now there was unspoken accusation in his eyes. "There are at least two dead—thrown from the prow. They can't be alive, twisted like that. And, of course, there's Mirri, and Crovax, and Ertai—"

"Ertai?" Gerrard asked, scanning the deck with anxious eyes.

"Not here. He must not have made it."

Gerrard slapped a hand against the railing. "You're saying he's still in Rath? Damn it, how could he not have made it onto the ship? All he had to do was jump as *Weatherlight* passed under him."

"He did manage to close the portal behind us." The minotaur pointed behind Gerrard to the empty sky. "The opening is gone."

Taking in the news, Gerrard said solemnly, "Even if it weren't, we'd have to fix the spar before we could fly back to get him."

"It's worse than that," came a new voice, rumbling behind them. The two turned to see a massive man of silver haul himself up from the engine room hatch. Smoke wreathed the metal golem and coiled into the early morning sky. Karn was a living part of *Weatherlight*'s engine, and no one but Hanna knew the ship better than he. "Systems throughout the ship are burned out. Hull integrity in the bow is compromised. The left landing spine is jammed. A split has opened in the subreactor manifold. And, of course, the Thran Crystal is still damaged. Everything else will have to be fixed before we can fly, and the Thran Crystal before we can planeshift—"

Gerrard licked his lips and tasted the coppery sweetness of blood. Impatiently, he wiped his sleeve across his face. "Well, wherever we are, we're stuck for a while."

"Hoy! You up there!" a man shouted below.

The minotaur glanced thoughtfully over the rail. "Someone wants to talk to us."

"Hoy! Who are you, and what in the name of the Nine Spheres are you doing crashing into my farm?"

Gerrard took a deep breath and shrugged to the minotaur. "Now for a bit of diplomacy." He secured a coil of rope to a bulkhead and dropped one end over the side of the ship. With practiced ease, he slid down the line and stood facing the farmer. Gerrard extended a hand in greeting. "My name's Gerrard Capashen. This is my ship, *Weatherlight*."

The farmer, whose smock and bare feet indicated that the crash had awakened him, looked at Gerrard stolidly. His arms dangled at his sides. Beyond him, huddled in the doorway of the house, Gerrard could see a woman and the head and shoulders of a small boy.

"*Weatherlight?*" the farmer repeated at last.

Gerrard slowly lowered his proffered hand. "Yes."

"What . . . what is it? What are you doing here?"

Gerrard smiled humorlessly. "We crashed. That was what all that noise was."

"How in hell does a ship fly? I once heard of a Rishadan dirigible but this ain't got an air sack . . ." the farmer continued, staring incredulously at *Weatherlight*. He looked at Gerrard, fear flaring behind his coal-black eyes. "Where in all the worlds did you come from?" he whispered. Although the air around them was cool, the farmer was perspiring nervously. "Are . . . you gods?"

Gerrard's voice rose. "We're not any sort of gods. But you wouldn't understand where we came from if I told you.

Suffice it to say, we want to get our ship out of your field as much as you do. That means repairs—"

There was a loud thump as another figure, sliding down the line, landed on the ground beside him. Sisay's ebony skin gleamed in the bright light of early morning. She turned a winsome smile on the farmer. "I'm Sisay, captain of his ship—and from now on the one at her helm." Gerrard nodded a little sheepishly at that. "We apologize for any damage we've done. May I know your name, good sir?"

The farmer looked at her a moment more, then cleared his throat. "I am Tavoot."

Sisay repeated the name several times, as if digesting a fact of great importance. "Tavoot. Tavoot. And do I see behind you your wife and son?"

Tavoot gave a grunt. "Sesharral—my wife—and my son Atalla." His eyes remained on Sisay's face.

For her part, Sisay continued to beam cheerfully at the woman and boy. "I hope we didn't frighten you too much. I'm sure—"

Tavoot interrupted. "Who sent you? Are you Mercadians? You don't look Mercadian."

"No one sent us. We were fleeing from a being called Volrath," Sisay replied. "His ship was chasing ours, and we went through a portal to elude him." She looked around, taking in the cottage, the orderly garden, and the neat rows of crops surrounded by dust-covered flats, which stretched in every direction. "We need to repair our ship. Can you advise us as to where we might get some mechanical assistance?"

Tavoot turned to look east. Against the lemon-colored sky, beyond the graceful lines of the cottage, loomed a great, gray shape. Its contours were softened by the dust that blew like a fine sand through the morning air. It was a dark triangle, its tip embedded in the ground and its long, flat edge hovering above the horizon. "Maybe you ain't from Mercadia, but that's where you'll end up. Everybody in trouble ends up in Mercadia."

Staring at the strange sight, Sisay said, "The Mercadians could help us?"

"They could." A rueful smile crossed Tavoot's face. "But Mercadians only ever help themselves."

*   *   *   *   *

Atalla was a bright lad—bright and a little enterprising. He and Gerrard stood in an empty pen in the jhovall stables. The space had been shoveled and swept, and new grasses lay in a bed across the floor.

"I imagine Father would rent this space to you as cheaply as he would rent our jhovalls," the boy said, eyes ingenuous beneath his tousled black hair. "Even with the hole in the roof."

Gerrard set hands on his hips and stared up at the rafters where a large section of thatch had been torn loose. The lemon-colored sky showed beyond—dust kept this world's sky from ever looking blue. Sunlight streamed down through the hole in the roof to splash against one wall of the stables. "It won't keep out the rain."

"Oh, there won't be rain for another few moonturnings. It will keep out most of the sun. Besides, you were the ones who ripped that hole in the roof."

"Just so," Gerrard admitted. "And we do need the space to get the more severely wounded out of the sun. But as I told you—we have no Mercadian currency and little in the way of precious metals or gems to pay."

"The issue of payment needn't come up," Atalla assured him. "There is always a trade to be made."

Blinking, Gerrard said, "What do we have that you could possibly want?"

"Take me with you to Mercadia."

"Out of the question."

"I've always wanted to see the city."

"Your father wouldn't allow it."

"He needn't know. I'll leave him a note. It would only be a few days."

Gerrard turned and set a hand on the shoulder of the boy. Atalla was in fact on the verge of being a young man, he thought. He was a bright lad and knew the languages and customs of the people. A local guide and interpreter could be helpful, but there was one flaw in him. Atalla craved adventure, and young men craving adventure tend to find it. He was, all in all, a little too much like a young Gerrard. "I'm sorry, Atalla. I wouldn't want to risk it. Where I go, trouble follows. We'll find something from the ship—an old sextant or something—that you'd like in exchange for the stall—"

Atalla's young eyes grew very hard in the dim space. "Don't bother," he said, stomping out the stable door.

Just as he left, another figure entered—two figures, in fact: Takara and her blinded father, Starke. The woman's red hair was flame bright in the sun, and her muscular figure was bent to aid the shuffling man beside her. Starke was not an old man, but he seemed one now. Blinded in Rath, he wore a white bandage about his eyes. He had not shaved since the incident and had eaten little. Starke was withering daily—the wages of guilt—and now, atop his craggy head, there was a bright sheen of sunburn.

"It's in here, Father," Takara said gently. "Gerrard has found a place out of the sun, in here."

"Gerrard!" Starke growled. "He wants me dead. They all want me dead, after what I did to Sisay."

"You cannot blame them. Treachery on any ship is a capital crime," Takara replied quietly.

"I did it only to save you, my dear," Starke pleaded, miserable.

"Yes, Father, I know," Takara replied. "But the rest of the crew does not know me. They would never have sold out Sisay to rescue a complete stranger."

Starke let out an exhausted hiss. "Then get them to know you, Takara. They hate me, and if they start to hate you, they'll kill us both."

As he shuffled along, a jhovall stretched in a catnap within one stall. It rolled massively to one side, released a rumbling purr, and licked its dagger teeth.

"What is that sound!" Starke gasped. "What sort of animals are in this stable?"

"You'll be perfectly safe," Takara said.

"I'm surrounded by monsters, vicious monsters. You say I'll be safe, but every last one is after me. If you don't protect me, Takara, you're as much a monster as the rest."

Gerrard at last stepped from the empty stall, motioning Takara toward it. "You are safe, Starke. No one is out to harm you. The wrongs you committed toward Sisay have been undone, and I think even she would agree that your blinding is punishment enough for everything."

Starke visibly trembled. He seemed more terrified of Gerrard than he had been of the jhovall. Sullenly, he said, "Yes, Commander."

"I know you don't trust me," Gerrard replied easily, laying out a saddle blanket on the grassy floor, "but trust your own daughter." He glanced at the lithe and muscular woman. "Takara was imprisoned in hell, but she emerged stronger than she had been before. She was annealed by Rath, not destroyed by it."

As she helped her father sit on the saddle blanket, Takara locked eyes with Gerrard. She mouthed a silent thanks.

Gerrard nodded. He felt a sudden strong connection to this woman. It was not the heady wine of desire—though Takara had a fiery beauty, to be sure. Instead, this was the wordless understanding that comes between folk who have

faced down the same foes. It was the strange, sudden cama-
raderie of strangers.

"Sleep now, Father. You are exhausted. Others will rest
here too—those with the worst injuries. You won't be alone.
You needn't fear monsters."

Petulant to the last, Starke rolled away from her. Tears
emerged from beneath his bandage and bore in them red
flecks of dried blood.

Takara patted his shoulder once more and then stood to
leave.

Gerrard joined her. As they walked away, past stalls of
six-legged tigers, he whispered quietly, "You are showing a
great deal of grace under pressure."

She continued a few more paces before responding. "My
father—the father I loved and grew up with—is a different
man than this husk. My father is dead. That doesn't mean I
shouldn't honor him by caring for this . . . poor creature."

Shaking his head in wonder, Gerrard felt again the sense of
connection. "You have lost so much, and still you fight on."

"What else is there for heroes to do?"

* * * * *

It had taken all day to empty the wounded vessel. Five
crew members had been killed in the crash. Four others
were wounded badly enough to need bed rest in the stables.
Two had such severe head and neck injuries that Orim had
refused to let them be moved from the ship. She tended
them throughout the long day in *Weatherlight*'s own sickbay.

The rest of the crew had to make themselves at home in
the open air. They had off-loaded the stores of food and
drink that would see them through and had rigged makeshift shelters with torn sections of sailcloth. All the while,
Gerrard moved among them, planning the next day's expe-
dition to Mercadia.

When the sun set on the dust flats, the air quickly grew uncomfortably cold. The crew huddled around a bonfire built from shattered hunks of *Weatherlight*'s hull and simsass stalks ruined in the crash. The fire lit five graves dug that afternoon on the hillside. Already, the bodies lay within, and three sailors, sweaty and stripped to the waist despite the cold night, waited with shovels to fill in the spots.

Atalla watched it all from a shattered window.

The crew of the vessel stood to attention as Gerrard, Hanna, and Sisay passed in front of them, followed by Karn and Tahngarth. The bridge crew of *Weatherlight* stood to one side of Hanna as she spoke solemnly.

"We lost dear friends this morning—Danis, Groud, Steepen Willm, Erkika, and Bevela. We lost dear friends on Rath—Ertai, Crovax, and Mirri. We have spoken their names to each other in grief, and all have mourned according to our own traditions. I want now to speak the name of my grief, the name of my dear friend and companion Mirri." Her eyes glistened in the firelight.

Sisay put out a hand to gently touch hers.

"Mirri gave her life that we might live," Hanna continued. "She did this without thought. That was the way she lived her beliefs. It was during this last journey that I came to know her best. We became friends when she and I traveled through the Skyshroud Forest on Rath. It was a friendship born of mutual respect. She passed through the dangers of the Stronghold," she continued, "was wounded defending Crovax, and slain defending the rest of us. . . ."

Karn spoke into the choked silence. "I join in mourning Mirri, for I remember her life and the brave deeds she did, but now she is gone."

Sisay said, "Mirri is dead, but we, her friends, her comrades, will always remember her. In our memories, she will live."

Tahngarth said simply, "I salute you, Mirri, a warrior worthy of Talruaa."

Last, all eyes turned to Gerrard. He had been standing in the shadows behind Hanna, shaking his head quietly. As the silence stretched, he looked up, caught unaware, and blurted the first thing that came to his mind. "So many lost. We have lost so many friends. . . ." Uncertain what else to say, Gerrard peered numbly out at the crew. Orange light illuminated Takara's hair, and her face shone white in the firelight. The fine bones beneath her skin were lit as though from within. Her green eyes returned his gaze. He said at last, "We have lost so much, but we must keep fighting. What else is there for heroes to do?"

The ranks of the sailors bent and rose, tossing handfuls of dust into the air where it briefly formed a black cloud before falling back to earth. They also scooped dirt into each of the five graves. Their voices murmured together an orison for their fallen comrades.

A sudden, loud rumble broke the quiet. A fine spray hissed above the fire.

"That sound came from the ship," Gerrard said.

Cries rose in the distance.

Sisay seized a burning branch from the fire and rushed into the night. Gerrard and Hanna followed, Tahngarth and Karn bringing up the rear.

From the direction of the dry riverbed, perhaps fifty yards to the north of the farm, they saw a strange, ghostly light. Clouds of fine mist sparkled, turning blue and green. Figures moved in that mist. They were the size of men but had wings of skin like dragons. The advancing cloud cast a dark and sinuous shadow on the ground beneath it. Within that shadow more figures darted.

But it wasn't a shadow. The river was running—

That was impossible. Hours ago the bed had been dry and cracked. The blazing sun had evaporated every drop of moisture from the soil, leaving it baked and gritty. Yet now, a torrent of water flooded down the center of it, splashing

over the banks and washing in puddles out over the field—
the field where *Weatherlight* lay.

"All hands to the ship!" Gerrard shouted even as they
ran.

"What is it?" Hanna gasped as she clambered over a brake
of simsass and climbed down toward the field.

"Water," Gerrard answered.

"I've never seen water like this," Hanna replied.

The flood swirled and lapped as if it were alive, driven
by conscious purpose. It was limned with light, each wave-
let shining with a glow that seemed to amplify the light of
the twin moons overhead in the starry sky. Through the
flood, figures moved like darting merfolk. Atop it came
dark shapes—craft of some sort propelled rapidly over the
waves. In the mists above, winged, semi-human figures
soared and dove.

Gerrard and Hanna reached the field, near the *Weatherlight*. Something long and heavy thudded into the ground
next to Hanna's feet. With a kind of slow-motion detach-
ment, she saw that it was a spear, a slender stone head bound
tightly to a wooden shaft. She looked up. The riverbank,
deserted a moment before, was filling with dark figures.

They rose from the deep, descended from the mists, and
shot across the crests of the waves in canoes. The force of
the waters propelled them forward, and they steered with
slim paddles, wielded by oarsmen in the rear of the craft.
Those in the front of the boats were clearly warriors, who
wore headdresses made of woven grass, colored by dyes in
brilliant reds and oranges. They were bare-chested, clad in
loincloths, and armed with spears, bows, and arrows. Some
stood in the prows of their canoes, and others leaped to the
shore, hurling missiles. There seemed to be hundreds of the
dark figures.

With bare fists, Gerrard attacked one of the warriors.
With a quick punch to the temple, he sent the man to the

ground. The warrior rolled, groaning. Gerrard smashed him in the jaw, knocking him out. He yanked up the warrior's spear and tossed it back toward Hanna. "You think you can make use of this?"

"Sure," she said, grasping the haft of the weapon. "I've wielded slightly more sophisticated artifacts in my time."

"Good," Gerrard said, grinning. "I'll go get me one."

As he dashed off, Hanna advanced on another warrior. His back was to her. Oddly, he was kneeling next to the ship's hull, placing his palms flat against the ground. In the distance, Hanna glimpsed several of the other attackers making the same mysterious gesture.

"That's my ship!" she growled, and rushed at the man.

The ground rocked. Hanna was thrown from her feet. Dirt and pebbles stung her face. The soil sank. Cold wetness rushed in around her. Water rose, lapping at *Weatherlight*'s hull. Hanna splashed, struggling to keep her face above water.

Figures teemed through the sudden flood. In moments they grasped and bore away the man Gerrard had knocked unconscious. The pool widened and deepened.

Hanna cried out as a hand grasped her leg and pulled her under. Lashing out with the spear, she bashed her attacker and swam to the surface, spluttering and coughing. The edge of the widening pool was twenty feet away. She struck out, swimming vigorously, kicking off her sandals and fighting the weight of her sodden clothing. Nearby, she could see the bobbing heads of several fellow crewmen.

Hanna swam harder, but the shore receded continuously. For some moments, all was shouting blackness and cold struggle. Then she threw both arms over the edge of the pool and pulled herself onto the bank. Staggering up the slope, she turned to look behind her.

Weatherlight was floating on the small pond that had somehow been created by the attackers. Its damage made it list heavily to one side. The repair crews had done a partial job of patching the rent in the ship's side, but Hanna suspected the vessel was taking on water. She wondered how long it would be before the water reached the engine room.

All around *Weatherlight* surged canoes and swimmers and gliders. They cast lines about the hapless craft and began hauling it toward the river. The waters boiled with the struggles of crewmen caught in the sudden collapse of solid ground. Hanna reached out to help her companions to shore.

She felt a hand on her shoulder and turned to see Sisay's dark face, almost invisible against the backdrop of night.

"Who are they? What are they after?" shouted the young woman. Her voice was trembling.

Frantically, Hanna scanned the scene for some sign of Gerrard. At last she saw him. He was wrestling with one of the attackers, whom he had evidently captured and pinned to the ground. Just as she spotted him, he reared back and, with a great blow, laid his opponent senseless.

"They're taking the ship!" she shouted to him.

Looking up, his eyes gleaming in the darkness, Gerrard rose and rushed toward her.

Already, *Weatherlight* was in the clutch of the river, which had reversed its course. It flowed away from the cottage, almost due west into the blackness of the plains. The ship was drawn along with the current.

"Run," Gerrard said. "It's speeding up!"

"We'll never catch it now," Hanna said as she fell into step beside him.

"We might! Look!"

The massive ship seemed to hang up on something, as if caught on a sandbar. Streaming water piled up behind it, but *Weatherlight* stalled for a moment in the flood. Something glimmered in the moonlit waters at the prow—a shiny boulder? No. It had eyes. Its mouth opened, and an almighty roar of exertion bellowed across the waves.

"Bless you, Karn," Hanna said, darting across the dark grasses toward the spot.

It was too much for the silver golem. The weight of the ship drove him down into the muck. His fingers scraped uselessly along the keel. *Weatherlight* won free and shivered away atop the receding flood.

"No!" Gerrard shouted. He ran futilely onward. "No!"

Panting, Hanna stomped to a halt. She gazed hopelessly toward the disappearing vessel. Her heart stood still as she spotted a small, turbaned figure clutching the rail and shouting.

It was Orim. She had remained on the ship with her two charges.

Gerrard had seen her as well. With a shout that rose to the skies, he pursued the ship. It moved all the faster now, swiftly vanishing from him. The river dried up as swiftly as it had swelled. Pools and rivulets of water splashed beneath his feet, and his face was stained with mud. All was in vain.

Weatherlight was gone.

CHAPTER 2

In her trips aboard *Weatherlight*, Orim had experienced many unpleasantries but nothing quite this bad. The ship creaked and groaned as it raced along the river. The bed was narrow, and *Weatherlight* lurched from side to side, occasionally blundering into the banks. Each impact jolted the ship and almost hurled the healer from her precarious perch at the rail.

Short and scrappy, Orim clung on. Her turban had padded her head against the worst knocks. The pockets in her healer's cloak helped absorb some of the body blows—and promised her salves and poultices aplenty when this all was done. She only wished her knee-high calfskin boots would have better footing on the rolling deck. Orim desperately wanted to get below and check on her patients.

She could see nothing behind her but the foaming water of the river, which receded as the ship passed. She turned to look ahead and was rewarded with nothing more than an onrush of blackness. Over the top of the pilothouse she could see dim forms moving about the ship's deck—attackers. The ones who abducted her patients, her ship, herself.

Orim struggled toward them along the rail. One figure—more surefooted than she—ascended the stairs and clung to the siding before her. He was tall and slender. Dark hair flew before his face. Hundreds of coins were braided into the long strands. The man's eyebrows drew tightly together. His eyes glinted like onyx in the night. He wore white robes that draped his shoulders and his waist but left his muscular chest bare.

The man spoke in a language she had never before heard.

She shook her head. "What do you want? Where are you taking me?"

He grabbed her elbow and hauled her to the hatch leading below decks. At the bottom of the ladder she could see him more clearly. His hands were glowing strangely—a silvery light that flooded the familiar passage. He urged her on toward the infirmary.

She entered and found two other strangers already occupying the cramped space, standing guard over Klaars and Drianan. Klaars was suffering acutely the effects of having been pitched from side to side in his bunk. In the crash, the thin young sailor had suffered a concussion. A large black knot hovered beneath his shock of auburn hair. In addition, his arm had been broken just below the elbow, and it was bound with a splint. In all the sloshing mayhem, the sling had fallen off, and the splint had been battered to pieces.

Drianan was in worse shape. His spinal injury had been severe, and despite Orim's neck splint, the man lolled back and forth on his bunk as if already dead.

Orim tried to remember some god to pray to.

From outside, over the noise of the ship, she could hear shouts from the others above decks. From time to time men climbed into the small room to consult with the coin-haired man, evidently the leader of the raiders. He answered them perfunctorily, all the time keeping his unwavering eyes on Orim as she moved between the two patients, trying to minister to them. He did his best to help, holding on to Drianan while Orim tended Klaars, and vice versa. Even that aid soon was unneeded. Drianan was dead before midnight.

It was a long and horrible night, traveling that way. Just when Orim was certain the ordeal would never end, the lurching motion abruptly stopped. There were further shouted exchanges from above. *Weatherlight* shivered. Klaars slipped from his bunk with a crash against the bulkhead. Mercifully, he struck his head and fell unconscious.

The ship shivered again and heeled upward. The list was gone. *Weatherlight* floated, buoyed on water.

There was a faint cheer from above, and then a clamor of feet across the deck. A hatch was thrown back with a crash. Silvery-green light spilled downward. The chief of the raiders strode to the hatch and called up into it.

Orim backed up, trying to shield Klaars with her body.

Two more raiders came into the sickbay and stood with their chief. One was a thin young man with straight, brown, shoulder-length hair. Coins were braided among the strands, though not nearly as many as in the chief's hair. Medallions and pouches hung about his neck. The other was a stocky warrior with black shoulder armor. They stood beside the chieftain and stared at Orim.

"You have the ship. Leave us alone," she said nervously.

They pushed past her. She tried to stop the plated warrior,

but he brushed her aside impatiently, as though she were a child. He drew a long, thin knife. Orim stifled a scream. The warrior slashed away some bedding that had tangled Drianan's body. Then, with surprising gentleness, he lifted the dead sailor. His companion hoisted Klaars. Orim sprang forward to support Klaars's arm, and the procession moved cautiously above deck.

Orim looked around in amazement. The open plain was gone. Around the ship rose huge trees, each trunk as wide around as a small village. They rose to a lofty canopy, far above which the yellow-orange sky of morning could be glimpsed. *Weatherlight* itself was floating on the edge of a vast lagoon whose dimensions were impossible to determine, and whose waters stretched off into distant oblivion. Everything was dark and cool. Festooned vines and moss draped from the lower branches of the trees, trailing across the deck of the ship.

All around her, Orim sensed a vast, living presence—a being beside whom she and all the humans with her were insignificant. After the long, horrific night, this magnificent presence was a balm. She stretched cramped limbs. Likewise, her spirit seemed to stretch outward, reaching up and up until it emerged from the topmost leaves to find itself pressed against the warm body of the sky. She wanted to cry out at the pain and beauty around her. With an almost audible sigh, her spirit slowly sank back into the soft bed of the trees, drifting lower and lower until the warm waters of the earth received and caressed it. She shivered with a sudden chill and blinked her eyes. The vision faded, and she found herself once again standing on the deck of the ship. The enormous trees all around were limned in silver fire.

"A prisoner in paradise," she muttered.

She was not the only one. Klaars had been moved to the other side of the deck, where he lay unconscious on a woven pallet of reeds. The medallion-wearing young man tended him, working over his arm. A vine rope was meanwhile wrapped around Drianan's body. Three men lifted him and gently lowered the corpse over the side of the craft. Below waited a canoe filled with fern boughs. Women in adjacent canoes received the body and arrayed his arms and legs, laying flowering ivy atop his chest and wreathing his head in blossoms. They cared for him as though he were one of their own fallen.

Other figures swarmed over the rails to stand dripping on *Weatherlight's* polished planks. With their chieftain, they approached Orim.

She took a deep breath and murmured, "Now what?"

The leader gazed levelly at her. His eyes glinted with the same light as the coins braided into his hair. He was handsome, yes, but proud and commanding. He gestured Orim toward the side rail. There, she saw a slender canoe, evidently there to take her to shore.

A line was swiftly passed over the side, and she clambered down. Even as she descended, other raiders who had swum from shore to meet the ship were scrambling up the sides of *Weatherlight*. She seated herself in the middle of the canoe. Warriors climbed down fore and aft. The chieftain of the raiders meanwhile dove from the rail and struck out for shore. The warriors paddled out behind him.

As they pulled away from the swimmers and canoes, they entered very still waters. Despite the dim light, Orim could easily see the slender ripples that bled away from either side of the canoe. Around her hung a vast silence, broken only by the soft calls of the raiders and the rhythmic swish of the paddles. Here and there on the lagoon crouched huts, linked by bamboo causeways.

There was a sudden fluttering from above. A dark winged form passed close overhead. Orim ducked and gasped. The tribesmen chuckled. They halted their paddling for a moment, and one held up his hand, making an odd chirruping noise with his tongue. There was another flapping of wings, and something settled on his arm. It hung there upside down, apparently a very large bat, but its eyes were enormous and gleaming. Its ears perked sharply in her direction, and it cocked its head to one side, as if deciding what this new creature was doing in its domain.

The paddler reached into a hidden pocket of his cape and plucked forth some morsel, which he offered to the bat. The creature, without taking its eyes from Orim, snapped it up in a mouth gleaming with sharp, white teeth. The man who held it crooned to it in a soft voice. It chittered briefly, then flitted off into the darkness.

A few more strokes of the paddle, and the canoe ran aground. The warrior at the prow climbed out and motioned for Orim to do the same. She alighted on a level bank formed not of soil but of mossy wood. The vast trees were so thickly clustered in this portion of the forest that their root bulbs merged. Trunks rose all around like pillars in a temple—except that each trunk was itself as wide as a whole temple. Bark gleamed silvery beneath robes of lichen.

The warriors took Orim's arms and escorted her in among the trees. The hush deepened, though here and there she glimpsed more tribesfolk. Soon, the forest was full of them. They waited furtively among the crowded boles. With their white robes and their coin-coifed hair, they were dwarfed by the gigantic boles. Folk peered at her out of mossy hollows. The men stared suspiciously, the women quizzically, and the children with curious grins.

Countless feet had worn footpaths along the root bulbs. Though the green ceiling overhead was lofty, it cast all below in a purple murk. Even at midday, the yellow sky would give little light this deep. In most places, only the silver glow of the ever-present trees lit the darkness.

Ahead was an exception—a bright clearing. One of the millennial trees had fallen, perhaps centuries ago, and torn a vast hole in the oppressive canopy. The downed tree now was no more than a huge, mossy hill that ran through the forest. Young trees grew in straight lines from the decaying bulk. The villagers had burrowed into the side of it, excavating cave homes for themselves. Windows and doors were dug into that log. They leaked silvery-green light out into the clearing. Other villagers dwelt in eroded root bulbs or lived in hovels so encased in lichen as to seem only knobs on the forest floor.

"We are like mere insects in this place," Orim thought aloud.

At the center of the clearing was a welcome sight. A great bonfire flamed. Its warm, red light was almost blinding after the forest's ghostly illumination. Klaars sat on a pallet near the fire, his auburn hair seeming a manifestation of its flame. He had reawakened, and he cradled his broken arm as though it pained him greatly. A metal-plated guard stood on either side of him.

Orim pulled free of her own guards and hurried over to him.

Klaars's arm bore a crude splint, probably devised by the man with the medallions. His skin had been pasted with a thick orange goo. It clearly agonized him. His eyes rolled in his head.

Orim patted his healthy shoulder and spoke soothingly. "Stay calm. I don't think these people mean to hurt us. They could have done so quite a while ago if that's what they intended."

The young crewman continued to breathe unevenly. The vein in his neck pulsed in a violent rhythm.

The leader of the raiders arrived, stepping into the firelight. His coin-braided black hair dripped lagoon water. He said something to Orim and pointed to himself.

"What? What is it? I don't understand." The healer spread her hands in a gesture of frustration.

Patiently he repeated the phrase, again pointing first to

people around him, then to himself. "Yo shava Cho-Arrim. Ja shav Cho-Manno."

Orim shook her head in frustration. Beside her, Klaars gave a moan of fear and pain.

The chief reached down to Orim. His hand gently lifted Orim's chin. She found herself staring into deep brown eyes that contained a flash of humor. Satisfied he had her attention, the man pointed to himself. "Cho-Manno."

Orim nodded slowly, repeating, "Cho-Manno."

He smiled and gestured to the crowd. "Cho-Arrim."

"Cho-Arrim." Deep within her, Orim felt a long-dormant excitement begin to build.

He pointed to her and cocked his head.

"Orim," she said.

"O-leem."

"No, Orim."

"O-reem."

"Yes. That's it. Orim."

He flashed white teeth at her and glanced swiftly around the gathering. His hair shimmered with hundreds of coins. Striding toward the gawking villagers, he drew forth a pretty teenaged girl. "Is-Shada."

"Is-Shada."

Is-Shada smiled nervously. She was beautiful, with long dark hair, a smooth olive complexion, and dressed in a knee-length white shift. She approached Orim, took her hand, and stroked it gently. Then she lifted it to touch her forehead.

"O-reem. Is-Shada. Do chrano 'stva o'meer." Her hand glowed faintly.

To her surprise, Orim saw that some of the silver light from Is-Shada's hand passed momentarily to her own fingers. She smiled and gently released her hand.

The girl knelt next to Klaars.

"Can you do something for him?" Orim looked from Cho-Manno to Is-Shada.

The former looked grave and pointed across the fire.

From the other side of the clearing came the thin, brown-haired young man she had seen on *Weatherlight*. Orim suddenly realized the pouches about his neck were medicine bags, not unlike her own, and the medallions symbols of healing.

The young man knelt beside Klaars and gingerly probed his wounded arm. Releasing a shriek of pain that echoed through the forest, Klaars fell back on the pallet and writhed in agony. The young healer shook his head in concern, raised the largest amulet at his neck, and touched it to Klaars's forehead. He spoke a brief word.

Klaars immediately sank limp, a faint snore emerging from his lips.

Orim stared in astonishment at the young healer. "Thank you," she said, hoping he could hear the gratitude in her voice.

The young Cho-Arrim stepped back a pace and said something to the leader.

Orim watched their grave faces as they spoke. "The things I could learn from these people," she whispered in amazement.

Cho-Manno nodded in decision.

In a single fluid motion, the young healer turned, drew from beneath his robes a weighty cleaver, and slashed it down and across Klaars's arm.

The crewman awoke, giving another wild scream of pain. The arm fell away from his side.

"No!" Orim shouted, reaching out. Her warrior escorts dragged her back.

Three more warriors held down Klaars as the healer knelt with a cloth and bound the spurting stump. He placed a stick in the rag and twisted it until the tourniquet shut off the blood flow.

Orim fought the warriors who hauled her away. She stared in horror at Klaars's maimed body. "No! You monster! You're all monsters!"

Is-Shada was suddenly there, wrapping Orim in a tight embrace. Even as the warriors pinned Orim's arms, the young woman held her tightly, patting her back and whispering soothingly in her ear.

"O-reem, Is-Shada 'stva o'meer. Is-Shada 'stva o'meer. . . ."

* * * * *

Night came to the village of the Cho-Arrim—though night was little different than day. The yellow-orange sky had gone dark, yes, but even during the day, little of its illumination reached the forest floor. Day or night, most of the light came from the silvery gleam of the ubiquitous trees.

That gleam was the only source of light in Orim and Klaars's cell. The room lay deep in the root cluster of an ancient tree. Though the chamber had neither door nor lock, it was clearly a prison. Stout roots formed a cage all around them, receding fifty feet in each direction. There was only one pathway down into that thicket of roots, and Orim and Klaars had been forced to descend it despite the man's amputation. At the top and the bottom of the path, a guard had been posted. No door, no lock—and no way out.

"Monsters," Klaars said, gripping the tourniquet on his arm. He paced across the foot-smoothed cluster of roots, his teeth grinding angrily. "Savage monsters!"

Orim shook her head. She had been trying for hours to calm the man, to comfort him, but he would not sit down beside her or listen to her. "I think they just didn't understand. They didn't realize the limb could be saved. Perhaps gangrene is worse here—"

"I'm going to get up there and kill one of them. I'm going to find that healer and chop *his* arm off!"

"No, Klaars," Orim said. "That wouldn't do any good."

"It sure would feel good!" Klaars hissed. He made a vicious chopping motion with his remaining hand. "How do you like that, you Cho-Arrim bastard!"

A new voice spoke out of the murk. "O-reem?" Soundlessly, Is-Shada had descended past the two guards to visit her new friend. "O-reem? O'meer Is-Shada." She stepped furtively into the chamber.

Orim hadn't the chance to warn the young woman. Klaars leaped like a wolf upon her. He knocked her down and wrapped his good arm about her neck. He flexed his elbow, but not before she released a strangled shriek.

Through the doorway came a guard—a huge and metal-plated manifestation of the night. A sword flashed out from his belt.

"Fight him, Orim," Klaars shouted, swinging Is-Shada out as a shield before him. "Fight the guard! Get his sword!"

Orim stood there, imploring, "What are you doing, Klaars?"

"Getting us out of here! Take his sword!"

"Let her go!"

The guard sized up Orim, who stood with hands trembling before her. He decided she was not a threat and lunged at Klaars. The sword darted in.

Klaars pivoted, flinging Is-Shada into the guard's way. Steel bit into her side. Blood welled forth.

The soldier withdrew, staring in disbelief at the blood he had drawn.

Growling, Klaars only tightened his hold. Is-Shada's face went from crimson to purple. In moments, she ceased struggling and hung limp in his grasp. Snarling like a cornered beast, Klaars shouted, "Drop the sword, or I'll kill her! I'll do it! I'll kill Eeeshadda!"

Somehow, the guard understood. He dropped the sword on the floor and lifted his hands. He nodded in supplication.

Klaars dragged the limp young woman across the floor

and picked up the sword. Once its hilt was in his hand, he brusquely dropped Is-Shada.

The guard stooped to grab her, but suddenly, red gore sprayed all across the motionless young woman.

"No, Klaars!" Orim shouted.

The guard stood. His severed arm flopped grotesquely atop Is-Shada. He staggered, blood jetting from his stump.

"Take that, Cho-Arrim bastard!"

Orim shucked her healer's cloak and wrapped it around the spurting limb, applying pressure. "Damn it, Klaars! Put down the sword!"

"Get away from him!" Klaars shouted.

"He'll die!"

"Get away from him, or you'll die!"

It was too late anyway. The bulky warrior went to his knees and collapsed in a bloody heap on the floor.

Klaars stared avidly at the two bodies. "Let's go, Orim."

She knelt, struggling to stanch the blood flow. "I'm not going anywhere with you."

"Suit yourself," Klaars spat. He strode out the door and began climbing toward the forest floor.

Meanwhile, Orim checked the guard. Pools of red life lay on the floor of the chamber. He was dead—irretrievably dead. But Is-Shada . . .

Orim reached the young woman. Her neck was not broken. Orim rolled her onto her back. Neither was she breathing or her heart beating. Orim pounded thrice on the young woman's sternum, tilted her head back, inhaled deeply, and filled Is-Shada's lungs with the breath of life.

"Live, damn it. Live."

As she compressed Is-Shada's chest again, Orim whispered, "Is-Shada, Orim 'stva o'meer. Is-Shada, Orim 'stva o'meer. . . ."

* * * * *

The killing had ended by morning. Klaars had slain two warriors, a young man, and an old woman before he had finally been wrestled to the ground. Now he knelt there at sword point. Beside him knelt Orim. She had been discovered in the cell, bloodstained beside the body of the first guard. Is-Shada lay unconscious but alive nearby. Without the ability to explain her appearance, she seemed as guilty as Klaars.

Morning had come—the time for executions.

Ta-Spon was the executioner, a hulking man as tall as Gerrard and as muscular as Tahngarth. A mane of long black hair spilled back from his head to his shoulder blades, and a crimson mask covered his features. He bore a wickedly sharp and heavy blade, which just now he held at Klaars's throat.

"They were always planning to kill us, you know," Klaars whispered to Orim. His eyes hatefully raked across the white-robed crowd that surrounded them. Cho-Manno stood in their midst, returning the man's vicious glare. To his right, in the space where Is-Shada would have stood, there was only an unsheathed sword. Klaars spit toward the chieftain. "At least I killed some of them before they killed me."

"At least I saved one of them," Orim answered stoically.

"Yes, but the one you saved can't save you," Klaars noted.

As if understanding the conversation, Ta-Spon glanced at Cho-Manno.

The chieftain nodded.

Steel flashed. It hummed in air. It sliced through skin, muscle, and bone as though through water. Klaars's head bounded free.

Orim saw no more. She buried her face in her hands and wept. The sound of her sobbing spread out through the hushed throng. The slump and spatter of her comrade only fueled her cries.

Ominously, Ta-Spon stepped up beside her. His blade cast a crimson light across Orim.

She did not lift her head. If he would kill her, he could do it easily enough as she lay there.

Ta-Spon seemed to wait for the signal. His feet shifted.

The sword rose into the air. Utter silence gripped the forest.

Then came the hum of the blade . . . and another sound—someone rushing up the path. A great weight fell on Orim's neck—not the weight of steel, but of arms. Someone crouched over her, weeping.

"O-reem, Is-Shada 'stva o'meer. . . . O-reem, Is-Shada 'stva o'meer. . . ."

CHAPTER 3

Gerrard himself dug the new graves. Whoever had stolen *Weatherlight* had killed three of his sailors—and abducted three more. He wondered if he ought to be digging six holes in the gloaming hillside. It was a solitary penance. Others had volunteered to help him, but Gerrard felt he owed it to these crew members— and to all the others he had lost.

"Dig them deep," came a warm voice in the chill morning.

Gerrard glanced up, flinging another shovelful of dirt onto the mound. Atop shifting soil stood Takara. Her flame-red hair blended with the crimson sky . . . what was the old saying?—*Red sky at morning, sailor take warning.*

"Dig them deep, Gerrard. The dead have a way of rising to haunt you."

Gerrard shook his head grimly, and droplets of sweat pattered across his bare shoulders. "Is that what's next? Black magic raising the dead?"

She nodded and smiled. "Yes, black magic. The blackest magic there is. Regret. You've become a master of it."

It was as though she saw right into his soul. With a grim laugh, he said, "I've had lots of occasions like this to practice it."

Takara grabbed a shovel that had been abandoned in the pile of dirt and dropped down into the grave beside Gerrard.

"I don't want any help."

"I know," Takara said, even as she flung a shovelful out of the hole. "But you don't want the others to help because they don't understand what you are doing. They tell you to let go of guilt and regret, but I know you can't. I know you can't because I couldn't either. I survived Rath not by letting go of guilt, regret, and anger, but by clinging to them. They are powerful magic, indeed—black and powerful. You can't get rid of them, Gerrard, so you have two choices— you can let them rule you, or you can rule them."

He paused and stared amazedly at Takara. Rivulets of sweat ran down his back.

She returned his gaze. "Every time I think of Father, of the man I loved, who was stolen away from me by a spoiled and vengeful monster, my hatred strengthens me. Hatred and fury. They perfect me, prepare me to kill that monster." She lifted her hand, fingers forming a trembling claw just before Gerrard's neck. "And when the black magic is complete, I will rip his throat out!"

Gerrard stared into Takara's eyes. They blazed like twin furnaces—steel and fire. "Yes," he said, nodding. "Yes. I have the same score to settle. I will use my anger. I will use it to get back my ship and escape this strange world and defend my own world. I'll use it to kill Volrath."

Takara's eyes narrowed, and she drew back, lowering her hand. "That's right, Gerrard. Take possession of your hatred. It will refine your soul—"

"What's going on?" came a new voice above—Atalla. The lad stood silhouetted against the morning. His homespun work trousers and patched tunic riffled in the breeze. "I thought you didn't want help."

"I changed my mind," Gerrard said, glancing at Takara, "about help, and about other things."

"So, I can go with you to Mercadia?" Atalla asked hopefully.

"We're not going to Mercadia. We're going to—what was the name of that forest you spoke of?"

"The Rushwood—land of the Cho-Arrim," the boy replied.

"Right. That's where we march, as soon as I'm done here."

A call came up over the hill. Atalla turned, cupping a hand behind his ear. He relayed the message. "They say there are riders approaching—a whole army."

"Damn," Gerrard said, planting his shovel in the dirt and hauling himself forth. "Sorry about my language, kid."

Atalla looked affronted. "I'm not a damn kid!"

Gerrard laughed a bit at that. He slipped his waistcoat over sweating shoulders and buckled on his sword belt. Takara's words rang in his head as she, too, armed herself. Gerrard felt anger like a forge fire stoking within him. "Let's go see who's coming."

With Takara and Atalla beside him, Gerrard headed out across the encampment and to the edge of the farm.

Karn stood there, watching the east. Beside his motionless form huddled the tiny green shape of Squee. The goblin clung to one of the golem's great silver legs, cowering almost out of sight.

On the dim horizon stood a strange shape—a gigantic, inverted mountain. When they had first glimpsed Mount Mercadia yesterday—a huge conic stone with its tip embedded in the wide plain—Gerrard had been sure the vision was a desert mirage. It must have been a normal mountain, its image flipped by a trick of the hot air. Tavoot had assured them that Mercadia was indeed inverted, and so were all its dealings. Now, from the shadow of the mountain came a cloud of dust, approaching fast. Within the dust storm rode a large contingent of soldiers.

Reaching Karn, Gerrard stared at the army, shading his eyes against the growing light. "What can you see?"

"There are perhaps two hundred riders," the golem replied. "They are riding jhovalls, but they do not appear to be keeping a close formation. I cannot tell if they are in uniform or not."

"Mercadians," Atalla said, spitting to one side. "They would have seen your ship when it shot across the sky. They saw it just like the Cho-Arrim. They've probably come to take it."

"They're a little late," Gerrard said wearily. "Nothing left to take."

Atalla shrugged. "They could always take you."

Behind him, Tahngarth sounded a call-to-arms through his cupped hands. The loud hooting rang through the camp. Men and women leaped to their feet and raced to the brow of the hill.

Across the flat, dirt-covered plain, the dark shapes rapidly advanced. They shimmered in the heat rising from the baked earth. There were hundreds against *Weatherlight's* twoscore crew.

Tahngarth barked orders. "Form a semicircle here, two lines. Get your arms ready." The minotaur thrust Gerrard and Hanna to one side as he prodded the crew into place, almost tripping over Squee.

Gerrard spoke to them next, his tone soft and confident after Tahngarth's barking roar. "All right, listen. This would be a battle better not fought. We're outnumbered five to one, and we've got more important things to do than bang swords. Don't make a move unless you hear a specific order.

Let's find out if these people are friendly—"

Atalla hid a small smile behind his hand.

"—and if not, let's find out how to make them friendly—"

"—and if not that either," Tahngarth interrupted, "then we fight."

"Just so," Gerrard affirmed.

The faint sound of tinkling harness bells intruded on the conversation. Soon the tintinnabulation was drowned out by the thunder of clawed feet on dry earth. The bounding jhovalls flung up dust. Grit clung to tawny, matted fur on the beasts' flanks. The six-legged tiger-creatures looked miserable in their cerements of dust.

The riders were little better off. Dust dimmed their saffron-yellow riding cloaks and the red and blue uniforms beneath. Their long, steel tridents glimmered only where sweating hands had grasped them. The lead rider's pennant streamed behind him, its white dimmed to dun, its blue to brown. He and many of the other soldiers were corpulent. Jowls waggled with each bound of their mounts. Almond eyes watered, bloodshot. Noses were red from sneezing and sun. Sloping foreheads and sunken cheeks wore dirt as thick as face powder. As they arrived, the soldiers brought the dust cloud with them, and also a faint stink that did not smell like jhovalls. The riders, more than two hundred of them, surrounded the *Weatherlight* party and halted.

Tahngarth hastily directed the crew to bend their line into a complete circle, swords held in a thicket outward.

Gerrard and the bridge crew stood outside the circle, just before the lead rider. As the Mercadians arrayed themselves, Gerrard noted the clumsiness of their maneuver, the unkempt state of their uniforms and animals, and the rust on their weapons. The tridents, Gerrard observed hopefully, were still held skyward.

There was a short silence, and then the leader spoke in a long string of syllables that tripped out unpleasantly.

Gerrard shook his head. "We don't understand you," he said.

The leader repeated his statement with an air of irritation.

"He speaks High Mercadian—I think," Atalla offered. "All the nobles do. They think it's the only language worth speaking."

"You mean, he understands us?"

Atalla shrugged. "I don't know, but you better act like he does."

Takara tugged Gerrard's sleeve. "I think I know what he's saying. Their language is similar to some dialects spoken on Rath."

"Interesting," Gerrard said, his eyes narrowing. "I wonder what connection the two places have. Can you interpret for us?"

"I can try," Takara said.

Turning to the leader, she spoke a sentence or two in the same curiously dissonant flow of words, ending in an abrupt crescendo. The leader uttered a reply. They exchanged a few more words, anger rising.

"They claim our ship as property of the Chief Magistrate of Mercadia, gods bless and keep his name in their eternal roll of glory." She couldn't entirely remove the sarcasm from her voice. "I told him he was too late, that the Cho-Arrim had already taken the ship. He then declared us under arrest and commanded us to lay down our arms and surrender."

"Arrest? On what charge?" Gerrard hissed.

Takara spoke once more to the soldier, who replied with an imperious air.

She translated, "The charges include—but are not limited to—invasion, illegal migration, arms smuggling, trafficking with the enemies of Mercadia, refusal to speak High Mercadian—"

Gerrard raked his sword from its scabbard. "Better damned well add resisting arrest! Attack!"

He vaulted directly toward the lead jhovall. His sword slashed down.

The Mercadian captain hauled hard on the reins. His cat mount reared back, mouth gaping to lunge for Gerrard's head. Before it could, he sliced downward, cutting the beast's halter. Leather traces dragged across the cat-creature's face, yanking it aside. Reins suddenly went loose. The rider tumbled back in the saddle. Gerrard lunged beneath the rearing beast and sliced the saddle strap too. He scrambled out from beneath the jhovall even as its rider spilled to the ground.

"Understand me now, Captain?" Gerrard growled, leaping at him.

He never reached the man. Mercadian troops surged into the gap. Jhovalls hissed and nipped. Tridents jabbed. Dust flew.

Gerrard found himself facing two troopers. They thrust inexpertly at him with their forked pikes. His sword parried the stroke of one guard member, while he caught the weapon of the other and pulled it hard, yanking the soldier off-balance. The man flopped in the dust beneath his jhovall. The other soldier stabbed at Gerrard again. The master-at-arms beat back this blow too, but pain erupted in his shoulder.

The man's jhovall sank its jaws into him and lifted him from the ground.

Gerrard roared, thrusting his sword directly into the flank of the tiger-creature. The jhovall released him and reared away, blood gushing from its teeth. Eyes rolled and ears flattened in pain, it rose again, almost hurling its rider loose.

Gerrard pursued. "Mean puss, aye?" He stabbed the feline's heart.

With a magnificent roar, the jhovall crashed lifeless to the ground, its rider pinned beneath it.

Protected on one side by the fallen creature, Gerrard knelt to rip loose a hunk of shirt and stanch the blood flow from his shoulder. There was no question these Mercadians were poor fighters. Their weapons were badly tended and poorly wielded. Nonetheless, their sheer numbers had broken *Weatherlight*'s line, and these jhovalls were fierce beasts.

Even now, Karn the pacifist wrestled one of the tiger-creatures. It was not fighting. The silver man could not have been truly injured by the monstrous feline, nor would he do anything to hurt the beast. Even so, he wouldn't allow teeth and fangs to tear his friends apart. It was an impressive tussle, solemn and quick like cats rolling in an alley. Matted fur and gleaming silver entwined. Razor claws screeched across impassive metal. Vast, stubby fingers clutched masses of hair. The jhovall gnawed hopelessly on Karn's head. For Karn, this tumbling match was play, but the cat meant to dismantle the silver man. Karn made himself a distracting—and maddening—cat toy.

Despite his efforts, the rest of the crew had their hands full. Tahngarth was doing the best of any of them. His curved blade slashed one Mercadian, dropping him at the minotaur's feet. He caught a second with a swift elbow to the eye and bulled a third onto his craggy horns. Tahngarth lived to fight. He would say he lived for honor and loyalty, but for Tahngarth, honor and loyalty invariably led to fights. A fourth Mercadian found that out when Tahngarth butted heads with his jhovall. The tiger staggered and slumped. The minotaur charged on, clambering up the beast's neck and attacking the man in the saddle.

If all Gerrard's crew could fight like Tahngarth, they would win. Takara and Sisay came damned close, with three fallen Mercadians at each of their feet. Hanna did her best with a trident she'd wrangled from her single victim. Squee darted about, tripping any Mercadian he could reach. But the rest of the crew were falling like grass.

Gerrard suddenly remembered the dry grass thrashing at the edge of the graves he had dug. . . . How many more graves after this hopeless fight?

"We surrender! Stop the fight! Ground arms!"

The guard captain barked out similar orders.

The combat quickly faded. Swords froze in the air. Tahngarth let the latest Mercadian slump from his horns. Karn released the jhovall, who backed away, hissing and spitting, its pelt standing all down its back. In moments, Gerrard and his crew were surrounded by grim troopers, their weapons bristling. He looked around for his interpreter.

"Takara!" he called.

The woman emerged from beside a pile of dead. Her eyes glowed with the same fiery light as her hair. She wore an angry grin and wiped her bloodied blade lazily on one of the dead Mercadians. "Do you think they'll be more likely to listen now that we've killed some of them?"

"Perhaps not, but the fight was hopeless. They wouldn't have listened if we were all dead."

Gerrard drew her to his side and directed her attention to the guard captain. The man was even dustier after his fall from the jhovall, but there was no blood on his saffron robes. He had never rejoined the fray.

Gerrard said to Takara, "Tell him we submit. We'll lay down our weapons and go with him on condition that our sick will be treated—well treated—and our dead buried with proper ceremony."

Takara translated.

The captain bowed his head in acceptance. In the common tongue, he said, "You honor my master, the chief magistrate, with your decision. Order your folk to disarm."

Brow furrowing, Gerrard said, "Do as he says."

Most of the crew flung down their weapons with alacrity and raised their hands. Tahngarth was more reluctant. His curved crystal sword was one of a kind, and the assortment of daggers in his belt had taken years to accumulate. He flung each to the ground, where they stuck and shuddered angrily. The sound almost covered the minotaur's curses.

Meanwhile, Mercadian soldiers unpacked lengths of shackle and chain. They carried the shackles among their prisoners, fastening them over wrists. One whole set was wrapped about Karn, his arms bound to his sides and his legs connected so he could take only short steps. The crew members were chained in pairs to whomever was closest, so that they could ride jhovallback in tandem.

"You have killed just enough of our folk to each have a ride to the city," the captain said biliously as a soldier handed him the ring of shackle keys. He hung the ring on his belt and said with a flourish, "A fair payment for your fighting prowess. For my losses, I confiscate your weapons, to be kept or sold, as I will it." He gestured to another soldier, who gathered the swords and knives from the ground. The man scurried especially quickly as he snatched up Tahngarth's blades. He bundled them all together with rope and stowed them atop the captain's saddlebags.

Sitting aback their respective jhovalls, the crew at last received medical aid. Gerrard's shoulder was bandaged, a cut over Hanna's eye was cleaned and dressed, and Sisay's dislocated shoulder was reset rather brutally. Squee claimed to have gotten foot fungus from one of the soldiers he had tripped, and two Mercadians assiduously checked over his feet.

Gerrard watched them quizzically. He spoke over his shoulder to Takara, who sat behind him on the same jhovall. "They seem eager to live up to their end of the bargain. Look how they treat Squee."

"There's something else going on," Takara replied. "Look how they treat the dead." She nodded toward the bloody ground.

There, teams of Mercadians unceremoniously dragged away the dead—soldiers and sailors and six-legged cats. The workers grabbed whatever appendage presented itself and pulled. Heels, hips, backs, and faces rubbed the rocky ground as the bodies were dragged to a nearby ravine. The corpses were flung or rolled or kicked down the steep bank.

"What are you doing!" Gerrard roared at the guard captain. "I said due ceremony—"

"In Mercadia, we do not bury our trash, we dump it," came the bland reply.

"They aren't garbage! The deal is off!" Gerrard shouted, struggling against his chains. A trident jabbed beneath his neck, piercing shallowly. Gerrard stilled to keep the points from digging deeper.

"The deal is off?" the captain sniffed. "Your shackles would say otherwise. No, the bargain is good. The wounded are treated. The dead are disposed of. There is no more cause for delay. Off to Mercadia."

*　　*　　*　　*　　*

The procession wound across the land to the north. In all his travels aboard *Weatherlight*, Gerrard had never seen a place so utterly barren. There was no water anywhere, and what plants survived in the bare, hard ground grew in the myriad dry cracks that crisscrossed the land. It was as if a great plague had blasted almost every living thing from the soil. For hundreds of miles, the land stretched out flat. Only the distant wedge of Mount Mercadia broke the horizon. Throughout the afternoon it had loomed, dark and impossible against the lemon-colored sky.

Then a dust storm rose, obscuring the view. Similar clouds could be seen in the distance, moving with slow majesty back and forth across the hard, flat ground. This one roared straight for them. The guards did not hesitate, only lifting yellow hoods, buttoning cloaks, and veiling faces before they rode straight into the brown eddy. The riders were quickly obscured. The storm grew thicker and darker. The chain leading back from them dragged Gerrard's jhovall into the dust storm.

Gerrard shielded his eyes and looked back. Takara sat just behind him, and blind Starke hunched against her. A chain led back to the next jhovall, where Hanna and Sisay rode. The navigator was bent almost double in her saddle, her hand pressed against her eyes. Her blonde hair was turning a dirty gray. Beside them strode Karn, who was forced to march forward with short, shuffling steps. This storm could well freeze his joints with grit. On the third beast rode Tahngarth. He used his great white bulk to shield Squee. The rest of the crew stretched out across the prairie, armed Mercadians riding in columns to either side.

The maelstrom thickened until Gerrard could see only the beasts beside his own. Gritty winds hissed and sighed. Tan ghosts swirled in the air. Dust drained the breath from his lungs, scoured his face, packed his pockets, trickled down his collar, up his sleeves, and beneath his bandages. It was maddening.

Gerrard shouted over his shoulder to Takara. "How is your father?"

She shook her head. "We must find shelter soon."

Gerrard motioned to the guard riding alongside him. The man reluctantly guided his jhovall up beside Gerrard's. "How far to shelter? We'll die in this storm."

Takara translated and then listened to the man's shouts. "He says there's no place to shelter here and that we will be at our destination soon."

That wasn't possible. They had ridden only a dozen miles from the farm. Before the storm, the inverted mountain of Mercadia was at least forty miles distant. "He's lying."

Takara shrugged. "Does it matter? We've no other options."

Even as she spoke, the wind diminished. Gerrard felt a large presence looming before him. He looked up.

A vast shadow rose out of the wind and dust to blot out the sky—the mountain.

Gerrard stared, rubbed bloodshot eyes, and stared again. It was still there, still impossibly there—Mount Mercadia. He leaned back in his saddle and looked up through clear air. The mountain was at least five miles wide at the top but barely half a mile wide at the bottom. It was perfectly balanced, like a gigantic spinning top frozen in place.

"How could it stand there? And how could we have gotten here so fast?" he wondered hoarsely.

Takara leaned up against him. "You've been to Rath. You've seen the Stronghold floating within a volcano. You've rescued me and Sisay, seen Tahngarth transformed, and Karn turned into a meat cudgel, and then you've flown out of that hell into this one—and still you wonder how it can be?" A smile twisted onto her face. "We're on a different plane, Gerrard. The same laws of physics don't apply here. For all we know, gravity works differently."

Gerrard could think of a thousand possible consequences of that statement, none of them very heartening.

The mountain shielded them from the wind now. Suddenly Gerrard wished the breeze would return. A gagging stench rose from the shadow of the mountain.

"What's that smell?" Gerrard wondered, gagging.

"It seems to come from beyond that wall."

A high, thick wall circled the base of Mercadia. It was an amazing earthwork, thirty feet high, thirty feet wide, and five miles in diameter. Here and there, tall, conic towers stood. Roads converged on it, and there were numerous gates through the wall. It must have taken decades, if not centuries, to build, but whatever lay beyond smelled too rotten to deserve guarding.

The soldier escort led the prisoners up onto one of the main roads, crowded with travelers. Carts, barrows, pedestrians, and riders all converged on the city. Many were Mercadians, with their sloping foreheads and small, high ears. Others wore turbans and desert garb and had swarthy skin. Still more were not human at all—giant rat creatures, men with the heads of boars, women with the heads of eagles, grimy giants carrying crates, shambling slaves whipped by their masters. All of them walked toward a vast gate in the wall.

Gerrard could make out no more, his eyes watering.

"This is worse than the dust," he said, wiping away tears and gagging slightly. "What could possibly lie beyond that wall?"

"I'm beginning to think the stench doesn't lie beyond," Takara said into his ear. "It's the wall, itself." She pointed toward the cliff-edge of the inverted mountain. Gerrard looked up.

Something dribbled from the edge of the city. Globs of dark material plummeted. A few items flashed in the cascade. There was foul liquid and tumbling bits of paper—?

"Garbage?" Gerrard asked, his throat clenching. "That's a wall of garbage?" Even as he spoke, he saw more filth tumbling down in brief showers all along the perimeter of the city.

"The captain said they knew how to throw away their refuse. Perhaps this is what he meant," Takara said. Some runnels were clearly sewer mains.

There was no more talking as they approached the mound of garbage. In waves, the stench grew worse. Someone had thoughtfully inserted long black pipes that vented gases from below and burned them away in constant blue flames.

Miserable, Gerrard and his crew rode on toward the archway. That stonework gate was meant not to keep enemies out but to prevent filth from landing on those who walked the road. It piled atop the arch instead. A few of Gerrard's crew members leaned over the sides of their mounts to retch. Similar spots on the ground told that this was a common reaction from visitors. The prisoner caravan marched along beside merchants and slaves and slavers, all passing beneath the putrid gate.

Within the wall, the stench was somehow more diffuse—either that, or the crew's sense of smell was well nigh dead. The caravan continued onward, and after about a mile along the crowded main road, the stink had become only a pervasive sourness.

Gerrard looked at Takara and the others. All the crew were attempting to brush and clean themselves of the dust, which had swept into their every cranny and pore. Tahngarth was quietly cursing to himself in Talruum—quietly for a minotaur. As they drew nearer to the mountain, the crew saw that the base was the site of complex activity. They passed through a low brick wall with mounted guards stationed along it at regular intervals.

Ahead stood the base of Mount Mercadia. It was hewn with doors, evidently leading to storerooms. Folk constantly passed in and out, some carrying boxes and bundles. From this mass of people rose a constant hubbub. Clusters of small booths dotted the area, taking up all available space, and the competing cries of merchants rose into the air.

"Best pressed tralana!"

"Morkrain! Ground morkrain! Get it before it's gone!"

"Come now! Who wants some nice, fresh kava berries?"

Gerrard listened to the cries for a moment before something struck him. He turned to Takara. "I can understand them!" Though the barkers had a strange predominant accent, their words were perfectly recognizable.

She nodded. "Yes. The language the guard speaks must be unique to the ruling class of the city. To them, it is evidently a mark of distinction."

Gerrard looked around in some awe. In Benalia and Jamuraa he had often passed through city marketplaces. Among the Benalish infantry, with whom he'd trained, such places were extremely popular. Soldiers on leave could purchase food, drink, or more exotic diversions. The great market town of Triven Fralli in Benalia had always seemed to Gerrard a circuslike experience. Yet, had that fabled market been dropped into the middle of this scene, it would have been immediately swallowed up. This market extended in all directions around the mountain as far as the eye could see.

"Tell him—" Gerrard jerked his head toward the captain of the guard— "we're impressed with the size and wealth of the city."

Takara spoke a few halting sentences to the guard, who looked at Gerrard in some surprise and burst out laughing. He dispatched a long reply. Takara questioned him further before turning back to Gerrard.

"He says this isn't the city at all," she reported. "It's merely the outskirts. A camp."

"Then where is the city?"

The red-haired woman pointed silently upward.

"Up where? You mean on top of the mountain?"

Takara nodded yes.

"But how are we going to get up there?" Gerrard asked, craning his neck.

Before Takara could reply, a bellow came from Tahngarth. "They have strivas." He pointed emphatically toward a booth that contained a variety of steel-edged weapons. Short, intricately carved swords spread in a fan against the dark cloth that formed the backdrop to the booth. "Strivas!"

Gerrard gave the minotaur a blank look. He shouted back, "What are they?"

"It is the chosen weapon of the minotaurs of Talruum. Why would they be for sale here?"

That question was ringing in Gerrard's ears even as another question formed. He was watching a group of five goblins strutting between the stalls of the market. They wore long, flowing robes and carried slender golden rods in their hands. Their stance was proud and upright, and they glared menacingly at those foolish enough to cross their path, yet there was no mistaking their essential kinship with Squee. The goblins spotted *Weatherlight*'s cabin boy, sitting before Tahngarth. Clearly they were equally amazed. They exchanged glances. Then the largest one, fully as tall as Gerrard, bowed low to Squee and passed on. The others followed suit, leaving the crew to gape after them.

Gerrard felt his own jaw dropping and collected himself. He, along with the other members of *Weatherlight*'s crew, stared at Squee, who smiled uneasily and ducked his head.

Between the booths was a path that wound its way along the mountain base. Here and there, vast columns of stone extended down from the cliffs above. Some were smooth, as if the mountain had turned liquid and dripped onto the ground, while others were pitted and twisted like old tree trunks. Gerrard even saw a few pillars that supported stairways winding upward, vanishing into doorways high above the ground.

The jhovalls shouldered through the thick crowd. The Mercadian guards herded them along successfully, and the thronging buyers and sellers parted easily before them.

At last, the beasts drew up next to an area where there were no booths. Long lines of people waited, chattering among themselves. The soldiers made their captives dismount, tied the beasts to nearby posts, and led the prisoners through the throng.

They reached a series of cages resting on the ground. Each could comfortably accommodate forty people. Surrounding each cage were four slender metal columns that extended upward toward the looming cliffs. Just now, an attendant slammed shut the door of a crowded cage, throwing a locking bar across it. Those within continued their chatter unperturbed. The attendant stepped back. The cage emitted a gentle whir as it rose swiftly up the shaft.

Gerrard watched openmouthed as the folk soared out of sight into the jutting slope of the mountain. He turned to

Takara, hoping for an explanation. The red-haired woman made inquiries of the captain.

"He says they are 'lifts.' They will take us to the main city."

Two more cages became available, and the soldiers herded their captives within. Twenty chained crew and twenty soldiers occupied each. The doors clanged closed. There was a violent jerk. Gerrard felt his stomach plunge. He saw the ground suddenly drop away beneath him.

Hanna was nearby. She examined the device as best she could in the cramped space. "Wires," she said. "There may be wires in the supports that control the cage. Though how they're powered . . ." She shook her head. "It takes a lot of force to lift this many people. Pretty clever, though. This is obviously how they control access to the city. Unless you have an airship, it makes the top of the mountain practically impossible to invade."

Gerrard spotted the second cage ascending at roughly the same speed. He looked around at his companions. Some of the sailors were pale and nervous.

Hanna watched them too. "Well," she said to Gerrard and Takara, "it can't take very long at this speed."

It was taking long enough to suit everyone, thought Gerrard. Tahngarth appeared to be frozen in fear, as if this close confinement brought back memories of his imprisonment in the Stronghold. Gerrard looked for Squee, but the little goblin was nowhere in sight.

Even as they ascended, Gerrard found himself staring at the panorama unfolding before him. Farmland spread out on the east side of the mountain, intersected by stone walls that marked complex patterns on the land. To the west, clouds of dust rolled across the land. Far away, Gerrard could see the black stain of the Rushwood and a long black line that marked the dry course of the riverbed. To the south, the land was broken by a series of jagged canyons, punctuated by red and gold spires of rock. Those must be the Deep Lands Tavoot referred to, he decided. To the north, the dusty plain stretched to a far horizon obscured by yellow haze that merged land and sky.

Above them the sky glowed in brilliant orange and red. Thick clouds raced across it. Gerrard passed his hand over his eyes. How long was it since he had slept? It seemed a lifetime. Images rose unbidden before him: his battle with Volrath in the Dream Halls of the Stronghold, his flight to the Gardens. But overwhelming all the other memories was the recollection of Mirri the cat warrior in her final battle with Crovax, whose mad eyes turned red as he tore out her throat.

Those unwanted dreams were banished, though, when he glimpsed nearby an unexpected face—impish beneath black tousled hair. Gerrard smiled slowly at the lad.

"What are we going to do now?" Takara asked.

Gerrard leaned close to her. "I'm thinking about making an escape."

She smiled conspiratorially. "An escape? Why have you waited so long?"

"The chance only just presented itself," Gerrard replied. "We have a friend in the crowd. A young man who tailed us on his own jhovall, through storm and garbage and market, all."

Takara looked about the cage and smiled a sharp-toothed smile. "Atalla."

CHAPTER 4

The long, dark ride in the lift ended in a narrow stone chamber, brightly lit from some undetectable source. Ahead was a set of arched double doors. These the guard swung open.

Gerrard passed through and found himself in a wide corridor filled with similar doors, from which flowed a steady stream of humanity. A moment later, Gerrard caught sight of the second contingent of *Weatherlight* crew. The soldiers reassembled the prison caravan. Chains chattered on stone as the crew marched up the wide passage. Even here in the nooks and crannies of the wall, there were merchants calling out to the crowd to come and sample their wares.

Hanna pushed up beside Gerrard and touched his shoulder. "Have you seen the looks we're getting?"

He nodded. "We cut a pretty ragged picture compared to these people." Indeed the people around them were far better dressed than the *Weatherlight* crew. They were clad in flowing silk robes that were brightly dyed, elaborately folded, and piled high despite the heat and grit. Gerrard whispered to Hanna, "We'll have to find a laundry line once we escape—help us blend in. . . ."

"Escape?" Hanna whispered back.

"Atalla's tailing us—brave lad. He's the outside man. And the lifts have reduced our soldier escort from two hundred to twoscore. The time is right. Pass the word for the others to watch me and follow my lead."

Hanna nodded and fell back among the crew. The corridor widened farther and ascended a short flight of broad steps. The group emerged into bright daylight in the midst of Mercadia.

Gerrard's first impression was of incredible noise. At the foot of the mountain, the cries of the merchants had been nothing compared to the roar up here. It was omnipresent and almost deafening in its intensity.

"Hale nuts! Selling hale nuts! Brown roasted hale nuts!"

"Buying simsass for coldseason. Anyone have simsass for coldseason?"

"I have four bottles of raga wine. I'm looking for hale nuts. Any hale nuts for raga wine?"

On either side of the street were long stalls bursting with goods. In the center of the broad avenue was raised a circular set of stairs ending in a platform. On this platform sellers crowded, each waving a paper and yelling out the virtues of goods offered or wanted for purchase. Along the street at regular intervals were other such platforms, and beyond—more streets and platforms and noise.

Around the platforms the crowd ebbed and flowed,

looking over the items in the booths, picking them up, putting them down, touching, tasting, squeezing, stroking, asking the price, arguing over the price, paying the price—all in that unpleasant accent!

The stalls themselves were little more than temporary creations of wood and canvas, stretching out from the fronts of buildings. Behind the stalls stood dun-colored buildings with square windows and arched doorways. Structures crowded against each other, shouldering for space and forming rankling canyons that mazed away through the city. The dizzy chaos of mud walls was accentuated by the tiles and elaborate mosaics that covered them. No street was straight, no block was level. The roads climbed and shambled, dipped and drifted. The sense of vertigo that Gerrard had felt at the base of the impossible mountain now redoubled.

Heedless, the guard pushed through the crowd, conducting the *Weatherlight* crew through. Squee, his short green form unmistakable among the tall *Weatherlight* sailors, was several files back from the Benalian. Gerrard noticed that any time a Mercadian caught a glimpse of the goblin, he bowed low and touched his forehead. The little creature was both puzzled and impressed by this behavior, and he began to strut a bit.

Tahngarth wrinkled his nose and frowned. "They smell," he growled, gesturing at the Mercadians. "The whole place smells."

Sisay nodded her agreement. "There's a lot of incense burning around here." She stopped a moment, breathing hard, and wiped sweat from her forehead. "I don't know about the rest of you, but this place is giving me a splitting headache."

Gerrard rubbed his eyes. The street seemed to oscillate. He glanced at his companions and saw they were having similarly dazed sensations. Some of the crew were staggering. Hanna looked ready to pass out.

Gerrard knew it was now or never. He fell to his knees,

gasping, and vomited into the gutter—that much was not acting. "Water! I need some water!"

Takara's hands fidgeted on his shoulders as she relayed the message to the laughing guards.

"You, there, kid," Gerrard called, gesturing to a familiar lad with tousled black hair.

"I'm not a damned kid," Atalla spat back, though he gave a wink.

"Bring me something to drink! Wine would be good."

Nodding, Atalla darted away through the market. His cloak flashed tan beside a vintner's stall. His hands darted atop a pile of burgeoning wineskins, and he snatched one. Holding it high, he waved the skin overhead and darted back toward Gerrard.

A roar of protest rose behind him, and a morbidly obese wine seller trundled in fury after the thief.

Atalla arrived, sandals skidding on cobblestones.

"Great work, kid—sorry, Master Atalla," Gerrard said, his smile turned down into the gutter. "Quick, pull the cork, give me a sip, and dump the rest on the ground."

Atalla worked deftly.

"When the captain of the guard comes," Gerrard continued, "get his keys."

The merchant stomped up behind Atalla and caught him up by his collar. The wineskin lay empty on the pavement, and wine and vomit mingled in the gutter.

"Thief!" the wine seller roared. "I'll cut off your hand!"

Gerrard stood, towering over the merchant. "Let him go! He's no thief! I sent him to fetch some wine for my master."

"*Your* master?" the merchant asked.

Rattling the chains at his wrists, Gerrard said, "I am but a slave to the captain of the guard. He uses me to taste his food and wine, for he fears poisoning. Your wine tasted to me of poison, and I vomited it there, in the gutter." A wry light shone in his glinting eyes. "I know what to do with rubbish!"

"Rubbish? Poison?" the vintner shouted in a pique. He dropped Atalla like a rag doll. "Your master will pay for this poison!"

The captain of the guard arrived, barking questions in High Mercadian.

"Don't pay him, sir," Gerrard said, gesturing emphatically toward the gutter. His jangling chains helped to draw attention away from Atalla. "I've never tasted such putrid bile in all my life!"

"Putrid bile?" the merchant shouted. He quivered with rage. His burgundy-dyed robe swayed dangerously. "You'll pay! You'll pay!"

The captain glowered at the merchant, oblivious to the dangerous operation occurring even then at his own belt. He shouted an indecipherable warning.

"He wants to trade me for the wine," Gerrard proposed.

The merchant gasped, a breath like a huge hiccough. "I'd rather own a one-eyed syphilitic donkey than an idiot slave such as you!"

"A donkey might like your wine," Gerrard agreed.

More shouts indecipherable, more threats, more bluster . . .

Gerrard leaned conspiratorially toward the captain of the guard to whisper in his ear (in fact, he extended shackled hands to Atalla, who quickly tried key after key). "I think the vintner is calling you a syphilitic donkey."

Giving an inarticulate cry of rage, the captain raised his trident to skewer the merchant. Metal lanced downward.

The wine seller squealed and rolled back on his round haunch.

The shackles fell from Gerrard's wrists. He snatched the trident in the air before it could fall and brought its butt swinging about. The shaft struck the guard captain in the side of the face, sending up a cloud of dust.

The Mercadian tottered for a moment like a dizzy top and then went down.

Gerrard gave a whoop and whirled the trident again, bashing back the soldiers who swarmed him. Meanwhile, Atalla crawled among the other prisoners, fitting the master key to the shackles. Takara was free, and then Starke, Sisay, and Hanna . . .

Tahngarth was too impatient. He lunged toward a nearby stall, snatched up a striva, and brought the heavy blade smashing down on the chain. It clove the inferior metal easily. Tahngarth sloughed off the shackles and lifted the weapon high. Merchants, and soldiers, and even Squee fell fearfully back from him.

For his part, Squee scampered up a similarly imposing figure—Karn. Being a pacifist, Karn would probably be an island of calm in the sea of swords. Squee shinnied up the chains that wrapped Karn's torso and flung his arms around the silver man's massive neck.

Karn opened his mouth, apparently to console the goblin. Instead he bit down on the chain that held Squee. It severed in two places, and Karn spit out the shattered links.

"Return the favor?" he asked Squee. "Lift one of my chains into my mouth."

Squee did. In moments, the whole mass of chain—and the goblin clinging to it—cascaded down to the street. Karn lifted his arms. Dirt poured from the gritty joints. Sunlight gleamed off his massive figure, and the crowd fell back again.

Not all of the crowd. Though their captain lay in the middle of the road, feigning unconsciousness, other soldiers fought inward. Their tridents slashed and jabbed among canvas stalls.

Sisay, Takara, and Gerrard parried easily with the weapons they had snatched. Tahngarth's striva merely clove any haft that came nearby. Always ingenious, Hanna had retreated to a fruit cart and thrust vast purple melons onto the tridents. Inspired by her valor, Squee clambered behind the cart and pelted the soldiers with hale nuts and simsass fruits.

Karn found he need only bellow and wave his arms menacingly to keep the soldiers at bay.

"As soon as the rest are free," Gerrard hissed to Takara as he flung back a pair of attackers, "scatter and blend. We'll meet again tonight by that big tower. Pass the word."

She was telling Sisay and Hanna when a new threat arrived.

At the lower end of the road, a huge shadow appeared. The creature that cast it was larger still. The color, height, and general bulk of an adobe house, the giant lumbered up to survey the scene. Its black hair dripped grease across a rumpled forehead and squinting eyes. It blinked in indecision. Soldiers behind it prodded it forward with tridents. Muscles rippling across its broad chest, the giant strode toward the melee.

"Karn!" Gerrard shouted. "Engage that giant!"

"I will not fight!" the pacifist called back. It was a foolish announcement there and then. Soldiers approached the golem.

In exasperation, Gerrard flattened another guard and shouted. "If you won't fight him, detain him."

"How?"

"I don't know! Dance with him!"

"Dance?" Karn asked as the giant loomed up.

"Hold him tight! That's an order!"

With a deft move that belied his bulk, Karn reached out, grasped the giant about the waist, and flung him into a heady spin. Karn held on tightly. He whistled a hornpipe he'd heard aboard *Weatherlight*, and his feet pounded out a precise imitation of the reels he'd seen Sisay perform. However, the effect was somewhat different. The giant was not a good dancer. It did not even seem to be trying. When its feet were not stomping down atop Karn's, they were smashing bookstalls or overturning juice carts or caving walls. Its hand motions were also a bit abrupt, more roundhouse than rondo. Still, Karn did not give up on his student—as long as no one got hurt, what was the harm?

Laughing, Gerrard turned from that scene to one less funny.

On the high end of the road, Mercadian soldiers escorted another creature to the scene. This monster's eyes glowed orange within a skull that was molded in green muscle. Two pairs of buglike mandibles extended from its cheeks and jowls. They hungrily shivered beside its fangs. From its shoulders sprouted a pair of venous humanlike arms ending in claws. Another pair of arms emerged behind the first, these tipped in wicked barbs. The thing's muscular abdomen was perched atop legs worthy of a drake, complete with eviscerating talons.

"A cateran enforcer," hissed Atalla, scrambling up beside Gerrard. "They're the meanest mercenaries the Mercadians have. I'm getting out of here. You should too. Your folk are all free."

"Thanks ki—Atalla. I owe you one." Gerrard cupped his hands and shouted, "Scatter!"

Only too happily, most of the crew obliged. Only Karn remained, dancing with his giant, and Tahngarth, who strode up beside Gerrard.

"It has four arms, so I thought we should as well," the minotaur said.

Gerrard smiled grimly as the thing came on. "You could never resist a fight."

"Not when I have a good striva." Tahngarth lifted the curved blade overhead just as the cateran reached them.

It hurled itself hungrily atop the pair.

Tahngarth thrust the striva into the beast's belly. Metal clanged uselessly on the creature's hide. The blade that had severed iron could not penetrate that skin.

Gerrard meanwhile rammed his trident into the thing's fangs. It bit down, severing the prongs and swallowing them.

This was going badly.

In one clawed hand, the beast clutched Gerrard's head, and in the other, Tahngarth's. Its grip was implacably strong. Barbed arms entrapped them. There was no escape. Fangy jaws ratcheted wide. The beast shoved Gerrard's head toward its gullet as though his skull were a melon. It sank its teeth past the tough exterior and into red pulp and reared back. Its mouth was full of crimson chunks and seeds—

Seeds?

Squee hauled back the other half of the melon he had rammed in the thing's mouth. He shoved the ruined fruit in the cateran's eyes.

Enraged, the blinded beast dropped Gerrard and Tahngarth to rake pulp from its face. It roared, melon spewing in a red shower from its jaws.

"Squee!" Gerrard shouted, startled, "I thought I told you to scatter—"

"—I'm glad, for once, he didn't listen," Tahngarth panted, crouching to receive the beast's next attack.

The cateran scraped the last seeds from his face and lunged again.

* * * * *

"Squee shoulda listened," the little goblin shrieked as the thing launched at him. He closed his eyes, cringing back from death. Any moment, fangs and claws and barbs would descend and rip him to pieces. There would be nothing left of Squee but hunks of meat, which the merchants would probably skewer and cook and sell. . . . Yes, once this beast fell on him, he'd be done for. That would be the end of the story for Squee. A short life, over too soon . . . he rather wished the beast would get on with the killing part. The suspense was getting monotonous.

Squee opened his eyes to see something altogether unexpected. The cateran had stopped midlunge and fallen to its scabby knees. It looked up beseechingly at Squee. The goblin's incredulity was mirrored on the faces of Gerrard and Tahngarth.

Through jagged fangs, the cateran pleaded, "Forgive me, Master."

Squee looked over his shoulder to see who the beast addressed.

"He's talking to you, Squee," Gerrard hissed nervously.

Squee splayed a hand on his chest and mouthed, "To . . . Squee?"

Gerrard only nodded.

"I did not realize a Kyren sponsored these . . . worthies. I did not realize these were your friends."

Squee considered, folding arms over his chest and frowning disapprovingly. "Well, dey are! How 'bout dat!"

"I was only following orders," the beast buzzed out, still kowtowing. "Of course, my master was not Kyren. Your rank exceeds his. What are your orders, Master?"

Gerrard nodded encouragement to the goblin, his eyebrows lifted. "Yes, Master Squee. What are your orders?"

Tahngarth released a groan. "Your orders . . . Master?"

A broad smile on his face, Squee took a deep breath. "Yes. Orders. Master Squee's orders . . ."

"Yes . . ."

"Dance with dat giant," Squee said. "Karn's bushed. We're gonna go get something ta drink."

"Yes, Master."

There was no difficulty sneaking away after that. Even the reinforcement troops that arrived seemed to see nothing except the dance stylings of the cateran and the giant.

* * * * *

For a day and a night, *Weatherlight*'s crew hid out in the great city of Mercadia. All had procured Mercadian clothes, the better to blend with the crowd. Only Karn remained in his native garb of silver—though he kept to the back alleys, Squee running interference for him. As a Kyren—that is, a goblin—Squee had special rights and privileges in the city, though Gerrard still did not understand why. In time, Squee secured discreet lodgings for him and the other bridge crew members.

The streets outside buzzed with talk of the foreign warriors who had marched into the city, defeated five hundred—no, a thousand—of the city guards, fought off twenty giants, and killed a whole band of cateran enforcers. Tavern talk made them outlaw heroes, striking out against oppression. Garrison talk made them simply outlaws, but their names were mentioned only in tremulous whispers.

"Legendary Gerrard, giant killer!"

The legend of Gerrard and his band reached a fevered pitch by next afternoon. It was time to enact his plan.

Gerrard and Takara climbed the white limestone stairs of the Magistrate's Tower—the opulent building at the center of Mercadia. In this city of trade, Gerrard had heard that any citizen who had a worthwhile bargain could approach the chief magistrate. Of course, if the deal was found wanting, the citizen would probably not be found again at all. Gerrard and Takara would take that chance. The outlaws had in mind an impressive bargain.

They climbed the tower steps, which wound around the outside of the structure without a rail to guide them. Gerrard felt increasingly dizzy as the streets of Mercadia opened out below. Beyond the edge of the city, he could see forever. Far away, probably fifty miles distant, was a blurred line of yellow.

Gerrard called Takara's attention to it. "What is that?"

"The Outer Sea, I imagine," she said.

They passed a number of landings with doors into the tower. A steady stream of people were also climbing up and down the stairs, passing in and out of the various openings. None paid the slightest attention to Gerrard and Takara. Surprisingly, there was little wind. Sweat beaded on both humans' faces as they climbed.

At last, at the very top of the tower, when only the end-less sky beckoned above them, the stairs bent inward in a large landing. Its rail was inlaid with dark marble and pol-ished stones in elaborate patterns. The side of the tower was pierced by a tall wooden door framed in elaborately wrought metal.

"This is it. The audience chamber."

Gerrard pushed hard. The door swung back to reveal a dark, narrow opening. Gerrard and Takara passed through. They traveled down a short hallway hung with tapestries and decorated with mosaics, and entered a large circular chamber.

The ceiling was an open skylight through which the bright morning sun shone. A circle of pillars lined the edges of the room. In the very center was a small platform. On it rested a chair, carved of ivory, where sat the Chief Magis-trate of Mercadia.

He was short and fat, with dimpled cheeks and thinning blond hair plastered against his scalp. His robes were yellow, trimmed with scarlet. They clung closely to the rolls of fat that cascaded from his chin to his waist. Indeed, Gerrard could never remember having seen so fat a man. His flesh seemed to drip from his body, and his six chins quivered and shook. His fingers were thick and stubby, and Gerrard noticed with a flash of surprise that the nails were manifestly dirty. His mouth was a round, pursed splash of red, and his face was liberally coated with rouge and powder. A foul smell arose from him, as if he had not bathed in several weeks. It melded with the thick scent of incense that pervaded the chamber. About the magistrate's stout shoulders hung a heavy gold chain. Each of its links was a tiny casket. He rested his pudgy hands on his stomach and watched through small, piggish eyes as the visitors entered.

About the heavily perfumed room were courtiers. All were clad in shades of yellow. They lounged languidly around the chamber or relaxed on cushioned benches—on which many of them sprawled full-length—eating, drinking, and sleeping.

Something whizzed from the midst of one of these groups and struck Gerrard's foot. He leaped, startled.

There was a burst of laughter. A courtier lumbered toward him as quickly as his grotesquely fat body would permit. He bent with a grunt and retrieved a small, furry creature. Chuckling, he held it up for Gerrard's inspection. It appeared to be a species of rat, somewhat larger than Gerrard was used to seeing. Its tiny eyes glittered, and its whiskers moved back and forth as it twitched its nose. Its tail was at least a foot long and ended in a sharp cluster of spikes. Deftly, the Mercadian flipped the rat on its back and scratched its stomach. A small panel opened, showing a tangle of machinery and a tiny glowing stone.

Gerrard gasped and said to Takara, "It's a toy—with a powerstone."

"Yes." The Rathi woman stepped closer and stared intently at the mechanical creature.

Glancing around the room, Gerrard noticed a number of the other nobles were playing with toys. Many were in the shape of animals; others were fashioned in the likeness of engines and vehicles. All were small but animated by power stones. He looked at Takara and grinned. "Our terms have just gotten steeper."

Moving very little, the magistrate beckoned to Gerrard. His voice was high and strained, and Gerrard could barely hear it above the other noise in the room. The words were High Mercadian, but on the lips of the magistrate they sounded even more coarse and degenerate.

Takara translated. "The magistrate asks who you are and what you offer, to approach his exalted figure."

Lifting his eyes to the man, Gerrard said, "I am the legendary outlaw Gerrard, giant killer."

That caused a sensation. The courtiers paused in conversation and looked up. A few gathered their grapes, and cheese, and little mechanical toys, withdrawing along the wall. The guards in the room also tensed.

The magistrate's eyes darted nervously toward the door.

"Call them off, Magistrate. I have slain whole companies of your soldiers," Gerrard lied. "I will slay these and you, too, if you don't call them off."

With a pallid nod, the magistrate sent the soldiers back to their posts.

"Good," Gerrard said. "We have come to make a bargain."

"To make a bargain you came?" echoed a mocking little voice—a Kyren. He emerged from beside the ivory throne, where others of his kind stood. They were garbed in fine silks and shadows. This one walked very erect, its eyes pinning Gerrard's insolently as it approached. "Most respected Magistrate of Mercadia, may the gods bless and keep your name," observed the Kyren, "does not your ineffable wisdom truly spread wherever the name of Mercadia is known? Might a humble servant of your divine mightiness presume to offer some small tidbit of advice on the matter of this stranger?"

The magistrate gestured meaninglessly.

The goblin continued. "Would it not be proper and advisable to determine why we should give any audience to a brigand? Would it not be advisable to call the city wizards, or failing them, the city guard, or failing them, the city waste managers?"

The insouciant Kyren had ventured a little too close. Takara lunged, grabbed the beast by the throat, and hoisted it in one hand.

Guards who had not rushed to the magistrate's aid now ran toward Takara. Gerrard turned and drew a sword to ward them away.

Takara meanwhile stared into the goblin's bugging eyes. Her own eyes narrowed, and her mouth was a toothy gash across her face. "Look at me, you little bug. Look at me. Really look, and you will see why you must listen to us!"

Gerrard busily circled the pair, keeping guards at bay. Over his shoulder, he glimpsed the goblin's face. At first, there was only angry umbrage and the panic of suffocation. Then suddenly, there was something else—abject terror.

The Kyren waved the guards back.

Takara nodded, lowering the beast to the ground. She released him, and the Kyren staggered away slowly, clutching his neck.

Gerrard hissed to her, "What did you do?"

Through a humorless smile, Takara whispered, "Just let him see my hate. It is a powerful thing."

Coughing raggedly, the creature retreated toward the chief magistrate. "Might I suggest . . . the chief to treat these folk . . . as privileged citizens . . . instead of outlaws?"

The fat man's chins quivered like the wattle of a chicken. "Very well. The magistrate accepts your advice." He nodded to Gerrard.

Gerrard said, "I am the legendary Gerrard, giant killer. I would triumph no matter what forces you sent against me. My folk are as powerful as an army. Our prowess is not diminished by the fact that your troops are pathetic, listless, and hopeless. Are you satisfied with the state of your army?"

One of the goblins replied, his voice oily and unpleasant. "Is Mercadia not still threatened by enemies from abroad, and yet our armies are untrained? Is not their skill with arms poor? Are not the weapons they possess badly maintained? Have you weapons you can trade? Have you sufficient soldiers to fill our ranks?"

"Better. The legendary Gerrard will make a bargain with you," Gerrard said. "I will train your troops in the use of weaponry. I will train them how to train others. I will turn your army into a fighting machine that will be, itself, legendary."

"You will train our armies in return for what?" the Kyren asked.

"Freedom for my folk, first of all," Gerrard said. "I want them to walk the streets as citizens."

"Is there nothing more we can offer?"

"There is plenty more. When I have finished training a division of your troops, I will be granted them to march into the Rushwood to fight the Cho-Arrim. I seek to regain the airship I was falsely arrested for trading to them."

Avarice flared in the goblin's eyes. "Why would we refuse the offer of legendary Gerrard to lead our armies against our enemies?"

"Once I retrieve my ship, I want facilities here to repair it—"

"Why would we refuse to grant facil—"

"And assistance in gathering power stones to repair the ship."

"Do we not know legends of power stone troves?"

"And last, but certainly not least, I want a thousand gold coins given to the farm family of Tavoot, in payment for damages incurred."

"A thousand gold?"

"Are the terms of this bargain accepted?" Gerrard asked. "Think twice before you answer with another question!"

The Kyren's eyes grew wide.

The magistrate himself answered. "The bargain is accepted, O legendary Gerrard, giant killer. Train our troops, and your folk will be treated as citizens and honored guests. You will be granted the right to lead a division to regain your ship. If you regain your ship, you will be allowed to use our facilities to repair it and benefit from our assistance in obtaining power stones to complete the job. And a thousand gold pieces will be granted to the farm family you mentioned. Agreed."

Legendary Gerrard nodded, smiling with satisfaction. "Good."

Beside him, Takara whispered, "Good for now, but that was too easy. Nothing here is as it seems. We must proceed cautiously."

CHAPTER 5

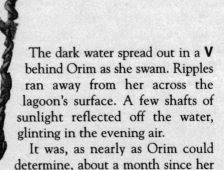

The dark water spread out in a **V** behind Orim as she swam. Ripples ran away from her across the lagoon's surface. A few shafts of sunlight reflected off the water, glinting in the evening air.

It was, as nearly as Orim could determine, about a month since her capture by the Cho-Arrim. On the forest floor it was difficult to be certain of the passage of day and night. The light was always the same soft, gray glow of the tree trunks. Within the village a fire burned at all times, and the Cho-Arrim moved about it immersed in their everyday routines. Orim slept when she was tired and awoke feeling rested and refreshed, but she had no idea whether she had been asleep two hours or ten. Perhaps the best measure of how much time had passed was how well she had picked up the Cho-Arrim language. Total immersion had taught her many words very quickly.

Total immersion . . . she dove deep and swam through dark spaces.

Orim now had full run of the settlement without accompanying guards. They would have been a useless expenditure of manpower, since Orim had no idea in which direction lay the forest's edge. If she went the wrong way and became lost, the Cho-Arrim told her, she would wander endlessly down the aisles of tall trees and never again feel the wind on her face. Certainly the forest looked the same to her wherever she walked: hoary, shaggy, vast, and vaguely threatening. Her sole clear landmarks were the village and the lagoon that bordered it—the lagoon whose waters seemed to swell and recede according to some strange rhythm. Odd sounds came from the water occasionally, noises too deep and remote to come from human or animal throats.

She surfaced. A few hundred feet from where Orim swam, *Weatherlight* floated peacefully. Figures moved casually on the upper deck. One waved to Orim, and she waved back.

To these folk, *Weatherlight* was not a ship. It was an oracle. Even down here among the trees, they had glimpsed *Weatherlight*'s cometary arrival across the sky and had believed the airship to be their god Ramos. An old myth told of Ramos falling from the heavens and breaking into pieces—soul, mind, and body. All the evils of Mercadia arose from his broken being. A prophecy told that Ramos would return, and if soul, mind, and body were reunited, he would unite the world and drive the evil away. To these folk, *Weatherlight* was not a warship but something altogether more valuable. It was a holy relic—the soul of a god.

There was no arguing with gods or their believers. Orim no longer tried to disabuse these folk of their strange notions about the ship. She only waved and smiled at the soldiers, turned, and swam for shore.

In the roots of the tree where she'd left her clothes, the healer found Is-Shada, her arms clasped about shapely knees, dark hair pulled back in a braid.

She giggled as Orim shivered. "I told you it was too cold."

"Cold water can be good for you," Orim said serenely. "At the university, we used to pour cold water over ourselves every morning and evening. In the winter we had to break the ice on the surface."

Is-Shada's giggles grew louder. "You were young and foolish. I'm young and sensible. You won't catch me swimming for at least another month. What was the 'university'?"

Orim had become accustomed to Is-Shada's rapid-fire questions. At first, when she only vaguely understood their meaning, she had labored over her answers, provoking still more questions and frustration on both sides. Now the healer had learned to pick and choose the questions to which she supplied detailed replies. Is-Shada never stopped asking, though.

"The university was a place at which I studied my art. My friend Hanna studied there as well."

"Hanna!" Is-Shada exclaimed. "What is she like? Is she pretty like you? Did she study the healing arts as you did? Where was the university?"

"Hanna is very pretty," Orim replied. She had not thought of *Weatherlight*'s navigator in some time. Is-Shada's question conjured up a mental picture of Hanna, her face grimy with grease, bent eagerly over a dissected component of the ship's engine—but pretty. Always pretty. "She was not a healer, though. At the university she studied artifacts."

"What is an artifact?"

Orim laughed. "It's—an artifact. A magical object." She pointed toward the ship. "*Weatherlight* is an artifact."

Is-Shada's eyes, always expressive, grew round and wide.

"An artifact? Really? It's more than that! Much more."

"Yes," Orim replied, her eyes faraway. "Yes, on that we agree."

Is-Shada looked troubled. "I think we should not speak of this." She lay back and watched as Orim bound her turban about her head. "Why do you wear your hair like that? It conceals your beauty."

"It marks my status as a healer," Orim replied.

Is-Shada looked serious. "Yes. You healed me that horrible night. Do you have chavala?"

"What is chavala?"

Is-Shada hesitated, struggling for the right words. "It is a gift from above," she replied slowly. "It is not given often, but those who possess it stand high in the favor of the tribe and of the gods. Ta-Karnst is so marked."

Orim put out a hand and pulled the younger woman to her feet. "Come on. Let's get back to the village before they think I've run off."

As they made their way through the trees, both women greeted the tribesmen they passed. Some sat industriously by the side of the lagoon, pulling gently on fishing nets. Much of the Cho-Arrim diet consisted of fish, supplemented by fruits, berries, and vegetables collected from various parts of the forest. Orim had not tasted red meat since she had been among the tribe, and she found the change a welcome one.

As a rule, Cho-Arrim preferred the cool, pale light that came from lanterns that each home possessed, or the gentle silver light of the forest itself. Tonight, though, the bonfire burning in the middle of the village was heaped high with fuel, driving away the cold and shadows. Around the fire, a large group had gathered.

Orim and Is-Shada approached curiously, and the younger woman gave a delighted clap of her hands.

"It's the separi! The storytellers. They are about to start!"

There were seven separi, three women and four men. They looked no different from the other Cho-Arrim Orim had met, but the village tribesfolk surrounded them, chattering cheerfully. One by one, villagers found seats around the fire. The very old and young were wrapped in shawls and blankets. Orim and Is-Shada settled in among them.

The separi began to perform. Around the fire they went, each carrying two masks, which they alternated as they assumed different characters. For the most part, the stories were simple fables, easy to follow, mostly comic. Orim laughed with the rest of the village, and when she had any trouble understanding, Is-Shada, curled up catlike at her side, explained.

In time, there came a short pause. The players gathered in front of the fire, upon which several villagers stacked more wood so that it blazed with a sudden ferocity. Then the separi began another play.

This was evidently not comic, and Orim had more difficulty following the action. It concerned some great conflict, for two men stood opposite one another, moving their hands in complex rhythms as their minions battled. Sometimes the fighters pretended to wield swords or spears; other times they moved swiftly, as if imitating machines that hacked and clawed at one another. The two sides separated, and Orim saw that the man on one side had been joined by a woman, from whose mask flowed a tangle of vines dyed bright red to simulate hair. On the opposing side were two figures, both male. In the middle, two separi surrounded a female, her mask trailing green vines. She swirled the tendrils around her, a whirling cloud of green and yellow. As the motions of the opposing men became more intense, supported by the players at their sides, the woman in the middle gradually sank to her knees. Her motions became slower, then ceased altogether.

Something about the performance touched the very edge

of Orim's memory. Dimly she recalled similar events: a mighty conflict between rival magicians, a conflict that ended in tragedy and death. She had heard the story back at the Argivian University, sitting in the library on a gloomy winter day, glancing through an obscure, age-old poem. . . .

Recognition came in a sudden shock. "It's the Brothers' War!"

"What?" Is-Shada had been lying on her stomach, intent on the play.

"The Brothers' War!" Orim slapped her hand against Is-Shada's foot in excitement. "I learned this legend at the university. Two brothers, Urza and Mishra, fought a war against one another on the continent of Terisiare. During the latter part of the war, they invaded the island of Argoth and fought until it was devastated. We were taught that the spirit of nature in Argoth died when the brothers had completed their battle. Then there was a huge explosion that killed both brothers and ended the war."

Is-Shada was plainly uninterested in her friend's story. "That's not what this is about," she said, turning back to the figures by the fire. "Watch."

The battle was reaching a climax. The gestures had become more violent. The red-haired woman slowly crossed the space between the two principal figures, her arms outstretched. Her former ally, whose mask was painted in dark, handsome features, lifted his hands and clapped. The red-haired woman dropped to the ground. The dark man lifted his arms in a gesture of triumph. He hefted three great stones waiting beside the fire, set them on his back, and began a whirling dance around the flames. At the height of one turn, he seemed struck by something, and the three stones flew outward, dropping among the fallen folk. Then, the man himself collapsed.

All the separi lay still on the ground now, save one, wearing a golden mask, who stepped over their bodies. She reached down and touched each of the fallen, and at her touch each one rose. Finally, when all were standing, they wove back and forth in an intricate dance until at last they joined in a single entity.

This episode brought the play to an end. The separi discarded their masks and stood grinning amid the plaudits of the watching Cho-Arrim.

Orim clapped with the rest of the crowd and then turned to Is-Shada. "All right. What is it about?"

Is-Shada shrugged. "It is the Peliam, the origin story," she said. "It tells us where everything came from and to where we'll return when we die."

"All right," said Orim after a pause. "Tell me."

Is-Shada spoke as if talking to a child. "The fight was between two gods, Ramos and Orhop. Each had pulled down a piece of the heavens, and each sought to use it to best the other. In the end, Ramos triumphed, and Orhop, the evil god, was vanquished. Ramos grieved for the ruin he had brought to his world. And so, he gathered the people of forest and plain and mountain and set them on his back and carried them to a new world, a better world. But when he arrived, he was struck from the sky and fell in three great pieces—soul, mind, and body. Borne atop his soul, the tribes of the Cho-Arrim landed in the forests. Those atop his mind—the Saprazzans—fell into the oceans. And those atop his body—some fell from the fiery corpse and struck the coastal lands, and they became the Rishadans. Those who held on to the blazing body were slain and lie now guarding the bones of Ramos. That is why when we die, we return to the heavens, the place from which we came. Once there, we are joined in the Great River that runs among the stars until at last it falls off the edge of the world into the great, everlasting dark."

Orim nodded thoughtfully. "And who in the play was the red-haired woman?"

"A demon who pretended to support Ramos in the conflict. In the end, she betrayed him, but he defeated her and so won the war. Her name was Hassno the Unrighteous."

"And the last part of the play?"

"Though the children of Ramos—Cho-Arrim, Rishadan, Saprazzan—were scattered through forest, plain, and sea, someday will come the Uniter. He will be a great metal serpent. When he returns, all the children of Ramos will be joined as one and will triumph over our enemies," Is-Shada said with conviction.

"And you believe *Weatherlight* is the soul of this Uniter?"

Is-Shada pushed back the dark hair that framed her heart-shaped face. "You would have to ask Cho-Manno."

"You know, there were other folk who thought the owner of *Weatherlight* was a uniter—the Korvecdal."

The woman only shrugged. "Truth is truth, wherever it is found."

* * * * *

Orim startled awake from a nightmare. Her heart pounded in her chest.

She had dreamed of monsters—inhuman beasts with four arms, boar-heads, scorpion tails. They scaled the vast forest wall, where tree trunks formed a barrier a hundred feet high. The monsters leaped upward, as nimble and bloodthirsty as fleas. They loped into the nighttime wood. Whenever they encountered a creature—whether coney-fox or wumpus or red wolf—the monsters fell upon it, tore it to pieces, ate their victim's innards, and flung away bone and muscle to rot. Their claws girdled ancient trees. Their talons tore up undergrowth. Worst of all, they arrowed straight through the forest toward the Cho-Arrim village.

"Just a nightmare," Orim said to herself, panting and clutching a hand to her chest. Her bed of leaves and moss lay, warm and familiar, beneath her. Solid walls of wood enclosed her. Is-Shada's room was just down the corridor, and Cho-Manno's beyond. She was safe. "Just a nightmare."

Feet came along the passage—probably Is-Shada, checking on her.

"You are awake," came a man's voice, basso in the darkness.

"Cho-Manno!" Orim gasped, grabbing a robe from a hook on the wall and holding it over herself. "What are you doing—?"

"You dreamed it too," he interrupted. His eyes glinted in the dark. "That's good. The Rushwood is getting its roots in you."

"You had the same nightmare?"

"Yes. Mercenaries. Monsters. They must be caterans," Cho-Manno answered. "But it was not our dream. It was Rushwood's. And it was not just a dream. The monsters are coming."

Orim stood. "Where can we flee? They can run, and climb—"

"We do not flee. We fight. The forest awoke us to mount a defense. Even now, it awakes other defenders—ancient things that have not walked the land in centuries—but they rouse slowly. We must go. We are the first line of defense."

"We?" Orim asked, astonished. "I'm not a fighter."

"You are a healer, like Ta-Karnst. The forest dreams in you, as in him—chavala. Where there are fighters, there must be healers."

Dropping her robe, Orim donned her healer's cloak, slipped on her leggings and boots, and wrapped the turban about sleep-tousled hair. "I'm ready."

"Good," Cho-Manno said, holding his hand out in the darksome room. She saw then that he himself wore only a loincloth. "My armor and sword wait by the door. Already, the skyscouts and wizards are on their way." Orim took his hand. It was strong and warm. A salty scent enveloped him. "Let us fight for the Rushwood."

A coney-fox darted, shrieking. Ears lay back along its shoulders. Gray haunches pumped furiously. Claws flung up the mossy ground. Hunks of lichen smacked the fangs of its pursuer.

The monstrous thing came on, heedless. Eyes glowed yellow deviltry in the night. Mandibles thrashed hungrily. Four arms raked out after its prey. Taloned feet tore the ground. A barb-tipped appendage stabbed down, pinning the coney-fox's bushy tail.

With another shriek, the terrified creature yanked free, leaving half its tail behind. It bled. Each bound flung a sanguine trail behind it. The monster would never give up now. It would follow the blood path across the forest floor. It was doomed. *To ground*—every coney-fox knew to go to ground to die. It vaulted over a root tangle and scrambled down into the vast hole that opened on the other side.

Darkness lay ahead. The silver glow of the tree trunks receded. The coney-fox bounded down a worn trail among roots. There was a strong smell ahead.

Another creature laired down here, a creature with massive claws, a scaly gray hide, huge muscles—a crouched and lumbering thing. Its mouth was filled with blunt, plant-eating teeth. This beast was a protector. The coney-fox leaped beneath it, flushing it from cover. The lumbering satyr jumped up the side of the hollow just as the fanged monster plunged down it.

The satyr lunged atop the cateran enforcer. Quicker and crueler, the cateran bit open the beast's belly and started feasting.

In its dying gasps, the satyr clasped the cateran's legs and yanked them apart as though it were breaking a wishbone. A messy moment followed, and then one dead beast collapsed atop the other.

The coney-fox cowered silently below.

More fanged horrors vaulted over the pit and raced on into the deep forest.

*   *   *   *   *

By the time Orim, Cho-Manno, Ta-Karnst, and Ta-Spon arrived at the battleground, the forest was bathed in blood.

Red shafts jutted from the bellies and brainpans of fallen monsters—boar-headed men, demon-eyed beasts, four-armed killers, things with scorpion tails, snake bodies, roach legs. . . . They lay thick across the ground behind the battle lines. Scores more had broken through, crashing against hastily entrenched Cho-Arrim warriors.

Black armor bashed black carapace. Darting swords of bone parried darting stingers of poison. The Cho-Arrim were outnumbered four to one, but they bravely fought on. Unarmored archers even waded into the midst, their arrows leaping a mere arm's length to pierce fiendish eyes. The Cho-Arrim made a valiant stand, but more inhuman monsters rushed from the dark woods.

A four-armed monster ripped the armor from one warrior's chest and plunged its claws through skin and muscle and rib to pierce the flailing heart within. A boar-headed beast drove its tusks up beneath a woman's jaw, impaling her and whipping her back and forth until her chin ripped off. A scorpion-man sunk its stingers in an archer's eyes and smiled lustfully as it pumped its red venom into his brain.

"I've got to get down there!" Orim gasped, clawing forward over a mossy root bulb.

Cho-Manno's hand pulled her back. "No. Wait here with Ta-Karnst. If my healers die, my warriors are doomed. First, let us drive them back. Then you emerge to tend the wounded." Drawing his bone sword, Cho-Manno strode down the embankment. Beside him went Ta-Spon, the gigantic executioner who had slain Klaars. Ta-Spon bore a massive spiked mace on his shoulder. Soon, those spikes would be running in blood.

"Drive them back?" Orim worried aloud as she watched the men's broad, armored shoulders. "How can they possibly drive them back?"

Young and lithe beside her, Ta-Karnst pointed to a rise of wood that overlooked the battlefield. "Watch. The wizards have arrived."

"What good is water magic in a dry place?"

"No place is truly dry," Ta-Karnst said. "Look!"

A spell leaped in white ribbons down from the hillside. It surged toward the center of the battle, where a four-armed beast tore apart warrior after warrior. The monster stood in a small swale between roots. Blood mantled the creature and filled the spot to cover its talons. Tendrils of force plunged into the blood pool, coiling through it, enlivening it. A sanguine vortex rose. As it gathered more liquid, the vortex formed into a man—a man of blood. With no sword, no armor, the man rammed his gory fist down the cateran's throat. His arm followed to the elbow, to the shoulder.

"What is it doing?" Orim asked.

"Drowning the beast in blood," Ta-Karnst said.

Gagging, clutching its throat, the cateran fell to its knees. Red bubbles gushed from its mouth, and it sank down in the pool of blood surrounding it. Gore disgorged from the monster's nostrils and mouth. The pool churned again, another vortex rising. The blood warrior drew more power from the pool and strode out to attack a second beast.

"We are, after all, creatures filled with water," Ta-Karnst said. "But we are not the only ones—see?"

Another spell lashed down from the wizards on the hill. Fingers of mist reached out and wrapped around a boar-headed invader. Droplets of water condensed out of air and

81

soaked into the beast's hide. Moments later, steam issued from its every pore. The monster shuddered, flesh seemed to boil. It opened its mouth to bellow, but only steam jetted angrily forth. With it came the unmistakable scent of roast boar. It, too, collapsed.

As more magic roared down from the hilltop, Cho-Manno and his warriors made brutal work of the beasts. The chieftain strode angrily against the foes, driving his sword into bellies and hearts and eyes. Ta-Spon's mace had become an aspergillum that laved the battlefield in blood. Beside him fought the blood warrior, empowered by the red rain in the air.

No new monsters joined the fray, and those already fighting fell back before the Cho-Arrim defenders.

"And now, they are trapped," Ta-Karnst said, gesturing behind the line of beasts.

From the treetops, on cords as long and sleek as spider webs, dropped the skyscouts. Others glided down on capes that draped from ankles to wrists. They reached the ground and drew their swords. In moments, as many Cho-Arrim stood behind the beasts as before them. The battlefield had become a vice.

"Let's go," Orim said. She vaulted over the root cluster and ran down the slope. Ta-Karnst followed behind.

They reached the first of the fallen warriors, many of them dead. For those who lived, there were bandages and salves, opiates to deaden local pain and soporifics to bring sleep. The work was brutal and busy. The number of wounded was overwhelming. Lacerations, amputations, eviscerations, poisonings . . .

Orim worked over her ninth patient when Cho-Manno strode to her side.

"The battle is won," he said heavily.

"I'm still fighting mine," Orim replied, cinching a tourniquet on a ruined arm. Panting, she asked, "Do we even know who the attackers were? Where they came from?"

Cho-Manno stooped, helping to tie the tourniquet in place. "They were cateran mercenaries, as I thought. They were hired by the Mercadians."

Shaking her head bitterly, Orim hissed, "Mercadians . . . they are not among the children of Ramos, are they?"

"No. Their origin is different than ours. But the forest knows them, now. They will not win so far inward again. As soon as Mercadians harm the forest again, greater powers will arise. The forest itself will destroy them."

"Vicious monsters. Why are the Mercadians attacking us?"

Cho-Manno's eyes were dark in his handsome face. "They came to capture *Weatherlight*."

CHAPTER 6

Tahngarth coughed and spat a gobbet of dust-blackened spit into the parched earth. The beads in his hair rattled in the dry wind. The minotaur reached up behind his neck and adjusted the straps of the pack riding high on his muscular shoulders. He twisted his other arm, reaching inside the heavy fabric of his brocaded jacket. His thick fingers scrabbled against his chest, reached his armpit, and gave a long, satisfying scratch.

Around him soldiers of the Mercadian Imperial Guard

Fifth Regiment groaned in the unrelenting heat. A stench rose from their sweating bodies, almost palpable in the dusty air. Around them, the broad plain before the city stretched away into nothingness. Far to the west, a thick brown eddy of dust swirled, spitting out long tendrils of dun-colored grit.

A thudding of claws nearby made the minotaur look up. Astride a nettled jhovall rode a familiar green form.

"Speed it up, men!" trumpeted Squee shrilly. "Keep dat line straight! Dress da front of the rear! Wheel behind da right of flank left!"

Since facing down a cateran enforcer a moonturning ago, Squee had pressed every advantage of his species. Goblins were accorded strange honors in Mercadia. It had taken Gerrard a whole week to convince his soldiers they did not need to listen to the "little commander"—that Squee in fact *wanted* them not to listen. After a month of training, the soldiers dutifully ignored Squee's commands. They marched steadily forward, looking neither left nor right.

With some difficulty, the goblin turned his large steed until he caught sight of the minotaur. "Hallo, Tahngarth. Didn't see you. Squee's having fun. How 'bout you?"

The minotaur's enhanced muscles bulged and swelled, and he bent his head without saying a word. He thought a good many words, though, and muttered a few under his breath.

Squee rode to the rear of the procession, where he found Gerrard, similarly mounted. The Benalian was sweating copiously. Near him, a group of young Mercadian nobles, dressed in the uniforms of brigadiers and generals, were being carried in litters by slaves. Other slaves walked alongside, waving large wood and parchment fans to create a continuous breeze upon the noble companions.

"Hoy, Squee! Everything going well up in front?" Gerrard asked, not expecting to get any real information from the goblin's answer.

"Oh, yeah. Great. Gerrard?"

"What?" The Benalian spoke through dry, cracked lips.

"Ain't you supposed to salute Squee when yer talking to Squee?"

Gerrard's lips moved, forming some of the same words Tahngarth spoke fifty yards away. Next, the Benalian thought sourly, the little goblin will expect to take Sisay's place as captain of *Weatherlight*.

That thought jolted Gerrard's mind back to the present. With a quick command he brought the party around in a right turn and then headed them back in the direction in which they'd come. Every day, every foray, the Mercadians improved a bit. He held up a finger, marking wind direction, and then rode up beside Tahngarth. "Well, what do you think? Are they ready?"

"No," the minotaur growled. "Their discipline is poor, and too many have not yet mastered fighting skills. If they were to confront properly trained soldiers, they would be slaughtered."

"I agree. From what Takara reports, the Cho-Arrim are more than trained soldiers. They're bloodthirsty head-hunters. It would be murder to march into Rushwood with unseasoned troops." Gerrard shook his head. "But from now on, we drive these enlistees harder. . . . Who knows what those inhuman monsters have done with Orim?"

The shrill voice of Squee broke into the conversation. "Play dead! Everybody, roll over 'n' play dead!"

In unison, Tahngarth and Gerrard spoke a curse.

* * * * *

The vendor ran a hand lovingly over his display. It was hard to imagine that anywhere in the lands ruled by Mercadia was a farm that could best these farfhallen melons: firm, ripe, an edge of green showing along the creases in the rind. He drew the morning air into his lungs and let loose a bellow heard across the entire marketplace. "Fresh scarlet melons! Beautiful farfhallen melons! Ripe for the taking! Who'll take some nice, ripe farfhallen melons?"

Out of the corner of his eye, he saw a long, thin arm reach for the fruit and pull one off the stand. Visions of adolescent boys, the bane of his existence, filled his mind, and he spun around, slapping down hard. An outraged squeal was heard, and the merchant found himself facing a small, green figure whose face showed surprise, anguish, and anger.

It was a goblin.

Yet this one was different. The merchant looked at the small green figure carefully. Like everyone else, he was well acquainted with Kyren, but this goblin was smaller than most. His eyes were dull and lacked the malicious glint of those who daily ascended the steps of the Tower of the Magistrate.

The farmer snatched back his hand as if it had been burned, his voice switching to a pleasant tenor. "I do beg your pardon, my good sir. I'm pleased my melons have found favor with you."

The thin, green face looked inquisitively at him. Behind the thief loomed an enormous brown figure, twisted horns brushing the top of the stall. The farmer gave a whimper of fear and stepped back away from his wares.

"Come, Squee. It's only a melon. Give it back and come along."

"But, Tahngarth, Squee's terrible hungry."

"You are always terribly hungry."

"Not always!" The goblin's face wore an injured expression. "But Squee ain't had a decent meal since we got ta this place." He looked disdainfully at the melon. "This place ain't got no proper goblin food. What 'bout bugs? What 'bout slugs? Squee ain't seen none around nowhere anyhow."

The farmer found his voice. "Pardon me, but the melons are scarce this season. There has been little rainfall in the lowlands, and Cho-Arrim raiders plague the caravans."

The minotaur gave a sour grunt. "Put it back and come."

"Sir, wait!" The merchant ignored the enormous brown creature and deferentially addressed Squee. "Allow me to offer you this melon—as a gift."

A young blonde woman, who had materialized by the minotaur's side, said to the merchant, "We apologize for our friend's behavior. We're a bit new to the city. We thank you for your generosity."

The fruit seller performed an obsequious obeisance. "Whatever our scaly friends desire."

The blonde woman wore an unsettled expression. "Yes, we've noticed."

* * * * *

"I can't believe they already sent a contingent after *Weatherlight!*" Gerrard growled, whirling his sword. The blade struck the practice dummy, shearing off its head. "I can't believe they didn't wait until our troops were trained!"

Takara took a deep breath of the dusty afternoon air. Gazing at the decapitated dummy, she said with dark humor, "If it is any consolation, the force they sent was slaughtered."

"Of course they were slaughtered!" Gerrard said. He kicked the post and snapped the thing in half. His troops on the practice grounds beyond stared with bald fear at their angry commander. "Of course they were slaughtered. Our fighters are the only fighters Mercadia has. It's taken us six weeks to turn these lazy sausages into fighting men. Anybody else would have been killed."

The Mercadians' eyes grew wider still. They stared down into the dust, practice swords hanging limp in their hands.

In six weeks, every last one had dropped in weight and bulked their muscles. They had learned to fight hard and bathe afterward. They were even beginning to be impressive with trident and sword, but still they feared their vitriolic commander.

Takara, on the other hand, seemed to thrive on his fury. He hissed, "They're trying to get to *Weatherlight* before we can. They're trying to renege on the deal."

Folding arms over her breastplate, Takara replied, "That's not reneging. They've met all the demands and will let you have your force when they are trained. The Mercadians never agreed to leave *Weatherlight* alone."

Gerrard nodded, sweat falling from his forehead. "Well, we'll just have to take these soldiers sooner."

"The Cho-Arrim aren't just cannibals. They're monsters, if you can believe these Mercadians. These Cho-Arrim are apparently vicious, inhuman beasts."

"All the more reason to whip these sad sacks into shape, and quickly. Orim is a prisoner among them—if she still lives," Gerrard said. "Go find Tahngarth and Sisay. I know this is their day off, but from now on none of us gets a day off until we have *Weatherlight* back."

"As you wish," Takara said, striding away.

Gerrard turned toward the Mercadian troops and barked out, "Back to the drill!"

* * * * *

The minotaur grumbled as they left the merchant's tent. Squee greedily seized another melon and began to munch on it, the juice dribbling over his chin.

A porter rushing along with a heavy basket of fruit on his shoulder barreled into the goblin and sprawled, the basket spilling bright red berries. Hanna and Tahngarth bent to retrieve what they could. Seeing Squee, the porter gave a sudden shriek and rushed off, leaving his basket and scattered wares behind him.

Tahngarth gave a snort, trying not to laugh. "Kyren goblins! What sort of place is ruled by goblins?"

Hanna shook her head. "I don't know. It's clear they're very important."

"Goblins! What 'bout goblins?" Squee appeared at her elbow, his nose and mouth smeared with red berries.

Hanna said sharply, "You shouldn't eat these things until you know what they are."

"Yeah, but how're you gonna know what they are without tasting 'em?"

The trio passed on down the street. Every few yards they were confronted with yet another merchant shouting and gesturing. It was a dizzying spectacle. The whole city was dizzying. During their six-week stay, the crew had come to realize the labyrinth of streets was ruled by a contorted, recursive geometry. A person could reach a landmark not by walking toward it but by walking away. A woman striding down a straight street would discover that she had been going in circles. A man wandering in circles would quickly reach his destination. It was as though a city of millions had been impossibly squeezed into a city of a hundred thousand. Space folded and refolded, maddeningly unpredictable. Sobriety led to utter confusion. Delirium led to truth.

Squee did quite well under these conditions. He did not even notice the disparities. Hanna's navigational sense was intrigued. She had plotted neighborhoods with various projections and found no system of coordinates adequate. Tahngarth—and other linear thinkers—spent their days hopelessly lost and suffering constant, raging headaches.

Tahngarth stumped irritably along. Buyers and sellers scattered before his hooves. The navigator looked at him and was struck at the change that had come over the minotaur. His bulky muscles were impressive, his frame more imposing than before his imprisonment in Volrath's Stronghold. Yet in his brown eyes there was a haunted look, as if something deep within him had died.

On an impulse, she put her hand on his broad arm and guided the minotaur to the base of a small tree. Here there were no stalls, and the noise was somewhat diminished. Hanna sank to the ground with a sigh of relief. Tahngarth remained standing. Squee squatted near them for a short time and then nosed off.

"Come, my friend. Sit down." She tugged at Tahngarth's tunic. He cleared his throat and knelt by her side with every appearance of reluctance.

"Do you want to tell me what the matter is, Tahngarth?"

"No. You would not understand."

"Perhaps I would. Suppose I tell you what I think is troubling you, and you tell me if I'm wrong?"

He stared sullenly into the middle distance where the Tower of the Magistrate rose against the lemon sky.

Hanna followed his gaze. "You were hurt in the Stronghold. However, Volrath didn't only torture you, he altered you. So much I've already heard from Gerrard, but I think there's something else to be said. I think you're afraid of something."

"Afraid!"

Hanna shrank back at the minotaur's roar.

"I am afraid of nothing!" He looked at her and blew a deep breath through his great nostrils. "Yet you are right. I would prefer I had died on Rath."

Hanna sighed in exasperation. "Oh, really? Well, that would be a lot of help to us here, wouldn't it? Then we'd be mourning you *and* Mirri." She leaned back, appraising the minotaur. "Is it the physical changes that bother you?"

Tahngarth stared silently into space. When Hanna started to get up, he spoke. "Ever since I was a tiny calf, I was told how handsome I was. I thought myself the handsomest of any minotaur in my tribe. I was more than handsome—I was beautiful." He turned and looked her full in the face. "Among my people, destinies are written in our faces, our bodies. I knew I would grow up to be a great warrior because I looked like a great warrior."

Hanna said thoughtfully, "Surely there must be more to being a warrior than looking the part?"

"There is, of course. One must train long and hard, hone one's fighting skills, prove oneself against others. But looks are by no means unimportant." He looked at her sharply. "Tell me this is not true among humans."

"It isn't," protested Hanna.

"Of course it is. Do you mean to tell me, Hanna, that when you look at Gerrard you do not see one who looks like a hero?" Though Hanna started to speak, the minotaur interrupted. "Sometimes during our journeys together I've heard you and others aboard *Weatherlight* speak of the great heroes of the past. Did you never notice that in all those tales the men are tall, strong, and handsome? That the women are exquisitely beautiful? Would you have enjoyed those stories just as much if the women had been ugly, and the men short, fat, and deformed? Would you still follow Gerrard if he looked like a rotten potato?"

Hanna spoke coldly. "I certainly hope that I can see beyond the surface. Gerrard is heir to the Legacy. That's why we follow him."

The minotaur shook his great head. "If Squee were heir to the Legacy, would you follow him?"

Hanna laughed. The idea of anyone following Squee anywhere was absurd. "But you're still exceedingly handsome, still young and strong."

"No. Strong but twisted. Volrath's soldiers placed me in a room where a beam of light shot from the ceiling. No matter which way I turned I could not avoid it." His voice cracked at the memory. "Finally it struck me, pinned me. I could feel it within me. My bones turned and twisted. My skin felt as if it was breaking. When it stopped, Greven il-Vec came. He looked at me and laughed. He said I might make a good first mate for him." The minotaur turned and stared at the blonde woman by his side. "And for a moment, I could see myself standing by his side. I could see myself, in my new, scarred body, standing on the deck of that dark ship as it swept across the skies of Rath. More than that, I *wanted* to be there." He lifted his great fist and slammed it into the ground. "Strong but twisted."

Hanna jumped as the earth quaked. There was a long silence, and then she said cautiously, "But you were rescued."

"Yes, yes, but I might have joined the dark ship had not Gerrard rescued me."

Hanna shook her head. "No, you wouldn't have, Tahngarth. Anyway, the past doesn't matter. What matters is what you are today, and right now you're the first mate of *Weatherlight*." She cleared her throat. "Maybe you have a point about appearances. But even if that's the case, I can tell you that you look like a first mate to me. Indeed, you look like a hero."

Tahngarth remained deep in thought for several minutes. Then he clapped Hanna on the shoulder. "Perhaps I have been brooding too much on this matter."

The conversation was ended abruptly by the arrival of Takara. "Tahngarth, Gerrard wants you and Sisay. He's ready to form up the troops for inspection. He's ready to march to the Rushwood."

* * * * *

Dust was everywhere. Grit filled sky and earth. It stung eyes and scoured noses. It clung to teeth and poured into ears. It clogged pores and tickled in necklines and filled the shaggy pelts of jhovalls.

Mercadian dust-magic moved whole armies rapidly across the plain, but they arrived looking like dirt clods.

Riding a great rust-colored jhovall, Gerrard led the Mercadian Imperial Guard Fifth Regiment through the dust cloud. To his right hand rode Takara, wrapped in a sandy scarf. To his left were Sisay and Tahngarth. Gerrard wanted his crew members beside and behind him—the best and most loyal fighters in his elite division. At their backs rode one hundred highly trained Mercadian warriors. Though grit covered their faces, they rode in even ranks. Amid swirling dust, the troops were mere shades of brown, yellow, and gray, but their weapons gleamed. Behind these riders came the most fearsome troops of all—caterans. The mercenaries were a motley and bloodthirsty band, some human but most inhuman, monstrous. They were cruel and unruly, loyal to Gerrard only through their commander, Xcric.

Gerrard whistled a distinctive trill. Out of the blinding cloud behind him rode Xcric. He was a cateran enforcer much like the one Squee had cowed in the marketplace that first day. Demonic eyes gleamed in his bulbous skull. Four mandibles plucked sand from a fangy mouth. Four arms jutted from his twisted shoulders. Clawed hands clutched the beast's reins, and barbed nubs held a lizard-skin cloak tight to his back. This taloned horror was no more than a brigand—and yet the Mercadians had hired him and insisted that he and his gang accompany the crew. Gerrard couldn't refuse.

"How close are we to the Rushwood?"

"Close." The creature's face was a mask of brown dirt. "Between a half mile and a quarter mile."

Gerrard nodded. "All right. Tell your people to fight only on my orders. We're counting on surprise and skill at arms, not brute force."

The fangy smile on Xcric's face was indecipherable. "Oh,

yes. I'll tell them." He reigned in his jhovall and dropped back through the ravening storm.

Takara leaned toward Gerrard, putting a hand on his knee. "You'd better be ready to fight, Gerrard."

"I don't trust the caterans," Gerrard replied. "They could just as easily kill Orim as the Cho-Arrim."

"And if the Cho-Arrim have already killed your friend—*our* friend—what then?"

Gerrard's smile was humorless. "Then I'll let the caterans kill as many as they want."

The dust cloud suddenly thinned and fell away entirely. The ever-present shroud of tan dissipated, replaced by a searing yellow sky, parched brown soil, and the vast green wall of the Rushwood.

The ancient forest was an imposing sight. Tree trunks, as wide around as mansions, reached to the sky. They were packed as tightly as teeth in a titan's smile. The lower boles and root bulbs had fused together into a smooth and sloping wall a hundred feet high. Above it, trunks divided and soared straight up, mossy columns in a colossal temple. They supported a lofty and dense ceiling of foliage and vines. Trees receded into dim infinity.

"Is this the right spot, Sisay?" Gerrard asked.

She nodded grimly, staring at a small map scroll. "Yes, if Mercadian cartography can be trusted." Sisay wiped dust from her face. The beautiful sheen of her skin appeared beneath it. She stared at the dark forest ahead. "It's another world in there, Gerrard. Outsiders are not welcome. It's no wonder the caterans before us got slaughtered."

Takara studied Sisay. "Those Cho-Arrim survive in a forest where caterans don't."

"Perhaps they survive because the forest wants them to," Sisay replied. "Stories in the Mercadian libraries tell that the Rushwood is a living entity, a great thinking thing. It will know we enter it. It will marshal defenses."

Gerrard nodded. "Then let us enter respectfully. Fight only if you are attacked. Relay the word." He set heels to his jhovall's flanks.

He rode up the slanting ground beneath the forest wall. His tawny mount flung back the bank easily. It bounded, weary of dust flats and eager for woodlands. The jhovall's claws sank in the loamy soil.

Takara, Sisay, and Tahngarth followed in his wake, and the Mercadian Guard and caterans brought up the rear. Though individually soft-footed, en masse the jhovalls made a vast rumble on the sloping ground.

Gerrard's mount reached a wooden wall and climbed. Claws gripped ancient bark. The beast hurled itself upward. Gerrard leaned forward in the saddle. With its six legs, the jhovall ascended with greater ease than a typical cat. In moments, it topped the forest wall and entered the cool, wet space between trees. Bounding over lichen and spongy humus, the tiger-creature led the mounted corps into the forest.

"So," Gerrard murmured to himself, "this is the Rush-wood."

Glaring dust gave way to damp murk. Sweat turned cold on necks. Shouts and rumbling footfalls were swallowed in a preternatural hush. The forest seemed to hold its breath as the army charged inward.

Gerrard motioned Sisay up beside his surging steed. Her mount matched his stride for stride. So quiet were their footfalls across moss and mushroom that the two old friends could speak to each other in hushed whispers.

"Where from here?" Gerrard asked.

"You should have brought your navigator," Sisay replied with a wry smile. "Though I wouldn't have flung Hanna into these fights, either." She consulted the map scroll. "We head southeast from here to the river. After we cross it, we head due south to reach the center of the wood. Then, of course, we hope *Weatherlight* is there."

"She's there, all right." Gerrard's eyes were faraway. "Does she call to you?"

"What?"

"*Weatherlight*. Does she call to you?" Gerrard asked.

Sisay blinked. "Maybe. Maybe I've just never listened. . . ."

"She calls to me," Gerrard said, his voice husky among the rushing boles. "Even when I fled away from her, *Weatherlight* called to me."

Sisay shrugged. The green murk grew deeper around them, and a ghostly silver glow shone among the vast trees. "That's why I'm *Weatherlight's* captain, and you're her comrade, her destiny."

"She's there, all right," Gerrard repeated, gazing into the darkness. "She's in the center of the forest. The Cho-Arrim took her there."

A speculative look crossed Sisay's face. "I think Takara's been listening too much to these Mercadians—all this inhuman monster nonsense. Those weren't monsters we fought at the farm. The way they appeared and took *Weatherlight*— it was like the ship called to them too." Hesitantly, she ventured, "Perhaps she is part of their destiny too."

A muscle in Gerrard's jaw leaped. "We'll see, soon enough. We'll ride until dark and then set up camp. No fires tonight. Nothing that might . . . offend the forest."

Sisay gave an appraising nod. The forest scrolled dizzily past her mount. "Yes. I think *Weatherlight* does call to you."

CHAPTER 7

"Orim!"

Weatherlight's healer turned on her bed of leaves and woven moss, murmuring inarticulately.

"Orim!"

"All ri'. All ri'. I'm 'wake. What is it?" She sat up, rubbing her eyes. Dim light shone through the window, illuminating the small room and its simple furnishings: the bed, a small hearth, a rough table, a chair. Before her squatted one of the Cho-Arrim whose name she did not know. He touched his forehead in salute.

"Is-Meisha's time comes. You must help her now."

Orim threw off the rough blanket that covered her and, without giving any thought to her nakedness, pulled on a simple shift. "Is Ta-Karnst with her?"

"Yes, but he wishes you to be there as well." He paused and added, "Cho-Manno and Is-Shada are already there."

Orim nodded, scarcely looking at him. Her mind was racing ahead. "Can you heat some water?" she asked, pushing back the door. She left, not waiting for an answer.

Orim made her way easily through the settlement. Many of the villagers' huts were grouped around the clearing in which the central fire burned. Others were tucked back within the trees, some nearer to the waters of the lagoon. A few, indeed, were built out over the lagoon itself, supported by wooden stilts, with narrow causeways connecting them to the land and each other.

The hut Is-Meisha shared with her mate was one of these. It took Orim only a few minutes to traverse the causeways to reach it. By the entrance, a small crowd had gathered, anticipating the new addition to the tribe. Is-Shada was among them, eager to help but uncertain what to do.

"Don't fear, everyone," Is-Shada said. "Orim is here. She will know what to do."

As Orim pushed her way through, she smiled nervously at her friend. The tribesmen respectfully gave way.

Inside the dwelling, she strained to make out the identity of the people. The executioner Ta-Spon, Is-Meisha's mate, was crouched next to the bed, on which lay a recumbent figure. Ta-Spon rose as Orim entered. A giant of a man, almost seven feet tall, his head brushed the top of the hut. Orim made a quick bow to him, feeling more than a little intimidated. Gratefully, she saw Cho-Manno standing motionless in one corner. He caught Orim's eye and smiled reassuringly at her.

Ta-Karnst was kneeling at the other side of the bed, his hands busy kneading Is-Meisha's muscles. He glanced up at Orim.

"The youngling is coming hard."

Orim joined him, putting a hand on Is-Meisha's swollen belly. She could feel contractions running along the smooth skin, straining the exhausted muscles. She lifted Is-Meisha's shift, already damp with sweat, and glanced beneath it.

"How long has she been in labor?"

"Four hours."

"Why did you not call me earlier?"

"There seemed no need to disturb your rest. I have birthed younglings many times before." He added, "I have seen this too. The mother strains and strains but cannot give birth. At last she may give birth, but the child is always dead, and often the mother dies as well."

Orim nodded. "I've seen it too, but it's a problem with a solution. The baby is breeched, turned in the womb. It's coming out wrong. We'll have to try to move it around inside." She looked about the hut and caught sight of the tribesman who had awoken her, bearing a large bowl.

From his place in the corner Cho-Manno stepped over to the man, placed his hands above the bowl, and murmured a word. Steam rose from the surface, and Orim plunged her hands into the hot water, almost scalding but barely tolerable.

"You too," she said to Ta-Karnst. "We don't want to cause infection."

The healer shrugged, immersing his hands. Then he knelt on one side of the struggling woman, holding her legs apart while Orim slowly forced her wet fingers inside. Is-Meisha cried out, a shudder convulsing her limbs. Ta-Spon growled something unintelligible and took a heavy step forward, but Cho-Manno put a hand on his big shoulder, restraining him.

Orim probed delicately. Only once before had she delivered a breeched baby, a number of years ago during one of *Weatherlight's* journeys. Now she touched the baby's tiny limbs, feeling it stir. She withdrew her hand and looked at Ta-Karnst.

"Definitely a breech. The baby is feetfirst."

"Can you suggest anything?"

"Let's try to rotate the child in the womb. But it's tricky, and it will hurt Is-Meisha."

The last phrase penetrated Ta-Spon's anxiety, and he tensed.

Cho-Manno tightened his grip on the big man's arm, saying quietly to Orim, "If you do nothing, will the child die?"

"Probably."

"And Is-Meisha?"

"Ta-Karnst is right." Orim washed her hands in the hot water, rubbing the blood and mucus off. "Often in such cases the mother dies as well."

Ta-Spon groaned, sweat dripping from his forehead. He bent over his mate, rocking back and forth in an agony of indecision. Is-Meisha shuddered as another contraction seized her, and a soft cry escaped her lips. Ta-Spon clutched her tiny hand in his enormous paw and nodded his assent to Orim.

The healer once again plunged her hand into the hot water, while Cho-Manno motioned to the big man to move back. He positioned himself behind Is-Meisha, stroking her head, murmuring a soft, slow chant. Outside the hut, the chant was taken up by the waiting crowd, filling the room. It washed away tension like a cleansing rain dragging dust from the air.

Again Ta-Karnst pushed apart the young woman's legs, and Orim reached in with her hand. She touched the tiny feet, pushing them gently back while at the same time her other hand pressed against the woman's belly, carefully manipulsting the baby's shoulder.

Another contraction came, nearly crushing her fingers, and her involuntary cry matched that of Is-Meisha. When the contraction subsided, Orim tried to will away the pain as she again worked her hands around the small body.

There! She pushed on the feet, while from the outside pressing on the upper torso of the child. For an agonizing second she met resistance, and the thought flickered through her mind that perhaps this was too much, perhaps the best thing was to remove the child in any way possible, to let it die and save Is-Meisha . . . but then, the fetus turned.

She withdrew her fingers with a gasp and plunged them into the bowl of water. "All right. Now let's try again, shall we, Is-Meisha? The next time there's a contraction, push. Push with all your might!"

The pregnant woman gave a scream as a fresh wave of contractions wracked her body, yet in the scream there was now a note of triumph. It was Ta-Karnst, leaning forward, eyes alert, who caught the tiny form as it emerged. He made a quick slashing motion, cutting the umbilical cord that bound baby to mother, and proudly lifted the newborn aloft.

Orim sat back, gasping for breath. Then, a second later, she realized something was wrong, very wrong. She turned to Cho-Manno. "Why isn't she crying? Why isn't she crying? What's wrong?"

Is-Meisha lay back, completely spent, her eyes closed, her mind oblivious to the fate of her child. Cho-Manno looked sadly at Orim, touching her hair gently. Orim felt the tears begin to trickle down her cheeks.

Ta-Karnst ignored both of them and showed no signs of mourning. Holding the child's body with one hand, he spread his other over the bowl in which he and Orim had washed their hands. His voice snapped out a command. Then, without hesitation, he plunged the child into the water.

Orim started forward in protest but was brought up short by the baby's squeal of outrage. The noise seemed to arouse Is-Meisha, who moaned and reached out her arms. Carefully Ta-Karnst wrapped the baby in a blanket and deposited her in her parent's arms. Ta-Spon, whose great hand had been pressed to his mouth during the birth, rushed forward to join his mate and baby daughter. He lay close by them, cradling them in his arms.

Orim rose and almost fell. Black spots swam before her eyes. She felt hands catch her arms, Cho-Manno on one side, Ta-Karnst on the other. Together they gently led her from the hut.

At the entrance, Cho-Manno halted and lifted his arms for silence from the crowd of Cho-Arrim. "She has come," he said. "Another soul to join the Great River of our people." There was a murmur of acclamation from those assembled, and they began to sing a welcoming song.

Cho-Manno looked from Ta-Karnst to Orim and said, "You did well. Both of you."

Orim turned to the Cho-Arrim healer. "I thought the child was dead."

Ta-Karnst shrugged. "Sometimes the child has a hard birth and will not breathe. But a little cold water helps."

"Of course," Orim chuckled. "You turned the hot water cold and then immersed the baby." She laid a hand on the healer's arm, but he pulled away as if embarrassed, touched a hand to his forehead, and slipped silently into the darkness beneath the trees.

Cho-Manno put an arm about Orim's slender shoulders. "Tired, chavala?"

She shook her head.

"Then come with me. We will sit by the waters and talk until our souls fall into the everlasting river that races through the sky."

He guided her footsteps over the causeway, over root and branch, until before them them Orim saw the soft glint of distant moonlight on the still waters of the lagoon. Cho-Manno sat down on a low stone. The water rippled about his dangling feet. He motioned for her to join him.

Orim did. Listening to the murmur of night noises, she felt a sense of peace such as she had never experienced.

Beside her Cho-Manno was silent, but she could feel the steady rhythm of his breathing. Orim watched his face in profile, the strong line of his jaw, the gentle curve of his brow, the thick, dark hair braided with countless coins.

He looked at her, his eyes gleaming. "You are strong, Orim, yet gentle. I admired you as you brought that child into the world tonight."

"As I helped," Orim corrected. "Ta-Karnst deserves credit."

"You are two sides of the same coin, chavala. Ta-Karnst is the head, while you are the heart. He himself has come to see this." Cho-Manno bent, his fingers barely touching the surface of the water. From his outstretched hand, a ripple of light ran away across the surface, flashing, diving, recombining in a hundred different forms. At last it faded away. Orim, in her days among the Cho-Arrim, had become used to such water magic, but it never ceased to delight her.

Cho-Manno leaned back against her and slumped wearily.

"You are tired."

"Yes. The watchers reported today, and I spoke long with them."

"Who are the watchers?"

"Those who watch from the eaves of the wood. They speak with the trees and the water and watch the people of the mountain."

"And what do these watchers say to you?"

Cho-Manno flicked another light pattern across the water. "They say there have been dust clouds on the horizon. Mercadians returning. The watchers will attack as soon as invaders harm the forest. The Mercadians haven't yet, but they will. They always do—and now, especially. They come for the soul of the Uniter." He motioned to where *Weatherlight* lay at anchor.

Orim felt a painful jolt, as if cold arms had suddenly embraced her. "What will you do?"

"Fight, again. Mercadians are not the children of Ramos.

They would destroy the soul of the Uniter before it could be joined with the mind and body."

"Tell me of the Uniter," Orim said, her eyes searching his. "Tell me."

"Your arrival on this ship, flaming through the nighttime sky, was foretold in the Sixth Prophecy of the Uniter. You saw the tale performed in part by the separi. It is the story of our creation and of our future. We came to this world riding on the back of a great god—Ramos. This great god carried us in an argosy—like this ship here—but the Mercadians flung it from the sky. It fell in three parts—soul, mind, and body—and so created Cho-Arrim, Saprazzan, and Rishadan. The Sixth Prophecy tells that the soul of Ramos will return again, blazing in the sky. Should his soul be reunited with his mind and body, he would live again and unite the people. Now, we Cho-Arrim have the soul of Ramos. The Saprazzans have his mind—called by them the Matrix. And in the ghoul-haunted Deepwood lie the Bones of Ramos. Unite these all, and the folk who possess them, and we shall drive off the evil of the land forever."

Cho-Manno rose abruptly and pulled her to her feet. "Come. I wish to show you something."

He found one of the small canoes the Cho-Arrim kept alongside the lagoon and boarded it. Orim sat in the prow, while Cho-Manno, with swift, sure strokes of his paddle, guided them across the still waters. The lights of the settlement dimmed behind them.

Orim felt sleep pulling at her. The journey became a dream in which she floated endlessly on a glass sea. There was no wind, and from time to time the trunk of a mighty tree thrust up high out of the waters. The trees were silver shafts in absolute blackness.

At last, before them, Orim saw a slender line of light that seemed to grow out of the water itself. As they drew nearer, she saw it was a small island, some fifty yards in breadth, ringed by trees. Unlike the other trees she had seen, these were mere saplings, no more than eight or nine feet in height. Curiously, their trunks shone with a brighter sheen than the larger trees, as if they were more vital, more alive—younger.

Cho-Manno carefully grounded the canoe, jumped out, and helped Orim come ashore. Between the water of the lagoon and the trees was a wide swath of moss. They paced across it, up the gently rising ground, and to the trees.

The light in the center of the circle was bright after the dim light of the forest. Orim stood still for a few moments rubbing her eyes. When she could see again, she observed that at the very center of the circle was a short stone pillar with a broad top and narrow bottom. As they came closer, she saw the pillar was carved with runes, many of them worn with age. From a broad, shallow bowl at the top bubbled a spring of clear water. It coursed over the edges of the disk and down to the earth in a sparkling mist. From there it ran through the circle of trees to the lagoon.

"This is the Fountain of Cho," Cho-Manno said. His voice, after such a long silence, rang strangely in Orim's ears. "It is the Navel of the World, the place from which we began, the place to which we return. It is the point around which all things revolve. It is here that our souls pass away from this world into the Great River."

"What is the writing on the stone?" the healer asked.

"It tells our story. The story I have just recounted to you." He smiled wryly. "I cannot read it, but its memory has been passed down from Cho to Cho."

"May I look closer?" Without waiting for an answer, Orim released his hand and neared the pillar. The characters on it had been deeply carved and wound around the stone in a spiral, but many of the carvings were faded, worn by the ceaseless action of the water. She reached a hand out to touch them.

"Orim, no! No one may touch the Fountain of Cho." He remained where he was, watching her intently.

Orim stared at the characters. Like the separi's performance around the village bonfire, they stirred a memory within her.

Cho-Manno advanced to stand by her side. He said, "I brought you here because I wish you to understand my people. This stone tells all our history. It tells us that once, long ago, our forest stretched from the base of the mountain of Mercadia all the way to the sea. All that vast forest was filled with the singing and light of the trees, and the waters of the Great River flowed freely.

"Then, gradually, the mountain people pushed back our boundaries, cut down trees, scarred the land. The plains of dust arose around their city, and only dust clouds lived on them." He shook his head sadly. "We live here, clinging to a tiny portion of what was once ours. It may be that a few generations hence, there will be nothing left of the Cho-Arrim. Do you see now why the Uniter is so important to us?"

Orim looked at him thoughtfully. There were depths to him that she never entirely appreciated. "Yes. All this—" she waved her hands about the sacred grove— "all this is somehow what I've looked for all my life."

Cho-Manno cupped her chin in his hand. "I was about to say the same of you." Their kiss warmed the chill morning.

CHAPTER 8

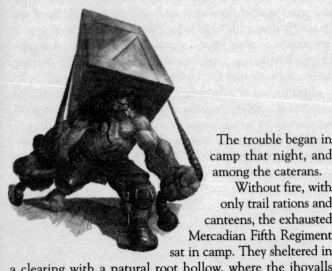

The trouble began in camp that night, and among the caterans.

Without fire, with only trail rations and canteens, the exhausted Mercadian Fifth Regiment sat in camp. They sheltered in a clearing with a natural root hollow, where the jhovalls could be corralled. The six-legged tigers slept in warm comfort in a feline pile, their saddles and packs removed and their coats brushed.

The soldiers and caterans were much less comfortable. They had washed during their river crossing, but their clothes had never fully dried. More layers of cloth only deepened the chill. Throughout the day, the forest's murk had been unnerving. Nighttime was worse. Only the cold gleam of the trees illuminated the dark. A fire would have been welcome, but Gerrard would not allow it for fear of "offending the forest." Instead, he offended his fighters. They grumbled angrily as they cleaned their weapons.

Soon around the camp appeared a circle of eyes—small, grim, glowering eyes. Minions of the Rushwood. It was more than the caterans could bear.

Their master, four-armed Xcric, had a crossbow. He cranked it quietly back, fitted a quarrel, and took bets from his comrades. "My orders from Gerrard were to command my troops not to fight unless attacked. I've done so. But Gerrard never forbade *me* to fight."

With a shuddering twang, the bolt launched free. It tore through undergrowth.

In the forest beyond, a set of eyes slammed shut. There came the agonized thrashing of something massive amid weeds. The beast's shrieks were piteous. Among vast, impassive trees, the cries echoed. They summoned the forest's myriad defenders.

Gerrard and his command crew came running. "What happened? What's going on?"

Xcric spoke proudly in the murk. "I got him right between the eyes."

"I ordered you not to fight unless—"

"*He* attacked *me*—looked at me wrong," Xcric replied.

"You bastard," Gerrard spat, raking his sword from its scabbard. "You've just declared war." Turning toward the camp, he shouted, "To arms! To arms! Light perimeter fires!"

In the anxious moments afterward, deadfalls were piled and sprinkled with rye spirits. Fires leaped up in an uneven ring around the camp. Orange light limned warriors as they rushed past abandoned packs. Jhovalls lolled awake and disentangled themselves from their sleeping kin.

Gerrard and his comrades meanwhile stared out into the darkness.

Tahngarth clutched a sword eagerly. "At least we have fires now. Our clothes will dry."

Sisay shook her head. "I'd rather have them wet with river water than wet with blood. What do you think is out there?"

"We'll find out soon enough," Takara said. She gestured beyond the fires, where flames glimmered in angry eyes. "They are converging."

From all sides, the beasts came. Hunched backs and stooped shoulders, twisted horns in shaggy brows, vast claws raking away undergrowth, footpads pounding ground . . .

"Lumbering satyrs and horned trolls," Sisay whispered in awe. "They're bigger than the books made them out. These are feral creatures—solitary. They must have been brought together by the mind of the forest."

Gerrard's face was grim as he watched the advance. The satyrs and trolls had nearly reached the outer fires. "If these are the forest's first defenses, what other monsters will follow?"

Xcric tugged on Gerrard's sleeve. "My crossbowmen are ready. Do we fire?"

"There's no sense in defending this camp. It'll be our grave. The beasts won't stop coming until we're dead or driven out. If we must fight, we fight forward," Gerrard said. "Clear a corridor. Open fire." Even as the first quarrels raced away, he shouted, "Troops! Mount up! Fight from jhovall-back!" He turned, heading for the corral. "Ride behind me, toward the center of the wood—"

These shouts were drowned out by another roar—the death throes of scores of beasts. Cateran quarrels sank in throats and eyes and brows. Many trolls and satyrs went down in that first volley. Many more charged. With bolts sticking from mounded backs and between grappling claws, they came on.

Gerrard and his comrades reached the jhovall corral. There was no time for saddles or packs. Gerrard yanked harness and bit from a nearby vine. He slipped the reins over the cat's head and clambered up. Caught between fire-light and silver tree glow, he whirled and met the attackers.

As quickly as that, the satyrs and trolls arrived. They flung themselves over root networks and down into the corral. Two tons of muscle and claw and horn—they landed, breaking soldiers' heads and jhovalls' backs. Roars of rage mixed with shrieks of pain.

In moments, five cats and ten warriors lay dead.

A huge monster dropped into the space beside Gerrard. His jhovall hissed and turned. Gerrard's sword sang in the darkness. It arced through screaming air to impact a great scaly skull. Steel bit through skin and muscle, lodging only on bone.

The satyr gathered its massive legs and lunged.

Roaring, Gerrard turned his blade. The sword pivoted across the beast's jaw and slid within the collarbone. Gerrard held tight to the reins. The satyr came on, impaling itself on his sword. Blood poured forth in a steaming torrent.

Gerrard wrenched his blade free and backed his spitting mount. The satyr plunged ponderously into the space where they had been. His jhovall reared and shrieked.

It barreled into the rump of Sisay's beast, which stood like a rampant lion. Her jhovall's claws raked the face of another satyr.

"Win free!" Gerrard shouted. "Then grab a torch and follow my lead!"

He barged past Sisay's mount, heading toward a nearby bonfire. Gerrard leaned down and snatched up a burning brand. No sooner had he righted himself than the bonfire erupted before him. Coals and sparks leaped up in a killing hail. Gerrard reined his mount back. Something vast had plunged into the midst of the blaze, driven there by a shriek-ing jhovall.

Tahngarth rode that jhovall. His sword was sanguine,

and his horns too. Though he spoke to Gerrard, his eyes were fixed on the fire. "There is no honor in this fight."

Gerrard saw why. In the bonfire, a horned troll thrashed. Fire flashed away its thick pelt, sending up acrid white smoke. Next moment, skin burst and peeled and blackened. The muscles beneath contracted moments more, until they, too, sizzled to stillness. Lids burned away from rolling eyes, which became as white and opaque as boiled eggs.

"No honor," Gerrard agreed, chopping the head from another satyr. The decapitated corpse went down sloppily before him. Holding high his torch, Gerrard drove his mount up over the enormous body. "No honor but to fight for Orim and *Weatherlight*. Follow me!"

Aback snarling six-legged cats, Tahngarth and Sisay fought in Gerrard's wake.

Ahead, Takara clung to the back of her dead jhovall, which draped across the horns of a troll. The massive monster had impaled her steed and lifted it into the air. Takara lashed at it with her sword but couldn't reach the troll's bent back. It bounded toward another bonfire, ready to fling jhovall and rider both into the flames.

"Get up!" Gerrard commanded his mount, digging heels into its sides.

The tiger-creature flung itself behind the troll. Huge feline claws sank into troll flesh, but they only propelled the beast faster toward the flames.

"Climb on!" Gerrard shouted to Takara, holding out his hand.

She sheathed her sword and rolled down the back of her dead mount, grasping Gerrard's hand. He swung her into place behind him. Gerrard reined hard. His mount reared.

Fires roared up ahead. The troll and the dead jhovall plunged into the flames. More putrid white smoke belched up.

"Thanks," Takara panted.

"Let's get out of this deathtrap."

With Takara sitting behind him and Tahngarth, Sisay,

and the Fifth Regiment following, Gerrard sent his mount bounding across the battlefield. Many of Gerrard's regiment were dead already, slain as they ran for their mounts. Their bodies lay savaged among forgotten packs. Not a few satyrs and trolls lay amid them. Some of the fighters who had slain them fought on. They seemed mere children waggling sticks at hulking bears.

One woman, who had killed two trolls, battled a third now, her strength flagging.

Gerrard's mount lunged beside the troll, and he clove the thing's brain between the horns. "Pick her up!" he shouted to Sisay, pointing to the weary soldier.

No sooner had Gerrard's jhovall leaped out of the space than Sisay's leaped into it. She grabbed the soldier's arm and dragged her onto the jhovall's back. Tahngarth likewise rescued another beleaguered guard. Soon, every soldier that lived rode a jhovall across the camp.

On the opposite end of the killing field, the caterans had been busy. They were not content merely to slay the beasts. They harvested trophies—sawing at horns and claws, hewing teeth, lopping off fingers, flaying skin and fur. Where a creature was cut open, the caterans thrust an arm in the gore—sign of a successful kill. When both—or all four—arms were red, the caterans painted their chests and foreheads and legs in the stuff. They fought like fiends, these caterans. Few if any of them had fallen, but the ground was thick with dead trolls and satyrs.

Gerrard's steed bounded past that abattoir and onward, into the murk. He held high his burning brand and charged on between silvery boles. With a glance back, he saw that most of his force remained—perhaps fifty jhovalls followed in his wake, bearing one or two soldiers each. The six-legged cats were faster and more agile than these lumbering, shuffling monsters. Soon, the Fifth Regiment would be beyond their reach.

"That was a near thing," Takara panted into his ear.

"Yes," Gerrard agreed in the rushing wind.

"Do you think Orim has . . . survived?"

"I hope so," Gerrard replied. "We drive on until we reach the center of the forest, and *Weatherlight*."

"At least we're safe for the moment." Takara said.

She had spoken too soon.

Something massive moved ahead—many somethings. As tall as five men, they lurked in the interstices between boles. Their bodies were black silhouettes against the silver gloaming—living shadows. They darted, positioning themselves in the path of the jhovalls. Here and there, true glimpses came of these vaguely human titans. In place of skin, leaves stood across their bulk. Mosses clumped in untidy mats of hair. Vines twined in veinwork. Fists of stone and stick bore huge clubs. Most horrible of all, though, were the creatures' eyes, glowing with the silver fire of the trees all around.

"Rushwood elementals!" Sisay shouted. "They are formed out of the leaves and boughs of the forest!"

Takara whispered sardonically, "What now?"

"What else?" Gerrard replied, feeling his fear turn to anger, and his anger to hatred. "We fight."

"That's what I like to hear."

"Hang on!" Gerrard kicked the flanks of his jhovall.

The tiger-creature snarled and leaped toward one of the looming shadows. Overhead, a club dropped with an awful roar. Gerrard drove the cat upward. The jhovall leaped. Claws sank into the moldy mass of the elemental's thigh. A vague roar came. The massive club descended toward jhovall and riders.

"Get up!" Gerrard shouted at his mount.

The jhovall bounded again.

The club struck. A shriek came, inhuman anguish. The elemental staggered. Its thigh—stones and sticks—had shattered beneath the blow of the club.

Rising still, the jhovall sank its claws in the monster's arm and hurled itself higher.

"Good work," Takara shouted.

But the elemental was not maimed for long. It pressed its club against the shattered thigh. The wood fused with its leg, solidifying it.

"Not good enough," Gerrard hissed.

The jhovall leaped from the elemental's shoulder toward its face. Feline claws sank into the elemental's skull. Standing in the saddle, Gerrard drove his sword into one of the titan's silver-glowing eyes. Takara rammed hers into the other. Mercurial flames danced out along the blades and burned their sleeves. Gerrard and Takara shouted in unison pain.

But the agonized shriek of the elemental overtopped their cries. Silver fire guttered and failed in its eyes. They went dark. The wailing ceased. The elemental died. With terrific and terrible motion, its corpse began to slump. Boughs and humus and rocks separated. No longer joined in a titanic body, the multifarious vines and mosses tumbled free of each other.

Growling, Gerrard drove heels into his jhovall's side. "Jump!"

The tiger-creature did, flinging itself across the wheeling heights. It bounded from the head of a dying elemental toward the shoulders of a living one. Trees flashed past in a dizzy spectacle. The jhovall extended its forepaws to grasp the next titan.

The elemental turned. Its club whirled about and struck the six-legged tiger in midair.

A whuff of breath exploded from the cat. With it came the snap of ribs. Blood boiled out of the creature's face. Broken, the jhovall spun through the air.

Gerrard and Takara clung miserably to its inert bulk. Trees whirled.

They struck one. The dead cat caught the brunt of the blow, but Takara was flung away. She fell toward the forest floor, landing atop a root-cluster and sprawling brokenly.

Gerrard meanwhile smacked up against rough bark. Something shattered in his chest, but he clung to the dead cat. It sloughed off the side of the tree and plunged beneath him. Cursing, Gerrard clawed atop the falling jhovall. It struck ground.

The impact was horrible. It drove the breath from Gerrard. He crumpled off the jhovall's corpse and flailed on the ground. He rolled across his torch. The wet fabric of his riding cloak—it was a flask of rye spirits that had shattered in his chest pocket—flared with sudden fire.

Gerrard staggered up and shucked the burning jacket. He flung it furiously away. The cloak wrapped itself around the elemental's leg.

Flame leaped to wood and dry moss. Fire spread up the looming titan. It shrieked, pounding the blaze. Flames roared onto its hands and arms. In moments, the elemental was engulfed—a living column of fire. It thrashed horribly among the boles, shying away from the trees lest it set them ablaze. Its screams were terrifying.

Gerrard could only grin grimly. He drew a hissing breath through gritted teeth and shouted, "Burn them! Burn every last one! Burn them!"

Even as the elemental fell to the ground, writhing in death throes, more fires awoke among the others.

A slim hand touched Gerrard's shoulder. "That was well done."

He turned, astonished. "Takara! How did you survive that fall? Your spine was broken."

"No. Hatred is my spine," she said, smiling a bloody smile. "As long as I keep it at the core of my being, I survive."

"Yes," Gerrard said, staring at her. "I've begun to see the definite benefits." There were four elementals burning now, their wails like music in the night. Gerrard cupped hands about his mouth and shouted through the chorus of moans. "Caterans to the fore! Clear a corridor! Kill anything that stands between us and *Weatherlight!*"

CHAPTER 9

The stillness of the wood was broken by shouts.

Orim rose, dropping the herbs she had been washing in the lagoon. She ran frantically, her mouth open in wordless horror. Even as she fled across the mossy forest floor, she saw hellish figures break through the surrounding trees.

On scaly legs they bounded forward. Claws ate up the ground. Bloody arms grasped villagers. Fangs sank into sides, shoulders, and heads. More blood painted the inhuman monsters.

"Mercadians!" Orim shouted. "Bar your doors! The Mercadians have come!"

More beasts arrived, monstrosities with boar heads, scorpion tails, and snake teeth. They rode horrific, six-legged tigers and bore swords and crossbows. As they filed into the clearing, the brutes hoisted their wicked bows.

"Left wing, pivot. Archers, loose!"

The battle commands, familiar and yet remote in Orim's memory, made her freeze. There was a whir from the line of beasts. Shafts streaked through the air to punch with deadly precision among the crowd of Cho-Arrim. The front ranks staggered and fell in disorderly rows. Tribesmen behind turned with a shout and hauled forth weapons, only to fall to a second volley of quarrels. Then came a third hail of deadly missiles.

Dimly, Orim heard Is-Shada shout something and run toward her.

Several of the crossbowmen pivoted toward the motion, bows at the ready.

Orim threw herself to the ground and felt the volley pass over her head.

Is-Shada ran across the clearing. Several of her playmates kept pace. She had almost reached Orim when an angry hiss sounded. Is-Shada stopped suddenly, staring at Orim. Two black-feathered shafts protruded from her chest and shoulder. She looked stupidly at them for a moment, and then fell face forward. Companions on either side caught her as she fell. One of them twisted and screamed in agony as a quarrel sprouted from her knee. She staggered and dropped Is-Shada, whose body bumped against Orim.

Orim wrapped the girl in her arms. The breath was already gone from Is-Shada's punctured lungs, the blood from her pierced heart.

Hands seized Orim and drew her away. She heard a voice shrieking and realized with astonishment that it was her own. Her lungs felt raw, her cheeks wet with tears.

"Is-Shada," Orim sobbed out, "*O-reem 'stva o'meer. Is-Shada, O-reem 'stva o'meer.*"

Ta-Karnst's firm hand was on her elbow, and he pulled her rapidly back toward the lagoon and the complex of huts that extended over the water. Wordlessly, the two healers ran up the causeway. The wickerwork strained beneath their pounding feet.

Another volley of quarrels whizzed overhead. Orim looked up and caught her breath. Before her, a wrinkled old woman slowly sank to the wooden platform. Three quarrels bristled from her chest, and another had pierced her leg.

The healers reached her. "Don't move," Orim commanded harshly. "We'll get those things out of you."

The old woman's fierce brown eyes, seemingly all dark pupils, glared at her. "*Svascho!* Traitor! You have betrayed us all! Rot forever in the Nine Circles!"

"No," whispered Orim. Then louder she cried, "No!"

The dying woman's face wrinkled up into a terrifying rictus meant as a smile. "You will never win, Svascho. We are Cho-Arrim. We are . . ." Her voice was drowned out by a stream of blood gushing from her mouth. Her old eyes clouded. Her head slipped sideways from Orim's lap.

"You must leave the dead," Ta-Karnst said urgently, "and tend the living—" He rushed off in the direction of fresh screams.

"Yes," Orim said, laying the old woman down gently.

A sudden cry came from a nearby hut. Is-Meisha stood in the doorway. In her arms was a tiny, wrapped bundle.

Orim raced up the causeway. A quarrel skimmed her leg and struck the wall. Ignoring it, Orim thrust the young mother back into the comparative safety of the hut. Another flight of quarrels smashed into the side of the structure. They were tipped with burning pitch. The forest was damp and would not easily burn, but the smoke would drive the Cho-Arrim from their huts. Already, the fire spread.

At her wits' end, Orim slammed her shoulder against the rear wall of the hut. The thick grass reeds swayed and bent. Orim struck the wall twice more and then, casting her eyes about the smoke-filled room, saw a thin stone knife lying near the empty cooking pot. She grasped it, slashing at the reeds. They yielded, and in a few moments she had a hole carved in the wall, overlooking the water.

"Come on," she gasped. "Through there, quick, or we'll suffocate."

"My baby," Is-Meisha wailed. As if in sympathy, the baby had begun crying.

"You'll have to swim," Orim said, panting. "Come on! You can do it. It's your only chance." There was a shout from below. A reed canoe passed beneath her, packed with tribesmen. "Hey," Orim called.

The paddler looked up. "Orim!"

"Wait." She bodily dragged Is-Meisha to the opening. "Look. You can go in the canoe. But hurry."

The paddler shook his head. "No. We will sink. There is another close behind. Take that one." He bent forward for another stroke.

Is-Meisha, with a shriek, stumbled to her knees. A bolt protruded from her chest. The quarrel had also pierced the baby's arm, and the child added her wail to her mother's dying gasps.

Orim tore the bloodied baby from Is-Meisha's arms and thrust it at the paddler. "Take the child!"

He did. "Where is Ta-Spon?"

Orim shook her head. "I do not know."

One of the other men in the canoe turned back. "Ta-Spon is . . ." He stopped, and Orim could see the unspoken words in his eyes. "He fell in the front lines, along with the archers and skyscouts and wizards. Along with Cho-Manno."

Orim reeled, almost falling through the gap. "No . . . he isn't . . ."

The canoe was already beyond reach of her words. Its paddlers propelled it rapidly away from the burning village.

Orim dropped to her knees and clutched the ragged opening in the side of the hut. All around her, flames crackled. One wall of the hut was a solid mass of fire. Smoke stung her eyes and raked her throat raw. She didn't care.

"Cho-Manno is dead. . . ."

Surrounded by killing fire, she felt only his warm arms around her. Despite roars and screams, she heard only his tender words in her ears. Through blinding smoke, she saw his smiling face, lit by the Fountain of Cho—by belief in the Uniter. . . .

"Cho-Manno is dead. . . ."

If Mercadian monsters filled the forest, *Weatherlight* was lost to them. The Uniter was lost. And if Cho-Manno lay dead in the woods, Orim would lie dead just here.

"*Cho-Manno, Orim 'stva o'meer.*"

* * * * *

Aback a new jhovall, Gerrard and Takara rode into the clearing and saw the atrocities performed by the caterans. "How could they . . . ?"

Women and children—*human* women and children—lay slaughtered everywhere. There were hundreds torn apart by cateran claws and fangs, pinned to ground by cateran quarrels, burned alive by cateran torches. Human flesh like so much refuse, human blood like so much sewage . . . Already the flies were gathering. The nearest corpses were missing hands, ears, scalps—trophies gathered. Surely those visceral cuts could only be for cateran blood rites.

"How could they . . . ?" Gerrard repeated, white-faced.

"The Cho-Arrim were human after all," Takara hissed.

Sisay rode up behind, turned in the saddle, and vomited.

"A massacre," Tahngarth gasped.

The survivors of the Mercadian Fifth Regiment flooded into the space as well.

Takara spoke a dread whisper in Gerrard's ear. "*You* ordered them to do this, Gerrard. *You* ordered the caterans to kill everything between you and *Weatherlight*. They followed your orders. Unknowing, you killed every man, woman, and child in this clearing."

"It must stop!" Gerrard shouted, standing in the saddle. "Forward, all of you. Fight the caterans. Kill them, if you must. Stop the massacre!"

* * * * *

Orim was nearly dead in smoke and flame when she felt Cho-Manno's hands upon her. She could not have spoken to him. Her lungs were suffused in smoke. Nor could she see him, but his rescuing arms were sure as they wrapped her and lifted her and carried her alive from the pyre. He strode from the oven-hot room and across wicker causeways.

Orim's eyes streamed, unseeing, beneath her turban and coin-braided hair. She clung to him, coughing poison from her lungs.

Then, they were clear, on shore. He laid her down on scorched reeds. The sounds of battle receded. The distant fighting slowly died.

"You're . . . alive," Orim choked out, her eyes swimming.

"*You're* alive," came the glad response. The voice was not Cho-Manno's. It was a woman's—strong and familiar.

"Sisay?" gasped Orim.

"Yes!" Sisay said, laughing happily. "Yes, it's me!"

Rubbing tears from her eyes, Orim said, "What are you . . . what are you doing here?"

"We came to rescue you," Sisay replied as she daubed a cloth at Orim's eyes. "And to get *Weatherlight*."

A look of dread crossed Orim's features. Her face went

very white. "You came . . . with Mercadians . . . with those killing . . . monsters?"

Sisay's eyes darkened. "Yes. But we didn't know about all of this. We thought the Cho-Arrim were the monsters. Even now, Gerrard is calling off the caterans. He even killed a few that wouldn't stop fighting."

Teeth gritting, Orim sat up at last. "Gerrard. I should have known. . . ." Eyes at last clear, she struggled to stand. "Take me to him."

"You're too weak," Sisay objected.

Orim wrenched her arm free, disproving the objection.

"All right. All right. I'll take you."

Weatherlight's captain and her healer walked arm in arm across the battlefield. The dead lay all around. With shame and despair, Sisay's eyes traced out shattered skulls and punctured hearts. Orim's eyes were full of death too, but they overflowed with tears of loss and fury. Scorch marks covered the sides of trees. Huts on the lagoon burned. Dead floated in the dark waters.

At least—at last—there were no more roars, no more screams.

Ahead, *Weatherlight's* deck swarmed with Mercadians and caterans. They had lashed the ship to shore, tossed off the scaling vines, and positioned a makeshift gangplank to one side. The vessel was well guarded. Even now, Tahngarth and Takara followed a cateran enforcer below decks.

On the nearby shore stood another familiar figure: Gerrard. He stared at his ship. His face was battle-scarred and weary, but he bore the look of a man seeing an old friend. As Orim and Sisay approached, Gerrard turned, and his glad look deepened. "Orim. You're alive! It's so good to see you!"

"*Kravchak!*" she hissed. "I wish I weren't alive. I would gladly die if I could bring back all the people you slaughtered today!"

"Orim?" Gerrard asked wonderingly.

The healer glared at him. Her eyes were dancing with sparks. "Look at what you have done, Gerrard. Look who you have brought with you." She gestured to the Mercadians and caterans, who stood watching her curiously.

"We came to rescue you, to recover the ship. What's the matter with you? I thought you'd be glad to see us. I thought—"

"You thought nothing! You're just like them. You only take things! You never give! Instead, you take and take, and always with the point of a sword! What about Is-Shada? Is-Meisha? Ta-Spon? And all the others?" She gestured to where a few of the Mercadian soldiers were still piling corpses. "What about Cho-Manno?" Her voice caught, and then she recovered herself. "They paid the price for your greed."

"Orim, I don't understand. . . ."

"No, of course not! How could you? You've never made an effort to understand anything."

"All right, that's enough!" Gerrard shouted. "A massacre occurred here today. An atrocity. I gave the order that set it off, yes, but as soon as I found out what was happening, I put an end to it. I didn't come for massacre. I came to rescue you and *Weatherlight*—"

"You don't even know what that ship is! You don't even know the power it has. You've spent all your life running from your Legacy, but now, when someone else finds the true worth of it, you come with swords and monsters to take it back?"

"I'm sorry for what happened here," Gerrard said contritely. He looked out over the fields of dead. "I am very sorry. But I didn't declare this war. These folk stole my ship, and I came to get it back."

"The ship is secure," said a new voice. So intent had the argument been that Gerrard and Orim had not noticed the approach of a four-armed cateran enforcer and his henchmen. The creature was crimson from his knobby head to his taloned feet. Only his fangs remained white, and they smiled gruesomely. "Per your orders."

"Thank you, Xcric," Gerrard replied coolly. "Just now, I'm in the middle of something." He turned back toward Orim.

"Yes, you are," the cateran hissed. He seized Gerrard's wrists and locked shackles over them.

Gerrard spun in sudden shock. "What is this?"

"You are under arrest, Commander," Xcric said, grinning.

Sisay reached for her sword, only to have shackles snap closed over her wrists too. A whole party of cateran enforcers surrounded them.

"Arrest? And what is the charge?"

"Murder of those in your command," Xcric said. "You ordered the Mercadian guard to attack my forces. You yourself killed two of my soldiers."

"This is ludicrous," Gerrard growled. Orim was also imprisoned now. Aboard *Weatherlight*, Tahngarth and Takara stood, similarly chained. "You have no authority—"

"On the contrary, the magistrate himself hired me and my band. He anticipated such treachery from you. I am empowered to imprison you and your coconspirators and press into service whatever Cho-Arrim wizards and workers are needed to convey *Weatherlight* back to Mercadia. Now, I am finished with you. Take him to the jhovall corral."

Gerrard struggled against the caterans that dragged him away. "You can't take my ship! The magistrate can't renege on the deal."

Xcric smiled. "He does not renege. You bargained for troops to regain your ship. You did not bargain for the ship itself."

Guards pushed Takara and Tahngarth up beside Sisay and Orim. Together, the bridge crew of *Weatherlight* staggered in chains across the field of the dead.

Takara's red hair gleamed with firelight. She said bitingly, "I knew it had been too easy. Nothing here is as it seems."

BOOK II

CHAPTER 10

Gerrard stood amid a huge, jeering throng. He'd been washed. His clothes were cleaned and pressed. The rust bands had been scrubbed from his wrists. The cuts and burns and bruises of the Rushwood now lurked beneath a thick coat of powder makeup. A Mercadian coiffeur had trimmed, polished, and set his hair and beard. He had never looked cleaner or more handsome.

Gerrard was not simply a military prisoner. He was a political prize.

"Behold, people of Mercadia!" cried a stout nobleman from a nearby dais. His gold-embroidered robes gleamed against the dark shadow of Mount Mercadia, towering above. His eyes swept the huge crowd that had gathered in the lower market. A sour turn of corpulent lips showed how little he enjoyed speaking the vulgar language of the commoners. "Behold our prisoner—Legendary Gerrard, giant killer!"

Boos and hisses came from the throng. The multifarious roar of the marketplace this morning had been stilled when the soldiers had returned with their prize. Now, the warring shouts united in a single purpose—the humiliation of the foreign traitor.

Even if Gerrard could have fought past the two hundred soldiers who hemmed him in, he would have had to battle a crowd of tens of thousands. His obedience was assured not by these hundreds or thousands, though, but by the daggers pressed to the shackled throats of three—Sisay, Takara, and Tahngarth. No, Gerrard would play out this perverse drama today, and his friends would live. Though unfettered, Gerrard was utterly trapped.

"Once, his fame echoed through these walls—the man who had single-handedly slain a thousand giants and two thousand cateran enforcers! So magnificent were his rumored deeds, the chief magistrate graciously provided him Mercadia's finest fighting force—the Fifth Regiment—to lead against his enemies." The nobleman smiled capaciously, his jowls glimmering like the wet pouches of a satisfied frog. "He took the Fifth Regiment to the Rushwood to rescue a friend, a comrade, who is here among us as well." He gestured expansively backward.

A crowd of soldiers parted, allowing a snow-white jhovall to stalk slowly into the clear space beside Gerrard. Tridents prodded the beast forward. It growled low and nipped at the points that jabbed its haunches.

Aback the beast rode Orim. Just like Gerrard, she had

been washed and primped for this public spectacle. Her turban was bleached to shine like a standard. Her hair had been elaborately braided with Cho-Arrim coins. Though she seemed unshackled, hidden chains bound her to the dazzling beast. Orim was a critical figure in the drama— Gerrard's crew member and friend, a convert of the Cho-Arrim, the damsel in distress that the giant killer had ridden to rescue. Her actions were as compelled as Gerrard's. Orim rode the gleaming jhovall toward Gerrard, but her eyes only watched the daggers that pinned the throats of her friends.

"Orim," Gerrard said. His eyes were slitted against the gleam of the plains. "I'm sorry for all that has happened."

She dropped her gaze from Sisay and the others. Pain, anger, and regret warred on her face. Whatever her true feelings, her part in the play was already scripted. Orim reached up, drew the turban from coin-coifed hair, and flung it at Gerrard's feet.

"Renunciation!" the noble shouted exultantly.

A roaring cheer answered from the crowd.

"Even the woman he rescued renounces the giant killer!" the nobleman cried above the furor.

Soldiers converged on Orim, fastening shackles over her wrists while removing the hidden ones on her ankles. They dragged her from the mount and drove her before their tridents. Dust rose in puffs from her feet as Orim staggered toward Tahngarth and the others.

"And here—do you see?—here are his other proud friends!" the noble said, gesturing toward the shackled crew.

They stood there only until Orim was driven into their midst. Then, impelled by blades, they turned their backs on Gerrard and marched under guard toward the lifts that waited beyond the crowd. In moments, they and their soldiers were within one of the golden cages that would take them to the city above.

"His friends renounce him as well. They turn their backs on the giant killer. But why? What could the Legendary Gerrard have done that was so horrible?"

In the pause, the question echoed against the mountain's base. It circulated in hisses among the crowd.

Nodding in mock indignation, the nobleman answered his own question. "There, first of all, is the matter of a massacre. The Cho-Arrim are our ancient enemies, yes, but they are still human. Gerrard did not act so. He ordered his troops to slaughter every man, woman, and child in the central village—ten thousand of them!"

Not even boos answered that, so deep was the shock.

"Even the cateran commander sent among the Fifth Regiment recognized the atrocity. When he tried to stop Gerrard, the giant killer turned his own troops on the caterans. He slew his own forces."

Groans turned to growls and then to roars.

Gerrard could only stand in their midst, head held high, eyes glinting darkly.

"For his acts, he and his coconspirators have been arrested, and all will face trial. For their crimes, they lose their freedom. For their atrocities, they lose the great treasure that they had marched to take from the Cho-Arrim. Their loss is our gain. Behold, Mercadians, our new airship, the glorious vessel—*Weatherlight!*" He flung his hand outward toward a great bulk covered in billowy shrouds.

Soldiers pulled down the obscuring canvas. Tan cloth fell away to reveal the long, sleek hull of *Weatherlight*. Her broken spar had been repaired, and both airfoils raked batlike back from slender rails. Her hull was sound again, seamless, as though the wood had healed itself. Her engines were still defunct, of course. The ship had to be brought arduously overland by giants with relays of rolling logs. Sweating crews of them stood beside it even now, clutching the vast ropes they had used to haul the ship forward. Some of the less tidy titans still had rubbish hanging from their heels after shoveling a path through the garbage wall. Despite filthy giants, shoving soldiers, and a gawking rabble, *Weatherlight* was a glorious vision there on the plains.

A cheer that was one part victory and one part avarice burst from the throng. Gerrard felt crushed beneath its omnipresent weight.

"Yes! This ship is now our ship—a defender of Mercadia. And, soon, the magistrate will complete its repairs and will send it out to conquer our foes in woods, and plains, and seas."

It was too much. As the greedy furor rose into the air, Gerrard went to his knees.

If the Mercadians succeeded, the massacres had only just begun.

* * * * *

For much of Gerrard's humiliation, Sisay had stood with a dagger at her throat. Now, within the golden cage of the lift, the dagger was gone, but shackles remained. So too did the horrible lump of dread. Takara, Tahngarth, and Orim seemed equally stunned by the events of the last days. They were doomed this time. The Mercadians and caterans had orchestrated every aspect of this day.

Almost every aspect . . .

Sisay's eyes widened in recognition and alarm when a certain goblin magnate arrived. She shook her head slightly, muttering to herself, "What are you up to, Squee?"

He strode imperiously onto the lift. Squee wore the full regalia of a Kyren: manifold robe in maroon with gold piping, double stole, and ermine hems that dragged in the dust. He was shorter and more rumpled than most Kyren, and he struggled to speak the lofty inquisitions that befitted his station. His words were singsong, as though he had rehearsed all night. "Aren't these the brave soldiers dat brought the giant killer from over there in the woods? Aren't these the *thirsty* guys dat bested a man not bested by the best—by the bestest of the best giantish fellows dat we've got hereabouts in Mercadia . . . ?" The words dribbled away in uncertainty.

Sisay leaped in, "They sure are! They bested Gerrard and all of us! But do they get any credit?"

"No. What do we get?" wondered the sandy-faced guard captain. He tried to spit some grit from his teeth, but there wasn't enough saliva to bear the grains away. The sputum landed in an ignominious glob on his yellow riding jacket. "We do all the work, and the traitor's the one that gets cleaned up. Is that right?"

"No—" Squee blurted, and then hurriedly turned the response into a question— "no, um, no drinks have been given ta you guys?" He tried to snap his fingers, though even that act seemed beyond him.

A nearby wine merchant heard, though—a mere boy with a wheelbarrow filled with wineskins. He lifted his face, nodded a head of tousled black hair, and wheeled his wares up beside the goblin. "Yes, Master? Do you wish to purchase a skin of wine?"

"A skin of wine? Do Squee look cheap to you, Atalla?" Squee asked. "Uh, dat is—do Squee look cheap ta you at all, huh?"

"No, Master!" the young man said, bowing obsequiously.

"Will this money purse buy dat whole cartful?" the goblin asked, pulling a bulging sack from his robes. He tossed it to Atalla, and it chinked with a sound like coins—or, perhaps, river stones.

Tucking the bag into his own robes, Atalla cried, "Wine for everyone!"

"Not the prisoners!" the sandy-faced man said greedily, grabbing two skins for himself.

"Why would Squee buy wine for filthy, scummy, stupid, ugly, bad-stinking prisoners?" the goblin asked, giving a big wink to Sisay.

She sneered in order to hide her smile.

"Might I also offer the work of my brush?" Atalla asked, producing a whisk broom and beginning to clean the dust from the guard captain. "That'll be just one copper more per soldier!"

"Ain't these guys worth a brush-off?" the goblin wondered amiably.

The captain squirted raga wine into his mouth, swallowed, and said, "You're going to earn this copper. I got dust everywhere."

Atalla quickly worked over the riding cloak and then coaxed it from the captain's shoulders. "I'll brush off your uniform too. Lift your arms. There. Your belt is really dirty." The whisk worked furiously over the set of keys hanging there. The captain began to look down.

Squee shouted in sudden startlement, "Is this here claptrap cage safe? Can it hoist these real good soldier guys up ta the uppity city? Doesn't dat console there look kind of banged up, like as if it'd been gotten into by somebody dat shouldn'ta gotten into it? Who's s'posed to fix this?"

A woman standing quietly nearby shoved forward. She didn't look very Mercadian—her face was suspiciously lean. Even so, she had greasy hair, grime on her cheeks, and a bit of a paunch beneath her yellow cloak.

Sisay's secret smile deepened—Hanna was in on this too?

Hanna bowed, her eyes averted toward the toolbox in her hand. "I am assigned to maintain this lift today, Master."

"Will you open dat console ta show me it's all right and not messed up by . . . guys trying ta . . . mess up things?"

"Saboteurs?" the woman supplied.

"Do Squee not know how ta talk?"

"Yes," the mechanic lied. She ducked past the goblin, set her tool case on the floor of the lift, and began working at the console.

Oblivious, the guards gulped their wine.

The boy had moved on from the captain to brush down Sisay. As clouds of dust went up from her shoulder, she whispered, "Surprised to see you, Atalla."

He flashed her a smile. In a wry murmur, he said, "Father told me I could come back to the city as long as I returned with another thousand gold."

"You will if you get us out of this," Sisay pledged. "What's the plan?"

"Drugged wine," Atalla replied. He brushed the shackles on her hands, and they clicked open. "A skeleton key . . . a rewired lift . . . Once Gerrard joins us, we'll soar to the city and disappear."

Sisay nodded. "The best place to hide in hundreds of miles—"

"Hey! What'th thith?" the guard captain slurred. "Why're you brushing off the prithoners?"

Atalla blurted, "To keep your hands clean when you grab them."

The captain nodded blearily and took another drink.

Atalla meanwhile moved swiftly to Tahngarth and Takara, intent on "cleaning" their shackles.

A soldier sprawled beside them, overcome by the drugged wine. Others turned on rubbery legs and stared down stupidly at the fallen man. One man tried to lift his comrade, but he fell too. Realization crossed the faces of the others.

"What thort of wine ith thith—?"

A third went down, and a fourth. The slumping soldiers were beginning to attract attention from the crowd nearby.

"I wish Gerrard would get here," Atalla growled as he unlocked Tahngarth's shackles.

"He's not coming," the minotaur rumbled, pointing toward the crowd.

In chains now, Gerrard rode away from the city aback the snow-white jhovall.

"The prithonerth are loothe!" shouted the guard captain even as he crumpled to the floor of the lift. "They're loothe! Guardth!"

Nearby, an officer heard the slurred call for help. He turned, gestured toward the lift, and barked orders to his contingent. Swords flashed out. Soldiers converged.

"Take us up, Hanna," Sisay shouted. She flung away her shackles, grabbed up a trident from one of the fallen guards, and swung it about, smashing the butt into the face of a new arrival. "Take us up!"

Sudden motion flung down the last of the drugged guards. The lift lurched upward. It pulled free of the ground. Its cage door clanged loose. Soldiers leaped, grabbing onto the gate, but Sisay kicked their hands away. They fell, and in moments, the lift rose out of their reach. It accelerated toward the city above.

"It'th no uthe," the guard captain laughed blearily. "They're going to exthecute your friend." He slowed down to speak more clearly. "They're going to bury him in the wall of garbage."

Tahngarth's eyes slitted. "Not if I can help it." With a roar, he flung himself from the soaring lift.

"No, Tahngarth!" Sisay shouted, extending her hand futilely after him. The lift was higher than he could have realized—a hundred feet and rising. As Sisay watched in horror, Tahngarth plunged toward ground. "Take us back down! Reverse, Hanna! Reverse!"

"I can't!" Hanna shouted. "It's hard wired now!"

"But Tahngarth!" Sisay shouted, staring down as his body shrank to a tiny point. Hands grasped her shoulders and pulled her back from the edge.

"Think of Gerrard!" Takara hissed as air rushed down over them. "If we can find the dump site, can stop them—we can save Gerrard."

Sisay collapsed atop her arms. "Yes. We can do nothing for Tahngarth. Think of Gerrard. Think of Gerrard."

* * * * *

Tahngarth had thought only of Gerrard when he flung himself from that lift. Now, he wished he'd thought of himself—and of basic physics.

Roughly speaking, every ten feet of a fall means another broken bone. This fall would leave Tahngarth with multiple contusions of legs, arms, spine, and skull. Those last two were the bad breaks. The shattered skull seemed almost a certainty since Tahngarth was flipping slowly over as he fell.

The marketplace spread out below him. Spectators crowded on either side of the road where *Weatherlight* rolled. Giants dragged the ship across logs and toward a huge door that gaped at the base of the mountain.

That was all Tahngarth saw before his face turned toward the spinning wall. Why had he thought of Gerrard? A few month ago, he couldn't stand the man, and now he would die for him?

Tahngarth somersaulted a second time. He glimpsed Gerrard's snow-white jhovall marching amid a military escort. Gerrard was headed for the rubbish wall, for the section dug out to allow *Weatherlight* through. He would be buried there, in more rubbish.

Just before flipping to the wall again, Tahngarth saw a silver flash below—Karn? And what did he hold? A canvas tent roof?

Karn ran to the base of the lift shaft and hurled the canvas upward. The cloth's upper edge snagged on a lift bracket. Karn yanked on the lower edge, drawing it into a taut, beautiful, slanting slide.

Tahngarth struck the canvas slide—face first—and shot down the fabric slope. The rug burn on his nose was agony, but it was better than a skull spattering on stone. In whizzing moments, he ran full speed into Karn, who clutched the base of the slide.

There came a terrible chime sound that jarred minotaur and golem, both. The two tumbled to the ground side by side, their ears ringing.

That tone might have been bearable if it weren't accompanied by the roar of hundreds of booted feet converging around them. In moments, Tahngarth and Karn gazed at a ring of tridents and angry faces.

"I could slay twenty of them . . . before going down . . ." Tahngarth panted breathlessly.

Karn gave a shuddering sigh. "I couldn't dance with more than three."

* * * * *

Where were Hanna, Orim, and Takara? They talked a big talk about responsibility and all that, but then they get themselves lost. And look who was left holding the bag? Look who got to save the day time and again! Squee, that's who. He'd faced down the cateran enforcer that first day, and he'd been saving Gerrard and the others ever since. Today was a perfect example. He'd played his part perfectly. He'd saved the whole crew. But did anybody talk about Squee, giant killer? And why not? Did anybody ever—

One of the best-looking bugs in Mercadia scuttled along the gutter. Squee stooped to watch it wobble. The wobblers were the tastiest. They had the most meat under their shells.

"Come on, Squee! It's right up here! No time to waste!" Atalla said, yanking on his arm.

Now, there was an impatient lad—Atalla. Nice, but impatient. He'd also helped the crew escape twice now, which was plenty nice, but he'd gotten paid a thousand gold for it. Did anybody ever offer a thousand gold to Squee for anything in his whole stinking life? Maybe if he got impatient once in a while—

"Come on!" Atalla said, bodily dragging Squee from the gutter.

For his part, Squee snatched the bug up and gobbled it down.

Atalla hauled him down a twisted lane to three huge wagons that stood side by side in stalls at the end of the road. Each wagon bore a massive bin brimming full of rubbish. Vegetable peels and hunks of splintered wood formed a slurry with broken plates and raw sewage. Above each of the bins swarmed ecstatic flies. Their tiny bodies jittered against the lemon sky. Just beyond the refuse wagons hung empty air—a drop of almost two miles straight down. Gerrard would be at the bottom of that drop, shackled and waiting to be slain by filth.

"Do you remember what you are supposed to say?" Atalla asked, shaking the goblin. "Do you remember?"

Squee tried to answer, but his mouth was full of bug.

Clutching Squee's arm tightly, Atalla approached the giant workers that milled about behind the wagons. "You see, Master Squee? These are the brigands I told you about!" Atalla said dramatically, pointing at the lead giant. "Illegal dumping!"

Gray-faced and massive, the giant jutted his jaw downward and compressed his brow. Beneath putrid locks, his eyes gleamed in confusion. "Illegal dumping? Ain't no such thing!"

"It's new," Squee replied, and then hastily added, "ain't it?"

The giant scratched a knobby torso. "We was told to bring this load of crap to this here street and dump it when we seen the flare."

"This-Here Street? This isn't This-Here Street." Atalla shook his head. "This street is That-There Street. Dumping's not allowed on That-There Street."

The giant shook his head, bedeviled. "This here street isn't This-Here Street?"

"No," Atalla affirmed. "This here street is That-There Street." He pointed to an adjacent road. "That there street is This-Here Street."

Gaping, the giant said, "I'll be damned."

"Is it not confusing?" Squee interjected.

"No—it *is* confusing," the giant replied.

"Don't it get more confusing with lots of street names?"

"I don't know what to say—"

"Don'tcha think we oughta call all streets by one name?"

"*Now* you're talking!"

"Wasn't Squee talking before?"

"Enough talking!" Atalla interrupted urgently. "By order of Master Squee, move these wagons to This-Here Street and prepare to dump them!"

"This here street, or This-Here—"

"Just do it!"

* * * * *

Gerrard, Tahngarth, and Karn knelt side by side in rubbish. Chains bound their wrists and necks and legs. To either side, a great wall of garbage rose. They would soon be part of that wall. Before and behind them stood whole regiments of men. Above it all, standing cockily atop the wall of filth, was none other than Xcric.

The cateran enforcer carried a crossbow and strolled idly back and forth along the mound. His talons gripped and released the pestilential muck. He relished this moment. As the officer who had captured Gerrard, he was given the honor of presiding over the execution. An execution by muck. It was an honor no Mercadian noble would have wanted.

"And now, we see the man for what he truly is! No giant killer, but rubbish!"

The cateran lifted his crossbow, lit the pitch-tipped quarrel, and fired a flaming shot into the sky. The bolt raced upward, disappearing except for the bright glow of fire it carried. All eyes except the prisoners' followed it upward. In time, even the fire was lost against the lemon sky.

Something else appeared to take its place. Along the rim of the city directly above, three bins of rubbish suddenly tilted. The vile stuff that disgorged from those bins sloughed down in a black and shapeless mass. Three muck-loads became one, spiraling toward ground like a black demon. It dropped straight down, not seeming to move but only to grow slowly larger.

"Won't you look up? Won't you see your coming doom?" hissed the cateran. "Judgment from the sky falls on each of us but once. Do you truly wish to miss the spectacle?"

Whether from the goading or from some impulse of their own, the three condemned men raised their eyes in unison. They saw the black monster of filth rushing down from sky. Faint smiles formed on their faces. Even Karn's jaw seemed to grin.

"Defiant to the last," Xcric growled, staring at his happy prisoners. "Smiles won't save you! Farewell forever, Giant Killer!" The cateran enforcer raised his arm in an angry fist.

And then Xcric was gone, buried under hundreds of tons of filth.

CHAPTER 11

"The *new* giant killers!" hissed a nobleman near the door of the magistrate's chambers. He startled from the bench where he had lain, scooped up a half-finished hunk of cheese, and withdrew among tapestries and tiles.

The four women who had just entered the chambers were a forbidding sight. Sisay wore black-metal armor and an indomitable look beneath her saffron riding cloak. She was clearly the warrior of the group. Beside her strode Orim, swathed in turban, veils, and healer's cloak. She shimmered with the silvery light of a Cho-Arrim mystic. Hanna wore an artificer's jump suit—the mastermind. And leather-armored Takara was the fiery will that united them all. Swords and tridents shone naked in their hands as they marched toward the magistrate's seat.

It wasn't weaponry or armor that made nobles scurry back and guards cringe. Since the women's escape, their fame had swelled. It was said each had slain twenty giants, hoisted a twenty-ton wagon of refuse on her back, and hurled it twenty yards beyond the rim to crash down atop the cateran, Xcric. Or was it forty giants, forty tons, and forty yards? Numbers are tricky but inconsequential. What mattered was that these women were unstoppable, cheered by the rabble and feared by the soldiery.

The deadly ladies passed by broad columns and entered the round glow of the rotunda. Unopposed, they came to a stop before the magistrate's dais.

He eyed them with trembling dread, and his gaze flitted hopelessly toward the guards at the door. They made no move.

Takara spoke for the foursome. "We come to bargain."

A Kyren appeared from behind the throne and began to speak.

Takara pointed angrily at it. "Get back! We've no time for nonsense. We deal with the magistrate only!"

With grinning fear, the Kyren backed away.

Corpulent and tremulous, the man on the dais said, "We are honored by the presence of the new giant killers and would be pleased to hear whatever bargain you might offer. Do you seek your freedom?"

Takara spoke with steel in her voice. "We have already won our freedom."

"Yes," the magistrate allowed uncomfortably. "On the other hand, your friends have not won their freedom, or even their lives."

"We ask only a stay of execution while we work out our bargain," Takara said.

"Speak on."

"You have our ship, but you cannot repair it. It is useless

to you. We offer this bargain—we will repair *Weatherlight* and fly it on a mission in service of Mercadia in exchange for our friends' freedom and possession of the ship once the mission is complete," Takara said.

The chief magistrate nodded in consideration. Behind his pursed lips lurked a smile. "Your friends would be held captive until the mission was complete? Their lives are held in security?"

"Yes. And if you wisely choose *Weatherlight*'s mission, you can make its singular appearance have an effect for centuries," Takara said.

The magistrate nodded, jowls rippling.

"There are conditions," Orim spoke up. "You cannot order *Weatherlight* to assault the Cho-Arrim in any way. They have suffered enough."

"Granted."

"And we need Mercadian assistance to repair the ship," Orim continued.

Shrugging, the magistrate said, "Whatever you require."

"We require passage to Saprazzo, realm of merfolk beyond the sea."

Brow furrowing, the magistrate said, "For what possible purpose?"

"To acquire the piece needed to repair the ship—an artifact called the Matrix."

A hiss of laughter came from the dais. "Do you truly believe you can steal the national treasure of the Saprazzans?"

"No," Orim said. "We will not steal it. We will bargain for it. And that is why we must be sent as ambassadors of Mercadia. We must be entrusted with the right to bargain on behalf of the city for this object."

"Outrageous! How shall foreigners represent Mercadia?"

"Send your own delegation along with us, if you must," Orim said. "They will assure the interests of Mercadia are guarded. We will function as ambassadors only in respect to acquiring the Matrix, and we will do so only to repair a ship that will perform a great service for Mercadia."

The hidden smile behind the magistrate's lips emerged now fully. "Perhaps we will merely acquire this item without you."

Takara spoke with a near sneer, "You have no idea how to incorporate it into the ship. And should you choose to deny us, perhaps we will simply orchestrate another escape, and bring old and new giant killers here to slay you and your Kyren court, and take back our ship and strafe this city until it is rubble." She smiled a dagger smile. "It is, as they say, your choice."

An ironic look crossed the magistrate's face. "Perhaps, and perhaps not. But the bargain is agreed to. You will go as emissaries to Saprazzo, in company with true ambassadors, will secure the Matrix and bring it to Mercadia to repair the ship, then will fly the ship on a mission of my choosing— not against any Cho-Arrim targets—and thereby win your friends' freedom and your ship."

"There is one more condition," Sisay said. "And this is nonnegotiable."

"What else could you possibly want?"

"A thousand gold to the family of farmer Tavoot . . ."

* * * * *

A week later, Sisay, Hanna, and Orim set out for Saprazzo. Takara remained in Mercadia to tend her father and make certain Gerrard and the other prisoners were treated well.

Though Sisay, Hanna, and Orim had intended to ride jhovalls to the sea, the Mercadians would not deign the dust and fur of such a transit. Instead, they rode in silk-veiled litters borne by gray-skinned giants. Retinues of servants conveyed wine and fans and cheese. The ambassadors seemed incapable of traveling more than two or three hours a day and that only in the cool of early morning. During much of the day they sat in their tents complaining about the heat, the dust, and the long hours.

At first Sisay and Hanna had ridden in the curtained litters. By the second day, however, they found they preferred to walk or ride jhovalls. Indeed, the pace was so leisurely that at the end of the day the only aches and pains they suffered were from sitting in one place too long.

Orim did not give up her private litter. She also spent evenings in her tent, meditating on the magic and mythology of the Cho-Arrim. When she spoke with her friends, she invariably directed the conversation toward the Power Matrix of the Saprazzans—what she called the "Mind of the Uniter."

Hanna knew of the Matrix from mentions in the *Thran Tome* and believed it could recharge—in fact *super*charge—*Weatherlight*'s damaged power stone. She sought the Matrix as one of the final pieces of the Legacy. Orim sought it as part of the Cho-Arrim Uniter. Sisay sought it just to get her ship and crew back. Discussions of the device gave the women common ground, but outside of these conversations, Orim spoke little with her comrades.

Onward they traveled. Gradually the scenery changed. The road wound out of flat, dusty plains and into a series of low hills, covered in scrub and broken by dry channels. The earth was a deep reddish brown, and the litter bearers often slipped when climbing down the sides of the chutes. Snakes slithered along the bottoms of the channels, red and black diamond patterns on their scaly backs. Near the mountain, the travelers had occasionally passed outlying farms, struggling to wrest crops from the inhospitable land. Farther from Mercadia, all signs of settlement ceased.

Wind swept over the hills, ruffling patches of long grass. The travelers made camp as best they could each night, servants clearing nettles. The ground was covered in harsh lava-like stones that poked through the bottoms of the tents and their thin blankets. Dry stalks rattled in night breezes, creating eerie moans and sighs that made sleep all but impossible. The hills grew steeper and the knifelike grass thicker.

Impatient with the slow pace, Sisay asked a servant why they did not conjure a dust cloud to take them to the shore.

"The clouds of hassim are present only on the west side of the mountain," the man replied. "Along this way, one must travel by the road." He sighed and looked about the desolate place. "My grandfather's grandfather could have told you of the days when it was lush and green, when water flowed in abundance. Trees rose overhead. Birds and beasts filled the land. But now . . ." He gestured at the dismal landscape.

Sisay rubbed her red and weary eyes. "So what happened?"

He was about to reply when a harsh cry from one of the Mercadian tents stopped him. He rose and hastily answered the call of his master.

As day after day passed, Sisay and Hanna succumbed to the boredom of the trip. The scenery changed little. After journeying a few hours, they would halt, pitch camp, and sit sweltering beneath the lemon sky and the merciless sun.

At last one morning, Sisay awoke from a restless sleep, emerged, and smelled on an east breeze a soothing scent: the tangy odor of salt water. The camp lay on the side of a long, ascending slope. The caravan had been climbing out of a broad basin, the bottom of which was broken by the crisscrossing dry water channels. Far to the north she saw a low, dark line that seemed to be a stone wall.

Hanna joined her and peered ahead. "The sea?" she asked.

"I think maybe over this ridge. I can smell it, but I can't hear it yet."

"Yes, the Mercadians say we're not far now. Perhaps another two or three days' travel."

The day's journey was somewhat longer than usual, and brought the party, shortly before noon, to the very top of the slope. When they crested it, Sisay stared in ecstasy at the vista spread before her.

As far as she could see stretched the ocean. On Dominaria, the seas were blue. Here, under yellow heavens, the waves were every shade of red, yellow, and orange. Along the horizon were low banks of clouds that promised of rain. The air was filled with sound that the hills had previously blocked: the cries of birds swooping to and fro over the water; the moan of wind as it swept along the shore and over the ridge. Distantly, breakers crashed against a rocky precipice.

A short distance before Sisay, the ground fell away precipitously, ending in a cliff, with the sea a thousand feet below. The road here ran north along the top of the ridge, its seaward side bordered by a wall. Sisay slipped from the saddle of her jhovall and approached one of the Mercadian servants.

"Where is Saprazzo?"

He gestured toward the sea. "There. Beyond the waters and within the waters."

Sisay shaded her eyes against the glare. "I can see something way off there, but it doesn't look high enough to be an island."

"Nonetheless, that is the isle of the unnatural and vile Saprazzans, may their names be cursed forever." The epithets rolled easily and unthinkingly off his tongue. "We will halt here and rest before traveling on to the great port city of Rishada."

"When will we get there?"

"It is hard to say. So many things are dictated by the gods, who may intervene in even the best-laid plans. Weather, accidents, enemy raids—"

"All right, all right!" Sisay, having had some experience with Mercadian answers to simple questions, beat a hasty retreat. She led her jhovall back to where Hanna sat looking at the sea.

"We're camping here, evidently."

The navigator nodded.

The curtain on Orim's litter drew aside, and the healer slowly emerged. She looked about, not seeing anyone in the traveling party, only the sea. It seemed to Sisay that Orim's face was changing. The expression of irredeemable grief she had worn since her return from the settlement had been replaced by something else. The sadness was still there, but now it was mixed with joy.

"Orim!" Hanna stepped toward the healer, hand outstretched.

Slowly the Samite turned to face her. Her eyes changed focus as she looked at the tall, blonde woman.

"Hanna." Her voice sounded like that of someone waking from a long dream. She turned. "Hello, Sisay."

Sisay smiled tentatively. "How are you doing?"

The healer made no reply, turning back to the sea. "Where are we?" she asked.

"Somewhere south of Rishada—another city-state. Kind of a jumping-off place for Saprazzo."

Orim nodded, seeming to lose interest. She turned to Sisay's jhovall, stroking its flank, patting it gently. Then she put her head close to its ear and whispered something. The beast gave a loud purr, as was its wont when contented, and arranged itself peacefully in a sitting position.

Sisay stared. "How did you do that? It took me a week of hard work and falls before I could even get the damn thing to let me sit on its back."

The healer ruffled the short fur on the top of the jhovall's head. She turned to her companions. "It's good to see you again. I haven't said that before."

Sisay looked at her thoughtfully. Orim was more than a friend. On *Weatherlight* she had been under Sisay's command. "Orim," she said quietly, "tell us what happened to you."

The healer shook her head. "No, Sisay. I'm not ready for

that yet. Maybe never. But regardless, I'm happy to see you and Hanna."

Next day, as they journeyed northward, Sisay, Hanna, and Orim grew accustomed to the spectacle of the Outer Sea on their left. On the third day, the road broadened. A low stone wall ran beside it, along which small empty guardhouses stood every mile or so. After perhaps fifteen miles, the road descended toward the water. Long, sweeping turns burrowed into the cliff wall, and Sisay sometimes closed her eyes as her jhovall's claws slipped on the spray-covered rock. The travelers' view to the north was blocked by a long spur of rock that thrust out into the sea. The sound of breakers filled the air all around, and many birds nested along the cliff wall.

A tunnel loomed before them, piercing the spur, barred by a great wrought-iron gate. The party came to a halt. One of the Mercadians approached the gate and placed his hand on the intricately carved iron plate at its center. He spoke a word, and there began a musical ringing that spread throughout the cavern and echoed above the crash of the waves below. Then, with a rumble, the great gates swung open, sliding into recesses in the rock. The party moved forward into the tunnel. As they entered, lights sprang up on the walls, illuminating the way. The passageway was long and straight, carved by picks. At the far end, a similar pair of gates opened as they approached. Sisay appreciated the military advantages of an approach that could trap invaders in a narrow space where they could be disposed of with impunity.

The caravan emerged from the tunnel, lights behind them fading into blackness. Before them, a steep, cobbled causeway descended into the main street of Rishada. Jhovalls' claws clicked along the street. Mercadians nodded condescendingly at the crowds that stared at them, shouting at the few foolish enough to block their way.

Rishada was a smaller version of Mercadia, with the same

profusion of market stalls, the same clamor of merchants—but all of it had a distinctly nautical flavor. Many folk roamed the streets with the rolling gait of sailors. Fresh fish were laid out on stone slabs, along with crabs, lobsters, squid, shrimp, and other, less identifiable creatures.

The Mercadian procession made its way through the confusing maze of streets, down to a broad, open square. Around three sides of the square were low stone buildings. The fourth side was open to the sea and extended outward in a long pier lined with docked ships. Most were small fishing smacks, but a few were sleek schooners.

It was beside one of these that the caravan paused. The ship *Facade* had been chartered to take the ambassadorial contingent. The company loaded on the ship and settled in for a night in the moorings.

One night's stay in Rishada was enough to last the *Weatherlight* companions a lifetime. The cabin in which they were housed was dark and narrow and smelled intolerably of fish. The beds were small, lumpy, and damp, and there was little privacy save the darkness. All three women—Sisay, Hanna, and Orim—were crowded together, and since Orim chose to speak no more than a few words, Sisay and Hanna felt constrained to silence as well. They slept as best they were able and were roused the next morning by a sense of motion.

Blinking the sleep from her eyes, Sisay rose and climbed to the deck. The crew had just cast off the lines, and *Facade* drew away from the city. Sisay breathed deeply. It felt wonderful once again to be aboard a ship under sail. Hanna came to join her, and the women traded quiet smiles.

On the water, the Mercadians seemed abnormally silent and tense. They huddled together on the deck while Sisay and Hanna stood in the prow of the ship, watching the water.

Rishada dropped quickly behind them. Before them the sea spread out in an endless horizon. Both women found the rush of air and water exhilarating after the long, hot, dusty journey. The wind filled the sails, and the flag of Rishada, gray with a red ship surmounted with a blue crest of arms, snapped smartly from the mast.

Along the surface of the water, small fish skimmed. One suddenly rose from the waves and, spreading a pair of broad fins from its sides, took to the air with a graceful swoop and soared away on air currents. Sisay and Hanna stood open-mouthed as an entire flight of the flying fish followed their leader and disappeared into the yellow sky. The water was very clear, and Sisay at times glimpsed stranger creatures moving about in the depths. When she stared hard at the distant forms, they seemed only shadows that flitted over the dimpled waves.

Gazing at the illimitable ocean, Sisay said to Hanna, "What wonders await us out there?"

Hanna's eyes too were filled with the oddly colored sea. "What wonders, and what horrors?"

* * * * *

Two nights hence, Orim was at the prow when the horrors began.

In the last gloaming of evening, a huge figure burst up from the distant, inky tide. It hung massively in the ribbon of dying light, and then crashed back into the wide sea—a breaching whale.

Orim gripped the rail. Through stout wood, she felt the profound thrumming of the waters across the beast, the compression wave flung from the leviathan's vast bulk, the rumble of tip vortices trailing enormous fins. Her own arms and legs remembered the blissful sensations of swimming and diving and surfacing in the lagoon. Closing her eyes, she could almost imagine stroking toward Cho-Manno. . . .

Another tremor moved through the rail—this one violent and shuddering.

Orim gasped, opening her eyes.

A harpoon sailed out from a deck-mounted gun. Its line uncoiled with a brutal whipping motion. The barbed shaft sank into the swell where the whale had disappeared. There came a muted shriek through the deeps. Rishadan crews cleated off the harpoon line, and it went taut with the agonized thrashing of the beast.

Orim staggered back from the rail, stunned. Gathering her strength, she stalked toward the harpooners, a pair of tall, thin, tan-skinned seamen. "What are you doing?"

One Rishadan flashed a glad smile. "Harpooning!" he said.

She shook her head. "This is a chartered vessel, an ambassadorial voyage—"

The young man shrugged narrow shoulders. The short gray vest across his chest leaped up. "This won't slow us. If we can kill it, we can drag it behind us and work it in the water while we make way. If it gets away, there's nothing lost."

"Nothing lost!" Orim said angrily. "What about the whale? What about its life? Nothing lost?"

The other seaman shouted a warning, pulling in slack rope. "It's coming about! It's heading straight for us. It's going to stave the ship!"

Orim turned back to the rail.

A massive mound of water angled across the billows, heading directly at the ship. Within the water rose a low roar. Fin tips broke the surface, and a massive figure shouldered through the darkness below. The harpoon stuck stupidly from the thing's back, slack rope trailing in the water behind.

"Fire!" the Rishadan cried.

That same shuddering violence moved through the rail.

Orim caught her breath as the second harpoon leaped outward. It met the surging bulk of the whale, embedding itself just behind the leviathan's head. Red streamed in the darkling water behind that jutting shaft. The beast did not slow. It came on, straight for the ship.

More amazing, though—a vast hand rose from the waters ahead of the whale. Huge fingers laid hold of the shaft and ripped it bloodily forth.

"That's no whale!" the harpooner muttered in dread. "It's a Saprazzan warrior beast!"

From the mounding waves rose a huge head, as large and knobby as a boulder. Kelplike hair streamed behind a sloping brow, which overshadowed small, angry, and intelligent eyes. The gray-green muzzle of the thing bristled with fangs that could bite a man in half. One vast hand clutched the gory harpoon above the waves. The other took a final stroke and then surged up to seize the gunwale of *Facade*. With an almighty rush, the warrior beast hurled itself on deck.

"Attack—!" one of the harpooners began.

His warning was cut short. The beast rammed the bloody head of the harpoon through the man. His chest cracked open and gushed like an egg. He riled on the shaft, gore making the deck slick beneath him.

Orim fell back.

More shouts rose.

Crew rushed forward with tridents and spears.

The vast beast hauled itself across the deck, clutched the second harpooner, and crushed him in an enormous fist. There was nothing left of the man but meat and bone meal.

This was a Saprazzan? Orim wondered numbly, clawing her way to the fo'c'sle. An ominous sight greeted her.

The black sea all around boiled angrily with fins. They converged on *Facade*. More monsters climbed the gunwales to slide onto the deck.

These were smaller—man-sized creatures. Their faces gleamed like mother-of-pearl, with hooked beaks and vast, staring eyes. Great mantles of seaweed draped the heads of some, while the heads of others were encrusted as with giant barnacles. Their torsos and arms were also very human beneath their conch armor, but from the waist down they had the long, scaly tail fins of fish. Pearlescent tridents were gripped in their webbed hands. As beautiful and otherworldly as these creatures seemed, they killed with an all-too-familiar savagery.

Orim staggered back. It was just like the attack on the Cho-Arrim village, this tide of killing monsters. They slashed and impaled and eviscerated. Dead crew littered the deck. Blood covered everything. Even *Facade* herself was being ripped apart. Soon, the ship and all hands living would be dragged to their deaths in the destroying sea.

Orim was surrounded. Saprazzans hemmed her in on all sides. She had no weapons. As they converged, rushing in to slay her, she could only hold up her silver-shimmering hands in futile supplication.

Then, the Saprazzan warrior beast surged up from amidships, grasped her in one huge and horrible hand, and dragged her overboard. Down, down into the dark waters of night they sounded.

Twilight waters receded above. *Facade* was only a black shadow there, only a slender leaf lying on the evening waves. The darkling sea below was bone cold and endless. It crushed Orim more viciously than the claws of the beast.

Already, light had quit the waters, and warmth with it. In moments, the sea would shatter her eardrums, burst her sinuses, and flood into her lungs. Only the Saprazzan beast remained—its fury, its agony. Orim reached up toward the creature's shoulder, and her hand settled on the harpoon wound there. A twitch of pain went through the creature. She could tear at that wound, perhaps win free as the beast spasmed—or she could show the Saprazzan that she was Cho-Arrim, that she was kin.

Silver light appeared in an aura about her hand. Magic awoke from streaming seawater. Warmth suffused her hand in a tingling glove. It sank into the harpoon wound, coursing deep along ruptured tissues. The glow intensified, and it stitched tissues together.

The warrior beast released a great moan that might have been anger or ecstasy. It only dove deeper.

Heedless, Orim continued healing its wound. She stopped only when the cold black deeps drew her own life away.

CHAPTER 12

Gerrard, Tahngarth, and Karn
might not have been crushed by rubbish,
but neither had they been coddled by it. The
three were spattered and smudged and foul-
smelling when they were yanked up from
their filthy knees. Soldiers further shackled
them, loaded them on their bellies on a wagon,
chained them yet again, and hauled them back
to the city. No baths—but neither were they executed.

Simple termination was not enough for these three. They
had publicly humiliated the chief magistrate and his minions. Their deaths would publicly repair the damage they
had done.

So, it was chains and more chains, dungeons, and dank
bread, nothing to drink but the septic swill that trickled

through the prison catacombs. No baths, and no escape—not by brute force or cunning contrivance, not by ruse or bribe. These rock-hewn cells were too hard, cold, and deep, their bars impassable, their guards implacable.

Then, suddenly, a few weeks into their imprisonment, there were baths. Gerrard, Tahngarth, and Karn were marched out of the hole. Washed, powdered, dressed—but still shackled—they were led by a full regiment of soldiers. Their escorts conducted them toward the Magistrate's Tower in the center of the city. Gerrard scanned the crowd for signs of Atalla, Takara, or Hanna—but no outside aid appeared. He twice tried to improvise an escape but only got yanked back in line and flogged.

The soldiers conveyed their prisoners into a small upper chamber, near the Magistrate's Tower. It was called an "ambassadorial apartment" and looked pleasant enough, though in truth it was as inescapable as the prison had been. Fifteen-foot-thick stone walls, a ceiling of plastered metal plates, triple-barred windows above a fifty-foot drop, three separate iron-banded doors, guard towers watching the four corners of the structure—whatever ambassadors resided here were in truth political hostages.

That's what Gerrard, Tahngarth, and Karn had become—political hostages. Someone had made a deal, and they were the security on the deal. Still, this was a cleaner, warmer, more comfortable prison than below—furniture and books, clothes and beds and—

"Wine anyone?" asked a familiar voice.

As the soldiers filed out the triple doors, Takara made her way in, carrying a wooden crate. Her red hair seemed flame in the dark entryway, and her lips were equally red around a smile.

Gerrard gaped at her, astonished. "What are you doing here—why have they let you—what is all this—?"

"What is all this?" Takara echoed. She lugged the crate

to a low table, set it down, and pulled on the top. Nails complained but were no match for her strength. The lid came away, revealing two dozen corked green bottles carefully packed in straw. "All this is wine."

Shaking his head in confusion, Gerrard approached. "No, I mean all of this? Why are they letting you in here—?"

"I made a deal, Gerrard," Takara replied, hefting a bottle and staring with admiration at it. "In Mercadia, deals are more powerful than armies. The deal I made brought you up out of the pit, sent Hanna, Orim, and Sisay off to get another piece of your Legacy—will even allow us to fix the ship and get out of here. You're still prisoners, of course, but part of the deal is visitation rights—and wine." Producing a corkscrew from her pocket, Takara yanked the cork from the first bottle. "Have some?"

Gerrard shrugged, taking the bottle in hand. "No wineglasses?"

"Don't get uppity," Takara replied, already working over a second bottle. "How about you, Tahngarth? I can't remember if minotaurs like this stuff—"

"Not in such piddling quantities," Tahngarth said, striding across the room to grasp the opened bottle. He smiled ruefully and took a long draw. "Gerrard will owe me a bottle from his case, when it arrives," he said dryly.

Takara laughed. "Then I'll owe you one, also." She lifted her own bottle. Only after a deep draught did she seem to notice Karn, standing like another piece of furniture near the window. "I don't imagine silver golems—"

"You are right," interrupted Karn, his voice a quiet rumble like distant thunder. "I require a different sort of . . . lubrication."

That brought laughter from everyone except the golem.

Gerrard smiled sadly and slouched into a low chair, his wine bottle hanging from his hand. He shook his head. "How did we ever end up here?"

Takara took a seat opposite him and drew a deep breath. "A dangerous question. I asked it often when I was a prisoner on Rath. The answer always came down to betrayal. I had been betrayed."

After a long swallow, Gerrard said, "Betrayal. Yes, that's awful stuff. Someone betrayed you into Volrath's hands, and then your father betrayed Sisay to get you back. It's the filthiest business—betrayal."

"It was my brother," Takara said, her eyes focused beyond the room. Embers smoldered in her gaze. "He betrayed me."

"Your brother? I didn't realize you had a brother."

"Ha! Of course you didn't," she said acidly. "I never talk of him. He wasn't really even my brother, only a usurping orphan. He was always jealous of me. He was always trying to steal what was mine. He betrayed me, cut me off from my father, destroyed my whole life, and sold me into slavery."

Shaking his head in compassionate outrage, Gerrard said, "That's horrible. You talk about your hatred, how it makes you strong. Now I see just how much reason you have to hate."

She stared directly at him, and her eyes were piercing, almost predatory. "So, how did you end up here? Betrayal?"

A speculative smile crossed Gerrard's face. "Well, there was that bastard Xcric—" he gently shook away the thought— "but, no. I'm through with blaming everyone else for my problems. I'm here because of my own failings, not someone else's."

Takara's look only intensified. "What failings?"

Gerrard laughed heavily, waving the question away. "You haven't time to hear all my failings." He took a long drink.

"Well, then tell me about the big one," Takara replied. "Tell me the first big mistake you made, the one that set up all the others."

"I don't know if there was just one."

"Oh, yes, there was. Every chain of misery has its first link, the one that binds you to all the others. What was it for you, Gerrard?"

He leaned back in his chair, took a deep breath and an even deeper draw, and said, "Of all the regrets I have, the deepest, the earliest, would be my father's death."

"Your father's death?" Takara said, seeming somewhat surprised and strangely angered. "What happened?"

"My brother—" Gerrard hissed— "gods, another wicked brother. He killed my father. He raised an army and marched on my father's village and killed my father and mother—the whole tribe."

Takara leaned forward, as if eager to hear the next bit. "Why?"

It was Gerrard's turn to stare into distant spaces. "He wanted to kill me. He killed the rest because he wanted to kill me. . . . He tried to kill me. He hated me. . . ."

Again, the single-word question. "Why?"

A bleary look was entering Gerrard's eyes, a sad muzziness that only thickened with his next drink. "Well, you see, I saved his life."

"You saved his life?"

"It was during his coming-of-age ceremony—a deadly climb up a nearby precipice. He was stuck, exhausted. He could go no farther. He was going to die. The tribe would have just let him die, but I wouldn't. I climbed up and carried him down. I saved his life."

"And for this, he hated you?"

"Well, yes, because in saving his life, I disrupted his coming-of-age ceremony. He could never be considered a full man from then on. He could never inherit the sidar's rule."

Takara's brow lowered. "Because of what you did, your brother could not inherit your father's kingdom? He could not ever rule?"

"Yes," Gerrard admitted heavily.

Sitting back in her chair, Takara took a drink, though her gaze remained on Gerrard. "I can understand his anger.

You stole his future. Whether you meant to or not, you took his inheritance."

"Yes, but after that, he came to take it back—no, not even to take it back, to destroy it so no one could have it. He murdered our father and burned the village. He took my Legacy—which was never his—and scattered it to the four winds. He joined the Phyrexians. He became Volrath—"

"Your brother . . . became Volrath?"

"Yes."

"And all because of you. Do you see what I mean?" Takara asked. "What you did to your brother led inexorably to your father's death and the village's destruction, to the scattering of your Legacy—even to my imprisonment in Rath, and Sisay's imprisonment in Rath, and the deaths of all those people who journeyed with you to Rath to save her. Do you see? The first link in a chain of misery. And it is a deep link, Gerrard. A deep, unbreakable link. Betrayal."

"That's enough," Karn rumbled from the window where he stood. "You weren't there, Takara. I was. You don't know what Vuel was like."

"No, Karn," Gerrard said, blinking in dread. "She's right. That's when it all began. All the misery started with that first betrayal."

With slow relish, Takara downed the dregs of her wine. She brought the bottle away from her lips. Wine hung bloodlike across them. A smile spread beneath the red liquid. "I told you, Gerrard, it was a dangerous question. Still, when you're locked away in a small room and there's wine aplenty, what other diversions are there than dangerous questions?"

Karn and Tahngarth stared intently at the woman.

Takara stood and languidly stretched. "I had better be going. I seem to have overstayed my welcome. I'll leave the wine, though. And there will be more. I see you've finished yours, Gerrard. Would you like another?"

He rested the empty wine bottle on the floor and tipped it over in resignation. "It's a bitter drink, but it's better than nothing." He reached his hand out. "Yes. Give me another."

* * * * *

By that evening, Gerrard and Tahngarth had each drained three bottles. As close as the space had seemed during daylight, when the windows were black and the only light came from a single candle beside the wine crate, it felt downright claustrophobic. The sheer bulk of man, minotaur, and golem put them forever in each other's way, and wine headaches put tempers on edge.

It was probably not the right time for Karn to express his doubts about Takara.

"Takara is wrong, Gerrard," Karn blurted. He plodded across the room and, knowing no chair would support his weight, knelt ponderously beside a slouching Gerrard. "You weren't the one who corrupted Vuel."

"What do you know about it?" Gerrard snapped.

"I know that after Vuel failed his test, a young, vicious, conniving man came to live in the village. I remember seeing him with Vuel. They spoke often," Karn rumbled quietly. "Do you remember?"

"Only vaguely," Gerrard replied, rubbing his temples, "but I'm not about to blame my troubles with Volrath on some sinister stranger."

"I had forgotten about that 'sinister stranger'—it had been so long—though now I recollect his face clearly. A young face, but familiar all the same."

"What are you talking about?"

"Starke," Karn said. "It was he who led your brother astray."

Shaking his head in disbelief, Gerrard said, "No, it can't have been. That's too much of a coincidence."

"There are other coincidences. Takara spoke of losing everything because of an orphan brother adopted into her family. You were adopted into Vuel's family, and he lost everything."

"What are you saying? That Starke masterminded every disaster in my life because Takara and her adopted brother didn't get along?"

"I don't know how this all fits together," Karn replied, "but I'm certain it does. And I no longer trust Takara. Why does she question you? Why does she dredge up such guilt and regret?"

Gerrard was suddenly angry. "Listen—Takara is the only reason we aren't dead now. She's our only advocate in the city. I think it unwise to alienate her." He scrubbed his head with sweaty fingers. "If you've got to talk, Karn, talk about something useful."

Karn leaned back on his heels, a sound like scrap metal settling. "Well, I suppose it is safe enough, now. . . ." From within his chest, from the cavity in which he stored the precious elements of the Legacy, he drew forth a wrinkled document. "I found this in the city archives," he remarked. "I feared to show it to you in the dungeon, or with Takara present."

"What were you doing in the archives?"

"Studying. I wished to learn more about the history of Mercadia." The golem shook his great head. "They are not meticulous record keepers. There are a number of documents that date from a very early period of the city's existence. At least, so I was told by the chief archivist. He had little real knowledge of the treasures in his vaults, and when I bore this paper away, I daresay he did not notice."

"All right. It's a piece of paper," Tahngarth said laconically. He had no especial interest in documents, but with no other entertainment, he moved the wine crate from its low table and settled in the seat opposite Gerrard. "Lay it out. What have you found?"

The golem spread the parchment on the table, smoothing it with his great hands. Gerrard and Tahngarth bent over it, puzzling over the symbols that seemed at once both cryptic and tantalizingly familiar.

Gerrard exclaimed, "Hallo!"

"What?" Tahngarth's eyes flicked back and forth over the unknown script.

"Look at Karn's chest."

On the golem's massive chest, a trio of symbols was inscribed by some unknown hand. Tahngarth had seen them hundreds of times but had never asked Karn about them.

"I do not know their meaning," said the golem as if in answer to the unspoken question. "But I know they are in the ancient language of the Thran."

"Thran?" Tahngarth snorted. "You mean you were made by the Thran?"

Again the massive head bowed. "I do not know. I know nothing of my origins. But I do know that in some fashion I am connected to the Thran and their mastery of artifice."

Gerrard looked at Tahngarth. "I don't know why it took me so long to see it. When I was a boy, I asked Karn what those symbols meant and got the same answer. But I've always imagined he was made by some Thran long ago." He turned back to the parchment. "So this document is written in the language of ancient Thran?"

"Not precisely, but there is an undoubted resemblance." His massive hand indicated the document. "It would seem that in some way the Thran are connected to the origins of Mercadia."

The Thran. Gerrard was swept away on a wave of thought. He remembered Multani, years before in his cave, lecturing him, Mirri, and Rofellos on the mysterious race who had lived on Dominaria millennia before. Thran artifacts were scattered across the land, hidden beneath the sands. Even the legendary Brothers' War had had something to do with the Thran, something to do with—

"Wait," Tahngarth growled, "are you saying these Mercadians are Thran?"

Karn said nothing, but looked to Gerrard, who rose and paced the room.

"No," he said at last. "Legend says the Thran became Phyrexians, the machine race that tried to invade Dominaria in the age of the Brothers' War. They were stopped by Urza the artificer."

Tahngarth's brow quirked in puzzlement. "But when we were shackled together, Orim told me the Cho-Arrim had a play about the Brothers' War."

Gerrard stopped pacing. "Then they would have to be . . ."

"Perhaps not all Thran became Phyrexians," Karn supposed. "Some might have come here. If they kept contact with the Phyrexians, they could have learned of the Brothers' War. Their earliest records, then, would have been kept in early Thran. That would explain this document."

"It would," Gerrard replied. "But did you hear what you just said?"

"Which part?"

"You just said the Mercadians must have kept in contact with the Phyrexians. If that's the case, Volrath may know we're here. Perhaps he has been watching us all along."

* * * * *

For nearly a week, Tahngarth had been drinking. The Mercadians, whatever their other vices, were well skilled in the art of producing alcohol. The minotaur had indulged himself considerably this evening.

The candle flared in its stick, and the room was stifling, smelling of its three inhabitants. Air from the windows was no relief. It smelled of hundreds of thousands of human bodies packed together into houses and courtyards, all sweating in the unbearable heat. A stillness had descended on Mercadia, and with it, heat that grew ever more oppressive. The very walls were sweating. Though the Mercadians seemed unaffected by the heat—trading in the marketplace below was as brisk and energetic as ever—the prisoners found themselves increasingly snappish.

The situation was not helped by the conduct of Squee. He visited only occasionally, always garbed in the robes of his kind. After "saving everybody's butt but not getting nothing for it," Squee had begun to spend more and more time with Kyren. That he was far less intelligent than they was patently obvious to everyone but Squee. The Kyren treated him as a dim but beloved cousin. He told stories of the practical jokes played on him, the incessant teasing, but indicated they also defended him against any perceived slight from non-goblins. All of this, he related in singsong questions, like his peers. Squee's ego flourished under these circumstances, and the minotaur had had to restrain himself on several occasions from taking the ship's cabin boy across his knee and giving him a sound thrashing.

And speaking of sound thrashings—what of Gerrard! Tahngarth frowned and took another deep draught of sweet wine. The young man who had stepped into the center of all their lives had been something of an enigma to the minotaur. Now, after regular visits from Takara, Tahngarth knew too much about Gerrard. Despite his outward calm, a great anger dwelt in Gerrard. Takara only enflamed it. He was angry about betraying his brother. He was angry about the deaths of Rofellos and Mirri. He was angry about everything, and every time Takara showed up, he grew angrier. At least she brought wine—and now, cups for drinking it.

Tahngarth poured a deep, dark-red stream into his cup and belched. The minotaur was rarely drunk, but on the few occasions on which he had let himself go, the results had usually been spectacular. His capacity for alcohol was amazing.

"Good wine!" The minotaur thumped his cup on the table for emphasis. Wine splashed from the cup and pooled on the heavy wood.

"Have you not had enough?" Karn asked, standing by the window.

Tahngarth growled in the back of his throat and drained his cup.

The silver golem stood impassively watching him. "Gerrard has slept all day today."

"So?"

"I think we should wake him."

"What's the point?" The minotaur scraped his cup along the table, drawing a long, raw gash in the wood. He rose and walked, albeit unsteadily, to the window and gazed out over the lights of the city. Even at night, it seemed to him he saw the waves of heat rising from the rooftops.

Behind him the golem's calm voice said, "We should be sure Gerrard is all right."

"Fine. Wake him. He'll just have another drink."

Karn strode to where Gerrard lay, sloppily tangled in a blanket. Stooping, the silver golem nudged his shoulder.

"Aw, c'mon, Hanna. Lemme sleep."

Tahngarth stomped up loudly, grasped Gerrard by both shoulders, and hauled him to his feet.

"All ri', all ri'." Gerrard stood unsteadily in the light of the room, his dark hair tousled and his clothing askew. He opened bleary eyes, and anger kindled there. "All right, Tahngarth! Challenge me, will you? All right!" Balling fists, he knocked away the minotaur's hands.

"Ah, at last, some entertainment!" Tahngarth said with relish.

Karn stepped back, leaving minotaur and man circling each other. "Fine entertainment for a pacifist," he rumbled.

Gerrard struck first, one hand darting out at Tahngarth's neck. The minotaur blocked the jab easily and countered with a swing to the head. Gerrard ducked under, came up, and brought both hands clenched together against Tahngarth's muzzle. It was a powerful blow, and the minotaur staggered. Gerrard snorted in satisfaction.

"Mutiny, is it?" Gerrard taunted. "You've wanted the ship ever since Sisay was kidnapped. Now she's gone, so you thought you'd have another try, eh?"

Tahngarth swung again. He connected with the Benalian's shoulder, sending him backward over the table and crashing to the ground. "You fool!" roared the minotaur. "You were never worthy to even lick Sisay's boots. You've done nothing for her ship and nothing for her!" He leaped at Gerrard.

The master-at-arms was too quick, rolling to one side and jumping to his feet. Tahngarth crashed past him. Gerrard spun, kicking him in the ribs. It was a blow that would have disabled a man, but a minotaur could shrug it off, and Tahngarth minded it little. He scrambled up, and he and Gerrard, each drawing a breath, rushed together.

Tahngarth was massive, but Gerrard was quicker and lighter on his feet. The Benalian had trained in hand-to-hand combat and had learned tricks that evened the odds.

Tahngarth grabbed him. Gerrard, with an agile twist, slipped through his huge arms and spun around behind him. One foot lashed out at the back of the minotaur's left knee. Tahngarth staggered forward with a cry and stumbled to the ground. Gerrard leaped on his back, clasping his arms around his opponent's throat.

"Admit it, you respect me," Gerrard growled.

Tahngarth merely flung Gerrard over his shoulders and onto the floor. "Admit it, you fear me."

Gasping, Gerrard rolled to his feet. "Who wouldn't fear . . . a walking pile of bullsh—?" The taunt was ended by a crushing blow to the stomach.

The minotaur smiled through bloodied lips. "Who

wouldn't respect a man *almost* worthy of the Legacy?" He got a foot in the teeth for that one.

The combatants reeled back a moment, gathered their strength, and lunged. Two fists carved the air. Two jaws cracked. Two sets of eyes spun. The fighters fell in opposite directions to the floor.

Brushing off his hands, Karn walked slowly between them and to the window. He peered out past the bars. "It's going to be a quiet night."

CHAPTER 13

Sisay staggered onto a blood-spattered deck. She hadn't time to see whom she fought—there were only pearly tridents and lashing scales—and then she was killing them.

The cutlass she had snatched below decks slashed down. It cut kelplike hair and clove a shoulder beneath. In fountaining gore, the beast crumpled. Sisay strode over it and caught a jabbing trident. She flung the iridescent prongs to the deck, where they stuck. Sisay's cutlass buried itself in a belly of scales and gutted the creature. It spilled messily at her feet, a net disgorging fish.

Another trident lanced in above the dead creature. Its twisted tines jabbed deeply into Sisay's side.

171

With a cry, she fell back, slipping on gore. She crashed down atop the two creatures she had slain. Her killer—that's what this scale-faced beast was—rammed the trident deeper. Sisay struggled, writhing back and forth on the impaling spikes. A hot gush came from her side, and she slumped.

The creature's fierce face changed not a whit. It hauled its trident back and spun to attack another crew member.

Sisay lay dying among the dead. She clutched the three ragged holes in her side but otherwise could not move.

The bloody battle all around became a dreamy thing . . . a masked dance. These fish creatures . . . they were beautiful in their clamshell armor and abalone masks. . . . Green and gold, orange and red, they danced. . . . What bright and flashing weapons they bore! The Rishadan crew—they were beautiful too. Tall, slim, bronze-skinned . . . Their cutlasses flashed in the dying evening. The players circled, fish and flesh. Steel joining them. Where it bridged the races, one would fall in red singing. . . . How alike they were, scale and skin, when they bled and died. How alike were Sisay and the fish corpses that pillowed her. . . .

She was death dreaming, she knew. This was the delirium of dying.

Amid the chorus of screams and the circling dance, there came a surreal figure. A beast as large as a whale vaulted onto the deck and clawed its way to the center of the fight. Warriors fell back in fear. The huge beast raised its fangy head and flung back green hair.

Stranger still—tangled amid that hair was a woman. She had ridden upon the beast's shoulders and now stood there streaming. She spoke to the stilled warriors. "Children of Ramos, fight no longer!"

It was Orim. Her voice was strained from the fist of the deep, and she was sodden to the bone, but it was she. In the tongue of the Cho-Arrim, she repeated the words. The vast beast beneath her roared something in kind.

The last tridents and cutlasses ceased their dance in air.

"We are not killers, but kin. The harpoon stroke that began this fight was given in error, and the second in terror. But those wounds are healed now. Already, too many of us lie dead from those absent strokes. Let no more die—"

Sisay smiled. This was not just a death dream. Orim and her Cho-Arrim magic had made allies of enemies. Even now, merfolk stripped feral masks from their very human faces. Their vast and scaly tails divided and reshaped into slender and very human legs. Where monsters had fought moments before stood only more humans.

This was not just a death dream, no—but it was a death . . . Sisay's death.

The last thing she saw in the twilight of her mind was Orim's face. The healer must have finished her speech, secured her alliance, for she had climbed from the beast's shoulder and traversed the deck of dead to kneel there beside her friend.

"Good-bye . . . Orim . . ."

"You cannot go," Orim replied firmly. "Not yet." Her hands settled on Sisay's side, and warm, silver, healing fire awoke.

* * * * *

Ever since she was a little girl, Hanna had had an intense dislike of water. Baths had been traumatic events, punctuated with shrieks and wails. As she grew older, she resisted all attempts to teach her to swim, and even, when possible, stayed away from the beaches and bluffs that bounded the shores of her native isle of Tolaria. Aboard *Weatherlight*, she had, to an extent, overcome this fear. Though, she felt herself fortunate the ship sailed through air rather than water.

Standing in the main street of Saprazzo, she was happy to be on dry land—or what seemed to be dry land. The city was built within a half-submerged volcanic caldera. A semi-circle of basalt mountains ringed one half of the metropolis, and a thick, stone seawall ringed the other half. Together, mountain and wall kept the sea out. Like other arriving ships, *Facade* had entered a channel bored through the mountainside and progressed down a series of locks to the deep harbor at the center of Saprazzo. Crews and cargoes were off-loaded there, hundreds of feet below sea level. Though the streets of the upper city were dry, they were below sea level, and every air-filled building had its foundations in deep waters. One could walk the streets above or swim the streets below. Hanna stood on dry land, yes, but it was dry land poised atop—and *beneath*—ever-present water.

It was not a great comfort for a woman with hydrophobia. She looked out at the shimmering city. Saprazzo was a vast inverted cone extending down into the caldera. Buildings and streets formed concentric rings in their descent toward the docks and the bay. Terraced houses in polished stones overlooked the central cone. A few of these dwellings were grand and dignified, with elaborate carvings and designs over the doors. Most were simple, with trailing plants hung over the pediments. These plants often bore bright blossoms or strangely shaped fruits. It would be difficult to imagine a greater contrast to the dry, dusty streets of Mercadia or the narrow, fishy lanes of Rishada.

Along the streets moved Saprazzans. They seemed completely at home on land or in water. From the docks the navigator had beheld groups of them sporting cheerfully among the waves. Most Saprazzans looked similar, having light blue skin and thick, flowing blue hair. The women wore their hair in cascades down their backs, save when they bound it up above the nape of the neck with exquisite silver filigrees. Saprazzan hands and feet were slightly webbed between fingers and toes, and about their necks was a suggestion of gills. They breathed water and air with equal ease and could transform their legs into fins. The Saprazzans who had attacked *Facade* in aquatic form had transformed into terrestrial bodies at the end of the battle, and stayed that way, tending the wounded and conducting rites for the dead. These same folk now walked with Hanna, Orim, Sisay, and the Mercadian contingent down a winding avenue in the heart of the city.

Hanna found herself stopping now and again to breathe the unusual air, damp and rich at the city's center. She felt as if she were inhaling an atmosphere that had somehow become liquid.

The broad pavement along which they made their way was intersected in places by little waterfalls that descended in a series of cascades from level to level. Hanna bent down to taste the water of one, and was surprised to find it fresh and pure. She straightened and caught one of the Saprazzans watching her. He smiled and said something.

Orim moved to her side. "He says these are the source of drinking water for the people here," the Samite healer said. She herself appeared to be more at ease than at any time since she had rejoined *Weatherlight*'s crew. Her dark, curious eyes took in every sight as they passed along the street.

Sisay, fully healed by Cho-Arrim and Saprazzan magic, looked happily intrigued as well. Hanna was glad for her friends. Their ease comforted her.

The lead Saprazzan turned into a broad doorway set with seashells. He stood to one side, gesturing to the visitors.

The Mercadians, who had been hanging back with expressions of disgust, shouldered past Sisay and Hanna. The women bit their tongues, let the Mercadians enter, and then followed.

The ambassadorial corps found themselves in a broad, descending hallway. The passage was lit by some means undetectable at first glance, and the walls were studded with shells. The hall ended in a pair of impressive double doors that the Saprazzans swung open, revealing a chamber beyond.

It was a large room, wide and tall. Its walls were adorned with shells and shapes of sea creatures hewn from the living rock. Most impressive though, and what took away the breath of the visitors, was the enormous window, fully fifty feet high. It stretched up and opened on an underwater vista of breathtaking beauty.

Outside the window teemed living coral beds that moved and swirled in the currents. Within their folds, small fish darted and swooped. Plants created a green fringe that swayed ponderously in the water. In the bay beyond, great schools of fish leaped into view and then swam away. A school of flying fish darted past, propelling themselves swiftly with their broad, winglike fins. Occasionally, stranger sea creatures appeared, undulating silently by the window as if observing the scene within.

As a child Hanna had seen the little fish her father kept in a bowl in his laboratory. Standing here, she began to appreciate the fish's point of view.

From a corner of the room, a woman came to greet them, also dressed in glittering blue robes. Though there was nothing to indicate her office, Hanna felt sure that here was the city's leader. Her face was lined, and silver streaked her hair, but her step was that of a young girl.

She stood before them, examining each member of the delegation. When she greeted the native Mercadians, her face was expressionless. She came next to Sisay, Hanna, and Orim, and a look of wonder appeared in her eyes. The woman spoke, and Orim translated haltingly, "I am the Grand Vizier of Saprazzo. I greet you, in the name of my people." She bowed deeply.

Sisay, Hanna, and Orim returned the gesture. The Mercadians only dipped their heads mildly.

The vizier continued, with Orim translating, "You claim to

come from Mercadia, but my folk say you know Cho-Arrim magic. To me, you seem neither Mercadian nor Cho-Arrim."

Sisay replied, "We are not native to Mercadia, but we speak with the authority of the chief magistrate. Nor are we native to the Cho-Arrim, but are friends of theirs."

The Saprazzan looked at her curiously as Orim translated. Then she said, "It is unusual for the Mercadians to allow women to speak for them. They have certain unaccountable—eccentricities."

Sisay smiled slightly. "I agree. But they've allowed it this time," she said.

The Saprazzan leader seemed momentarily perplexed, then smiled and touched Sisay's hand gently. Her eyes closed, and she seemed to enter a mild trance for a few seconds.

Sisay looked at her curiously, and then with amazement. She felt she had received a sudden shock.

The Saprazzan leader broke her connection and stepped back a pace. Her smile broadened, and she held up a hand, palm outward in greeting. In perfect Dominarian, she said, "I am glad. For too long women among the Mercadians have not spoken with us. I am pleased to have the opportunity to confer with one."

The others stared at her in amazement. Sisay's breath was coming hard, as if she had been running in some great race.

The vizier's expression changed to one of concern, and she said, "Please, sit down. I am sorry if I have caused you discomfort. Yet it seemed to me best that we be able to speak frankly, without interference, and without misunderstanding.

"You, my sister—" the Saprazzan leader turned to Orim— "you have a strong, familiar soul." She stared intensely into the Samite's eyes, then looked away to the Mercadian nobles. She gestured to them and said something in Mercadian that sounded placating.

The nobles, with what appeared to Hanna to be very bad grace, seated themselves on the chairs that were provided, carefully placing their backs to the window and its vast seascape.

The Saprazzan leader touched a bell that stood on a rack to one side of the chamber. Amid sweet chiming, she said to Sisay, "You have had a long journey hither. I have instructed chambers to be prepared for you and for your friends."

The captain nodded. "Thank you."

"We shall begin our discussions tomorrow. Meanwhile you and your companions are free to make your way about the city. If you like, I shall send some of my people with you to guide you and answer your questions."

"Your offer is most kind."

From a hidden recess a servant entered, bearing tall-fluted glasses on a silver tray. He distributed them, and the Saprazzan leader lifted hers in a toast. "To the success of our meeting."

"To success!"

Sisay, Orim, and Hanna lifted their cups. They contained water, but to Hanna it tasted like no water she knew. She could feel the liquid flowing deep down inside her, washing away the weariness of her journey, invigorating her. It had much the same effect on Orim and Sisay, who were drinking with eager delight. The Mercadian nobles had done no more than touch the rims of their cups to their fat lips and were now sitting silently, with expressions of disapproval.

The Saprazzan looked around, then addressed Sisay once more. "You come in the name of Mercadia, though our long-standing antagonism with them is no secret. You come aboard a Rishadan ship, and we have no love for their harpoons and nets. You come as friends of the Cho-Arrim, and though in ancient times we were great allies, it has been centuries since we have conversed with our forest brothers. Mercadian, Rishadan, Cho-Arrim—what message could you possibly bring to Saprazzo?"

Sisay replied, "It is a very important message we bear—very strange and wonderful. So important and strange, you will not believe if we tell you here, in this place of politics."

A look of concern crossed the vizier's face. "Where then?"

Sisay's gaze was level and bright. "A place of faith—for outside of faith, our message will be but foolishness."

"There are many places of faith in Saprazzo—sea shrines and sacred wells—but you seem to have one place in mind . . . ?"

"Yes," Sisay said. "We beg the favor of speaking to you tomorrow in the Shrine of the Matrix."

* * * * *

The Shrine of the Matrix lay, heavily guarded, at the center of Saprazzo's royal palace. The palace itself was a massive edifice poised above the docks. One bank of windows gazed out on the wide bay and the other on the spreading city above. The building was a vast jewel box, built of red oceanic marble, white limestone, and insets of onyx. Corals of fuchsia and mauve had been figured into bosses along the walls. Curtains of kelp, rugs of woven seaweed, sponge cushions, whale-bone archways, baleen screens—the majesty of the sea suffused the place. At its heart, in a small raised room done in crimson, the Power Matrix resided within a large case of thick glass. It was magnificent.

The main body of the Power Matrix was a single enormous white crystal, nearly the height of a man. All along its faceted outer edges, other smaller stones in blue, green, red, white, and black were affixed. They seemed to pluck each strand of the spectrum out of the room's dim light and send it lancing into the central crystal. A network of metal wires connected the stones, and along the wires moved scintillating jolts of energy. It was a mesmerizing sight.

"We must keep the room dark," the grand vizier told her guests, "for the Matrix stores and channels energy. Were it to be exposed to sunlight, the stored energy would quickly cause the Matrix to explode."

Hanna nodded, her eyes tracing out the device she had read about in the *Thran Tome*. Orim's gaze was less analytic, more worshipful. To her, this was the mind of the Uniter. The Mercadians could only gape in naked avarice.

Sisay spoke reverently, "Tell us, Grand Vizier, if you please—tell us the story of this glorious artifact."

The vizier replied, "This is our greatest treasure, a symbol of the Saprazzan people, of their origins in divinity. Have you heard of the myth of Ramos?"

Orim said, "Yes. Among the Cho-Arrim, I observed the separi and stood beside the Fountain of Cho."

"The separi and the Navel of the World are well-known legends among us," the grand vizier replied. "I cannot speak for the Cho-Arrim account, but among Saprazzans, the story we know is this." The vizier's voice sank low, vibrating through the room in a kind of singsong rhythm that grew more pronounced as her tale continued. "Ramos was a great king and artificer, born in the dim past in another world. Some say he ruled all of his world, and the people bent beneath his foot. He strode across mountain and sea, fen and forest. But one place eluded his rule. At night he beheld the stars shining in the sky, and he wept because he could never reach up to them, could never bring them within the folds of his power and wisdom.

"Ramos sought long and hard for a way to reach the stars and grew increasingly obsessed by his quest. Each night he sat in the top room of the highest tower of his castle by the sea and stared up at the night sky. He made machines that might lift him up to the stars, but all failed.

"His people began to suffer for his neglect. He ignored the ordinary affairs of state, and the kingdom fell into disarray. Cruel, ambitious men took advantage of his preoccupation and carved out kingdoms for themselves. The land and sea groaned under their depredations, and the people sent ambassadors to Ramos, begging him for help. Still he would not listen.

"At the height of his pride and the peril of his need, he began to delve into the deepest secrets of artifice, secrets long hidden and forbidden. The palace was filled with strange men in white robes, and his courtiers shrank away from them when they passed. Yet they were welcomed into Ramos's inner sanctum, and he spent more and more time with them and less time with his ministers, so the kingdom grew even more weakened and divided.

"There came a night when the smoke and oil reek from the sealed room at the top of the tower was especially noisome, the chants and exhortations especially foul. So horrible were these mad ministrations that the folk of the forest gathered below the castle to shout imprecations. A shipful of pirates drew near to shake their fists toward the castle. Even the people of the sea rose from the waves to cry in anger. All of them heard the artificers clamoring amid their unholy machines, and they saw flashes of light from within the tower.

"On the balcony of the tower, from which place he had been accustomed in times past to watch the skies, appeared Ramos himself. Yet it seemed not Ramos, for his body shone and glimmered from within as if he were on fire. He clutched to his body a strange device—this device, the Power Matrix. It gathered the light of moon and stars and channeled them into the king.

"With a mighty shout that was heard through all the corners of the kingdom, he leaped from the tower. But instead of falling down, as might a normal man, Ramos rose into the sky. As he did so, the light from his body grew more and more brilliant. The watchers trembled at the unnatural sight. The body of Ramos grew until it seemed titanic in size, filling all the sky, turning night to bright day.

"The false sun's beaming raiment rolled down to catch up the folk of the forest. They were lifted aloft in the hem of his glory. So, too, the rays of light grasped the pirates and their ship and hauled them skyward. Lines of radiance hooked the people of the sea and brought them aloft, as well. Ramos carried the people of forest and coastline and ocean into the heavens with him, beyond his world. They ascended to the emptiness between worlds.

"So high they rose, so far so fast, that cracks appeared in the visage of Ramos and spread throughout his body. His triumph turned to terror, and great rents opened within his body. His luciferous raiment unraveled as well, flinging away his folk of sea and coastline and forest. Their clothes burned away, so that the people were flung naked into a new world. The pirate ship arced, flaming across a new sky—harbinger of their coming. The folk of the forest fell in the deeps of the Rushwood. The folk of the coastline fell in the bay of Rishada. The folk of the sea fell here. So cometary was their arrival that they broke the basin of the sea, and a great volcano rose—the volcano of Saprazzo.

"Ramos dropped the Power Matrix. It fell from the heavens with such force that it ripped the top from Mount Saprazzo. That is how the mountain came to be as it is and how we came to have the Power Matrix.

"Even Ramos himself burned. His flesh drifted to earth in ashes and embers, flaming in the air. In a mighty explosion, the remains of Ramos burst apart in five great pieces. They burned as they shot through the sky, each coalescing into its crystal essence—the Eye, the Skull, the Heart, the Horn, and the Tooth of Ramos. Together, they are called the Bones of Ramos.

"It is said that should this Power Matrix be joined with the five crystalline bones of Ramos, that Ramos himself would rise again and carry his people of forest and coastline and sea back to the beautiful world before."

The vizier's words ceased. She breathed slowly, deeply, gazing with reverence at the device.

Orim glanced at her companions, a small smile playing about her mouth.

Taking her own deep breath, Sisay said, "Grand Vizier, you have spoken very eloquently about the Power Matrix, symbol of your people. So too has our own Orim spoken eloquently of Ramos. The myths differ, though they agree about a few central truths."

The vizier's slim eyebrow lifted as she listened. "What truths are shared among Cho-Arrim and Saprazzan?"

"These truths—that you came here from another world, that you are kin one to another, that you arrived in this world on the back of a god who burned across the sky, that if artifacts left by that god were brought back together in conjunction, the people who held those artifacts would be united once again, that they could transform the world into a truer, more beautiful one."

As Sisay finished relaying these words, the vizier's beautiful face changed. A solemn joy came to her features. "Yes. History is full of facts without much truth, and mythology is full of truth without much fact."

"A matter of faith," Sisay replied, "which is why we asked to see you here. Have there been rumors of Ramos's return? Have the people been speaking of a fiery ship that burned across the skies?"

A look of surprised realization came to the vizier's face. "They have."

"So have the Cho-Arrim. So have the Mercadians and Rishadans. Ramos has returned. His soul—that fiery ship— brought us to this place. It cannot rise to fly again unless Ramos's mind—this artifact, the Power Matrix—is joined with it and with the Bones of Ramos. We have come seeking the Power Matrix, to fit it to the core of the ship. Your stories, Cho-Arrim stories, even the stories in our own *Thran Tome* agree—if these pieces are but joined, Ramos will rise again."

The spell of hope that had entered the vizier's face suddenly vanished like a soap bubble popping. "No. Faith and myth are good as far as they go, but you cannot ask a people to sacrifice their greatest treasures on faith. You cannot ask us to give up who we are in order to be united with our foes."

"Don't make up your mind yet, I beg you," Sisay replied. "Let us provide proof of what we say. Let us propose ways that your treasure and the treasures of the rest of the world might be safeguarded."

"Now you are speaking politics. And this is no place for politics. We will meet again tomorrow, in the council hall." So saying, the grand vizier lifted her hands, ushering the ambassadorial corps out of the Shrine of the Matrix.

* * * * *

Later that evening, Orim left her room and walked quietly along the street. Her head was bent in meditation. The Saprazzans she encountered gave her room to pass and did not speak to her.

After two days in Saprazzo, Orim had determined the city's general geographic structure. Toward the top, nearest the seawall, was a large open-air market, not nearly as extensive as that of Mercadia but impressive nonetheless in the range of goods available. Farther down the descending spiral were the homes of the Saprazzans. As far as the healer could tell, the poorer families lived closer to the top, while the level of wealth and luxury increased the farther down one went. Toward the bottom, one encountered the buildings that housed the Saprazzan government. All were richly decorated. Like the Mercadians, the Saprazzans had a weakness for mosaic, but while the people of the mountain used colored bits of stone and glass, the sea people preferred shells.

Water was ever-present: it cascaded in streams from the top to the bottom of the city, creating a fine mist that shone like diamonds in the morning sunlight. The inhabitants drank water in preference to wine, and to Orim, the water seemed intoxicatingly fresh and strengthening.

The waters of Saprazzo were far different from those of the Rushwood. That water was dark and secret, and its strength lay in its stillness. This water was lively and sparkling, constantly changing and shifting as the sun's rays struck it, turning it to yellow, orange, scarlet, and violet. So too, the Cho-Arrim had been hidden and unchanging, preserving the life they had lived for centuries in the face of a changing world. The Saprazzans, meanwhile, had embraced change and become part of it. The Cho-Arrim had been interested in quiet, inward-directed philosophies. The Saprazzans were ever watching the horizon for what new adventures the sea would bring.

A short distance from Orim's room was a courtyard. There, graceful columns rose to an evening sky, and fresh greenery lined a small pool of clear, cold water. As the sun dipped behind the seawall and shadows lengthened, Orim sat beside one of the columns and listened to the gurgle of the stream that fed the pool. She could almost imagine she was back in the Rushwood, gazing out over the lagoon, Cho-Manno sitting peacefully at her side.

She knelt by the pool, legs and feet tucked beneath her, in what Cho-Manno had taught her was the proper position for meditation. She sought the inner peace and solitude that Cho-Arrim called vomannis, but lately she found not peace but pain.

Cho-Manno was dead. That thought haunted her. This time she did not push the thought aside. Instead, she reached out, embracing the pain. Her body shook with sobs. Damp hair clung to her cheeks. Her arms and legs trembled.

In her despair, she thought not of Cho-Manno but of the mystical place they had explored that last night before the attack, the Navel of the World, the Fountain of Cho, and its garden ringed by the lagoon.

Peace washed over her. As if in a trance, she heard the voice of her lover.

After death our souls are joined with the Great River to wind endlessly among the stars. The river has no final destination, just as it has no source. Amid its waters, all souls merge and become one. The river meanders through the heavens, redoubling upon itself until at last it merges with its beginning and the cycle returns. The river becomes the sky, which shelters the earth, embraces it, draws its strength and existence from it. True perfection lies in unity, the unity of all existence. True wisdom begins from the recognition of this unity. True happiness comes from participation in this unity.

As her lover's voice faded, Orim felt herself drifting. The stars wheeled above her. The sound of the stream merged with that of the sea. She reached toward the heavens, seeking to pluck down one of the bright stars that glittered there, to touch it, to taste it, to—

"No one comes here. We can discuss the plan here—"

Orim started from her dream and straightened. Her limbs were sore, her arms and legs full of pins and needles. She backed away, hiding behind a pillar.

The speaker had been one of the Mercadian ambassadors. There was a Saprazzan with him, clad in the light blue loincloth characteristic of the citizens. His face was in shadow, but Orim could see the moonlight glinting off his light blue skin. The men were speaking Saprazzan, slowly enough that Orim could understand their words.

"We need to act now," the Mercadian said. "They had the vizier in the palm of their hand today. Give them another few days, and she will surrender the Matrix to the foreigners. Our master would be very unforgiving of that outcome."

Orim ventured a glance from behind the pillar. She could

see the Mercadian, his white robes gleaming in the darkness. The Saprazzan bent toward him and said something Orim could not hear.

"Of course. Your treachery will be well repaid. You will be the richest Saprazzan in the city and all because of a simple theft. You'll have your money once the Matrix reaches Mercadia."

There was a pause, and the Saprazzan asked some question. The Mercadian shook his head. "It will be simple enough. The foreigners have already expressed great interest in the Matrix. They have been shown its resting place. They will be easy enough to frame."

Orim must have made a sound of which she was unaware, for she saw the Saprazzan half-turn in her direction, peering into the dusk.

The Mercadian turned also. "Who's there?"

She leaped up but was too slow. Out of the starry night, a club descended.

A loud crunch . . . the smell of blood in her nose . . . and she fell to the limestone floor. Dark waters closed over her, and she knew no more.

*   *   *   *   *

Orim awoke to blades and blood. She sat up and peered about in confusion. Merfolk soldiers surrounded her, their tridents forming a deadly circle. The dark courtyard had been replaced by a bright and ornate room.

"What . . . what's happening?" she asked in garbled Saprazzan, rising to her feet. "Where am I? Who are you?"

The commander of the soldiers said, "I am Guard Commander Oustrathmer. You are in the royal palace, and you are under arrest."

"Arrest?" Orim asked, clutching her throbbing head. "For what?"

"For murder," the commander said, pointing down beside Orim. A Saprazzan guard lay there, his throat slit. Gesturing toward a small raised room, the soldier said, "And for conspiracy to steal the Power Matrix."

The blood ran from Orim's face. "No. You don't mean—"

"The Power Matrix is gone," Oustrathmer replied flatly.

Only then did Orim recognize the man—he was the Saprazzan conspirator at the pool.

CHAPTER 14

Keys turned. A pair of doors opened. A visitor was coming to the cell of Gerrard, Tahngarth, and Karn.

"Is anybody home?" came a shrill shout through the final door. "Is any criminals wishing ta see a great magnanimity such as yours truly, eh?"

Standing at the opposite window, Gerrard shouted over his shoulder, "Go away, Squee." To Karn, he whispered, "The little maggot's gone completely over to the Kyren."

Karn shook his head and replied, "No, he's served on *Weatherlight* a long time. He's not smart, but he's loyal. What he needs is a good talking to. He might even be useful to us right now. He can go anywhere in the city, he can get into any room, he can probably find out more than the rest of us put together."

Gerrard sighed. "All right, all right. I'll talk to him, if you want."

"Does anybody stuck in there gots the smarts ta know they gotta see Squee, seeing as he's *Master* Squee?"

"Come in, Squee," Gerrard said with a sigh, not bothering to turn around.

The final door opened, and guards allowed the goblin into the room.

Those who had known Squee only as *Weatherlight*'s cabin boy would have been astonished at the change Mercadia had wrought in him. He stood taller, clad in rich silks. A band of gold was bound about his head, though its impressive effect was unfortunately ruined by its tendency to slip down over one eye. The ends of his robes were fur trimmed, though they, too, had suffered from Squee's insatiable curiosity and his tendency to follow tasty insects into inaccessible places. Even now, he was chewing on something, and the tiny wisp of a jointed leg protruded from one corner of his mouth.

"Squee don't gotta visit you in here, you know?" he said as the guard locked the door behind him.

Gerrard turned, regarding the goblin calmly. "Squee, I think it's high time you and I had a talk."

"Suits Squee. Whatcha wanna talk 'bout?" The little goblin seated himself in one of the chairs and propped his feet on the table. He toyed with a shiny bauble on his finger—a Kyren ring that showed his special status in the city.

Gerrard ambled over to Squee and stood looking down at him. "You've done pretty well for yourself since we've come to this place, haven't you?"

The goblin gave a final chew of his morsel before swallowing. "Squee's happy. People like Squee! Dat's good. Squee likes dat. Get some respect."

"Ah! Is that what you want, Squee? You want respect?"

The goblin nodded, but something in Gerrard's expression was troubling him, and his eyes, though never the brightest, narrowed suspiciously as the Benalian drew closer. "Yeah. Respect. Dat's what Squee's got here."

"Let me tell you what you've got here." Gerrard's arm came around in a blow that knocked the goblin's feet from the table and sent him sprawling on the ground beside the overturned chair. "You've got nothing! Nothing! Do you hear that?"

Squee rose, shaking, and started to back away toward the door.

"Don't you think you're going anywhere, mister! Stand at attention!"

Some dim memory penetrated the goblin's consciousness, and he drew up in a rough parody of a salute. Gerrard paced in front of him and stopped, his face lowered only inches from the goblin's.

"Now you listen to me, and don't speak until I give you permission. You're a cabin boy! Understand that? You're a cabin boy and nothing else! I don't care how goblins are treated in this city. You are a member of the crew of my ship, and you're subject to my command! You'll take your orders from me. When I say move, you'll move. When I say jump, you'll say how high, and that's final! Understand?"

Squee gave a strangled answer.

"What was that?" growled Gerrard.

Squee looked down, eyes rimmed in red. "Okey-dokey, Gerrard. Maybe Squee forgot all dat. Maybe Squee forgot you was in charge since you . . . since you turned so mean."

"Mean?" Gerrard said, his temper flaring. He raised his hand to strike.

Squee cringed back.

Someone grabbed Gerrard's arm and kept it from falling. "He's right, Gerrard," Tahngarth said, his voice a low rumble. "You've turned mean."

Gerrard spun on the minotaur and tried to break free, but Tahngarth's grip was too powerful. "So you want another fight?" Balling his free hand in a fist, Gerrard hurled a roundhouse toward Tahngarth's jaw.

Another hand grasped Gerrard's fist—this time a hand of silver. The pacifist Karn clutched Gerrard's arm implacably. "They're both right, Gerrard. Listen to them."

Gerrard stared at his three crew members, his three friends. He struggled a moment more but glimpsed his red-faced reflection in Karn's silvery chest. His eyes glowed like stoked embers. His brows were twisted demonically in the contours of the metal. His gritted teeth formed an ugly grimace.

Dropping his head, Gerrard gave an exhausted laugh. "I'm sorry. It's just being cooped up like this—not being able to fight our enemies, not knowing what's become of Hanna and the others . . ."

"All that's bad," Tahngarth said, "but it's none of that. It's Takara and her wine."

Gerrard lifted his eyes. "You don't mean she poisoned it?"

"No," Tahngarth said. "Not the wine. She's poisoning your thoughts. She's turning you into a monster, making you eat yourself away from the inside out. She made you mean, and if you keep listening to her, she'll destroy you."

Breathing heavily, Gerrard looked to his old friend Karn, who only nodded quietly. He stared down next at Squee.

The goblin said, "Let's both straighten up, eh?"

Gerrard smiled and nodded. "Eh." In a final act of violence, his leg lashed out. It struck none of his comrades, but instead a wine bottle that sat on the floor nearby. Glass shattered and wine spattered across the stones. "I'm drinking Takara's wine no longer."

Nodding their approval, Tahngarth and Karn released Gerrard.

Squee smiled and bent down to fetch something from the red mess. The mouth of the wine bottle had broken cleanly away, leaving a smooth ring of green glass. Squee poked the cork out from its center. "Squee like this ring." He slipped the Kyren ring from his finger, letting it fall carelessly to the floor, and reverently slid the green glass over his finger. "Squee wear this ring from now on."

* * * * *

"My father and I demand a private audience with the chief magistrate and his Kyren servants!" Takara shouted imperiously. Her voice filled the vast chamber, echoing among columns and through the rotunda above. Guards and nobles shrank back from the angry woman and the shivering blind man at her side. "Drive out the courtiers! Bar the doors! Pull the curtains!"

On his throne, the magistrate swallowed in dread. The action rippled bags of fat hanging from his chin. "Isn't your father receiving adequate care?"

"He will receive adequate care by the time I'm finished here!" She dragged a sword from her waist. "Now clear the chambers!"

In a move of uncommon athleticism, the magistrate clapped his hands twice. "You heard her. Out! All of you! Quickly. Guards, wait outside. Kyren, bar the doors!"

There was pandemonium in the next moments. Courtiers who had spent whole weeks lying about scampered as guards jabbed tridents at them. They gathered what they could— grapes and wine, cheese and games—and scuttled out into the glaring sun. More than a few wondered why this new giant killer should receive such special attention, but they knew better than to ask.

With a resonant boom, the main doors closed. The room darkened. A pair of goblins lifted a stout bar into its brackets over the doors. The courtiers and guards were gone. Even the gentle breezes that spent their days coiling among banners and veils died away to nothing.

"Better," Takara said, sheathing her sword.

With the departure of his court, the facade of command that veiled the magistrate unraveled. He trembled visibly, his neck shuddering in fearful anticipation. "H-How might I a-assure your f-father his d-due?"

Takara smiled wickedly and walked slowly around the blind man, gazing at his pathetic figure. "You needn't trouble yourself. I'll make sure he receives his due." Coming up behind her father, she shoved him. Her boot lashed out, catching Starke in the back of the knee. He crumpled to the floor.

"Takara!" he gasped piteously, clutching his bruised leg and kneeling. "Please, Takara. What are you doing?"

She continued to circle her father, staring hatefully at him. "I preach to Gerrard about his betrayals, but I should be preaching to you. You're the one who betrayed Vuel into the hands of Phyrexia, and Sisay and the rest of the crew too."

Starke's trembling fingers clutched at the bandage around his eyes. He was a broken man, sobbing into a stubbly beard. "I betrayed them for you, Takara. I betrayed them to get you back."

"And now, the traitor himself is betrayed," she said with relish. As she walked about him, a vulture circling a doomed man, she slowly drew a dagger from her belt. "I'm the one who blinded you, Starke, or didn't you know?"

His lips trembled, and he shook his head. "No! Madness! You didn't blind me. Volrath blinded me."

"You betrayed everyone to win back your daughter," Takara said, though her voice was changing, deepening. "And you thought you had won her back, but betrayal is a wager that wins only its own returns."

"Volrath!" hissed Starke in terror.

It was his last utterance. Behind him, Takara grabbed Starke's forehead with one hand and drew her knife in a

long, slow, deep line over his throat. It was almost a decap-
itating wound, so deep was her hatred. There came a wet,
red moment, and then the blind man slumped to his face on
the mosaic floor. His lifeblood made a bright sunburst around
him, what seemed a gleaming and fitting adornment in that
patterned place.

Takara stepped back, but she was no longer Takara. Her
red hair compressed into a gray mantle of skin, and bone,
and brain. It curled up from knife-edged brows, back around
pointed ears, and down to fuse along a tapered jaw. Small
black horns jutted from the ridge of these folds, and a tail of
flesh draped from the back of the knobby skull. Where once
there had been fiery eyes, now were white, inhuman orbs. A
masculine face replaced the feminine one. The muscled
body of a man replaced the wiry litheness of the woman.
Clothes became plates of gray armor across a tortured green-
black skin. At last, the body matched the voice . . . matched
the seething hate.

Volrath. The shapeshifting lord of Rath—and Mercadia.

Snickering gleefully, Kyren emerged from behind the
throne of the magistrate.

The fat man quivered there, staring in dread at the corpse
of Starke and the pool of his blood—but not for long. Kyren
hands laid hold of the magistrate, set after set, and claws
sunk in. Struggling, the crew of goblins hauled hard. With
a rubbery motion, the magistrate slipped from his seat and
spilled messily to the floor. His finery ended in a pile, and
his corpulence lolled out grotesquely beneath the fabric.
His hands and face slapped the floor in the pool of blood.
Powder makeup was painted in red. Gibbering in dread and
tears, the magistrate lifted his head.

Volrath strode slowly through the sanguine pool. His
armored feet dripped with each step. Lifting one of those
gory boots, he set it gently on the magistrate's head, forcing
it down into the blood.

With a contented breath, Volrath said, "It is good to be rid of masks once in a while. It is good, occasionally, for outward things to plainly reflect the things that lie within."

The chief of the Kyren gestured placatingly toward the empty chair of the magistrate. "Does Master Volrath's plan proceed well?"

Treading across the magistrate's head, Volrath slowly ascended the throne. He sat, easing himself into the chair. "Yes. My blood-brother Gerrard is half destroyed. His ship is in my grasp. His friends travel to retrieve the artifact that will repair it. Already, my agents have framed them for the theft of the device. Once it is in my hands, my people will repair the ship, and I will kill Gerrard and fly *Weatherlight* and the Legacy back to Rath." He smiled with vicious savor. "Yes. Master Volrath's plans proceed well."

"What would the Glorious Master have us do with the body of the blind man?" asked the lead Kyren obsequiously as he arrayed cushions about the master.

Volrath stared dispassionately at the corpse. He heaved a sigh. "Starke was the weightiest part of the mask I wear. Having to coddle him . . . having to walk slowly beside the old bastard . . . especially knowing he was the man who lured me into Phyrexia. I could not stand him." He made a dismissive gesture. "He'll have to be conveyed to the infirmary and discovered there, his throat slit by some hateful healer. Someone will have to be charged with the crime and killed for it, of course, and Takara will need to seem distraught—more repellent playacting. But it will all be worth it. Soon, Gerrard will be destroyed, and his Legacy will be mine."

Volrath's eyes glowed with a cold light beneath his brows. He turned his attention on the lead Kyren. "And what of your progress, Lord Griid? Last week you reported rebel uprisings in both the lower and upper markets. Have you rounded up the culprits? Have you put them to death?"

Griid recoiled from the pillows, and his head bowed.

"Has Master Volrath heard the rumors of the giant killers?"

Eyelids drooped angrily across Volrath's eyes, and his lips curled. "Don't hide your ineptitude behind tales of the rabble."

"Is it not remarkable how a fiction can rally the people? How the Ramosans have used lies to foment rebellion? Is it not astonishing how their leader Lahaime lays hold of vulgar minds?"

"Astonishing," Volrath echoed, his hand lunging like a cobra and gripping the Kyren's bowed head. "Isn't it astonishing how I have laid hold of your vulgar mind? Now, tell me what you are driving at—and tell me without any of your damned questions!"

Griid went to his knees. His eyes clamped shut against the pain. His brow pressed the edge of Volrath's throne. "The giant killers—Gerrard and Sisay and their friends—have rallied the people. They have become popular heroes. Hope has replaced fear. Folk who once were unquestioningly loyal are now harboring and aiding revolutionaries."

"Dispel these stories then," Volrath said, tightening his grip.

"Forgive, Master, but how can we dispel them while Gerrard and Sisay yet live? While you yet are Takara among them?"

Volrath hissed. "When *Weatherlight* is repaired, Gerrard and the whole crew will be killed. That will end these stories."

"Perhaps not," Griid replied miserably, his voice muffled by the edge of the chair. "The giant killer stories have banded the people together, have catalyzed the Ramosans. Lahaime leads them. While he lives, the revolution lives."

"We will find him, then, and kill him," Volrath replied.

"You can kill Lahaime, but you cannot kill the Uniter."

"The Uniter!" growled Volrath. In fury, his hand clenched, fingers piercing the Kyren's skull as if it were a ripe melon.

Griid convulsed, impaled on the man's clawlike hands. He slumped against the throne, and his riddled head gushed down his leg.

Volrath stood, abstracted. His fingers slid languidly from the mush that had been Griid's head.

He walked. Gore dripped from his claws. It fell with a quiet pattering sound on the floor, on the prostrate magistrate, on the puddle of Starke's own lifeblood. "I should have anticipated this. *Weatherlight* is an oracle wherever it goes. I should have seen that Lahaime and his Ramosans would be whipped into a frenzy by it." He strode calmly over the body of Starke. "Everyone is after my prize. I shall simply have to rebuild it more quickly and defend it more . . . viciously." He neared the barred doors.

Kyren scurried to haul away the bodies, to mop up the blood, to cover the chief magistrate's bloodstained face and hands with powder.

Meanwhile Volrath himself transformed armor to clothes, black muscle to pink flesh, gray skull to red hair. In midstride, the master of Rath and Mercadia had once again become Takara.

She placed one hand beneath the stout bar on the door and with a single gesture, hurled it up from its brackets. The bar rattled loudly across the tiled floor. Takara hauled the doors open, spilling nobles and guards who had been listening there. As they fell to the ground in seeming obeisance, Takara strode through their midst, out into the deepening night of fomenting rebellion.

"Defend my prize more viciously . . ."

CHAPTER 15

After much effort, Sisay obtained an interview with Orim, who was being held in a small suite of rooms beneath the statehouse. If a makeshift prison, it was a spacious one, but the lack of growing things and the forced confinement had pushed *Weatherlight*'s healer back into a state of acute depression. Under Sisay's prodding, she repeated the conversation she had overheard. She vigorously expressed her opinion that Guard Commander Oustrathmer and the Mercadian ambassador were responsible for the theft and murder. They had made off with the Power Matrix, framed Orim, and left the *Weatherlight* officers virtual captives in the city.

"One thing's sure," Orim said bitterly. "The Mercadians have accomplished what they intended. We're stuck here, and they've got the Matrix."

Sisay nodded. "I'm afraid so. There's a hearing scheduled for two weeks from today, and the gods know how long that will drag on."

"What about the Mercadians? What are they doing?"

"They're gone. They disappeared just after your arrest." Sisay slammed a hand angrily on the arm of her chair. "Can you believe it? They couldn't have left the city without help from within—the Saprazzan commander you mentioned. The Mercadians are gone with the Matrix, and we're stuck here."

"What do we do?"

Sisay began to pace restlessly, kicking pieces of furniture as she passed. "Well, we've got to do something. I'm going to talk to the vizier."

Though in the past Sisay had had little difficulty obtaining an audience with the Saprazzan leader, today she found her way barred by Guard Commander Oustrathmer. When she insisted on seeing the vizier, he motioned several guards over and stood implacably before the door.

Sisay grew belligerent. "Look, just take her the message that I need to see her! Is that too much to ask?"

He replied in an unmistakable Saprazzan negative.

"She'll damn well see me, and you know it! Of all the—"

"What is the matter?" came the vizier's gentle voice. She came to the doorway. Her face seemed older, wearier.

The dark woman drew a breath and fought to control her emotions. "Vizier, I must speak with you."

"I cannot free your friend. We have already discussed this matter."

"Vizier, that's not what I'm asking. I understand she must stand trial. But what I have to say, I would rather say—" she shot a venomous look at the commander— "in private."

Oustrathmer spoke coldly to his vizier. The Saprazzan leader put a hand on his arm and made a request in Saprazzan. He replied in the negative, but the tone of her final words brooked no resistance. Oustrathmer's face turned pale. With a brief salute, he marched away from the door, allowing Sisay through.

The vizier beckoned Sisay to follow into the counsel chamber. They seated themselves on either side of the table. At a gesture from the vizier, a servant brought them each a tall glass of clear, cold water and then retired from the room.

The Saprazzan looked at the Dominarian silently, waiting for her to speak.

Sisay spread a hand on the table before her. "Excellency, I am as concerned about this theft and murder as you. Now the Matrix is in the hands of those who do not believe. If Orim had conspired to steal the artifact, at least she would have stolen it to raise Ramos. But those who have the Matrix wish only to prevent him from rising."

"We do not know yet who stole the Matrix."

"Orim was attacked by a Mercadian and your guard commander."

"So she says," interrupted the vizier.

Sisay nodded. "Yes, but assume for a moment her story is true. If that's the case, your enemies have our ship and your Matrix. If they can acquire the Bones of Ramos too, we'll all be doomed."

The vizier shook her head skeptically. "And if you had the Matrix and could join it with your ship and the Bones of Ramos, what is to say you would use your ship to help us? We Saprazzans might be doomed anyway."

"No," Sisay said, clear eyed. "I give you my word. If Ramos rises, his children—Cho-Arrim, Rishadan, and Saprazzan—will rise too."

* * * * *

Even after two weeks, Orim found sleeping difficult in Saprazzo. The soft, diffuse light that came through her underwater window made her feel sleepy and sluggish, and the perpetual damp gave her the feeling she risked molding. Her bedclothes felt damp as well, and she often shivered beneath them half the night, or avoided them altogether, rising to pace back and forth across the room, waiting impatiently for morning.

Even the coming of day brought no change in her restlessness. The Saprazzans were continuing their investigation of the theft and murder, but at a leisurely pace, characteristic of everything that happened in the city. Orim was permitted to leave her quarters and move freely about Saprazzo, but she was invariably accompanied by a guard, who never left her side. She could talk to whomever she pleased, and though she spent time with Hanna and Sisay, she found she had little to say to them. Most days she spent meditating in her cell or sitting on the seawall and staring at the ever-changing water.

This morning, in what had become a disturbingly familiar routine, she rose, dressed, and rang the bell that signaled she was ready for breakfast. Having completed the meal, she opened the door and, the guard at her side, walked up into the city.

Unlike Dominarian merfolk, Saprazzans were excessively friendly, even with a prisoner. Orim had several times been invited to dine with the vizier, who questioned her extensively about Dominaria and the journeys of *Weatherlight*. Orim answered the questions as best she could, trying to avoid explaining too much about the Legacy or Gerrard. The vizier never seemed to take offense when her questions were turned aside. Instead, she moved politely on to some less sensitive topic.

Orim's daily meditation in the little courtyard had reduced the pain of Cho-Manno's death to a dull heartache. It no longer overwhelmed her, as it had in the first weeks since it occurred, but it was always with her, always a sadness that rose up behind every thought and action.

Now, as she sat in the courtyard, the sun slowly rose over the city. Orim emptied her mind as the Cho-Arrim had taught her. She let her senses flow out around her, embracing her surroundings. The voice of Cho-Manno returned to her.

To live is to grow. We live only because we are growing. Even death is a kind of growth. Growth is more than mere change. To grow is to become one with those things around you. All existence—the sky, the earth, the water—strives to become one. All things yearn to be united to one another. Thus to grow is to progress toward a state of oneness, of unity.

Intellectually it had been easier for Orim to grasp this idea than to understand all its spiritual implications. The desire for unity was common to many religious systems. She had encountered such beliefs many years before at the Argivian University. What she found more difficult was the Cho-Arrim conviction that to actually attain unity with one's surroundings meant rejecting the logical connections formed by the conscious mind and surrendering to those elements she had always rejected as irrational and ineffable. Nonetheless, each time she practiced the meditation Cho-Manno taught, she felt closer to a moment of revelation, a flash of insight in which all creation would suddenly come into focus and, for the first time, she would become complete. This feeling was still a dim anticipation, but she now found meditation a delicious rest rather than a vain striving against some distant, unattainable goal.

She felt, rather than heard, a step behind her on the stones of the courtyard. Her concentration broke, and she rose, a reproof on her lips.

Silence enveloped her. The world rushed away, and all she knew was concentrated in the face before her.

Cho-Manno.

He stood exactly as she remembered him, one eyebrow slightly raised, his mouth drooping half-humorously. He was clad as he had been that day of the raid—in a short skirt, his chest bare, and coins flashing in the braids of his hair. She could see the fine beads of sweat on his breast, the gentle rhythm of his breathing as he looked silently at her.

She gave a wordless cry and held up a hand, blocking him from her sight. Then, cautiously, she lowered her hand and saw that he was still there, still gazing at her. His soft brown eyes reflected all the world in their deep pools.

Without another sound, she ran to him and was gathered into the warmth of his embrace. She heard his voice, just as she'd remembered it so many times.

"Orim. Chavala."

She pressed into his chest until she could hear his heart beating. His hands caressed her hair. He knelt, pulling her down with him, and covered her mouth with his lips in a kiss that lasted forever.

The healer pushed away from him, suddenly, thrusting herself back with rigid arms. "No! No! You're not here! You're dead! You died in the Mercadian raid!" She bent almost double, weeping. All the pain of that tragedy returned, as fresh as it had been a month ago.

Cho-Manno reached out for her, and again she backed away. "Orim," he said, his voice calm and reasonable. "I am not dead. How could I be, when you see me here, when you touch me? I am not dead, chavala. It is you who have been dead and are now alive."

Still crying, the healer shook her head. "You can't be alive. Everyone saw you die."

"They saw what they thought they saw. I was not dead, and here I am to prove it to you." He drew Orim to him, and this time she did not resist. Their kisses were gentler this time, less urgent.

At last Orim withdrew. "What happened?"

The Cho-Arrim leader shrugged. "I was badly hurt, but not, as they thought, killed. It is more difficult for my people to die than you suppose, Orim. We have such a strong life-urge within us. Yet we can be killed, and many were that day."

"Is-Shada?"

"Yes, she and others. We fled across the lagoon to the Navel of the World and from there into the Inner Waters. It is a dangerous place, and we do not like to go there, but I knew that once there none would find us." Cho-Manno chuckled grimly. "If the Inner Waters frighten a Cho-Arrim, how much more will it frighten a Mercadian?"

"What is it?"

"It is a bad place, Orim." For the first time, Cho-Manno looked troubled. "Do not ask me about it. It is a place of decay and rot. Others died there. There, we lost Ta-Karnst."

"Ta-Karnst." Orim closed her eyes, remembering the Cho-Arrim healer.

Cho-Manno nodded. "His soul is with the river now." He rose and stretched, one hand absently stroking Orim's hair as she gazed up at him. "At last we fled that place. We could not return to the village. The Mercadians had destroyed it and placed guards about the site, and I knew that if any of us appeared, they would never rest until they brought us down. We traveled south for many days until we came to where the Rushwood ends and the Endless Water begins."

Orim nodded. "The Outer Sea."

Cho-Manno repeated the words to himself, and Orim was reminded of his habit of learning new words and phrases, almost as a compulsion.

"The waters of this place are not as friendly to us," he resumed. "They are bitter rather than sweet. Nonetheless, we dwelt for a few days at the very edge of the Rushwood while we debated what to do. While we were there, we captured a traveler, who proved to be Ramosan. He—"

Orim lifted her hand. "What is a Ramosan?"

"A society of Mercadians who fight against the kho-voshtvo." Cho-Manno used the Cho-Arrim word for goblins, a word charged with contempt. "They are few and secret, but we know something of them. This man was one of them. From him we learned of what had happened to you after the attack. The Ramosans told us you and your comrades had headed to Saprazzo. I told him you must have sought the mind of the Uniter. He warned that the Mercadians would take it before you could, in hopes of destroying the Uniter, or using it for their own gain."

Orim nodded. "Prophetic words . . ."

"We determined to come to Saprazzo to aid you. In the past, Saprazzans have given help to the Ramosans. We came, but not soon enough."

"How long have you been in the city?"

"Since yesterday." Cho-Manno anticipated her next question. "I have waited to see you, chavala, because I needed first to be sure of my reception by the Saprazzans. Dear as you are to me, I have a political responsibility to my people."

He linked Orim's arm through his and walked slowly about the courtyard. They stopped near a stream, and Cho-Manno let the fresh sparkling water run over his hand. It seemed to give him new strength, and he smiled and laughed as it bubbled over his fingers.

* * * * *

The vizier gathered them all—Orim, Cho-Manno, Sisay, Hanna, and several Saprazzan officials and advisors—in her rooms. Also present was a thin, dark man, with a long angled scar running from the corner of one eyebrow to his chin. Orim deduced correctly that this must be the Ramosan Cho-Manno had told her about.

The vizier's face was serious as she addressed them. "I

have spoken with my Circle, with Cho-Manno of the Cho-Arrim, and with Lahaime of the Ramosans. We have pondered why the Matrix was stolen and its guard slain, and who would perpetrate such a crime in the heart of the city." She rose and stood before Orim, looking the healer full in the face. "Orim, Cho-Manno of the Cho-Arrim tells me he is certain you had nothing to do with this crime. Will you truth-speak with him to confirm your innocence?"

Orim hesitated. Truth-speaking, she knew from her time among the Cho-Arrim, was a practice that was used only in the cases of most extreme crimes. The merging of two minds was a difficult and often extremely unpleasant business. She looked at Cho-Manno's dark face as he sat expressionless, then turned to the vizier and nodded wordlessly.

The Cho-Arrim leader came before her. He did not touch her, but instead looked long into her eyes. He began a low, soft chant and closed his own eyes.

Orim felt the chant run through her mind, but instead of soothing her as Cho-Arrim ritual chants had done in the past, his words beat against her brain, forcing it open. She felt violated and started to protest, but could not break away from his power.

Cho-Manno's presence suffused her. Into her mind poured his entire life—not merely its events but its emotions. She saw his mother and father, his brother, his sisters. She felt his pain when his sister Is-Mashtsun was lost in the dark places of the Rushwood and never found. She heard the great weeping of his mother and father. She experienced his joy when he came of age, and the awe with which he realized that he, of all the tribe, had been chosen as leader.

Then, with an odd feeling, she relived his first meeting with her, and the feelings that stirred within him as he beheld her, as he desired her. She felt all this, and in some part of her mind knew that he was exploring her life too, experiencing her emotions.

A cool hand touched her forehead. Orim opened her eyes. Tears streamed down her cheeks.

The vizier gazed at her with great pity.

"Cho-Manno has assured me of your innocence in this matter, Orim," said the woman. "We are sorry for the pain you have experienced at our hands. You are free to go where you will."

Orim bowed her head in acknowledgment.

The Saprazzan leader continued, "Cho-Manno has also confirmed to us the truth of your vision of the thieves and murderers. We will act upon this."

She turned to her guard and spoke several short, harsh sentences in Saprazzan. The guard bowed his head in a brief salute and went out.

The vizier turned back to Orim and Cho-Manno. "I have instructed the guard to place a watch upon Guard Commander Oustrathmer. He must not yet know we have received evidence of his guilt in this matter. There is something going on, something much more complex than I first suspected. I think we have been caught in a great web, and the more we struggle against it, the tighter it will bind us to it."

Orim asked, "What about Oustrathmer? What will you do with him?"

The vizier smiled grimly. "It would be foolish not to take advantage of a tool so ready at hand," she said. "Clearly the guard commander has had considerable dealings with the Mercadians. He likely has already reported that leaders of the Cho-Arrim and of the Ramosan rebels are seeking the help of Saprazzo. Perhaps we can use our spy to spread misinformation to the Mercadians."

She looked thoughtfully at the Ramosan, whose face split in a wicked grin.

* * * * *

Along the seawall, a large group of Saprazzan officials gathered. Next to the vizier were Sisay, Hanna, and Orim. On a separate, lower platform stood Guard Commander Oustrathmer. All were stern faced as they stood watching a line of storm clouds slowly taking shape along the western horizon of the lemon sky.

There was a loud rumble of drums, and from out of a guardhouse came a file of soldiers. In their midst, bound with chains, was a thin, dark figure. His face was red with bruising, and a line of blood trickled from the corner of his mouth. A scar stood out in scarlet against his pale face.

A guard at each elbow, he shuffled to a narrow, enclosed stone pit that stood on the outer section of the wall. The cover that normally sealed the pit had been placed to one side, and the crowd collected about the edges. As the prisoner reached the side of the well, a guard bent and fastened a large block of stone to his leg by a weighty chain.

The vizier turned to the assembly. "See, citizens of Saprazzo," she said in a clear voice, "that justice is done upon those who commit thievery and murder in our midst. This Mercadian has conspired to steal our Matrix. He has killed a guard in the commission of his act. For the loss of our national treasure, and for the death of this comrade, I am heartily sorry."

The tall figure of Oustrathmer stood watching the scene impassively. A close observer might have noticed that his webbed fingers twitched nervously.

The vizier looked at the Ramosan and said, "I have been satisfied of this man's guilt in the crime. Sentence against him is passed. Let him return to the sea from which we all came, and let the centuries wash his bones free of guilt."

She nodded to the guards. Two of them seized the heavy stone, while another propelled the prisoner to the edge of the well. His last despairing cry was cut off by a splash. Bubbles sparkled along the surface of the water.

The vizier spoke once more. "I understand this thief and murderer was a member of a secret organization that would overthrow legitimate government in Mercadia. This execution provides a clear message to such conspirators—Saprazzo will tolerate no subversive activity within its walls."

Orim looked on worriedly. A guard was busy securing the lid over the well. She turned to the vizier, who stood beside her, and whispered, "Do you think he's . . ."

The vizier smiled and spoke quietly. "He is fine. Trust me, Orim. We had our folk waiting below for him, and they will ensure that no harm comes to him. But Oustrathmer will send word that Lahaime of the Ramosans is dead and that Saprazzo is on the side of Mercadia. It will allow Lahaime and I both to operate without intense scrutiny." Her face grew grim. "More such false information will be borne by this spy, and we will use him to weaken the Mercadians. Once Oustrathmer's purpose is at an end, we will be certain he receives his due for betrayal. There will be no return to the sea for him."

She looked at Orim, and her face softened. "Now, let us talk with Cho-Manno. We must pool our strengths—the people of the waters—and end the evil that has gripped Mercadia."

* * * * *

The long quay leading out into nighttime waters bustled with activity. Wagon trains were drawn by sweating workers. Iron bands surrounded their upper arms, and cloths tied about their foreheads kept the sweat from their eyes. Their muscles bulged and strained as they hauled their loads over the flagstones toward a waiting vessel.

Accompanying the men were four figures, hooded and cloaked. They halted when a gigantic captain raised a hand before them. The captain walked slowly around them, stopping before a dark-skinned woman.

"Where to?"

"Mercadia. Our passage has already been paid." She brought out a piece of paper.

The captain took it, scowled at it, turned it around several times, and spat to one side on the slippery cobbles. "To Mercadia? Very well. But I have no cabin space left. You'll have to ride in steerage."

"Steerage!" a blonde-haired woman said indignantly. "But this paper guarantees us—"

The captain crumpled the paper, tossing it away. "That's what I think of that," he growled. "You paid only for passage to Rishada and Mercadia. You'll travel in the style available, and I tell you you'll journey to Rishada in steerage and no other way. Understand?"

A man with the tawny skin of a Cho-Arrim said, "Look me in the eye and tell me that."

The captain permitted himself a small chuckle. "All right." He stared intently into the man's eyes.

A quiet chant began on the Cho-Arrim's lips.

The captain pulled away, frightened. "What did you do?"

"Where did you say we were riding?"

Blinking in confusion, the captain said, "You can have my quarters. I was planning on sleeping with the crew."

With a sly smile, the Cho-Arrim man nodded. "That's what I had thought. Now, can you show us to our quarters?"

The captain nodded, at a loss for words. He led the four hooded figures along the quay and to one of the ships that bobbed in its moorings beneath a star-filled sky.

CHAPTER 16

Atop the great engine block of *Weatherlight* perched the Power Matrix. It seemed a huge, crystalline squid clinging to a vast whale of silver and ivory, glass and wire. The two artifacts were clearly kin, clearly fashioned by the same hand in some ancient time. Their polished brass panels, their networks of wire, their elegantly turned support structures, their enormous arrays of crystal—all of it showed the same genius for artifice. Matrix and engine were of a piece, fashioned for each other.

But the crystals of both were utterly dark.

"Where is the power?" roared Volrath. His voice echoed through the long, narrow engine room. He lurked back in the darkness amid the ribs of the hull. Teams of Mercadian artificers meanwhile swarmed the inert bulk, lifting their examination lanterns for a better look. Volrath hissed. "This is supposed to be a *Power* Matrix! Where is the power?"

The chief artificer cringed beneath the verbal assault. She was one of twelve workers holding the Matrix in position. Her fingers struggled to find a grip along the lateral crystals. They were slick with the gore of the former chief artificer. Volrath had been unimpressed with the man's results and had forced his successor to drag the corpse to the deck and fling it overboard. Now, the new chief artificer's life depended on the same faulty piece of equipment.

"Forgive me, Master Volrath," she ventured quietly. "But might I make an observation?"

From the darkness behind came the growled response. "It is your job to make this machine run, not to make observations."

If she was going to die anyway, she might as well die speaking the truth so that her successor might be spared. "There are crystals missing—five large and irregular crystals." With a bloodstained finger, she pointed. "Here, here, here . . . do you see where the conduits converge on empty spaces? Crystals must be inserted here before the Matrix will function. And not just any crystals—these are irregular, one of a kind. Once they are in place, the Matrix will fuse with the main body of the engine, and—"

She could speak no more. It is hard to speak when a cutlass is lodged in one's lungs. There was a red fountain, and the chief artificer slumped brokenly on the machine she was unable to fix. In her last glimpse of the world, she saw the eyes of her assistant—the next chief artificer. Horror, despair, and sadness mixed on his features, with something else—gratitude. The woman slid, dead, to the floor of the engine room.

"Well, haul her out of here," Volrath growled. "And clean this place. I want it to be sparkling by the time I return with these . . . these crystals she spoke of."

The new chief artificer lifted his dead mentor and carried her toward the hatch. The other workers gaped at the horrible sight.

"Clean this place!" Volrath ordered. "How can you fix anything when there's so much blood in here?"

* * * * *

A freak thunderstorm rose from the evening seas beside Rishada. It formed misty hills and then massive mountains and then anvil-headed continents. At their heights, lightning argued like gods.

Fitful, hot winds crowded beneath the clouds. Ships shook in their moorings. Lines and stays moaned in dread. Rishadans packed up the last of their market goods and fastened shutters and rushed for the safety of cellars.

The storm was not intent on them, though. A tan wind came off the plains and tried to shove the storm back out to sea, but it was not intent on Saprazzo either. Like a huge black wolf, the front only gathered on its haunches and leaped over the wind, out onto the vast plains. High in the sky it went, bounding, sending down cyclones like clawed legs and hurling itself forward—toward Mercadia.

Like a wolf, it ran toward the city. . . . Or like a vast, running river, leaping its starry banks.

It had been centuries since such a storm hit Mercadia. The dusty plains ate away most moisture before it could arrive, but this storm had a predatory instinct. It fell upon the city, blackening the already deep night. It flung down its drops in a trillion pounding fists. The few folk left in the streets ran as though from murdering brigands. Some even barred their doors, as though the rain might ram them open. White ghosts of mist danced through the streets. At their feet, water sank into every dry crevice and joined and mingled to wash away ancient dust. Soon, torrents followed the recursive roads, some streams spiraling endlessly back upon themselves, growing deeper and faster as liquid sought escape. Yellow and brown serpents of water ruled the street. They coiled and slithered, fusing into a vast and multi-limbed creature that gripped the whole city.

The tower at the center of the city was held tightest of all. Cyclones descended from the black heart of the storm to coil about the tower. Sand grit mixed with rain, scouring stone walls and bedeviling guards.

The storm was cruelest to them. They had to stay out in it, at their posts. At first, they had thought their thick yellow riding cloaks would be proof against the drops, but fabric that kept out dust only greedily soaked up rain. Soon each cloak dragged like a fully loaded pack on the backs of the guards. Scarves protected faces from the slapping fingers of water but also channeled the stuff down necks and across spines and shoulder blades. Eyes squinted, near blind. Ears strained to pick orders from the shouting air. Mouths streamed. Throats shouted. Every patch of exposed flesh was pounded to numbness.

The guards outside Gerrard's tower prison were no exception. Indeed, the storm converged with a particular vengeance on that spot. They couldn't see farther than ten feet up or down the stairway. The guards in the corner towers were driven away from their windows.

All the while, Gerrard, Tahngarth, and Karn were warm and dry within.

"Who's the prisoners here?" shouted one guard to his comrade. Though the man stood just opposite him beside the triple doors to the cell, there was no hope of hearing. "I said, who's the prisoners here . . . them, or us?"

The other man only shook his head, mouth clamped grimly shut.

Soldiers approached from below. Yellow cloaks shouldered up the stairs. They were led by a half-collapsed parasol, a cringing Kyren beneath. A relief contingent? At least somebody was thinking of the soldiers out in this storm. Already, the relief troops were bedraggled. Their hair was plastered to their faces. Some looked dark with bruises, others pale with fear. Three of the guards were so young they seemed mere women within their voluminous riding cloaks. Another had a long scar on his cheek. The goblin ahead of them was the most pathetic of the lot, though. He seemed to have shrunk within his bedraggled robes, and his rain-lashed face looked pugnacious. As he approached, his worthless little parasol was ripped from his hands and carried away to smack a nearby rooftop.

The goblin was in a bad mood. He shouted something to the guard at the door. The guard leaned closer, cupping a hand. Again came the shout. "Aren't you sick of this?"

"Sick to hell, sir!"

"How 'bout if you stand down?"

"Love to, sir."

The guard motioned to his partner and headed down the stairs. Two of the relief soldiers took their posts. Eager to get out from under the hammering heavens, the guards descended to the street.

"Glad somebody thought of us."

"What?"

"It's unusual . . . somebody thinking of us . . . "

"What?"

Instead of responding, the guard glanced back up the tower, where the relief soldiers stood their posts. In the dim heart of the storm, a light shone, as though the door had opened to the prison cell. Perhaps the goblin had some word for the prisoners. Or perhaps this was an escape. Ha, that was a funny one. Who would leave a warm, dry cell to come out in this?

"We were the real prisoners," the guard shouted.

"I can't hear you!"

"Never mind." Already, the guard could think only of his warm, dry bed.

* * * * *

"Ain't you ready ta get outta here?" came a shout at the door. It swung open, and in came a drenched Squee.

Gerrard had been leaning next to the window. He came away from the wall and smiled, shaking his head. "You couldn't wait until after the storm?"

"We brought the storm," said a new voice—Orim. She strode into the room, her riding cloak streaming on the floor. At her side came a handsome olive-skinned man with coins braided through his hair. "Water magic. Cho-Arrim can bring rivers coursing over dry land and rivers coursing across the sky."

Gerrard strode toward the pair. He smiled happily, embracing Orim despite her dripping cloak. "I'm so glad you're safe. There were terrible rumors. Takara heard you'd been imprisoned, the Power Matrix stolen."

"All that did happen," Orim said. "I would still be imprisoned if it weren't for Cho-Manno."

Reverent eyed, Gerrard regarded the chief of the Cho-Arrim and extended his hand. "So, at last, we meet face-to-face. I have much to apologize for."

"The regrets of the past are many—too many. We cannot allow them to doom the future," Cho-Manno interrupted, taking Gerrard's hand.

"How did you get into the city?"

Cho-Manno gestured upward. "We can move in rivers and storms just as the Mercadians move in clouds of dust. Our skyscouts and wizards have mastered the warm air currents. This storm brought us and rained us down into abandoned streets. The rain fills the city with my folk." He nodded toward a scar-faced man who came in beside him.

"We will join the Ramosans and prepare an uprising."

"Great news!" Gerrard said.

"Not all great," interjected a new voice. "After all, the Mercadians do have the Power Matrix."

"Hanna!" Gerrard cried, wrapping her in a happy embrace. He kissed her, stopping only to stare into her eyes. "You can't imagine how much I've missed you."

"And I you." Hanna's face was beautiful despite the rain that dripped from her blonde hair. Her expression turned sad. "Even so, we'll be apart again soon, I fear. I must seek out *Weatherlight* and find out what they've done with the Power Matrix."

"I'll help you. It's my ship after all."

"No, you've got to go after the Bones of Ramos," said Sisay, behind. "I'll go along, and Tahngarth, and whatever fighters we can scrounge up from the ship's crew—Chamas, Tallakaster, Fewsteem . . ."

Hanna supplied the names of three others. "Dabis, Ilcaster, Takara."

Tahngarth rumbled, "I think we'll leave Takara out of this one."

"Hold on, everyone," Gerrard interjected, gripping the sides of his head. "What's all this about the Bones of Ramos?"

Hanna answered, "They are the final pieces that will complete repair and overhaul of *Weatherlight*. They will allow the engine and the Power Matrix to fuse. The ship will be faster, more powerful than ever."

"But, what are these bones, and where are they?" Gerrard asked.

Cho-Manno said, "We will explain all as we make our escape. There is no time to stand and talk. Gather your things. The storm cannot last much longer. Nor can Mercadian stupidity."

Gerrard glanced back at his cellmates.

Tahngarth eagerly pushed his way out the door and stood

in the pounding rain. He howled into the heavens.

Karn meanwhile said simply, "Let us go, Gerrard. *Weatherlight* awaits me, and the Bones of Ramos await you."

* * * * *

From the Magistrate's Tower, Volrath watched the storm. His fingers dug into the stone windowsill where he stood. It was one of the subtler powers of a shapechanger, to make his flesh as thin and sharp and strong as razors, to insinuate his being into whatever fault might present itself and swell in those cracks to split them wider. Solid stones became sifting sand in his grip. His flesh could flow, and freeze, and destroy like water. It was how he ruled the rock of Mercadia. His grip had split the mountain to its core.

These rebels, though, were not rock. Ramosan, Cho-Arrim, Saprazzan, Rishadan—they were all folk with affinity for water. They brought this storm down upon Mercadia. They would grip it in a fist larger and more powerful than Volrath's. They would break the rock of Mercadia to shifting sand.

Why, though, did they bring this storm now? What did they seek?

Volrath saw. Through the shredding curtains of rain, he saw. Dark figures descended amid those cascades. They were human, though they had billowing cloaks above them that seemed the wings of bats. On the warm currents of the storm they rode, dropping where they would, where they could—rooftops, streets, gardens, awnings. Like the water that had borne them hence, they went to ground. Following channels invisible to the eye, they gathered and went below. One by one, each of the invaders escaped into gutters and rebel safe houses.

"Not safe for long," Volrath muttered to himself, flinging limestone sand out into the night. He would send a regiment of the guard around next morning on a house-to-house search. Invaders and anyone harboring them would be summarily executed, their property seized by the state. Whatever uprising they planned would be put down before it could even occur.

"I shall defend my interests viciously."

Something else moved in the stormy night. Another group of rebels streamed down a stairway and into the winding streets. Gerrard and his crew.

Volrath watched angrily. He had planned just such an escape—Takara had planned it to send Gerrard after the crystals he needed to repair *Weatherlight*. Now, the ingrates were escaping on their own. Their plans were already discussed, and Takara had neither been consulted nor thanked. It mattered little.

Gerrard was doing just what Volrath had planned. Gerrard had always been his own worst enemy. His betrayals and his blunders led inevitably to ruin.

Smiling, Volrath released the crushed windowsill. He turned and took a step. In midstride, he transformed into a lithe, fire-haired woman.

"Gerrard will lead me straight to the crystals I need, and I will destroy him in the process."

* * * * *

Squee led his companions on a ridiculously jogging path. The pounding rain and lightning flashes made Mercadia's mad maze only madder still. Hanna, whose direction sense was the best of anyone's, was hopelessly confused. Squee insisted he knew where he was going, and his errant rout proved very quick. The company traversed the two-and-a-half miles from the Magistrate's Tower to the outer rim of the city in only half an hour.

"Dis here street is Dat-Dere-Street," Squee announced proudly.

Gerrard and his comrades arrived at the dumping station where Squee and Atalla had fooled the giants. In the pelting storm, there were no giants or wagons, only the yawning blackness of a nearly two-mile drop to the storm-lit plains below.

Reunited again for the rescue, the company would soon be sundered. Hanna, Squee, and Karn would remain behind to search for *Weatherlight*. Orim, Cho-Manno, and Lahaime would rendezvous with the Ramosans and begin to foment rebellion against the ruling Mercadians and their Kyren. Meanwhile, Gerrard, Sisay, Tahngarth, and five other crew members would take the maps and lore provided by Cho-Manno and set out in search of Ouramos, where lay the Bones of Ramos.

Parting was no easy thing, especially for the commander and the navigator.

"Listen," Hanna said, staring into Gerrard's eyes. "Don't just bring back Ramos's bones. Bring back your own, as well. And all in one piece."

His smile glinted with lightning. He stroked a sodden lock of hair back from her face. "Don't I always?" Glancing over the precipice, he said, "If I survive the next few minutes, I can survive anything." He lifted his arms. The cape of a Cho-Arrim skyscout draped, dripping, from wrists to ankles. "Orim, are you sure these things are safe?"

"Safe enough," Orim replied, sheltered in Cho-Manno's arms. "Just glide like a flying squirrel and let the Cho-Arrim wizards do the rest. Don't try anything fancy."

Gerrard gave a flap of the wings. "I'm not sure I'll even breathe on the way down."

Tahngarth stood nearby, snorting white plumes of irritation in the air. "I'm no squirrel." He stared down at his own cloak—two skyscout capes sewn together.

With a light laugh, a similarly winged Sisay recited, "Birdie, birdie in the sky, what just dropped down in my eye? I'm sure glad that cows don't fly!"

"I'm not a squirrel or a cow," Tahngarth growled. If anyone but his captain had made the remark, there would have been a brawl.

Cho-Manno said, "The storm is losing its force. You had better get going."

"Yes," Gerrard replied. Leaning forward, he kissed Hanna one last time. "I'll bring back my bones and Ramos's. Don't worry about me. You just find *Weatherlight* and get ready to put the stones in place."

"I will."

"And we'll make sure the revolution is ready," Orim pledged.

"Good," Gerrard said. He cast a glance toward Sisay, shrugged, and said, "Well, here goes."

Taking a deep breath and spreading his arms, Gerrard did a swan dive off the edge of Mount Mercadia.

The ridge of solid ground disappeared beneath him. He plunged toward the blackness beyond. Spreading arms and legs, he felt the skyscout cloak snap outward. Air filled the garment. Insistent cloth yanked on wrists and ankles. Gerrard's back hyperextended. Gritting his teeth, he brought arms and legs to full extension and entered a steady glide.

Rain pelted down. Winds roared up. The black plains swayed nauseatingly as they stretched away toward the hills.

A sharp crack came nearby. Gerrard glanced over to see Sisay hanging there on the wind, like a spider drifting down on a thread too gossamer to see. To the other side came a sound like a shot. It was followed by a long roar in concert with the winds. Tahngarth was taking the descent less well than his mates. Six other crew drifted downward in a tenuous flock.

Gerrard smiled grimly. The sooner they were on the ground, the better. He dipped his arms and banked toward the marketplace below. There, under cover of dark, they would "requisition" jhovalls and supplies. Before daybreak, they would charge out of the city, on the way to Ouramos.

The other gliders followed. They crossed above the vast, putrid circle of the garbage wall. Beneath the sheltering edge of the inverted mountain, the rain ceased. Still, mists followed them—the conjurations of Cho-Manno's wizards. Cho-Manno had said he would take care of the flight, but Gerrard would have to take care of the landing.

Selecting a likely corral of jhovalls, Gerrard soared down. What seemed at first to be only specks of white pepper slowly swelled upward to scraps of paper and then to large tents. Gerrard brought his team down among them, near the corral.

He tried to land upright, but the ground stole his feet, and he rolled in the dirt. A fence post of the corral caught him short. Fouled in his cloak, muddy, and somewhat bruised, Gerrard staggered up and turned to see his crew land.

Sisay soared up beside him, flung her cloak out to catch one last hold on the air, and landed easily on her feet. Tahngarth came to ground like a great black comet. He flopped facefirst, his horns digging twin furrows in the dirt. Chamas, Tallakaster, Fewsteem, Dabis, and Ilcaster arrived less gracefully than Sisay—but less catastrophically than Tahngarth.

Last of all alighted a thin, strong figure, who folded the cloak behind her as though she were used to having wings. "Sorry I'm late. Squee sent word you'd arrived and told me what you were up to. I figured you could use another fighter."

Gerrard only shook his head in disbelief. "Takara . . ."

BOOK III

CHAPTER 17

In the dark before dawn, a caravan moved slowly away from Mercadia, through circling walls of stone and garbage. Gerrard and his companions trailed in its wake. Here in the shadow of the mountain, the ground was dry enough to produce dust, which masked the rebels and their stolen jhovalls.

The corral Gerrard had landed next to had turned out to belong to the city guard. He had "borrowed" several mounts from the stables. It seemed poetic justice. The guard was in such disarray they were unlikely to miss the jhovalls until it was far too late to do anything about the theft.

"They should have learned from my training," Gerrard told himself dryly, spitting dust from his teeth. It was not the first or last time he would spit on that long, dusty journey.

226

Despite the inevitable grit, *Weatherlight*'s crew members rode with a glad ease. For Gerrard and Tahngarth, the journey meant freedom after long incarceration. For Sisay, it was a chance to negotiate with sword instead of word. For Dabis, Tallakaster, Fewsteem, Chamas, and Ilcaster, the smell of clean dirt was welcome after months in the perfumed fetor of Mercadia. All were glad to be riding—and soon, fighting—together. It was like old times.

Only Takara rode apart. Since her mysterious arrival, she had hung back in the pack, lending aid where it was required but offering little comment. Perhaps she sensed the crew's growing distrust of her. Perhaps she knew that Gerrard no longer welcomed her advice. The others left the fiery Rathi alone. By the dawn of the second day, her reticence was beginning to wear on her comrades.

In the dusty morning, Gerrard's curiosity at last awakened. He let his jhovall fall back among the other steeds until he came even with Takara. Keeping his eyes trained on the road ahead, Gerrard said, "You've been pretty quiet on this trip."

Takara's mount stalked easily forward. "Yes."

"Is something bothering you?" Gerrard pressed. "You seemed happy enough to join us."

"My father is dead."

Gerrard's eyes grew wide. He stammered, "H-He's dead?"

"Murdered in the infirmary. It was one of those Ramosan assassins."

"Ramosan . . . assassins?" Gerrard echoed amazedly.

"The city is rife with them. The guards are worthless. They haven't the first clue where to find the killer."

Gerrard's eyes followed the rumpled ground. "I'm sorry, Takara. I shouldn't have . . . intruded on your grief."

"Oh, I don't grieve," she said bitterly. "I never grieve. I only hate. I'm going to corner the man who killed my father. I'm going to wrap my fingers around his neck and rip his throat out." She turned her gaze toward Gerrard. Her eyes were as sharp as poniards. "Do you know where the Ramosans hide out?"

Pursing his lips, Gerrard said quietly, "No, I couldn't help you there."

Jaw flexing grimly, Takara peered toward the front of the caravan. "Aren't you needed up there?"

Gerrard nodded, nudging his jhovall with his heels. "I'm sorry to have intruded on your . . . on your hatred."

Two days out, the caravan they'd been following turned off to the north. The *Weatherlight* brigade continued to the west. The directions to Ouramos, such as Gerrard had managed to ascertain, were tantalizingly vague. The Cho-Arrim had provided their best map scrolls, but even those were only approximates. By Sisay's reckoning, a jhovall journey of five days west, bearing along the line of the Great Scales at darkest night, would bring them in sight of the fabled place.

The plains rose in a long, gentle slope and then fell away into a valley. At the far end, the road curved through a series of high paths. The earth was very black and moist but with surprisingly little vegetation. The road they followed grew narrower and less used. Finally, they could follow it only by tracking along a widely spaced series of huge, gray stones on its edge.

At the mouth of a wide, swampy gorge, Gerrard halted, and the others stopped behind him.

"What's the matter?" Sisay wiped her forehead.

The day had been hot, and the sun was only just beginning to sink into the south, amid a striated series of clouds. They were facing a long passage between two mesas. The high cliffs, made of blood-red rocks, dropped to foul-smelling fens at their feet. Drowned forests stood white amid marshy grasses. Clouds of insects hovered in the air. The stillness and the unpleasant odor that lingered in the air contributed to the atmosphere of rot and decay that hung over everything and bore down on the travelers.

Gerrard said, "We're not alone here." He looked at Tahngarth.

The minotaur nodded. "Yes. Someone is watching us."

"Who?" Instinctively, the party drew their mounts closer together, and Gerrard loosened his sword in its sheath.

Before the minotaur could reply, a black shape surged up from behind a dead tree that bordered the road. As it raced toward them, it gave an unearthly, ululating cry. The shout was echoed a few seconds later by other creatures emerging from the swampy forest. They rose from the muck, gray-skinned manifestations of it. Once men, these withered and shambling monsters were draped in whatever clothes had survived the ravages of rot. Here and there, bone showed through sloughing flesh. The creatures shrieked as they stormed the party. Their screams rebounded from the white ghosts of drowned trees.

"Deepwood ghouls!" Takara shouted as her sword raked free.

Tahngarth's striva slashed off the head of the foremost ghoul. Rather than collapsing, the body of the creature pushed its way blindly forward, groping in a horrid parody of human action. Its arms embraced Tahngarth's jhovall. The six-legged tiger-creature reared, slashing its forepaws across gray flesh. Claws tore open the undead thing's belly, as if ripping a sack of old leather. Out tumbled desiccated organs. Parts quivered on the ground, but still the ghoul raked forward.

With a shout of disgust, Tahngarth kicked the headless monster away from him.

Another group of ghouls converged from the other side of the road.

Swiftly *Weatherlight's* crew backed their steeds into a circle. Swords menaced above the snarling and spitting heads of the jhovalls.

The ghouls showed no fear, leaping inward.

Sisay bent from her saddle, thrusting her blade into the

heart of the nearest ghoul. Steel crackled through dead flesh and snapped ribs as though they were twigs. Her sword sunk deep. A full foot of blade protruded from the monster's back. It kept coming. Its decaying fingers gripped Sisay about her waist and pulled her down into the dust. White bones with shredded flesh sank into Sisay's neck. It squeezed, strangling her.

A jhovall bounded up beside her, and a sword flashed down. Gerrard's blade slashed the arm from the ghoul's body.

From the other side, Fewsteem attacked with a heavy mace. Spikes fell, impaling the thing's skull. Powdery brain ghosted out on the air. The strike smashed the ghoul's body to the earth.

Sisay pried the dead hand from her neck and retreated among shouldering jhovalls.

The party was fighting perhaps twenty of the flesh eaters. The ghouls were impervious to mortal wounds. They bore on, regardless of the injuries they suffered. Survival did not matter to them, only destruction of their foes. Despite their obvious mindlessness, the ghouls seemed to attack in concert. Two ghouls would slash at adjacent jhovalls, opening a space into which a third could charge. It was as though they were the dumb pawns of a much larger mind, playing out the battle like a game of chess. And every good chess player guards his king.

"They fight with a vengeance!" Gerrard shouted above the melee. As his sword split the head of another creature, he yelled, "They fight like guardians!"

He heard a shriek to his right and saw that one of the ghouls had plunged a rusting sword into the heart of Fewsteem's jhovall. The great tiger sank to its knees, its head jerking back and forth as lifeblood poured out. Fewsteem was flung from his saddle, and a pair of ghouls dragged the hapless crewman toward the swamp beyond the road. His eyes rolled back in panic.

With a shout, Gerrard leaped from his own mount, which was hemmed in by a circle of slashing, clawing ghouls. He vaulted over their heads. Even as he did so, he heard a squeal of agony from his jhovall. It too fell victim to the bloodbath. The Benalian reached the fen. He swung his sword and cut in half one of the ghouls holding Fewsteem. Sisay ran up behind him and disposed of the other creature. They dragged Fewsteem out of the muck.

On the road above, the situation was improving. The crew had destroyed a dozen attackers, at the cost of three jhovalls. The other ghouls continued to press forward without hesitation, but the tide of the battle had clearly turned.

Despite a dozen small cuts on his chest and arms, Tahngarth scooped up a ghoul and threw it some twenty feet away to smash against a twisted tree. Takara cut the legs out from beneath another at the same moment that Ilcaster chopped its head from its shoulders. The severed head bounded along the road into the ditch, where it sank beneath the muck, its eyes rolling in their sockets.

Gerrard, Sisay, and Fewsteem rejoined the others to destroy the remaining beasts. In a few minutes, the crewmen were panting, wiping their weapons, and binding up each others' wounds. Without visible effort, Tahngarth picked up the various pieces of ghoul left on the road and tossed them into the festering swamp. Gerrard looked sadly at the mangled body of his jhovall. The two surviving jhovalls were so seriously injured that their suffering called for mercy. At a nod from Gerrard, Tahngarth walked them to the side of the road and swiftly, efficiently dispatched them.

Sisay looked at Gerrard and sighed. "Well," she said philosophically, "I suppose we could all do with a long walk to get back in shape."

"Did you notice how the ghouls fought?" Gerrard asked amazedly. "I got the distinct impression they were servants of some higher being."

Sisay worried her lip a little. "Cho-Manno had warned me that the road to Ouramos was protected by the dead comrades of Ramos—his soldiers who were burned alive when he fell flaming from the sky. I'd just taken the comment as a bit of folklore, but perhaps he meant these ghouls. I should have passed on the warnings."

Gerrard smiled appreciatively, patting her shoulder. "Your reticence was understandable, but from now on, if you remember any more of Cho-Manno's warnings, make sure you tell us. In a legendary land, myth may prove truer than truth."

* * * * *

None of the party was seriously injured, but the claws and teeth of the foul beings had evidently been infected with the water of the swamps. Next day, Sisay and Fewsteem both ran high fevers. The party camped in the shadow of cliffs far removed from the fens. Gerrard soaked a rag in canteen water and pressed it to Sisay's forehead. Chamas performed a similar service for Fewsteem. They spent a miserable, uncomfortable day and night before the two ill travelers had recovered sufficiently to move on.

The next day, much to their relief, they left both swamps and cliffs behind. They had reached the top of a large plateau. The land stretched before them, dotted with clumps of trees and other vegetation. On the far horizon was a ridge of mountains, their tops capped with snow. Looking back, the party could see they had come through a long series of broken defiles that led down to the eastern plains. That night, they found plenty of wood for a fire and built a cheerful blaze to guard against the brisk wind that swept over this higher land.

Sisay and Fewsteem huddled close to the fire. Both had recovered from their infection, but neither was as hardy as before the ghoul attack. Against the darkness, the flames made fantastic, leaping shapes. Tahngarth picked up a long stick from the ground and stirred the fire. A shower of sparks spat and leaped up, rising into the ebony sky. To himself, the minotaur chanted softly a Talruum battle song. Gerrard looked at him with affection.

"What are you smiling about?" asked Sisay, a blanket wrapped tightly about her.

"I was just thinking," Gerrard returned.

She moved a bit closer to him on the log. "About what?"

Gerrard rubbed his chin, feeling the rough bristle of his beard. "I've forgotten how much I miss this."

"Miss what? Sitting miles away from your home with nothing to eat but dry rations, nothing to do but hope you'll make the next day's march without some disaster, nothing to wear but the clothes on your back that you haven't washed for a week." Sisay wrinkled her nose. "I hope to the gods we find a stream tomorrow. You need a bath."

Gerrard laughed. "I know. You're pretty ripe yourself. No, that's not what I meant."

"What, then?"

He waved a hand around him. "All this. Companionship. Searching for something but not knowing whether you'll ever find it." He shook his head. "Nothing. Never mind."

Sisay put a hand on his arm. He could feel the tough calluses on her palm. "I know what you mean. Believe me, I do. There's something special about the search itself, even if you don't find what you're looking for. I think sometimes that's what I was really looking for, rather than for the Legacy. I was looking for . . . for the looking itself. Is that stupid?"

"No. No, it's not." Gerrard turned and looked Sisay full in the face. Since he'd found her in Volrath's Dream Halls, this was the first time he'd looked closely at her. Fine lines surrounded her eyes. A tiny streak of gray had appeared in her hair. A delicate scar—almost a decoration, it was so fine—ran from the edge of her mouth back along the line of her jaw to her ear. Her skin was weather roughened, not the fine blush that mantled Hanna's face. Yet it had a kind of unearthly beauty that was all Sisay's own. Her eyes were brown, set deep in her face, filled with pain, with joy, with a kind of wild hope.

"Do you know something?" Gerrard asked. "Rath made you stronger. Made you wiser. More beautiful."

"It's the power of hate," interrupted Takara, sitting nearby, tossing pebbles sullenly in the fire. "Hate makes you stronger, wiser, more beautiful."

Without looking at the Rathi, Gerrard shook his head. "No. There you're wrong. Hate eats you up from the inside. It makes you weak and stupid and ugly. It's hope that makes you strong. There were two ways to survive Rath—hate and hope. Only hope makes heroes."

* * * * *

The next two days, the road wound among trees of increasing girth and height, with branches that began fifty or sixty feet up the trunk. They were of a kind completely unfamiliar to anyone in the party. In some places, the path was completely overgrown. It took all of Tahngarth's and Sisay's tracking skills to keep them going in the right direction.

From the lower branches of the trees, moss draped like tattered clothing, casting mysterious shadows across the path. Wherever upper branches let sun penetrate to the forest floor, lizards scuttled across the roadway or sunned themselves on rocks.

At night the party lit fires that drove back the shadows but attracted thousands of huge moths. During the still watches of the night, the rumble of vast hooves came from the forest, and huge pairs of eyes gleamed distantly with reflected firelight. It was easy enough for watchmen to stay awake, but no beast ever came close enough to be identified.

On the second day in the forest, they came upon the ruin of a large stone tower among the trees. Its walls were limned with moss and ivy, and the roof had fallen in. When new, the tower must have been impressive, but now it was merely a sad reminder of a long-ago glory. The crew found themselves speaking in hushed tones as they examined the ruins.

It was Ilcaster who drew Gerrard's attention to the glyph carved in the stone arch.

The Benalian examined it carefully. "Yes. No doubt about it. It's another Thran glyph. Whoever built this place knew something about the Thran." Gerrard looked about them at the tall trees, silent witnesses to the unknown past. "I think," he said finally, "we can safely say we've entered Ouramos."

The following day saw the number and size of the ruins increase. The Thran glyphs engraved on the fallen edifices were now so common that they ceased to provoke comment. The buildings were closer together, bigger and more impressive, but all were in a state of decay and ruin.

Gerrard saw Sisay looking about her with a slightly puzzled expression. "What's the matter?" he asked.

She pointed to a series of walls that extended along one side of the path for a quarter mile before ceasing abruptly. "These ruins. There's something odd about them."

Gerrard glanced around. "I don't see it."

"That's right," chimed in Tallakaster from behind them. The large blond sailor, bare to the waist, shifted his pack on massive shoulders. "I mean, Cap'n, if you were standing out here all alone for years, you'd be falling to pieces too."

Sisay chuckled. "I daresay you're right. But that's not what I mean. They're not just falling to pieces; they've been destroyed."

"What do you mean?" asked Gerrard.

"I mean something happened to this city."

"Like Ramos falling on it from the sky?".

"Well, perhaps a figurative Ramos. The myth might mask a historical truth. Look." Sisay grabbed Gerrard's arm and led him toward the wall. She touched the stone, which crumbled beneath her fingers. She rubbed her fingertips, and the stuff turned to a white powder.

"I've seen something like this before, on Dominaria." She pushed a few of the stones, and they fell with a thump to the forest floor. "This wall's been blasted by sudden heat—"

"Gerrard! Sisay! Tahngarth! Come look at this!"

The three turned, making their way to where Ilcaster and Dabis stood near a large mound. Both were holding their hands before their faces, warding off the stench that rose from the mound.

"Phew! What have you two found?" Gerrard's eyes watered.

Tahngarth spat once. "Taumalangah!"

"Spoor!" Sisay translated for Gerrard's benefit. "Droppings from something."

"Humph! Well, whatever it is, it's huge." Gerrard walked around the pile of excrement, careful to keep his distance. "Everybody keep your eyes open—and your noses covered."

The travelers moved on down the road into dim, green recesses.

Another hour of silent tramping brought them to a small clearing. There, they halted for a moment to rest. Sisay sank to the ground, head between her hands, knees drawn up. Although she had largely recovered from the fever of a few days previously, neither she nor Fewsteem were quite as healthy as the others. Tahngarth moved restlessly about the glade, while Gerrard took a long pull from his waterskin. In the forest, they had found several streams, all of which seemed excellent sources of drinking water.

"Sir!" Dabis ran up. The dark-haired Icatian was about as excited as Gerrard had ever seen him. He opened his clenched fist. "Look, sir!"

Gerrard gasped. A powerstone. Tiny, no more than a mere speck compared to the crystal that powered *Weatherlight*, but it was nonetheless a glowing powerstone, shining with its own source of internal fire.

"Excellent!" He clapped Dabis on the shoulder. "Where was it?"

"Just lying on the g-ground." Dabis, almost too excited to speak, stuttered. "I saw a glow from off to the side, and there it was, just lying on the ground like somebody dropped it."

In an instant, the group was down on its knees in the spot Dabis had indicated, clawing through the undergrowth. After a frantic, silent ten minutes of searching, Gerrard gave up with a sigh.

"All right. This is only one. But the important thing is we know we're on the right track." He lifted his pack to his shoulders. "Let's go."

The companions proceeded, in single file, Gerrard leading the way and Tahngarth, his sword drawn, bringing up the rear. Before them, the path grew more obscure, the trees denser. To either side, they heard a series of deep rumbles, with an occasional hiss that sounded like the heavy breathing of some mighty creature.

Without a word, the party halted, and swords were drawn from scabbards. Gerrard placed a finger on his lips, and they stole cautiously forward.

Suddenly the trees parted. A great vista opened. They found themselves blinking in the unexpected sunlight.

Before them, the land dipped in a wide bowl carved from the living rock, a great arena overrun by weed and creeper. In the center, perhaps a thousand feet from where the party stood, was a great circle of raised sand, low but baked and gleaming in the bright sunlight. Standing stones, carved with Thran glyphs, ringed the sandy circle. In the center of the circle was a large, flat stone table, resembling an altar. The altar stone in turn held five large crystals, glinting in the sunlight.

"Ouramos," Gerrard said in awe.

Sisay looked at him and nodded. "Yes. Those must be the powerstones. The Bones of Ramos."

Takara said, "It's not likely those stones would remain undisturbed all these years unless they were pretty well guarded. Magic. Or worse . . ."

The Benalian cast a quick glance around. "All right. There's no point in all of us going down there. If ever there were a place likely to be rigged with traps of some kind, this is it. Sisay and Tahngarth, you're with me. The rest of you stay here and keep a sharp eye out—"

His instructions were interrupted by a terrified scream behind him. Gerrard turned.

Ilcaster's dark, handsome face contorted with pain. He was caught in the grip of two vines that had snaked across the path, entwining his feet. The lad fell to the ground, drew his knife, and hacked at the green tendrils.

Gerrard darted in and chopped down with his sword. It clanged away. The vines were as hard as steel.

Ilcaster gave a yell of horror. There was a spurt of blood from a severed artery as the clinging vines cut through flesh and bone in his ankles. Another vine, writhing as if it were a snake, shot across the path and gripped him around the throat, cutting off his cry. A moment later his head rolled free beside Gerrard's feet.

Sisay and the others curved in a tight circle, facing outward. Gerrard joined them. From the woods, more vines groped inward. The crew bashed them back with ringing blades.

A young sapling lashed down atop the crew like a scourge.

Tahngarth reached up, grasped the bole, and viciously snapped off the top. The rest of the tree sprang back. It seemed to give a shriek of pain. Thick green sap surged from the wound.

A vine yanked Sisay's feet from under her. Gerrard jerked her upright and battered the tendril until it let go.

A tree trunk smashed to the ground beside Tallakaster, missing him by a hairsbreadth. Below the feet of the crewman, the ground boiled and turned to mud, imprisoning his feet. He screamed and sank farther into the morass.

Gerrard pulled at his arms in a vain attempt to pry him loose. Gerrard's fingers dug into the sailor's flesh. Tallakaster's eyes bulged with fear. The sailor slipped another few inches, pulling Gerrard with him. In a moment, he too would be trapped by the mud. Gerrard felt the man's hands slip away. The Benalian had a last brief glance of Tallakaster's fear-crazed face sinking below the mud, and then he was gone.

A blast of wind trembled the treetops and rose to a screaming gale. The trees shook. Leaves, pine needles, and fir cones beat on their heads. The very ground bucked and swayed beneath their staggering feet.

"We can't last here!" Gerrard shouted. "Retreat!"

They did, moving cautiously away from the great bowl of Ouramos.

"Look!" Sisay yelled, stopping short.

The crew were suddenly surrounded by fantastical figures. Roughly human in shape, they had green hair and pale, green skin. Long, slender fingers waved as if branches. They were clad in leaves, twigs, and vines, knitted together in sheaths that barely covered their lean bodies. Their hands were raised, crossed together and linked in a curious pattern. As if from a great distance, Gerrard heard a sound that could only be described as singing.

"More defenders . . ." Sisay said breathlessly as Gerrard staggered up beside her. "Dryads."

CHAPTER 18

The two guards lounging about the lower story of the Magistrate's Tower were drunk. Duty shifts among the city guard were observed rarely, if at all, but yesterday Samanalashakal had had the bad luck of beating the sergeant at a game of bones and tosses. This morning when Sama entered guard headquarters, he found the sergeant waiting for him, an unpleasant grin on his face.

That was how Sama came to be sitting on the first landing of the tower, passing a wineskin back and forth with Dromelasthamarab. Above them, the sun rose slowly in the sky, and the shadow of the tower thinned and disappeared entirely, leaving them awash in brilliant light.

The heat made them even more thirsty, so they drank to quench their thirst, and then they drank to forget their troubles, and then they drank because the wine was plentiful and good and neither cared anymore.

Indeed, Sama was so intoxicated that he almost did not notice the small green form that descended the tower steps, poking and prying, flicking long greasy fingers into the nooks and crannies of the staircase and sucking greedily on them. Eventually, the goblin bumped into one of the guard's legs and started back.

Sama and Drome drew aside from the door, their hands rising in clumsy salutes.

The goblin stared at them.

In their sodden haze, they noticed he seemed reluctant to give the counter salute. "Enter, Master," Drome said, bowing deeply.

The goblin seemed to take the invitation as a command and scuttled through the dark door they guarded.

Drome laughed and seized the wineskin from his compatriot. "Here's to the—" he used a vulgar Mercadian term for goblin, one that was carefully kept from earshot of the green race "—and may he fall down the stairs and break his neck!"

Sama grabbed for the skin and missed, almost tumbling off the balcony. "Go to the Nine Spheres! Don't shout that stuff so loud, or you'll get us in hot water!" He rubbed his eyes, and somewhere in his wine-soaked brain a worry stirred. "Wasn't that one awful small?"

Drome shook his head and hiccuped. Belching loudly, he sank back into his seat. "Who cares? They're all green buggers! Look a' me! I do my job, and wha's it get me? Nothing! Because green buggers are the ones that count. I been fifteen years in the guard, getting nothing but trouble. 'Cause I won't kiss up, tha's why. Know why I don' get ahead?"

" 'Cause you don't kiss up?"

"Damn right!"

Francis Lebaron

* * * * *

Squee, meanwhile, was intent on following the trail of a bug—not just any bug, but an enormous insect. Squee's nose fairly quivered in anticipation of the delicious treat. His senses, poor of sight but keen of smell, drove him onward. The bug—almost three inches long, with a thick, juicy-looking body and long feelers protruding from its head—scurried along, heedless of its pursuer. His nose to the ground, Squee headed down a short passageway, through another door, and along a hallway. His light footsteps could scarcely be heard. He almost had it now. Just another few feet, another few inches, another—

Thump!

His head struck hard stone, and he fell sprawling. He had run squarely into a brightly patterned mosaic. Similar bright patterns flashed dizzily within Squee's head. After a few moments, he was able to rise and look about. His quarry was gone.

"Damn."

The passage bent left, and Squee blinked away the flashing tiles. Curious to see what might lie beyond, he ambled along the corridor to a flight of stairs that descend in a great sweeping curve. In three gentle turns, it reached a large doorway with a decorated lintel in a pointed arch. Squee pushed open the doors and found himself in a big chamber, empty except for a singular platform at one end.

A more discerning observer would have considered the room a shrine, altar to an unknown god. Squee considered the room merely inviting. He pushed and poked at the strange carvings on the altar. One, done in colored stone, depicted a large snakelike creature with a snouted, horned head. Outlined in flashing gems, its horns caught his attention. Without conscious thought, he touched them and was surprised to feel the stone beneath his feet move.

Hinged to pivot, the altar swung back slowly to reveal a broad stair plunging to unknown depths. Dark, deep places were good for bugs. This place didn't look oozy—dark, deep, and oozy was the best—but dark and deep was good enough. There was sure to be plenty of fat grubs and worms below, a tasty midday snack.

Squee scampered swiftly down the steps. The stairs were steep, but steep was good because it meant you got to the bottom quicker. Even so, it seemed to take a very long time. Miles of stairs. It would've been nice if they'd made these stairs straight up and down—then you'd get to the bottom real fast.

Voices echoed up to Squee from around a bend. Some instinct for self-preservation made him slip into a convenient niche and stand as still as he knew how. Ears pricking, he listened to the voices as they drew closer.

". . . two weeks at most?"

"Not bad, but is not it possible that the schedule could be moved up to allow for a completion date in one week?"

"Is that not only possible but desirable? Will I not attempt to finish by this date? Do not the workers require some extra . . . encouragement?"

There was a long, drawn-out chuckle accompanying this last remark. Two dark figures brushed by the hollow where Squee stood concealed, trembling for reasons even he did not understand. The voices faded into the distance.

"Has anyone discovered what has become of the prisoners?"

"Has the master not sent them to gather the stones for him?"

"Are they not stupid pawns?" Their laughter retreated with them.

Silence once more mantled the stairs. Slowly, Squee extricated himself from the cleft in the wall. He was not sure of the entire import of what he had overheard, but he would try to remember it to recount to Hanna.

In fact, it was tempting to retreat back up the stairs and tell her now. At the best of times, Squee was a coward; he remained in *Weatherlight*'s crew only because he amused Sisay and Gerrard. Still, the goblin had virtues even Sisay and Gerrard did not suspect. The events of Rath had deeply stirred him, and after the scolding he'd received from Gerrard, he took pride in his fierce loyalty to *Weatherlight* and Dominaria. Though fear nudged him back up the stairs, duty pushed him forward. Duty won.

Squee headed around the corner. A few minutes brought him to another doorway—this one even larger than the first. He slipped through it, moved to one side, and gasped in wonder.

He was standing on one side of a vast underground cavern, miles across and miles deep. Huge stone columns descended through the space, joining ceiling to floor. In some places, the columns had been carved out, and light gleamed from windows within. Scaffolds ran around the columns, and huge horns projected outward from them in a stony thicket. Catwalks clung to stalactites and stalagmites. Aerial platforms and bridges stretched across the huge, dark reaches.

"What kinda place is dis?"

It was like staring out through a nighttime thicket and seeing a complex of cobwebs joining thorn to thorn. Globe lights gleamed like golden dew along the webs. Humans, Kyren, machines, and . . . other things ambled spiderlike on the walkways. Some folk carried supplies. Others bore tools. Still more clambered over great, hoary things that seemed like flies caught in the giant web.

They were not flies, though. They were ships—aerial ships, most of them larger than *Weatherlight*. Vessels hung from the jutting thorns.

Squee had discovered an enormous underground hangar, bristling with piers and moored airships. Long and sleek, with wings of skin and carapace shells, the vessels reminded Squee of something . . . his small brain wracked itself trying to remember what. Then he seized upon it: the ship they'd met on Rath—*Predator*. That was it! Some of these ships were even larger than *Predator*.

Squee had once thought *Weatherlight* the mightiest warship. Then, they encountered *Predator* on Rath. Now, though, amid this multitude of mammoth vessels, *Weatherlight* seemed a grain of sand on an endless beach.

There were ships with two and three masts, ships whose foredecks were bigger than the entire deck of *Weatherlight*. There were ships that seemed to move even as they stood still. All were coppery brown or black in color. The larger ships were moored, floating impossibly in the air, line after line, layer after layer. Several smaller dinghies busily ferried workers and supplies about the hangar. Workers moved from ship to ship, ignoring the vast space over which they hung suspended.

Cannons jutted above and below decks on those ships closest to Squee. Curious, he left the wall and trotted across the stone floor toward a rail.

Squee was out in plain view before he thought better of it. He skidded to a halt, freezing in fear. A pair of human workers approached. He was sure they would haul him away. Instead, they merely bowed deferentially as they passed by.

It was good to be a goblin.

Squee continued toward the rail. En route, he came across two metallic beings—squat, roughly spherical, with a variety of legs extending in many directions. They stank of oil, and liquids flowed through tubes that bounded their bodies. The creatures' eyes jutted on long stalks and rotated slowly to look at him.

Squee squealed in alarm, cowering as the metal spiders scuttled up to inspect him. Feelers, pincers, and antennae methodically prodded the shivering little goblin. He'd spent his life poking bugs, but now the bugs were poking him. The scent of oil was overwhelming as they bent over him.

"Squee wasn't doing nothing," he said defensively.

Neither creature gave the slightest heed. The one on his left put out a long, jointed feeler and touched the goblin. A sharp, brief pain, like an electric shock, coursed through Squee's veins. Then the two beings turned toward one another. The one that had touched him reached out an arm to the other and inserted it into an available socket in the top part of its spiderlike body. There was a long moment of silence between the creatures, and then they moved away, apparently satisfied.

Squee heaved a sigh of relief and proceeded on his way, licking his arm. "Least Squee didn't get ate."

He reached the rail. A ship slowly and gracefully rose just beyond. It glided through the air like a fish feeling its way through unfamiliar waters. Its decks were crowded with workers—Kyren, human, and otherwise. The craft passed overhead and moved through an enormous arch on the far side of the cave, disappearing from Squee's view.

He rose to his feet, rubbing his head in a desperate attempt to stimulate his thought processes. "Gotta follow da boat," he muttered to himself, scurrying after the ship.

As much as possible, he kept within the great shadows along the edges of the cave. He rounded the arch, raced along a huge passageway, and then emerged through a second doorway into another chamber, equally large.

Here he saw additional lines of ships moored, their runners resting on the cave floor. There were fewer here than he'd seen in the first cavern, but the size of the complete fleet was immense beyond his imagining.

Stunned, Squee wandered down aisle after aisle of vessels, staring, stroking, tapping, poking. No one questioned him, no one stopped him. There were fewer workers here, but those who did pass between the ships carried bundles and boxes of supplies, which they were loading onto the ships.

Then he saw the ship—*Weatherlight*, resting on her landing spines. She was moored there in the midst of the fleet. She seemed small and delicate next to the bristling monsters around her, but just now, Squee could think of no more beautiful sight in all the worlds.

"Squee found it! Squee saved everybody all over again! Gotta go tell Hanna!" A loud growling in Squee's stomach reminded him he'd not had a full meal in some time. With a pang, he thought of the huge bug he'd been pursuing earlier. "Get sumpthing ta eat and tell Hanna 'bout all this."

Squee's mind, as Hanna had once remarked to Gerrard, rarely had room for more than one idea at a time. Now all he could think of was a plate of tasty grubs and worms. Turning his back on the fleet, he headed back the way he'd come. Indeed, he was so intent on thoughts of eating that he paid little attention to where he was going and ran full-tilt into the stomach of a creature coming from the opposite direction.

Whuff!

Squee sat down quickly and looked up, a whine already forming on his lips.

A pair of Kyren looked down at him. Goblins might have looked alike to other races, but to each other, they were as distinct as goats and chickens. With a sinking feeling, Squee recognized the Kyren advisor to the chief magistrate, the one who'd insisted that Squee be made a captain in the Mercadian guard. Now the Kyren advisor was staring at Squee with a look both surprised and disapproving.

From his years of service aboard *Weatherlight*, Squee was thoroughly familiar with that look and was generally adept at evading its consequences. He rose, wheeled to one side, and dove across the cavern floor in a movement that ended in a roll and jump. With a loud parting squeal, he dashed into the passageway. Behind him he heard shouts and the beating of flat, flabby feet against the stone. As the sounds became more distant, Squee gave a gurgle of triumph.

Something slammed across his chest. He fell backward, striking his head against the stone floor. As blackness closed around him, he saw dimly the form of a Phyrexian dock worker—big, ugly, and dead looking.

"Phyrexians . . . h-here!" Squee stammered.

The monster's club struck him again. Squee slid across the floor and lay still, feeling the long arms of darkness embrace him.

CHAPTER 19

"Dryads," Sisay repeated breathlessly, staring at the surrounding thicket of creatures.

Attenuated limbs, oblong faces, features formed of wood grain and patterned bark—the dryads were beautiful, otherworldly. Beneath minimal clothing lurked skin as smooth and tough as birch bark. Their eyes were narrow and a deep green shade, though the color seemed to shift in the dappled sunlight. They sang a song that stilled the rioting forest and the roiling ground. As swiftly as the song had begun, it died away.

Gerrard cleared his throat and edged forward. Instantly, the ground beneath his feet grew soft, sucking his boots

249

down. He was mired to midcalf. The Benalian stopped and held up one hand, palm outward in a gesture of peace. "I'm Gerrard," he said. He indicated the rest of the party. "We come in the name of Ramos."

The creatures made no response. None of the dryads so much as lifted a finger.

Tahngarth brushed a hand over his horns.

His sudden motion alarmed their captors. From one dryad came a single soft note.

The minotaur looked sleepily at his comrades. "Must sleep," he said in a voice filled with weariness. "Tired. Must . . ." Without another word, he fell forward on the ground, almost flattening Sisay. He began to snore.

"What the . . . ?" The dark woman leaped back. "They enchanted him somehow."

The dryads regarded the sleeping minotaur stoically.

Gerrard quietly lowered himself to the ground and told the others, "Sit down."

"What?" Sisay stared at him. "Are they enchanting you, too? Chamas, take Gerrard's right hand, I'll take the left—"

"Belay that." Gerrard's voice was low but sharp. "Sit down, all of you."

Slowly, the crew sank to the ground.

Sisay glared at Gerrard, but she too followed suit. "What are we doing?"

"A long time ago, I overheard Multani tell Rofellos that among the tree people sitting is a sign of peaceful intentions. While we were standing, they thought we might attack them."

There was a long moment of silence. Then the dryad who had sounded the note glided a foot or two closer. His eyes were half-closed, as if in concentration. From his lips there came a series of notes, some long and languorous, others sharp and sparkling.

Gerrard bowed his head submissively. The dryad chieftain advanced to within a foot of the Benalian and slowly, tentatively, extended long fingers toward him. Gerrard's hand came out in response, and the two gently touched.

Something passed between their fingers—small, leaping energies. The others in the glade could see the tiny lightnings in the air. Auras roiled up Gerrard's arm and sparked in his eyes. He felt power jagging through his mind, and he suddenly knew this was the way whole forests thought—infinitely intricate networks of bough and vine, tangled masses of root, and energy leaping from one to the next. Each tree and plant was an individual being until those minute synapses were bridged, and then, each and all became one.

Gerrard suddenly understood. He understood this place, these people, the guardians of the wood. He rose. His boots pulled free of the entrapping earth.

The dryad chief took a step back. He too understood. He knew of *Weatherlight* and the Matrix, of the Cho-Arrim and Saprazzans and Rishadans, of the coming rebellion. . . .

"We have reached Ouramos," Gerrard told his crew. His voice sounded oracular in his own ears. "This place was shaped by the arrival of Ramos on this world."

"Ramos . . ." Sisay whispered in amazement.

Words rolled out of Gerrard in a steady, strong stream.

"Long, long ago, in the wake of the Brothers' War, Ramos fled Dominaria. He had been on the battlefield of Argoth when Urza unleashed the sylex blast. Ramos flew out before it. Naked energy pursued him. It leveled mountains and sank continents. It lifted oceans in killing waves. Ramos soared ahead of them.

"Beneath the waters, he spied merfolk fleeing in terror. Reaching one gigantic hand into the flood, Ramos bore the merfolk away with him. He flew on, ahead of the hand of death. Next, Ramos came upon a great galley packed with refugees. In his mercy, he reached down with his other hand and lifted the ship from the waves. He bore them away, that they too might be saved. Ramos flew on, ahead of the incinerating blast.

"Perhaps, though, Ramos sought to save too many. So weighty was the great galley and the host within it that Ramos—great Ramos—was slowed. He could not outrun the shattering wave. It struck him and the ship he carried. Chaos energies and magic vortices enveloped them. Madness dragged at reason. Falsity overwhelmed truth. In the malign irony of destruction, the wave flung Ramos and the ship beyond Dominaria to his former world—to Phyrexia.

"Yes, the great Ramos was himself Phyrexian. He had been brought out of Phyrexia by none other than Urza Planeswalker. Once created to hunt and destroy humans, Ramos was altered by Urza to save them. He had been redesigned to fight the malign leviathans of Mishra and to bear away from battle wagonloads of wounded. When the sylex blasted away the isle of Argoth, Ramos had only followed Urza's design and become a rescuer. Ramos had flown ahead of the blast, seeking someone to save. He had lifted the merfolk and the refugees in the great galley in hopes of saving them—but *this* was not saving them. Bearing them to Phyrexia was not saving them. In that horrible place, the folk would be mangled and mutated into monsters.

"Ramos knew of another world beyond Phyrexia, a fair place linked to that foul one. Gathering the last of his might—for the blast that had borne him to Phyrexia nearly destroyed him—Ramos soared through a near-forgotten portal that led from Phyrexia to Mercadia.

"It was truly the last measure of his saving power. Through a portal in the sky, Ramos emerged, bearing in one hand a school of merfolk and in the other a great galley. They all were mantled in fire. The folk Ramos sought to save were burning alive. Seeing their distress, Ramos's heart broke. It cracked away from the core of his being and fell into the sea. There it waited in the deeps, the great artifact called the Power Matrix.

"Hollow hearted, Ramos lowered the hand that bore the

merfolk. He released them gently into the ocean. Water hissed to steam, extinguishing the fires that burned the people. As the burning ship neared shore, Ramos reached onto the deck, where crew struggled among blazing lines and masts. He clutched them up and rolled them out on the beach of Rishada. Sand extinguished the fires that burned the people. As the ship soared over Mount Mercadia, Ramos reached into the hold where the refugees of Argoth cowered. He hauled them forth and spread them through the forests of Rushwood beyond. Leaves extinguished the fires that burned the people. When next his hand reached inside, there was nothing but corpses to be found. In his pity, Ramos lifted even them and sprinkled them through the fens of Deepwood.

"Only the ship and Ramos himself remained. Together, they burned like twin suns. Beneath them, the forests and cities flashed away. Buildings were shattered, stones turned to ash, and folk in the hundreds of thousands died. Hundreds of thousands died because Ramos sought to save hundreds.

"It was this last, cruel irony that shattered the core of great Ramos. The immortal's crystalline soul, which had withstood incendiary heat, could not bear the deaths of hundreds of thousands. His will fragmented. The burning ship fell from his hands. It struck ground just behind us, carving out the vast crater there. Fires erupted from the spot and blazed through the forest. Ramos fell into that burning bowl—his own killing sylex. He did not rise. He no longer had the will to.

"Fire is the bane of mortal things but not of things immortal. Ramos was not slain, though every living thing around him fell to black soot. In time, the flames died. Ramos was left alone among ashes. Shards from the shattered core of his being rattled loose within him. Five great pieces had chipped away, and for their lack, he could not muster the will to move.

"If fire is the bane of mortal things, time is their ally. Life always returns. Grass covered the torn earth. Saplings pushed up through the ashes. Black gave way to green. With the rise of life, Ramos rose too. He placed an altar stone at the center of the blast crater, and upon that stone, he set the five crystals that had broken away from the core of his being. He made those stones a symbol for the hundreds of thousands. He made Ouramos a temple, sacred to their memory.

"As the forests around had brought will and life back to Ramos, he brought will and life to them. He enlivened the trees with his spirit. He gathered the dryads from among them and made them into his people. He raised even the dead folk in the Deepwood and made them guardians of his realm. He longed to heal all the shattered world, to make it whole again, but such feats were beyond the ruined immortal. His will, his true power, lay in shards on the altar stone."

Gerrard blinked, seeming to awaken from the oracular trance that had taken hold of him. His crewmates stared at him in wonder.

Sisay approached reverently. "That was beautiful. Did the dryad chief tell you all that? All with a mere touch?"

Gerrard nodded. "And I have told him many things. He knows—all of them know—about our quest."

"And we know another version of the Ramos myth—"

"It is no myth," Gerrard interrupted. His eyes seemed like mirrors, they were so bright in his head. He gestured toward the crater. "You will see. He invites us to go below."

A chill went up Sisay's spine. "Who, the chief?"

"No, Ramos."

Gerrard turned and walked back toward the great stone crater. The wall of dryads parted to let him pass.

The other crewmen warily watched Gerrard go.

"Well, you heard him," Sisay said. Her voice quavered in the air. "Let's go meet Ramos."

Following Gerrard, Sisay and the crew walked reverently through the gap in the line of dryads. They began a slow, cautious journey down the cracked, broken stone edge of the crater, toward the sandy circle and the altar at its center. The sun's rays seemed to grow brighter, hotter as they went— or was it merely that they had traveled so long in the cool shade of the forest?

Gerrard wiped the sweat from his eyes and stared ahead. It might have been a trick of the heat or light, but to him, the stones around the altar wavered, as if they were emitting some sort of energy. He looked at his companions and saw they too were staring ahead. The very air grew thicker and more forbidding, and the silence more ominous.

He reached the circle of standing stones. Gerrard stepped between two of them. The air was resistant. It was as if he had encountered an invisible wall. He tried again and managed to slip between the stones but with an effort that left him gasping.

Sisay, Takara, and the others followed his example, the minotaur doing so with a great grunt of effort.

They climbed over the sand circle, which was no more than three feet high, though Gerrard guessed its total circumference at perhaps a hundred feet. The altar itself, unlike the ruins they had observed thus far, was undamaged. Its polished surface gleamed in the bright sunshine. In the center of the table was scooped a low bowl, and within it lay the five Bones of Ramos.

Powerstones. Gerrard stared at them, marveling. Before coming to Mercadia, he'd seen only the Thran crystal that powered *Weatherlight*, the most impressive stone of its kind, and a few smaller stones used to power ornithopters on Dominaria. The stones he had seen in Mercadia were tiny, barely more than gleaming pebbles. But these . . . each of the irregular shards of crystal was the size and general shape of a hand laid out flat. They glowed with lambent energy.

"The Bones of Ramos," Gerrard said reverently.

Sisay came up beside him, staring with hungry eyes. "I thought we had come to see Ramos himself, not just his bones."

"We have," Gerrard replied. He lifted his gaze beyond the altar.

The ground suddenly shook. The crew were nearly hurled from their feet. The stones that ringed the sand circle trembled.

Sisay grabbed Gerrard's arm. "What's happening!"

"Ramos is coming."

The sand beyond the altar exploded. Up from the ground jutted an enormous head, long snouted, with a sharp beak and lizardlike eyes. Polished metal scales gleamed. Two slender horns rose above a long, sinuous neck. Sand sifted from the gearwork shoulders of the beast, and a pair of enormous claws dragged the massive, winged body from his lair.

Ramos was a dragon.

No, Gerrard realized, even as the word shaped itself on his lips. Not a dragon. Ramos was a dragon engine. Dim memories of Multani's sketchbooks stirred. Dragon engines were the mightiest artifacts in the age of the Brothers' War. Armed with them, Urza and Mishra fought until the land of Terisiare sank beneath them. Ramos had been one of those engines, redesigned by Urza not to kill, but to save. . . .

Gerrard found himself bowing before the great beast. Sisay and the others followed suit.

Meanwhile, Ramos had risen to his full height—a hundred feet tall. He bent his head backward. Metal plates of armor gleamed. Oil streamed. His jaws opened.

Sisay winced, fearing a gout of flame.

Instead, Ramos only spoke. His voice was ancient. His words were barely recognizable—an accent that must have been common on Dominaria when Urza and Mishra walked the land. "Gerrard of *Weatherlight*—you have come to pillage a temple, to pillage a grave."

Lifting his head, Gerrard replied, "No, great Ramos. We have come to fulfill a prophecy."

A huge sound answered that, the ominous rumble of metal on metal. It was a fearful racket, though it could have been nothing but a laugh. "You forget, Gerrard of *Weatherlight*, that those prophecies are fictions about me. I am Ramos, whom you have come to raise. But I cannot rise, or I would have already. Your ship's arrival in this world—through the very portal I took from Phyrexia, now moved to Rath—only coincidentally resembles my own arrival. Both of us crashed upon this world. Neither will rise again."

Gerrard felt his insides sinking. Ramos knew everything. The dryad chief had conveyed it all to him. Ramos saw the masquerade and the truth that lay beneath it. Why ever would he allow Gerrard to take the sacred stones that had calved from his own power core?

"You are Ramos, yes," Gerrard replied, "but perhaps *Weatherlight* truly is the Uniter. Perhaps the prophecies are not mere whimsy."

"You do not believe in prophecies, Gerrard of *Weatherlight*," Ramos scolded. His voice had the timbre of shivering metal.

"No, I don't," Gerrard allowed. His eyes remained riveted to the dragon engine's. "But I do believe in hope. That's where these prophecies came from. Hope. The people who believe these stories remember how you brought their ancestors here. They remember that horrible day so long ago. They remember the death and destruction, but they have transformed horror into hope. They remember Ramos, yes, but they hope for the Uniter. No, these aren't prophecies, foretelling what was destined to happen. These are only hopes, wishes for what must happen."

Ramos's metallic eyes peered deeply, sharply into Gerrard's soul, but the dragon engine did not speak.

Gerrard continued. "You built this place as a memorial to the dead, but what about the living? You long to heal the hurt that you brought to this world, and here's your chance to do it. You've mourned the hundreds of thousands you killed, but mourning is not enough. What about the hundreds of thousands even now who suffer? The Bones of Ramos are only selfish relics lying here. Within *Weatherlight*, though, they can raise the Uniter. They can bring the world together. They can save those who are doomed."

Gerrard had never spoken with such passion in his life, and the tone of his own voice suddenly struck him as ludicrous. He began to laugh. At first, he only snickered, but attempts to stanch the giggles only made them worse. Soon, he guffawed, slapping his leg.

Ramos glowered at him. "What do you find funny about all this?"

Gerrard smiled through his laughter. "It's just that . . . it's just that I used to be like you, Ramos. People decided I was a Uniter. People said I had a Legacy, I had a mission to fulfill. They told me I was supposed to save the world. For a long time I dragged my heels. How does one man save the world? But then I gave up fighting. It was too hard to fight destiny. It was only just now, as I heard my own voice talking to you—it was just this moment when I realized my destiny had caught up with me. Without even knowing it, I'd become everything everybody said I was supposed to be." His explanation ended in a belly laugh.

A great shiver moved through the dragon engine. He seemed to slump in resignation. "You are right to laugh, Gerrard of *Weatherlight*. All of this is absurd. You have come here because of a myth that misremembers me and makes you something you are not. You came seeking these five simple stones, broken millennia ago from my power core. They cannot save you. They have power only because they lie here beside me, in the midst of my forest. Beyond the crater, they will be nothing." Ramos gestured dismissively. "I understand hope and know it does not die easily. You will not give up until you see for yourself. I will allow you to take these stones as far as the dryads' grove. There, you will see what I say. They will darken beyond the crater. They will be nothing more than useless shards of stone."

Bowing his head in thanks, Gerrard said, "I will take them to the dryad glade, great Ramos—but you are the one who will see. Hope can enliven even dead shards of stone."

"They cannot save you, Gerrard of *Weatherlight*. I cannot save you. And you cannot save Mercadia, or your own world."

Despite the dragon's words, Gerrard gazed down into the bowl at the center of the altar. There the Bones of Ramos rested. The central facet of each rough shard bore a resemblance to a body part—Skull, Eye, Heart, Horn, and Tooth.

Reverently, Gerrard lifted the Skull stone. It was warm to his touch, and its blue light glimmered on his palm. He turned and presented it to Sisay. "Keep this safe." She nodded her head and backed away, allowing the next crew member to step up. Gerrard picked up the rest of the stones, one by one, and presented them to his dear companions—Tahngarth, Takara, Chamas, and Dabis.

"Fewsteem, I want you to lead the march back up out of the crater."

"Yes, Cap'n."

"I'll bring up the rear." Then, turning back to Ramos, Gerrard said, "We thank you for this gift, great Ramos, and for the chance to prove you wrong."

"I dearly wish you could do so," the dragon engine said.

"Perhaps you can prove yourself wrong. Perhaps you can be united with the Uniter," Gerrard said.

"Perhaps." With that single mournful word, the ancient Phyrexian dragon engine coiled back into his nest. Wings flapped, stirring storms of sand to settle over him.

The crew of *Weatherlight* turned and started back across the bowl.

As they ascended the side of the crater, Ramos's warnings were borne out. One by one, the inner light of the stones guttered and failed.

Sisay's stone—the Skull of Ramos—flickered tepidly, its blue gleam disappearing by the time she stepped from the crater.

"It's dead, just as he said," Sisay muttered, sadly shaking her head.

The others gathered, showing similarly dark stones.

Gerrard joined them, staring down.

"Well, that's it," Takara said bleakly. "We've come all this way, chasing a lie."

Gerrard patting her and Sisay on the back. "No. It's not a lie. This morning I would have had doubts but not now. We'll camp with the dryads tonight. I need a night to think. The answer lies here somewhere."

Takara sighed angrily. "Well, while you're holding on to hope, I'll hold on to hate." She gestured toward the bloody ground where Ilcaster had died. "We'll be sleeping among the folk that killed your crew, Gerrard. I forgot how skillful you are at burying your friends."

* * * * *

The rest of the day was spent burying the remains of Ilcaster and holding a memorial for him and Tallakaster. Gerrard and *Weatherlight*'s crew made their camp in the dryad glade nearby. All the while, the tree folk watched them, hemming them in lest they should try to escape with the stones.

When night came, the dryads simply faded away into darkness. Gerrard had a vague impression that somehow they were absorbed into the trees themselves and remained there until they had renewed their energy. Only the elders of the wood folk remained visible—standing in a line at the edge of the clearing.

While the rest of the crew bedded down, Gerrard approached the chief of the dryads. He lifted his hands in a sign of peace and sank to the ground cross-legged. The chief imitated him, though the others remained standing.

The Benalian took the Heart of Ramos from his breast pocket. Holding it up, he pointed to it and tapped it sharply.

The dryad chief stretched out a slender, long-fingered hand. Gerrard held out the powerstone, and the chief took it. He held it up, closed his eyes, and made a sound that resembled a single, clear note of a bell. The tone resonated until it filled the air. The trees themselves seemed to vibrate.

The dryad lowered his hand. In its center was the powerstone, and within its heart there now glowed a distinct spark of energy.

Gerrard gave a whoop that brought the others running.

The dryad sprang back in alarm.

Weatherlight's commander gestured frantically to the others. "Sit," he hissed. "Look at this."

Sisay gasped. "It works. How did you—"

"I didn't do anything. He did it." Gerrard jerked his head in the direction of the dryad, who had now been joined by several of his fellows and was looking nervously at them. They conversed between themselves with the soft musical tones that served as their speech.

Tahngarth was examining the powerstone more closely. "It is fading," he observed.

Sure enough, the glow within the stone had diminished appreciably. Even as they watched, it flickered, flared briefly, and then went out. Gerrard held out the stone to the dryad again and spread his hands in an interrogative gesture. The creature carefully picked up the stone and made a sweeping gesture toward the forest, accompanying it with a low quiver of sound.

Chamas spoke up. "I think he means to say something about a circle—a gathering."

Sisay asked, "How do you know?"

"I've been watching them and listening to them," the woman replied. She extended a hand toward the dryad, two fingers outstretched in a **V**. At the same time, she gave a ululation ending in a kind of squeak.

The dryads watched attentively and replied with a series of motions and trills.

"What did you just say?" Sisay asked.

"I think I said thank you," returned Chamas. "It's an odd language. They've developed a relationship between words and gestures. I'm not sure, but I think if you make the same sound but match it with a different hand movement, it will have a completely different meaning."

Gerrard said, "Everybody, pull out the stones I gave you and give them to the chief."

They did, and the chief received them, beginning a keening song.

In the cold, clear night all around, dryads shifted. They emerged from the trees and gathered, adding their voices to the song of the chief.

Gerrard and his crew remained where they sat. He felt Sisay shivering and heard her teeth chatter. Earlier, she'd wanted to light a fire, but Chamas had warned her against it.

"What are they doing?" Sisay whispered.

"I don't know." Gerrard turned to Chamas. "Any ideas?" She shook her head.

Soon, dryads surrounded the crew in a dense thicket. The tree folk seemed to root themselves. They stood unmoving, their faces lifted to the stars that shone brightly down from the cloudless sky.

The dryad song fell away into a low humming noise, so

faint at first Gerrard thought it was the sound of night insects. Then it grew in intensity, a vibration that made the ground quiver. It was as if they were at the center of an enormous drum, its tense surface trembling with suppressed power.

From the north, Gerrard felt an answering call. With a start, he realized it came from the dragon engine. Unutterable loneliness infused the sound, as if Ramos had waited an eternity for this moment. For millennia, he had been alone, truly alone. Phyrexians had built him, and Urza had given him a purpose, but for eons, Ramos had dwelt beyond any purpose. He had waited. The folk he had saved remembered him in myth, not truth—the folk he longed to help lingered forever beyond his reach. The cry of the dragon filled Gerrard with overwhelming sorrow.

In other parts of the forest, new minds awoke. Ramos's loneliness gave thought, being, to the forest around him. Animated by visions of the dreaming dragon, the denizens of the forest were woven together in a pattern of increasing complexity, drawing their power from the land itself. Trees became individual neurons in a great mind. A circle of wolves lifted their throats in howling. Flora and fauna raised a single song of many voices, swelling into a triumphant anthem.

A new light awoke. In the hands of the dryad chief, the Bones of Ramos were beginning to glow. Dimly at first, then brighter they shone. Light splashed across the circle of dryads, across the waiting crew. Sun bright, the stones beamed.

Gerrard turned his face away. He saw his companions shielding their eyes, their faces bathed in the brilliant light. Waves of power surged from the stones, far stronger even than fluxes from the Thran crystal at the core of *Weatherlight*.

"Ramos is joining us!" he shouted to Sisay through the omnipresent song. "He is joining himself with the stones. He is joining the Uniter."

The stones were linked to the dragon. None could function alone for long, but when joined together by the power of Ramos, they formed an inexhaustible source of energy. It was as if five unique worlds had been united in the stones, and each universe within the stone was a part of the greater multiverse.

Suddenly, Gerrard knew with certainty that the struggle he was engaged in—the enemies he faced on Rath and here in this reality—were part of a cosmic struggle that was being played out across the entirety of existence. These stones connected him and Ramos to that struggle. Each stone was a cosmos, and within each cosmos were myriad worlds.

The song of the dryads slowly faded. As it did, the glow within each stone lessened. When the music ended at last, the powerstones each retained some portion of their inner fire.

Silence settled like a blanket on the grove. A hush extended across the land for miles, a stillness that embraced every living creature. For a long moment, it stretched outward. Gradually, normal night noises resumed.

Gerrard found, to his surprise, that he was breathing rapidly. Beside him Sisay sat, head bowed to her knees. When Gerrard touched her arm, she stirred and looked at him, her eyes dark pools in the night. Tears glinted on her cheeks.

"Did you hear it?" she whispered. "Did you?"

He nodded.

The chief dryad approached, laying the stones at Gerrard's feet. Twiglike fingers reached toward the Benalian. He held his hand out as well. Small, snapping surges of power arced between them, and Gerrard once again understood.

"Ramos has given us his blessing," he told the crew reverently. "Ramos has joined the Uniter. Within these stones, he will return with us to Mercadia."

While Gerrard spoke, the dryads faded into the trees that ringed the grove. The crew rose to their feet. No one said anything else; nothing was needed. Gerrard gathered the Bones of Ramos, placing them in his pack.

"We will remain here through the night," Gerrard said quietly, "and hike out for Mercadia in the morning."

* * * * *

By morning, the pack, the bones, and Takara all were gone.

CHAPTER 20

Darkness gripped the deck of *Weatherlight*. Squee awoke, soaking wet and tied hand and foot to a chair. He turned and twisted, trying to free himself. Water splashed coldly over him, drawing a cry of protest from his throat.

"Is not that enough? Is he not awake once more?"

Unfamiliar voices. Squee struggled again. Shapes moved before him in the murk and slowly took form and substance.

Two Kyren were standing there, both in rich robes. To one side was a Mercadian, tall and slender, his simple robes indicating his servile status. The Mercadian held an empty bowl, which he had evidently just emptied over Squee. The dark cave ceiling hovered far above.

Squee struggled against the ropes. He gave a piteous yelp as they scraped his flesh. His chest and head ached. Tiny shapes swam before his eyes.

The Kyren paid no attention to him.

"Will not his companions miss him if he is gone?"

"Is it not possible, though, that they sent him away on purpose, knowing his nature to be superior to their own?"

"May your words not be truthful, but even so, is it not equally possible that he was sent by his party to spy upon us and to bring word of this to those who must not know?"

"Should we not question him to learn the truth of this matter?"

Both Kyren nodded solemnly and turned to Squee.

"Do your companions know of your whereabouts?" asked one, whose slightly larger size and more authoritative demeanor made Squee think of him as the leader.

The little goblin shook his head. The larger Kyren took Squee's chin in his long, slender fingers and twisted it back and forth. Squee gave a loud yelp and bit the hand. The Kyren jerked back, slapping the prisoner soundly across the mouth. Squee wailed and felt blood running down his chin.

The other Kyren stepped forward. "Are not we your friends, Squee?" he asked. His voice was gentle, and he patted the cabin boy's shoulder. "Are we not of one people? Are we not all klomahamin?"

Squee nodded without speaking.

The other, larger Kyren, who had been nursing his hand, suddenly grabbed the bowl from the Mercadian and with a shout brought it down on Squee's bony knee. The bowl shattered.

Squee felt something pop in his leg. A wave of agony shot through him, and he screamed until his throat felt raw.

Both Kyren stood watching him impassively. When he'd shouted himself hoarse, Squee slumped in the chair, and the smaller of the two Kyren stepped forward again.

"Again I ask, do your companions know of your whereabouts?" he asked calmly.

Again Squee shook his head.

"Do you know where Gerrard and his companions have gone?"

Another headshake.

"Do you know when they will return?"

Squee tried to shake his head a third time, but the pain in his leg was so great that he found himself falling into the comfortable, dark shadow world. His eyes rolled back in his head. His body sagged against the ropes that bound him to the chair. He felt the room falling away. At the same time, as from a great distance, he heard the conversation in the room.

"Must we not revive him and continue?"

"Have we not received answers?"

"Is he not lying? Does he not know where his friends have gone? Do we not have a clear obligation to continue until we are satisfied he truly knows nothing?"

From farther away, Squee heard another voice break in. The voice was tantalizingly familiar. "He knows nothing."

"Is one completely sure?" The Kyren's reply was deferential.

"I am sure."

"Shall we release him, then?"

"No. Keep him here. Question him again. Above all, he must not be allowed to communicate with his companions."

"Is it not easier to kill him?"

Squee struggled to remain conscious. Amid the pain, he felt a new pressure in the air, as if some being, vast beyond his conception, was bearing down on him, pulling at his mind, seeking to dominate it, to tear it apart. The presence was strong, growing stronger.

"No. I do not wish him killed. He will provide useful leverage against his comrades, and when this is over, it may amuse me to have him serve me."

A hand touched Squee's forehead, and he suddenly saw a great hallway filled with gleaming mirrors. He turned this way and that, and each of the mirrors he saw reflected a small, frightened face—his own. Slowly, he walked down the endless hallway. Each image of himself became subtly different. As he progressed, the images grew leaner, the skin tighter. With each reluctant step, Squee felt his body contract and contort.

He was starving. He was alone. He would never again see his friends. He would never again taste food. The goblin knew with certainty that in all the multiverse, in all the countless planes and worlds, there was no one but him. Through space and time, there was no one but him.

No one.

He cried out in despair. His scream, high and plaintive, echoed down the mirror corridors and found no listener. Try as he might, Squee could see nothing but his own endlessly repeated image.

Kneeling, he wept, his tears puddling on the floor. They congealed into sparkling ice and spread out on either side of him, forming a gleaming pool rimed with frost. Within the ice, Squee saw his own frozen shadow, trapped forever in sorrow. He knew with a horrible certainty that he would never escape, that he was imprisoned for eternity.

With a kind of relief, he felt his mind slip away. He heard the goblins ask the same questions as before, but this time he did not hear his answers. The dream world faded, and the tiny flame that was his mind flickered with one final thought before it went out.

Volrath . . .

* * * * *

Hanna and Karn waited nervously in their latest hideout in the lower city. It was a deep cellar hewn from rock, small and solid and dark. A single candle burned by the stairs— the last of the candles. It cast the cellar in a dingy light. The place was better suited for potatoes than people, which made it perfect for Karn. He had a tendency to break through the floors and walls of rundown shacks, and no disguise allowed him to move safely about the daytime streets. At night, he made his way by wrapping sackcloth over his silver skin and pretending to be a runty giant. Hanna was almost as conspicuous—slim, blonde, and clean. Only in the company of Squee could Karn and Hanna safely navigate the nighttime streets, and Squee had been missing now for days.

Sitting beside a bushel basket of carrots—her main sustenance since Squee's disappearance—Hanna shook her head. "He's been captured, Karn. That's the only explanation."

"I fear as much," the silver golem replied from the dark corner where he crouched, donning sackcloth. "It should be night by now. We'd better brave the streets and rendezvous with the Ramosans. They might have word of Squee."

"Do we dare risk it? We don't want to lead the Mercadians to the rebels."

Karn shrugged. "We haven't much choice. We're out of water—"

"Shhh," Hanna hissed. She glared toward the dark stairway that led above. Metal shifted, and a latch furtively drew back. "Someone's coming." She drew away from the bushel basket of carrots and moved toward Karn.

Hinges complained as the shabby doors above lifted away. A foot quietly settled on the top stair. Grit crackled beneath that furtive tread. A few more steps, and the doors swung closed above.

Hanna whispered to Karn. "I don't imagine you're ready for a fight?"

Silver flesh shuddered beneath half-donned cloths. "I've learned to bluff."

Down the dark wedge of stairway stalked a slim, muscular figure—as lithe and brutal as a bullwhip. The shadow reached the last stair and ducked into the cellar. Even in the murk, the fiery shock of red hair was unmistakable.

"Takara!" Hanna blurted, clutching her panting chest. "You scared the daylights out of us."

"There you are," Takara said, striding into the room. She bore a bag in one hand. "What are you doing hiding in the dark—and under those . . . rags?"

"We didn't know who you were," Hanna responded, emerging from the corner.

Karn drew the sackcloth from his shoulders. "How did you find us?"

"Squee told me where you were," Takara said levelly. "He's been living it up in the Magistrate's Tower."

Hissing, Hanna said, "And I thought he'd been reformed."

"I was *sure* he'd been reformed," Karn said suspiciously.

"I've come to take you out of here." Takara upended her bag. Its contents emptied atop a bulging grain sack. Out tumbled five stones, the size and general shape of hands laid out flat. They glowed brightly, red and white, green and blue—one even cast a purple-black tone over everything around. The candle's light was tepid murk beside the stones' collective gleam.

"The Bones of Ramos!" Hanna knelt down beside the grain sack. Her hands trembled above the stones, shaking with awe and excitement and hope. "They're beautiful."

Karn loomed up behind her, staring down at the glimmering crystals. "More than that. There is an intelligence in these stones."

"That's Ramos himself. He has infused the crystals with power," Takara said.

Hanna gingerly lifted the Heart of Ramos. "I can feel

it—a warm vitality." She looked up at Karn and Takara, her eyes full of wonder. "Now, we need only find *Weatherlight*, insert the stones, and get everyone aboard—"

"That's the sad news . . ." Takara interrupted. "We can't gather everyone."

Karn's jaw dropped slowly open.

A cloud of worry passed over Hanna's face. She lowered the Heart of Ramos among the other gleaming stones. They cast inverted shadows under her eyes. She stammered, "Wh-what are you s-s— Where is everybody else? Wh-where is Gerrard?"

"Dead," Takara said. She stared unblinkingly down at *Weatherlight*'s navigator. "They gave their lives for these stones."

"Dead?" Hanna echoed unbelievingly.

"Ghouls attacked us." A faraway look came to Takara's eyes. "Deepwood ghouls. Tahngarth fought five of them himself. They surrounded him. He hacked off their limbs, but it wasn't enough. They sank their claws into him. They ripped open his stomach and ate his guts. He fought on. They clawed out his eyes. They split open his head. They ate his brains." Takara trembled violently and dropped to her knees, burying her face in her hands.

"No," Hanna gasped out in horror. Tears streamed down her cheeks. "Killed by ghouls . . ."

Takara sobbed into her hands. "That was just Tahngarth. Sisay was . . . Sisay was . . . It's too horrible to say. . . ."

"What?" Karn asked mournfully. "What happened to Sisay?"

"A wumpus attacked her," Takara said, shaking her mantle of gleaming hair. "A hulking beast, all hair and claws. It leaped down on her from the treetops. It crushed her body. She split open like a burst sausage. And then the wumpus plucked her head loose as though it were simply a grape. It bit her face in half and . . ." The horrific account ended with more wracking sobs.

Through tears, Hanna said, "What about Gerrard? What happened to Gerrard?"

Takara's voice was muffled by her hands. "That was the worst of all."

"Tell me!" Hanna cried desperately. "I have to know."

"He and I were the only ones who had survived the ghouls and the wumpuses. We reached Ouramos. We were gathering the stones from the altar where they lay. Ramos appeared."

"Ramos!" Hanna echoed.

"He was a huge dragon engine, a hundred feet tall, with rending talons and fiery breath."

"Gerrard was burned alive!" Hanna said miserably.

"Worse."

"He was ripped to pieces. . . ."

"No," Takara said, choking on her tears. "He died of fear."

"What?"

"As soon as the dragon engine appeared, Gerrard fell down dead. He died of fear."

"He died of fear?"

"Yes." Takara shook with weeping. "Of course, he soiled himself first." She lifted her head. In the weird light of the Bones of Ramos, Takara seemed to be laughing instead of sobbing. Her face seemed a hateful, leering mask. She drew a deep, raking breath, and then sobs transformed into gales of mocking mirth.

Hanna shook her head, tears streaming down. "What is it? What are you saying?"

"Gerrard soiled himself and died!" Takara shouted exultantly.

A vast silver hand struck her face, and the red-haired woman spun away. She was thrown like a rag doll into the corner.

"Vicious monster!" Karn growled, looming before the woman. "Hateful, vicious monster!"

Takara rose, blood replacing laughter on her lips. Fearlessly, she stared at the silver golem and growled, "Strike me again, Karn. Strike me again!"

Shivering in fury, Karn backed away. He hissed. "I want to, but I will not. If I struck you again, I would kill you."

Wiping the blood from her lip, Takara said, "Oh, no you wouldn't." In the strange light of candle and powerstones, her face changed. Red hair turned to gray skin and bone. Small black horns traced out the ridges of a rumpled skull. Human eyes became white, piercing orbs. The woman's whiplike body bulked into a powerful torso. Only Takara's mocking, bleeding smile remained the same. Otherwise, in her place stood Volrath.

"Strike me again, Karn! Strike me again!"

With a shout of animal rage, Karn lunged at the hateful figure. Volrath was too quick. He leaped aside, and Karn smashed into a stack of empty crates. He turned, bashing them aside. Wood hit the wall and fell in splintery showers. "I'm going to kill you, Volrath!"

"No, you aren't," Volrath replied placidly. He stood behind Hanna, one clawed hand clutching her neck and the other clutching her stomach. He held her up like a human shield. "If you try, your precious navigator dies of strangulation, and a broken neck, and decapitation, and evisceration right before your eyes."

Karn stood, quivering, his hands hungry to tear the monster apart. "You are a coward, Volrath. Skulking, sneaking, hiding, pretending to be a friend only because you feared to fight us openly. You are a snake and a coward. You have always been one, since the time you were Vuel, you have always been a coward."

With his face pressed up beside Hanna's, Volrath smiled wickedly. "Perhaps, but what does cowardice matter when one always wins? I always win." He whistled once sharply. The cellar doors flung back, and down the stairs flooded a regiment of Mercadian guards.

* * * * *

There was a strange parade through the city streets that night. Mercadians surrounded a pair of pathetic figures. Both were shackled at ankles and wrists, prodded forward by a swarm of tridents. The woman, thin and blonde, stared unseeing as she hobbled up the street. Her face was wan, her eyes empty, her soul dead. Beside her clomped a massive man of silver. His arms hung hopeless at his sides. His head draped forward in defeat.

Before them capered the strangest figure of all. His muscular frame and gleaming gray armor showed that he was a warrior, and yet tonight, he seemed a taunting jester. In his hands, he held a pair of gleaming crystals, which he waved in front of the unseeing eyes of his captives.

Orim saw it all. Her heart broke to see Hanna and Karn captured this way. Spies had told her that Squee, too, was a prisoner within the city. Had she been within reach of her Ramosan allies, she would have mustered them to fight this regiment. Her heart broke for her friends, but it stopped altogether when she recognized the one who tormented them—Volrath.

He could not so openly parade through the streets unless he ruled them, and all of Mercadian. He would not so openly parade through the streets unless he did it to flush out Orim and her rebel friends.

As much as her heart ached, Orim would not be drawn into Volrath's trap. No. Her despair and anger would not make her weak. She would not bring out her allies now. She would only better prepare them for the coming revolt.

* * * * *

It was a horrible night for Hanna.

First, there was the awful news of Gerrard's death— graphically described—and Sisay's death, and Tahngarth's. Then, Takara herself did worse than die. She transformed into Volrath. The villainous creature paraded Hanna and Karn through the streets, taunting them with his destruction of Gerrard, with the ways he manipulated the crew to gain *Weatherlight*, the Power Matrix, the Bones of Ramos. He regained them all, and then he captured the two crew members who would know how to bring them together.

All the while that they marched through the dark, twisting streets of Mercadia, Hanna watched the rankling roof line. She hoped at least that Orim and Cho-Manno would not be drawn into this latest trap of Volrath's. In dark archways and from shuttered windows, many eyes watched, but no one emerged to help.

Volrath led them to ground. As snaking as were the ways above ground, the caverns beneath were a mesmerizing labyrinth. Endless spirals, dipping shafts, shambling stairways, coiling corridors—the tread of the soldiers' boots echoed over blind and seeping stone. At least Volrath's taunts ceased the moment that they entered the caves.

Hanna staggered along as if descending into a delirious dream. At last, the passage opened up, and Hanna felt her heart leap in hope.

There, before her on a wide cavern floor, stood *Weatherlight*. She was beautiful. The ship's sleek rails gleamed like gold in the murk. Her spars jutted in solid newness. Her twin airfoils raked boldly outward. Her helm glimmered in torchlight. The once-shattered hull was smooth and whole, a vast black bulk on the floor of the great hangar. The ship was beautiful, and now with the Power Matrix and the Bones of Ramos, it was only hours away from flying again.

Hanna and Karn halted before the great airship, guards hurrying to surround the pair. Volrath walked up beside Hanna, resting his arm on her shoulder as though he were an old friend. The twisted evincar took a deep, contented breath, and his black plate armor crackled quietly.

"A glorious vessel, isn't she?" Volrath asked.

"Yes," Hanna replied reflexively. She shied beneath his arm but couldn't escape the clawlike grip on her shoulder. "But she isn't your ship. She's Gerrard's."

"My brother never deserved his Legacy. Not this ship, not Karn, not the *Thran Tome*—none of it. He is a toad dressed up to be a king. *Weatherlight* was never his, and now she is mine."

Hanna glanced at the Phyrexian armada that filled the hangar all about, receding into vast distance. "You have all these ships. Hundreds. Most are larger than *Weatherlight*. You want this ship only because you are jealous of Gerrard, only because it is his."

Volrath's hand struck her cheek with such force it flung her to the ground amid the chains. "The Legacy is mine. I have every piece of it. And now you will put those pieces together for me."

Looking up in anger, Hanna dragged a shackled hand over her bleeding mouth. "You can torture me, but you can't make me repair *Weatherlight* for you."

"Can't I?" Volrath asked with a smile. He gestured toward the spars raking out beside and behind the ship. A chain connected the ends of the two spars, and something dangled on that chain. Not something—someone.

"Squee!" Hanna gasped out.

"Yes," Volrath replied. "Are you familiar with this form of execution? It is gradual and agonizing, a type of crucifixion. Squee's whole weight is held aloft by the shackles that bind his wrists. At first, the pain isn't too bad, but every moment, muscles and tendons grow weaker. Circulation ceases in the hands. Shoulders slowly pull from their sockets. Viscera stretch out the diaphragm. Chest muscles grow so weary they can no longer force air outward. Squee will eventually suffocate because he won't be able to exhale. He'll suffocate though his lungs are full of air."

"You bastard."

Volrath blinked placidly at that. "If, however, you repair the engines, you can use them to lower the masts and save your friend. You see? I impose no time limit on you. Only Squee does. And if you allow him to die, I'll simply have to bring your friend Orim down here and do the same to her, and Tahngarth, and Sisay, and Gerrard. It's up to you how many crew you'd like to kill as you repair this ship—*my* ship."

"So, they *are* alive!" Hanna said, hope rising in her.

"For the time being," Volrath said. "Let Squee die, and you'll see the others, one by one."

Karn's joints grated massively as he stooped to lift Hanna. "Come. Let us do this quickly. We haven't much time."

*   *   *   *   *

"We haven't much time," Orim shouted to the vast assembly gathered in another subterranean chamber.

It was a motley group—Ramosan rebels assembled by Lahaime; Cho-Arrim skyscouts and water wizards who had arrived on the night of the great storm; an elite contingent of Saprazzan warriors sent by the grand vizier; a Rishadan ship crew converted to the cause during Cho-Manno's sea crossing; and bull-men, boar-men, griffins, and other non-humans and non-goblins disparaged in Mercadia—a ragtag, rebel army. These few hundred would hardly be a match for the Mercadian guard with its cateran mercenaries—and its master Volrath.

"We have a new enemy," Orim continued. "This rebellion began against the corruption of the nobles and the vicious manipulation of the Kyren. We have felt ourselves mere pawns in their great game. Now it is clear that even these great enemies are pawns of a much more malevolent master. The Phyrexian steward, Volrath, is here in Mercadia. He rules the city through Kyren and nobles. He has captured the airship *Weatherlight*, the national treasure of

Saprazzo, and the very Bones of Ramos. In mere days, perhaps hours, he will combine these weapons and train them upon us and slay us. We haven't much time."

A voice rose from among the Cho-Arrim skyscouts. "How can we fight if the Uniter has not risen?"

Cho-Manno stepped up beside Orim and declared, "We can no longer wait for the Uniter to rise. The Uniter is in the hands of our greatest foe. We must be our own uniters, our own saviors. If we do not fight now, the Uniter will rise to fight against us."

A collective groan echoed through the stony cavern.

The Rishadan captain interrupted. "These allies have told that their airship was hauled through doors at the base of the city. I will lead my forces through those doors and find your Uniter. Perhaps it'll yet rise—and fight for us."

Scar-faced Lahaime spoke next. "I will lead the Ramosans into position to strike against the Magistrate's Tower and the seats of government."

"My skyscouts and water wizards will produce another storm," Cho-Manno pledged. "The water will empower us and the Saprazzans to take the streets."

"What about the market?" someone shouted. "You can't win a battle in Mercadia unless you can take the market."

Among the rebel leaders on the dais was a young man with tousled black hair, a man who many of the folks in the chamber had taken to be a mere page. His voice was still young, though he spoke with a calm confidence that impressed them all. "I am Atalla of Tavoot's farm. As with many other farmers, I have come to Mercadia with this season's harvest of simsass fruit. As with many other farmers, I am fed up with Mercadian rule. We farmers are united with your cause, and we fill the markets. I will lead my comrades to take the marketplaces, high and low."

"How can you, a mere boy, lead an army of peasants?" someone asked.

Orim grasped Atalla's shoulders and squeezed them affectionately. "He may seem young to you, but Atalla here is the man who made Gerrard and his comrades into heroes of the common people. Atalla is the man who made us into giant killers."

CHAPTER 21

Behind them, the group of jhovall
traders kicked up a cloud of dust that
looked gray beneath the gathering storm.
The jingle of harness bells and the purrs
that came from the herd of several hundred mounts were accompanied by dis-
contented rumbles from the clouds
above. In the marketplace beyond
the wall, tents flapped in rising winds, cold with unnatural
mist. Workers pounded tent stakes deeper to keep canvas
from pulling loose. The guards along the wall crouched in
surly array and glanced skyward with each distant growl of
thunder.

The fattest of the Mercadian guards approached the
leader of the traders. "How many beasts do you bring to

market?" Speaking the patois common to traders, his voice had a supercilious, sneering edge to it.

The trader, whose dark face and nose rings proclaimed him a Tsaritsa of the northern plains, chewed stolidly on a wad of klavaa leaves. "Two hundred."

"Six pieces of copper to bring them into the city."

"Two."

"Five."

"Four."

"Done." The trader pulled a greasy leather pouch from his saddle and extracted the price. The guard tucked the money away in the recesses of his uniform and waved the traders ahead. His lip curled. He eyed the dirty, unshaven figures as they passed, their robes drawn up tight around their faces to keep out the dust. "Hurry up there! Storm's coming!"

One trader, considerably taller than the others, paused and lifted a pair of dark eyes to stare back. There was reproach in his gaze. The trader moved on.

Spitting into the dirt, the guard looked down the road at the next party approaching.

The traders circled around the base of the mountain before finding a clear space in which to pitch their tents. They hastily erected the canvas, close together and clustered as near to the mountain as possible, hoping it would shield them from the coming deluge. The jhovalls were enclosed in a rough pen, erected of wooden posts and ropes. The beasts settled down to feed.

Leaving a few of their number to keep an eye on the herd, the traders gathered within the largest tent for their evening repast. In the center of the space, a brazier burned. The traders squatted around it, their robes trailing on the floor, as bits of meat roasted on skewers. A large communal bowl of rice sat nearby, and the meal was washed down with draughts of thick red wine.

The herdsmen ate in silence, broken only by the sound of chewing, swallowing, and sucking on fingers. Outside, the ever-present hum of the mountain rose and fell in regular rhythms, as if some great beast was breathing heavily. Distant thunder came with the ominous portent of war drums. When the meal was complete and the dishes removed, the traders sat cross-legged on the floor of the tent and passed pipes of tobacco. After a long time, the leader spoke.

"We are arrived at your destination," he said to one of the herdsmen. "You have paid us for our help, and we have taken you through the outer guard as we agreed. Do you now wish to leave us?"

The herder cast back the hood of his robe, revealing a head of dark hair and a long, thin scar running along his cheek. His companions did likewise, one shaking out a long braid that dangled down her back. The tallest one carefully disentangled his hood from a magnificent pair of horns.

"We must leave you and find our companions in the city," Gerrard said. "We are grateful for your assistance, but now we must find a way above."

The leader drew deeply on the pipe and spat into a convenient brass cuspidor that had been placed near his side. "Not an easy task."

"Nevertheless, we must try."

The leader nodded slightly. "I can show you a way into the city," he said after long contemplation of the fire. "It is a secret known to my people. In the past it has allowed us to enter the city without paying the entrance fees and taxes that are charged by the magistrate. In the lifts, you would be quickly discovered by the guard. But if you and your friends take the way I show to you, you will go undetected."

"Is the way safe?"

The leader shrugged. "We have not traveled to the surface that way in some seasons. The last time I passed through that way, I experienced no difficulties."

Gerrard glanced at the others of his party. "What do you wish in return?"

The leader stroked his chin, his eyes bright and glittering. "You have said little of what you wish to do in the city."

"If I said less than I knew, Most Respected Shi'ka, it was because I did not wish to put you and your friends in danger."

"But I suspect what you intend will threaten the chief magistrate and those who support him." He lifted a hand, stopping the other's protest. "I will be satisfied if the rule of the magistrate is weakened. Such a thing would be of great service to the people of my tribe, who suffer beneath the taxes and bribes of his rule."

Gerrard looked at him for a time in silence. "I can promise you, Shi'ka, that whatever we do in the city, the magistrate isn't going to like it."

Shi'ka nodded solemnly. "Very well. Let us sleep. Then, in the deeps of night, long before morningsinging, I will bring you to the secret way."

He motioned for his fellow tribesmen to clear away their meal. Weary with the long jhovall drive, Shi'ka rolled himself up in a blanket and began to snore heavily. The others of his tribe followed suit.

Around the tent, the business of Mercadia went on unabated. The markets never closed, and the busy trading and selling at the foot of the mountain did not slow. The coming storm only added urgency to the marketplace. Through all the dark hours, peals of thunder were echoed in the hustle and bustle of the stalls.

A few hours after nightsinging had resounded from the minarets of the city far above, the black night was pregnant with rain. Shi'ka roused Gerrard and his companions from sleep and led them through the crowds of merchants and traders who thronged the area. After a walk of considerable distance, they reached a series of stalls hung with rich rugs of complex design. Shi'ka hastily pushed Gerrard and the others through the stall and into a tiny room in back, hung with rugs and smelling of musk and the oil used to polish rug racks.

The jhovall trader grasped one edge of a large heap of carpets and indicated Tahngarth should take the other. With a grunt, they lifted the pile and moved it aside, revealing a small trapdoor studded with heavy nails. Shi'ka pulled up the door and gestured Gerrard toward the dark hole. The Benalian could see a slender ladder leading down into blackness.

"Here is the way of which I spoke," Shi'ka said quietly. "Though you have torches, if I may offer advice to you, risk no light within the passage unless absolutely necessary. The burrows beneath the mountain have many rambling ways, and it is possible that a light might be noticed by one whom you would not wish to encounter. Keep your voices still and travel as quickly as you can. May the face of Gho'miko shine ever upon you."

Gerrard clapped Shi'ka briefly on the shoulder. He shucked his jhovall trader's robe and climbed onto the ladder. As he descended, Sisay, Tahngarth, and the sailors of *Weatherlight* removed their cloaks and followed. Shi'ka closed the trapdoor behind them.

The first part of the climb was made in an intense darkness. After a dozen yards, the ladder ended in a narrow, circular chamber, from which there appeared to be only one exit. Along this tunnel the company passed, hands extended on either side, ears cocked for the slightest sound. Their own footsteps sounded alarmingly loud, rattling and echoing against the stone floor.

The passage was rough and narrow, so that Tahngarth had to stoop to fit through it. The minotaur softly grumbled to himself.

After a few turns, Gerrard felt the floor begin to ascend. The upward slope continued for some time, the passageway climbing in a series of great, sweeping turns. There was still no light, but echoes told of a wider, taller corridor. In one or two spots, the darkness grew less intense. Gerrard made out several side passages that led off to unknown destinations.

Groping along the main passage, his hands fully extended before him, Gerrard encountered a pile of boulders. They felt rough and irregular, and they completely blocked the way. The others crowded behind.

"Well," Gerrard whispered. "I think this is where we take a risk. Sisay, light the torch, but keep it shielded as much as possible."

There was a faint scrape of steel against flint. A spark landed on the torch's head, and Sisay blew it into a flame. Soon, the brand glowed brightly. The party saw they had come to a cave-in that completely filled the tunnel through which they had been traveling. Many of the stones were of great size, and there was little hope of clearing the passage easily or quietly.

Sisay smothered the torch, and they were back in the darkness, their eyes spotting from the sudden light. "Well," she whispered. "What do you think? Do we go back or try to find some other way through?"

Gerrard sensed the sentiments of the others: none liked this dark passage and they would prefer to take their chances with the guards in the lifts. Nonetheless . . .

"We try to find another way through," he whispered. "It's our best hope of getting into Mercadia without anyone knowing we've come back." He heard a faint sigh in the blackness and led the way back down the tunnel toward the first of the side passages.

The new tunnel felt smaller and narrower than the one they had been traversing. Tahngarth had to crouch to make his way along, and even Gerrard began to feel oppressed by the vast mountain overhead. At last, a faint glow appeared in the distance before them. As they drew closer, Gerrard spied the outline of a wooden door. He reached it and cautiously pressed his weight against it. The door yielded, opening into another passage.

Gerrard peered out. This hall was surprisingly wide and broad. Every fifty feet or so, an iron sconce on the wall held a flaring torch. To the left, the path angled upward. To the right, it bent down around a curve.

Sisay touched Gerrard's arm. "Well?" she asked. "It looks as if this particular road is no secret."

Gerrard nodded. "I think we have to chance it." He looked at the others crowding behind him. "Try not to make much noise, and go as quickly as you can. We've probably climbed about fifteen hundred feet from the base of the mountain, so we've got a long way to go."

The ascent was faster but tinged with urgency and trepidation. From far below, echoes occasionally resounded—machinery at work in the bowels of the mountain. Sometimes, disturbingly, they heard voices.

Dabis crouched and retrieved something from the side of the road. "Sir," he called in a whisper.

"What?" Gerrard stopped, as the others gathered around the sailor.

"Look." Dabis held out his hand.

Gerrard stared at the tiny object in his palm—a ring of green glass. "It's Squee's ring. It would seem he's been down here. But how?"

Tahngarth said disapprovingly, "If there is trouble to be found, Squee will find it."

"He was searching for *Weatherlight*," Sisay remarked. "Maybe he found it down here."

Gerrard thought a moment. "Yes, perhaps *Weatherlight* and Squee are both down here somewhere."

His voice found an echo, this time from up the tunnel. Someone approached around the next bend. The party glanced quickly around. The walls surrounding them were solid, unbroken by any nooks or crannies. Gerrard shook his head grimly and loosened his sword.

A moment later, a group of Mercadians appeared and stopped dead at the sight of *Weatherlight*'s crew. Four in front wore the livery of the city guards. The others were courtiers, but Gerrard caught sight of a flash of green skin from the middle of the group. At least one Kyren.

With a shout, Sisay dashed forward, Tahngarth leaping behind her. There was a ringing that echoed up and down the tunnel. The guard drew their swords in time to parry the first attack. Sisay and Tahngarth closed with two of them.

Gerrard engaged the third guard, and Dabis the fourth.

Chamas rushed forward to aid her shipmates but fell with a cry of pain. A silver shaft emerged from her thigh.

The courtiers edged back. Two Kyren lifted blowpipes to their lips. They were aimed at Fewsteem.

With a slashing blow, Gerrard drove his opponent back so that the Mercadian was interposed between the goblins and their target.

Tahngarth meanwhile chopped sword and hand away from a guard. The Mercadian stared in shock. The minotaur's blade finished the job. In a mighty backstroke, it lopped off the man's head and hurled it down the corridor.

Sisay was having a bit more trouble. Unlike most Mercadian guards, her opponent knew how to handle a sword. He delivered a powerful blow that would have forced a lesser foe to her knees. Sisay parried successfully and shoved the man back. The guard aimed a stroke at her head. She ducked just as a shaft from the blowpipes whistled over her to thump uselessly against the wall.

Gerrard's duel was also more prolonged than he had hoped. He forced his opponent back against the wall. Desperate in terror, the man erected a whirling dervish of steel before him. The Benalian's best strokes could not penetrate it.

There was a wild yell from one of the Kyren. A dagger,

thrown by Fewsteem, stuck out of the creature's wrist. He clutched his wound, howling in pain. Sword in hand, Fewsteem leaped over the body of the decapitated guard and attacked.

Tahngarth rushed up beside him, grabbed the Mercadian courtiers, and knocked their heads together. They fell unconscious—at the least—to the floor.

Gerrard feinted toward his opponent and brought his sword up in a sharp thrust that finally struck home. He felt the blade enter flesh and grate against bone. Then the man went to his knees. He sank slowly to the floor and clutched at his throat, from which poured a fountain of blood. The Mercadian's eyes rolled back in their sockets. His legs thrashed twice, and he was still.

In the same instant, Sisay came in over her opponent's guard. Her sword made a deep gash in his chest. As he staggered back, she lunged at him, twice plunging her blade through his body. He fell without further sound.

Tahngarth's striva hovered at the throat of the remaining goblin, whose companion had been cut down by Fewsteem. Dabis held Chamas in his arms. Her lips had turned blue, and she was shaking uncontrollably. Dabis looked up, tears in his eyes.

"The dart must have been poisoned. Can't we do something for her?"

Gerrard knelt by Chamas's side. She looked at him and spoke through chattering teeth. "S-S-Sorry, Commander. I c-can't feel my l-l-legs anymore."

"Hang on, Chamas! We'll try to do something for you."

She shook her head. "N-No good. I c-can't feel . . ." Her voice faded. Her eyes closed.

Gerrard rose and looked about. The tunnel walls and floor were stained with blood. Sisay was tying a bandage around her arm. The bodies of the Mercadians lay sprawled. From the surviving Kyren came a low, chittering whine.

The Benalian walked to where Tahngarth held the creature pinned against the wall. "Where were you going?" he snapped.

The Kyren said nothing.

"Where does this corridor lead?"

Again, the goblin was silent.

Gerrard turned to Sisay. "Are those two alive?" he asked, jerking his head at the Mercadians.

She examined each briefly. "This one is. I'm not sure about the other."

"Wake him up."

The dark woman slapped the Mercadian's face once, twice. He groaned and lifted his head. He groaned again when he saw who stood over him.

"Come on, you. On your feet!" Sisay jerked him up by the front of his robes and dragged him over to stand next to the Kyren.

Gerrard bent and picked up one of the darts from the Kyren blowpipes. He held it up to the Mercadian's face. "You know what this is?"

The Mercadian turned pale. His lip quivered. Gerrard brought the dart closer, until its point was resting on the Mercadian's fat cheek. "Where does this corridor lead?"

Tears rolled down the Mercadian's face. He tried to turn his head to look at the Kyren but was prevented by the pressure of the dart. He opened his mouth, his eyes pleading.

The goblin's body twisted. A long-fingered green hand slapped Gerrard's, driving the dart deep into the Mercadian's cheek.

The man shrieked and fell to the ground, clawing at his face.

Tahngarth's blade sliced the Kyren's throat, spilling lifeblood.

Gerrard leaped back, not in time to avoid a sharp kick from the dying goblin. He turned toward the Mercadian, but the man was already stiffening.

Sisay stared at the bodies around her. "Where in the Nine bloody Hells were they going?"

Gerrard shook his head. "I don't know, but we need to find out. Let's get these bodies out of sight."

"Captain," Dabis broke in, "what about her?" He indicated the body of Chamas, lying still on the corridor floor. The sailor had done his best to straighten her limbs and wipe away the white foam that had gushed through her teeth.

Gerrard laid a hand on his shoulder. "I'm sorry, but we'll have to leave her with the other bodies for now."

Dabis swallowed and then nodded. He bent and tore a piece of clothing from one of the dead Mercadians and spread it over the young woman's face. Then he picked her up and followed after the others.

The hiding of the bodies was a messy business, and none spoke during it. When they had cleaned the site as best they could, Gerrard removed the closest torches. With luck, no one would notice the bloodstained rocks in the dim light.

Carefully retracing their steps, the crew moved stealthily downward until they reached the bottom of the tunnel. They crouched in a pool of shadows just beyond the passage's mouth. It opened on a vast chamber suffused with a thin blue smoke.

"By Urza's Rack and Mishra's Ruin!" Gerrard muttered.

The crew looked out wonderingly on a mighty fleet of aerial ships being assembled in the huge cavern. A mile high and miles across, that enormous subterranean space was filled with vessels—Phyrexian vessels. Workers moved along web-thin causeways, building, repairing, testing, preparing. . . . Two ships rose through a wide opening in the floor and moved across the vast tunnel.

"What does it all mean?" Tahngarth asked.

Gerrard shook his head. "A lot of these vessels look like *Predator*, the one that attacked us in Rath. Most of them are bigger, but you can see they have the same general design features. I'd guess this fleet is being built for Rath, for Volrath's use."

"Why?" Sisay asked. Her eyes were hard as she heard Volrath's name. "Why do they need a fleet this big?"

"Only one reason," the Benalian returned. "This must be for the invasion of Dominaria. This is Volrath's invasion fleet."

Tahngarth shook his head. "That does not make sense. Why build a fleet in a place other than Rath? And why here, in a place that is not controlled by Volrath?"

Gerrard rubbed his beard. "Perhaps it *is* controlled by him." A chill moved through them all. "Perhaps it is."

"They brought *Weatherlight* through doors below," Sisay said. "What if they brought it here?"

"*Weatherlight* is here," Gerrard said with sudden certainty. "She calls to me."

Tahngarth said, "Then let's go find her."

"Yes," Gerrard said, pulling his sword. "We'll find the ship and do our best to create some mayhem on the way."

* * * * *

Karn stood on the main deck of *Weatherlight* and gazed aft, toward the panting figure who hung on chains there. "Poor Squee," Karn whispered mournfully to himself.

There was no sense speaking to the goblin. Squee had hung unconscious for a day now. At least he still breathed, but for how much longer? In his silent suffering, Squee was doing more to save *Weatherlight* than any of his crewmates. Thrice, Karn had fought toward the spars, hoping to save his friend, and thrice been prevented by the guards that surrounded and filled the ship. It was no use. Squee would hang there while he lived—but how much longer would that be?

"Gerrard will come soon, Squee, and we will bring you down among us. Gerrard will come soon."

A figure approached through the moored armada—but it was not Gerrard.

"Volrath," Karn groaned beneath his breath. He turned away from his suffering friend and descended through a hatch to the engine room.

The cramped space was littered with tools. Oily rags hung across the engine's enameled fuselage. Cogwork lay arrayed on towels on the floor. Grease smudged, Hanna sat paging fitfully through the *Thran Tome*, muttering uncertainly about which part went where. All of the mess was for show, meant to impress the Mercadian guards who watched her. Within the first hour of work, Hanna had effected the correct configuration of Power Matrix and Bones of Ramos. She had even fitted the Juju Bubble, a Legacy item stored in Karn, into its position at the center of the Matrix. By merely inserting the Horn of Ramos into its position, she could power up the whole ship . . . but then *Weatherlight* would be Volrath's. . . .

"He's coming," Karn rumbled ominously.

Hanna looked up, startled. "Who?"

"Volrath," Karn replied.

No sooner than the name was spoken, the gray-armored evincar descended the stairs into the engine room. He wore a wicked smile that split his gray-skulled head, and in his hand he held a cocked crossbow. He swung it jauntily up to his shoulder. "How does the work progress on my ship?"

Hanna looked away, her face hardening. "Not well. The myths were wrong. These devices weren't fashioned to fit together. The construct has to be joined by a series of cogs and conduits."

"Nonsense," Volrath responded, kicking the loose gear-work aside. "I had not thought your goblin friend would last this long. My patience has died before him. But only just . . . Start up the ship, or I will kill him."

Hanna looked up, her face as white as paper. "I'm telling you, I . . . I'm working as fast as—"

Volrath spun on his heel, marching up the stairs.

Karn followed, his massive hands spread beseechingly. "Patience, Master Volrath. *Weatherlight* is no mere machine. She is a being—as complex as a living body. She cannot simply be repaired. She must be healed. The Matrix cannot simply be fastened in place. It must grow into the engine."

Volrath was heedless. He gained the main deck and strode to one rail, lifting the crossbow before him. Taking a deep breath, he trained the bolt on Squee's small, panting figure.

"Please, be patient," Karn implored behind him. "Please, Vuel."

Volrath hissed, turning angrily on the silver golem. "Vuel? Vuel! Vuel is dead! He was killed by your blessed master. I am not Vuel. I am Volrath. Volrath is Vuel's corpse, a corpse that wouldn't lie down and die when Gerrard killed it. Do not call me Vuel!" The crossbow trembled in his grasp.

"You are not dead, Vuel," Karn replied placidly. "You still live inside this monstrous shell. Perhaps there is only one nerve of you alive, but I've touched that nerve. Come back, Vuel. If you fire that shot, you'll kill Squee, yes, but you'll also kill Vuel—forever. Put down the crossbow. Come back to life, Vuel!" He reached out and grasped Volrath's shoulder.

Cold steel tore free from warm silver. Snarling, Volrath leveled the crossbow. The trembling was gone. He squeezed the trigger. The bolt leaped out, straight for Squee's heart.

"No!" Karn shouted, his arms flashing out too late.

A thud sounded. Chains rattled plaintively. The spars shivered. A hum shivered through the decks and lights flashed on along the rail. Masts descended. Chains sagged. The crossbow bolt shot over the goblin's drooping head.

Hissing in triumph, Volrath dropped the crossbow. "So, *Weatherlight* is repaired at last!"

Karn heard no more. He left Volrath there and clambered up over the glassy bridge of the ship, heading toward Squee.

Volrath smiled wickedly and barked orders to the guard captain on the deck. "Summon my crew. *Weatherlight* launches within the hour!"

CHAPTER 22

Silently, the team crept up the passageway alongside the subterranean hangar. Gerrard led the way, accompanied by Sisay, Dabis, and Fewsteem. Some distance behind, at rear guard, stalked the hulking figure of Tahngarth. It was five swords against a Phyrexian armada—but these five swords had faced down ghouls and dryads and dragon engines, and they had won. They had surprise on their side, and *Weatherlight* called to Gerrard.

"She's above—in the cavern on that side," he had said, gesturing beyond the huge columns of stone that spanned a mile from ceiling to floor. "They must have moored her where she could rest on the ground. She's there. I'm sure of it."

Gerrard was not given to mysticism, and so these spoken certainties had seemed nothing short of oracles. He had insisted the group retreat up the side passage, taking the fastest route around the huge cavern. Thrice along the way, they had encountered more Mercadians, and thrice more had cleaned up the resultant mess and removed the torches from their sconces. So far, no alarm had been raised.

In time, they reached the entrance to the upper cavern. As they watched, a ship rose in stately grandeur from the central pit and sailed gracefully down the tunnel to the side.

The level of activity within was remarkable. Along one wall lay an armory, with bin after bin of goblin bombs. Human workers gingerly loaded the incendiary devices into crates and set the crates on skids with rollers on their bottoms. Phyrexian dock workers—mindless creatures—stooped in their traces, pulling the skids down long aisles to various ships. Crews conveyed thousands upon thousands of bombs into bomb bays. There was a sense of urgent activity, the feeling of a vast project nearing completion. Each of those explosives had been fashioned with the intent of killing someone—or many folk—the folk of Dominaria.

Gerrard turned to the crew members gathered about him in the shadows. He gestured. "*Weatherlight* is there—about a hundred ships in. Do you see?"

Sisay's eyes were grim as she marked the spot. "Yes, and a whole army of Phyrexians between us and the ship."

"We'll use that army to our advantage," Gerrard replied. "Between the armory and the bombs loaded on the ships, we should be able to start a good sized chain reaction. I want the blasts to lead out into the main cavern—see how many of the finished ships we can destroy. We'll create an avenue that'll let us fly out of here. Perhaps we'll destroy the entire fleet."

"This is a plan I can wholeheartedly approve," Tahngarth said, eagerly gripping his striva.

"Here at the entrance is an unguarded vessel, loaded with bombs. We'll sneak over to it and take as many as we can carry. Sisay and I will set charges leading out into the main cavern. Tahngarth, Fewsteem, and Dabis, you'll set charges in this cavern. Target especially ships with full payloads. Head toward *Weatherlight*, set off the charges, and when the guards go to investigate, take the ship. See if you can get it up and running."

"What if we can't?" Tahngarth asked.

"Then abandon the ship, get more bombs, and blow the whole cavern," Gerrard said decisively. "Better to lose *Weatherlight* than to let this armada attack Dominaria." He smiled humorlessly. "Are you still so wholehearted, Tahngarth?"

"No," growled the minotaur. "It's the right plan, though. Of course, blowing the whole cavern might bring the entire mountain down on our heads." He was speaking also for Dabis and Fewsteem, who glanced uneasily up at the vast stone roof that arched above them.

Gerrard nodded. "Yes, it might. That's a risk we'll have to take. Is everyone ready?"

Heads nodded.

"Okay. Let's go."

Watchful and stealthy, they darted to a nearby ship. It was a one-person skiff with a long, bony prow and orange wings that folded like paper fans to aft. Sisay scrambled up the leathery fuselage and into a goblin-sized cockpit. Her practiced eye soon identified the bomb bay door controls. She triggered them. Bombs spilled out across the floor. Gerrard and the others cringed back a moment before swiftly loading their arms. Laden with the heavy black goblin bombs, Tahngarth, Dabis, and Fewsteem moved swiftly and silently along the wall of the cavern toward *Weatherlight*.

Gerrard looked at Sisay. "Ready?"

Before she could respond, a klaxon suddenly shrieked. A brazen voice squalled, echoing off the cavern walls. "Intruder alert. All troops to battle posts! Intruder alert!"

With a shout, Gerrard led Sisay down the corridor to the main cavern.

Ahead, two goblin skiffs rose beyond the railed causeway. Gerrard hurled one of his bombs, catching the leading craft squarely. There was a loud explosion. The skiff tipped sharply, spilling most of its passengers into the abyss. They screamed as they fell, their cries fading into the vast pit below them. The injured craft turned twice and slipped below the level of the causeway.

At the same instant, Sisay threw a bomb that enveloped the second shuttle in a cloud of white-orange flame. The vehicle dropped to the cavern floor, and the goblins aboard fell or stumbled away from it. The air was filled with the nauseating smell of burning flesh.

Gerrard and Sisay reached the edge of the pit and looked down. The plummeting skiffs had struck several other ships. At least one was alight, burning brightly some seventy-five feet below where they stood. Gerrard could see the forms of the dock workers running to and fro attempting to stifle the flames.

"So much for stealth," Sisay commented wryly.

"Aim for the biggest ships!" Gerrard bellowed. He threw his remaining bombs one by one.

The first struck a massive ship two hundred feet below. Its deck exploded. Gerrard could feel the force echo through the floor of the cavern. Flames shot up from the ship, scorching the hull of the craft immediately above it. The rigging and ropes of the second vessel caught fire, and in a few moments, it too was ablaze. The first ship shivered from stem to stern with another enormous explosion. Its bow tipped downward, and then it fell, a fiery meteor streaking down into darkness. As it went, it rebounded from several other vessels, and they also caught fire.

Other bombs rained down. The sound of explosions was magnified by the cavern until Gerrard felt as if he were being shaken to pieces. Flames leaped upward. Ship after ship twisted in its death agony and fell, amid the cries of those who had been working on them. Some, bearing full payloads of bombs, exploded in white-hot sunbursts. They flung flaming shrapnel out to slice causeways and slay workers and ignite more vessels.

A skiff wound its way upward, turning and twisting to avoid the explosions and fires. It burst from the pit.

Gerrard hurled his last bomb, which caromed off the skiff's side and exploded harmlessly in air beyond. "I'm out."

"Me too."

"Here's where the fun begins."

Kyren dropped from the vessel onto the causeway, accompanied by several Mercadian guards, whose livery smoked and smoldered. Each guard bore a trident and the fiery will to use it.

Gerrard found himself facing a massive Mercadian. Easily seven feet tall, the man had a face streaked with soot and oil. He gave a yell of rage as he brought his trident down on Gerrard. The arms master dodged and parried with his sword. Its blade rang against the trident's metal handle. He drew back his sword for another stroke and was pushed violently from behind. His weapon almost flew from his hand, and he stumbled forward, tearing the skin of his knuckles against the stone floor.

There was a whiz and a thud above his head, and a peculiar choking gurgle. Gerrard looked up. The Mercadian stood stunned. Blood trickled from the corner of his mouth. His hands clutched a trident whose spines were imbedded in his chest. The Mercadian coughed, and more blood came from his mouth. Then he fell backward and lay still.

Sisay had pushed Gerrard out of the way of the thrown trident. Now she came to her feet in a quick roll and swung her sword at the weaponless warrior. His head bounced along the floor as his body collapsed at her feet.

With a roar, Gerrard rejoined the fight. His sword darted like a swooping falcon. Where it sank its tip, bodies went down in spray.

In moments, most of the goblins fell. Three broke away and ran for their lives toward the surface tunnels. Gerrard and Sisay let them go, busy with the guards that remained on their feet.

Gerrard attacked one with a blow so powerful it flung his enemy back against the causeway rail. The guard wavered for a moment on the edge of the pit and then, with a scream, toppled and plunged.

Sisay meanwhile ran another guard through with a single thrust. In the follow-through of that stroke, she bashed the final guard to the ground with her elbow. A quick sword jab ended his struggle.

The battle was over. Thirteen dead Mercadians and Kyren lay in a bloody mess on the causeway. Beyond, explosions and flames were spreading. Most of the ships were burning. A few skiffs maneuvered among them, but flaming vessels plummeted all around. One skiff, packed with refugee goblins, went down beneath the blazing hull of a huge warship. The Kyren were thrown from their craft and fell squealing into oblivion.

"Nice work . . ." Gerrard said breathlessly, clapping Sisay on the back.

"Let's get . . . to the ship," Sisay panted.

"That's a plan I approve . . . wholeheartedly."

The cavern rocked with another massive blast. Stones fell from the ceiling and bashed the already burning ships. Cracks spread along the roof. On the far side of the hangar, a tunnel collapsed in a cloud of dust and rubble.

Gerrard and Sisay turned and raced toward *Weatherlight*. Even as they did, the floor beneath them shivered. Great boulders fell from the ceiling. A crack split the floor, extending from the edge of the pit. Sisay stumbled and almost fell, but Gerrard pulled her to her feet and ran on. They pelted up the passage.

Behind them, a skiff rose from the pit. Goblin faces twisted in grimaces of fear. With a deafening crash, a section of the cavern roof caved in. It fell like a huge hammer atop the skiff, pulverizing Kyren and flattening the top of the craft even as it flung it to the floor. The skiff struck rocky ground, which in turn buckled. The floor dropped into the space below it. The mountain trembled.

Gerrard and Sisay fled up the passageway as the tunnel collapsed in their wake. Up they ran, their legs aching. The way seemed endless, and their shadows leaped wildly in the flickering torchlight.

"Even if we reach the ship . . . how do we fly it out?" Sisay panted.

"We'll worry about that . . . if we live long enough. . . ."

* * * * *

All day and all night, a storm had gathered above the city. Its black bulk blotted out moon and star and bore down on the mountain below. Unlike most storms, this one did not hover overhead. It crouched on the shoulders of the people. It gave weight to the ominous musings in every heart. It squeezed every pair of lungs until bitter introspection oozed forth in whispers of dread.

"The Kyren have captured the Uniter."

"They have killed Ramos."

"This storm is his wrath."

"He will crash to earth again—not in fire, but in flood."

Where private dreads mingled, they admixed and became

public fury. The storm that mounded itself atop the city awoke a second storm in the streets below—a storm of rage . . . of revolution.

"The Kyren are parasites!"

"They are apostates!"

"They can kill Ramos, but they cannot kill us!"

"We can kill them!"

Morning light did not come to storm-swathed Mercadia. The sun's rays could not dispel clouds so deep. Nor did peace return to the streets. Tridents were impotent against such rage. Thunderheads rumbled their ominous threats, and mobs shouted their calls to arms. Lightning flicked across the sky in awesome anticipation, and Ramosans marched along the streets in open rebellion.

Lahaime lifted his voice to the heavens: "People of the mountain, arise! You have nothing to lose but your chains!"

The storm broke.

A gigantic fist of water fell from the skies and smashed into the city. The bashing torrents of rain bore among them winged skyscouts, who dropped on soldiers in the street. Water wizards descended, lightning bright, and sent jags of power to blaze through guard towers. Smoking corpses tumbled from parapets. Other Cho-Arrim—warriors and archers—rose from storm drains to join the rebellion. Cho-Manno led them, with the healer Orim at his side.

In the deluge, fountains across the city overflowed. From their deeps rose merfolk. Limned in storm light, they were glorious and horrific. Conch masks streamed rainwater. Iridescent scales gleamed goblin blood. Pearly tridents skewered boar men and cateran enforcers. Fish had become spear-fishers. Rishadan harpooners had joined the vengeful spirits of the sea. Wind-lashed and water-soaked, slim seafarers slew giants and bull-men and monsters.

The markets, too, rebelled. Farmers loosed jhovalls upon the very soldiers who had extorted money to allow them into the city. Traders dropped tally sheets, and lifted swords, and drove the guard out. Slaves rose from their hypnotic stupor to pull to pieces the caterans who had captured them for sale. At the head of the common army was a most uncommon young man, Atalla of the tousled black hair.

Some who glimpsed these rebel farmers and exotic warriors might have thought this a coup from without, but the main body of rebels were Mercadians themselves—Ramosans and the common folk they had rallied. Scar-faced Lahaime led his marching minions through the streets. They took prisoners wherever they might. They made guards swear loyalty to the people and disavow Kyren rule. Many civilians joined them, and the rebel army grew more mighty as it moved along. Whenever rebels found a Phyrexian, it was borne in chains to one of the dumping stations and hurled from the mountain.

When the mayhem in the streets was complete, when the storms above and below were in full fury, an elite squad of rebels marched on the center of the corruption in Mercadia—the Magistrate's Tower.

* * * * *

Cho-Manno was gone.

Orim lifted her eyes from the wounded skyscout she tended. In the streaming rain, she could see no more than ten feet in any direction, but she knew Cho-Manno was gone. She sensed it. There was only one place Cho-Manno would have gone.

First, Orim must heal this fallen scout. . . .

Drawing a deep breath of the watery air, Orim set her hands on the man's severed side. Her fingers glowed with silver fire, fueled by cascading rain. Warmth suffused the wound. Water mingled with blood and knit tissue to tissue. Pressing her eyelids together in concentration, Orim felt muscles and skin fuse. In a few moments, the young man was whole again.

Sitting back, Orim helped the scout rise. "Go. Fight for the Rushwood. Fight for the Uniter. Fight for all of us." Orim rose with him. She gave his hand one last squeeze and then released him. As the man moved off toward the raging battle, Orim headed up the street, toward the Magistrate's Tower.

Toward Cho-Manno.

She ran across the gray lawn to the tower steps. She drew her sword and moved cautiously up the winding stair.

Storm clouds wreathed the tower. Cyclones battered its walls. Rain washed in a regular cascade down the stairs, making them treacherous. Lightning danced from cloud to ground and ground to cloud. Buildings burned with voracious fire, red flames rivaling blue bolts. Deep cracks appeared in the street, and from them emerged orange flashes and booms—explosions in underground caverns. It seemed all of Mercadia would disintegrate in the clutch of this storm.

Orim climbed into the shrieking heavens. Through several doors, she could hear the sound of fighting, but continued on until she was near the top. At last, she reached the apex of the tower. The great doors to the chamber of the chief magistrate were broken open, and a clash of swords came from within.

Orim burst into the room. The chamber was in disarray. Tables and many of the low couches lay overturned. Before the throne were three goblins—advisors to the chief magistrate. They wielded short, crooked swords and were slashing at the figure who stood before them.

Cho-Manno.

His dark face was contorted in anger, and his blade—long, curved, and slender—flashed in and out in a gleaming curtain of steel. He parried the blows of the creatures before him. At least one of the goblin blades was stained with blood, but the Cho-Arrim leader did not appear to be wounded.

Someone cowered behind the throne—the chief magistrate. The white flesh about his throat jiggled in dozens of small pouches, and his great belly quivered with panting fear. In one fat hand, he held something long and slender—a goblin blowpipe. He lifted the pipe, pointing it at Cho-Manno's back.

Orim threw her sword. It left her hand, trailing silver magic. The blade sang through the air, revolving in a great circle. It struck.

The magistrate screamed. He stared stupidly at his severed wrist. A fountain of blood gushed from the wound. Blowpipe, sword, and hand thumped together to the ground.

Orim gave him no time to recover. She rushed across the room and snatched up the blowpipe. Clapping it to her lips, she blew. The dart whispered as it left the pipe. It appeared in the magistrate's fat neck.

The Mercadian's eyes rolled up into his skull. He gasped, gurgled, and fell to the ground with a thump that shook the room. His remaining hand clasped spasmodically for a moment before it fell still.

Cho-Manno had made good use of the momentary distraction. With one stroke he slashed open the chest of the Kyren before him. His backstroke lopped off the head of the second. The third turned to run, but the Cho-Arrim leader made a tremendous cut downward. His saber clanged against the ground, and the two halves of the goblin fell apart from one another in a cloud of blood and bone fragments.

With a great bound, Cho-Manno sprang over one of the couches and bent over a figure lying on the floor. Orim joined him and gazed down at Lahaime. The Ramosan leader lay on his back, a blood-soaked cloth clutched to his left shoulder. His face was pale, and he was unconscious.

Orim pulled back the bloody cloth and pressed her hand to the wound. Silver fire emerged from her fingertips. Flesh slowly knitted.

Cho-Manno stroked her face. "I am glad you came. You saved the leaders of the Cho-Arrim and of the Ramosans, both."

Lahaime's anguished expression faded. He gently awoke.

Orim said to Cho-Manno, "I was only repaying the favor."

* * * * *

In chains, Hanna staggered up the engine room stairs. Her guards hauled her upward with an unusual brusqueness. Her shackles made such a clangor in the passage that she had not heard the explosions in the cavern until she gained the deck. Then, the blasts were omnipresent.

The cavern's mouth was collapsing in a shower of stone and sand. Figures rushed up the path, just ahead of the killing cascade. They ran from a crushing death toward a fiery one. In a regular line from the entryway, Phyrexian ships exploded. Red blasts awoke beneath their keels. They bounded up, hull carapaces cracking like eggshells. Ram-headed prows tipped forward. Horn-studded sterns flipped backward. Amid shattered glass and rent steel and scorched wood flew the crushed bodies of Kyren, Mercadians, Phyrexians. . . . Where fire reached bomb payloads, the results were even more spectacular. In shattering succession, small blasts awoke large ones. Nearer and nearer the armory they went, until a blooming sun awoke on one side of the chamber. It was blinding, deafening, and for a moment it obliterated all. All.

The few guards who remained on *Weatherlight* ducked, covering their heads. Hanna shied back. On the cavern floor below, Volrath and the rest of the guard fell to their faces. As suddenly as the blast had begun, it ended. Blue smoke belched out across a cracking ceiling. The smell of lightning filled the chamber.

Hanna's guard barked orders. His shouts were whisper quiet after the blast. He hauled Hanna to *Weatherlight*'s rail and forced her to kneel. Her chained hands struck the deck before her. The guard pressed her head to the wood.

Another Mercadian, tall and muscular, stomped up along the planks. His sword had a cleaverlike head, as heavy as an ax. His massive boots ground to a halt beside Hanna.

"Put your neck on the rail," the man shouted.

Without moving, Hanna replied, "What if the ship breaks down again? Who will fix it?"

"Put your neck on the rail!" The order was followed by a kick from one of those massive boots.

Swallowing, perhaps for the last time, Hanna lifted her neck into position.

The executioner's sword flashed firelight as it rose. With an almighty roar, steel descended. Razor-sharp metal cut through nape, and spine, and throat to emerge, streaming gore. The severed head vaulted free, bounced once on the rail, and tumbled in a sanguine spray toward the floor of the cavern.

But it was not Hanna's head. Nor was it the executioner's sword that had severed it. A bloody striva swooped harmlessly over Hanna's neck, and she gaped down at her executioner's blinking skull. Turning, Hanna saw her liberator.

"Tahngarth!" she exclaimed in amazement.

He did not return the greeting, too busy hoisting a guard who was impaled on his striva. Tahngarth hurled the struggling figure toward the rail. The body struck a pair of goblins and bore them overboard.

Nearby, Fewsteem and Dabis fought two more guards. Unmade by unison strokes, the soldiers fell. One of them landed atop the keys to Hanna's shackles.

"Get the keys!" she shouted.

Tahngarth finished a final guard and went to fetch them.

He returned and knelt beside Hanna, fitting metal into the lock.

"You arrived just in time," she said.

"How's the ship?" he asked as he worked.

"Fixed. Perfected. More powerful than ever," she replied. "It's complete at last, Tahngarth. Get these chains off me, and the ones off Karn—he's below—and we'll get this ship into the air. We'll fly out of here."

No sooner had she said these words than the shackles clicked. Chains tumbled to the planks. "It won't be so easy. The flight path is blocked."

Rising, Hanna stared out bleakly beyond the rail. The entry to the cavern was completely sealed by a landslide. Her gaze lingered only a moment on that impediment, though. "It's worse than that." She pointed.

Below, in the midst of smoldering ships, stood Volrath and his company. Forty-some soldiers surrounded two figures—Sisay and Gerrard.

CHAPTER 23

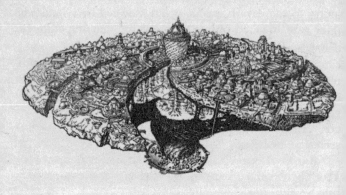

Volrath. Twin mantles of gray skin and bulbous bone arched back from white-gleaming eyes. Black barbs jutted from a thin sagittal crest, and gray armor clung like a second skin to muscles of twisted wire.

The evincar's form was all too familiar to Gerrard—and not just because of the battles and dungeons of Rath. Even after leaving that place, Gerrard had seen Volrath's wicked grin, had felt his predatory gaze parse his soul.

"Takara," Gerrard hissed in amazed realization. He held his sword out before him, keeping the ring of Mercadian soldiers and Phyrexian dock workers at bay.

At his back, Sisay whispered. "Takara? She's here, with Volrath?"

"She *is* Volrath," Gerrard replied grimly. His mind fled back over all his conversations with the red-haired Rathi—the confidences shared, the guilt unearthed, the talk of hatred giving spine to a hero. It had been Volrath all along.

Gerrard growled at the evincar, "So that's where you've been hiding—in someone else's skin—afraid to face me. You truly are a coward, Vuel."

An edge of anger entered the man's supercilious eyes, but lingered only a moment before dissipating. "I was not hiding, Brother. I was ripping your spine out from the inside and taking your Legacy from the outside. I did not take the form of Takara because I feared you but because I hated you, and I wanted you to hate yourself. On Rath, I've made a career of ripping out heroes' spines and replacing them with mimetic hatred. That's what I was doing to you. I am no coward—more a counselor, more a friend pointing out your great and chronic failings, and empowering you to overcome them. It would seem you are incorrigible. It would seem you are determined to fail."

"You are the one who has failed. Your fleet is destroyed. Your Phyrexian monsters are burning among the ships. Your rule beneath this mountain has ended."

Volrath laughed. Pacing back and forth within his circle of soldiers, he actually laughed. "You and Sisay are surrounded and outnumbered twenty to one, your lover Hanna is executed, your guardian Karn is shackled and held captive, your perfected ship is mine." The evincar spun on his heels, looking directly at Gerrard. "You dare pretend *I* have failed. What is this measly fleet in flames? It was a cheap price to pay for so diverting a masquerade, for this pleasant dance in which I have systematically stripped away everything you loved until you stood naked and helpless—until I killed you." Volrath drew his own sword. "This moment was inevitable from the time you stole my birthright, Brother. Your death was inevitable."

"All death is inevitable," Gerrard said, lunging forward and swinging his sword.

Volrath easily batted the blade back. Smiling, he dipped his head. His troops surged up behind Gerrard, swarming Sisay. Three Mercadians and one Phyrexian lost their lives before her sword was wrenched away and she was wrestled to the floor.

Gerrard turned, seeing Sisay lying prone, arms and legs held down and a trident jabbing her neck. He growled, stalking toward the Mercadians. Something sharp and heavy struck his shoulder, spinning him around.

"You deal with me, first," Volrath said, raking a bloodied blade from the wound he had just inflicted. "They'll not kill her until I kill you. I want her to see this." He attacked in a humming overhead stroke that crashed down janglingly on Gerrard's sword. Steel skittered on steel, throwing sparks.

With a roar, Gerrard caught the evincar's blade on his hilt and flung it back. "Mercadia is no longer yours. It never will be again. I've denied you this world."

Volrath chuckled. The sound resembled the soft mirth of the boy Vuel when he had roamed the Jamuraan landscape in search of adventure. There was nothing left of Vuel now—nothing boyish except remorseless cruelty. "Mercadians! They can play their little games, or they can perish. It doesn't matter to me what they do." He circled slowly to the left.

Gerrard matched his maneuver. "I've denied you this world, and I'll deny you Dominaria."

Volrath halted, threw back his head, and yelled aloud. Not a yell of anger, but a shout of scathing laughter. "You idiot! You cannot deny me anything. And even if you could, you cannot deny my master."

"Who is your master?" Gerrard felt his heart hammering against his chest.

"The Ineffable, the Lord of Phyrexia and God of the Multiverse. He has spent millennia plotting the invasion of Dominaria. It is his homeland. It is his holy land. He came from Dominaria, you know, with his people, the Thran. With his people, the Phyrexians, he will return. Do you think for a minute you're going to stop him? Do you think this fleet that you're so proud of having wrecked was the whole of his force? What you saw beneath this mountain is the tiniest part, the merest forefinger of the hand of Phyrexia. That hand is stretching out for your world, and there's not a thing you can do to stop it." Volrath's sword vaulted through the air.

Gerrard barely parried the blow. The Benalian returned it with one of his own, and the clash of steel rang through the hangar as the two blades battered each other. The brothers circled. Volrath lunged wildly. Gerrard stepped back and dashed the sword aside.

As steel skirled again, some long dormant part of Gerrard's mind remembered an identical duel. He and Vuel, mere boys, fought in the bright Jamuraan sun. Beside them stood Vuel's father, the Sidar Kondo. "Remember, boys, no swordsman is invulnerable. Every strength casts a shadow of weakness. Strike there. Gerrard, you're an aggressive fighter with an instinct to attack. Your defenses are weak, cast in shadow. Vuel, you favor your left side. Your blows are powerful and deadly when they fall on the left. Your right is cast in shadow—less guarded and more open to attack."

As Volrath stabbed toward his left, Gerrard consciously gave way. Again, Volrath bore in. Gerrard fell back. Twice, Volrath's attacks sank home. Gerrard felt blood stream down his left arm. His brother smiled hungrily to see the blood, and lunged more recklessly to the left, leaving his right side open.

Careful, Gerrard told himself. He beat back a blow and measured the distance between them. You'll get only one chance. If you strike and fail, he'll realize what you are doing, and you'll perhaps be dead.

Gerrard lowered his guard and feinted.

Volrath's blade swung back, aiming squarely for his exposed left side.

Quick as thought, Gerrard struck at the right. His steel lanced through the breastplate, punched past metal and muscle and bone, and plunged into pink lung.

Volrath fell back, winning free. He howled in pain, the hole in his chest gushing blood even as it sucked air. Golden foam boiled up from his lips as he gasped, "You . . . wounded . . . me!"

Mercilessly, Gerrard advanced, his sword raised high. "No, my brother. I killed you!" Like an axe, his sword plunged down.

Volrath winced back, lifting his blade to guard. Too late. It clanged from his hand, useless.

Gerrard's weapon landed with the weight of a cudgel—but it cut like a razor.

The sword struck Volrath's right collar bone, severing it. It clove a trench eight inches deep. The evincar was laid open. Rib marrow, severed halves of meat, and flayed tendons showed clearly on either side of the sword before blood poured out in a killing tempest. So deep the blade went that it met the previous stab wound in gurgling lungs.

Volrath stood a moment more, only because the attack had been so swift he hadn't had time to crumple. Then he went down sloppily, sprawling to his face, legs twisted beneath him and haunch jutting up.

Gerrard's brother Vuel—Gerrard's nemesis Volrath—at last was dead.

Gerrard raked his sword free and spun, knowing the same fate awaited him. Phyrexian dock workers and Mercadian guards flocked inward. He cared about none of them, but only about Sisay.

With a shriek, Gerrard hurled his blade as though it were a scythe. It harvested the heads of Sisay's captors. They fell as their master had, in streaming gore. Red blood and glistening oil mingled on the floor. The few that survived this first stroke bolted or did not survive the second. Hand slick with the life of his foes, Gerrard reached down and hauled Sisay to her feet.

She had the presence of mind to snatch up a trident from one of the fallen guards. Shaking, she turned back-to-back with Gerrard. The old friends warily watched the circle of soldiers tighten.

"Just like . . . old times," Gerrard spat out between labored breaths.

"Outnumbered twenty to one?" asked Sisay.

"Well, there's that."

"Surrounded by idiots?"

"There's that, too."

"About to die?"

"Yeah," Gerrard said with feigned ease. "That's the part I meant."

There was no more time for jokes. A wall of tridents and swords converged around the two. Gerrard's sword trailed red, painting the faces of soldiers even as it flung back their killing steel. An edge flashed past his defense and caught Gerrard in the side, but its wielder paid with a sudden debilitating gush of guts.

At his back, Sisay was equally pressed. Her trident was an inferior weapon—rusted and dull—but she made devastating use of it. Prongs blinded one warrior while simultaneously skewering the skull of another. Wrenching the tines free, she brought the butt end up to crack a soldier in the jaw.

In the first press, Gerrard and Sisay each downed five foes, but twenty-five fresh ones remained. The sheer weight of descending metal dragged Gerrard and Sisay down. Prong by prong, Mercadian guards and Phyrexian dock workers slew them.

"It's been good!" Gerrard shouted above clanging metal.

"The fight?" Sisay yelled back.

"Knowing you."

"Same here."

The conversation was cut short by converging blades. From both sides, the unstoppable foes surged in. Gerrard made one final swipe with his sword, knowing it could not fend off even one of the killers.

His blade met no resistance. It swung through empty air. Not empty—full of energy.

A wide, red beam, bright as the sun, surged into being before Gerrard. It flash-burned Mercadian flesh, melted Phyrexian armor and weapons, turned skeletons of both races to puffs of ash. Awash in that destroying beam, Gerrard's sword wilted and fell to the ground in a silvery puddle. There, it mingled with the watery weapons and armor of his foes.

He pivoted back from the killing blast and saw that a second beam vaporized the warriors in front of Sisay. Mercadian and Phyrexian, they were dead. Only Gerrard, Sisay, and a handful of soldiers survived in the trough between the twin rays. A few of them staggered into the incinerating light and burned away to nothing.

Gerrard and Sisay embraced, steadying each other lest either of them tumble into death.

As suddenly as they had appeared, the blinding rays of destruction were gone. They had flashed away more than a score of warriors, their armor and weapons, and even melted the stone floor into magma. In the gloom, two hovering points of light remained—a pair of cooling lenses in the ray cannons aboard a certain ship.

"*Weatherlight!*" Gerrard sighed gratefully.

The ship was the most beautiful thing he'd ever seen.

She floated above, swathed in the gloomy deeps of the hangar cavern. Her hull shone as if it had been polished, her sails were furled along the great masts that stretched like wings on either side of her. Her intakes set a healthy roar in the air. Fires from burning hulks cast a lurid light across the hull of the ship, but *Weatherlight* was whole. She was once again flying . . . and fighting.

The remaining few Mercadians and Phyrexians beat a quick retreat from the warship.

More bolts of death could have leaped from the ship's rail, transfixing them. Instead, a coil of line dropped down. It snaked from the bow and waved within reach of Gerrard. A head peered down beside the rope, and Gerrard realized the ship was only the second most beautiful thing he had ever seen.

"Hanna!" Gerrard cried happily. "Volrath said you'd been executed!"

"He's a liar," the blonde navigator shouted back. She nodded toward the evincar's lifeless corpse. "Or, he *was* a liar. Grab the rope and climb up!"

Shaking his head, Gerrard gave a rueful laugh. "I'll not be climbing for a while. Not with this shoulder in ribbons."

"Then tie it around you, and I'll pull you up."

Gerrard dropped the hilt of his melted sword, fed the rope beneath his arms, and struggled to tie it over his breastbone. His hands were shaking too much, and his left arm was weak.

Sisay stepped up, completing the knot. "There you go."

"Oh, Sisay—what am I thinking? I should have let you go first. You're the captain, after all."

She smiled. "I'll catch the next lift." Even as she said it, the rope went taut, and Gerrard started lurching upward.

"After she brings me up," he quipped, "you might have to wait awhile for the next lift."

Sisay laughed happily. Another line dropped down

within her reach. She glanced up to see a pair of horns above. "Permission to come aboard, First Mate Tahngarth?" she asked as she secured the rope.

The minotaur replied, "Permission granted." He hauled her aloft.

Despite Tahngarth's bulk and Sisay's light heft, Hanna was quicker at hauling Gerrard to the deck. She set one foot on the rail and dragged the rope rapidly upward. Hands accustomed to bolts and wrenches greedily hauled hemp.

In moments, Gerrard slid up the gunwale and over the rail, spilling atop Hanna. They tumbled to the deck, ropes coiling all around them. Their glad laughter gave way to kisses, which again gave way to laughter.

"It's nice to see you," Gerrard said in understatement. His fingers stroked her grease-decorated face and hair. "But you shouldn't have spent so much time primping."

Hanna smiled as she rolled him over. This time she landed on top, straddling him. Her hands gingerly probed the lacerations in his shoulder. "Don't you know it's bad manners to go on a date with an open wound?" Insistently, she dragged his shirt from his shoulder, and the lightness in her voice ceased. "I wish Orim were here . . ."

"I'm just glad you are," Gerrard said, pulling her fingers away. "It's not bleeding much now. I'll grab some rags and wrap it. Orim can look at it once we get above." He looked about at the ship. "You've been doing some healing of your own. *Weatherlight* looks terrific."

"Let's go get you and Sisay some bandages, and then let me show you what I've done."

Sisay had gained the deck by then—with a bit more decorum. Together, Sisay, Tahngarth, Gerrard, and Hanna made their way into the bowels of the ship. Down a ladder and along a passage, they reached the sickbay. There, Hanna dressed Gerrard and Sisay's wounds. On a nearby pallet lay Squee, sleeping fitfully after his long ordeal. Fewsteem and

Dabis happened in, lending two more sets of hands. With light but weary voices, the crew members each told of what had happened to them since their parting. They were, Gerrard reflected, like school kids returning after a long holiday, happy to see familiar things once more.

Once the bandages were in place, the crew moved to the engine room, jammed with humming machinery. There, they found Karn, looking immaculate as usual. His hands were sunk into a pair of twin ports in the engine. Within lay handles, which he gripped. Metal filaments jutted from the console into the joints in his metal fingers, hardwiring him to the power core. With a thought, he could control all the engine's levels, harness and shunt its power, even sense the outside world through the ship's lanterns and weapons and hull. It was his concentration that kept *Weatherlight* floating in midair in the smoky cavern. Karn gave no acknowledgment of his friends' entry, for his silver shell had gone inert. While engaged this way, *Weatherlight* became his body.

Passing him, Hanna reached the forward casement of the engine, where the Power Matrix rested. She gestured the rest of the crew up beside her and pointed within. Her face beamed for the first time in weeks. "I used the Juju Bubble!"

"What are you talking about?" Gerrard asked.

"The bubble. Karn's been carrying it about in his guts for—how long has it been?"

"A long time," Sisay said. Unbidden, there rose to her mind an image of First Mate Meida, killed when they retrieved the Juju Bubble from the Adarkar Wastes. "What did you do?"

Hanna grabbed her arm, leaving a thick, greasy palm mark on Sisay's skin. "Look. I took the Bones of Ramos and fastened them into the framework of the Power Matrix, but it wasn't enough. I'd hoped they would provide the final link that would channel their power into the Thran Crystal. They didn't until the Juju Bubble was added."

Sisay shook her head. "I don't understand."

"It was Karn's idea. He brought it out from his chest and realize what it was for. When we placed the bubble over the framework of stones, it acted as a kind of lens. It focused the power. The Power Matrix spontaneously grew to incorporate it. It was beautiful!"

Sisay laughed. "All right. I'll take your word for it. But can we planeshift?"

Hanna nodded. "I don't see any reason why not. The ship actually seems stronger than it ever has been. It might be the result of having this new power system combined with the Skyshaper that Karn installed just before we left Rath. But all indications are that we can travel probably twice as fast as we could before."

"We can't reach enough speed to planeshift out of here—" Sisay began.

"We'll have to blast our way into the main cavern and then out the doors at the base," interrupted Gerrard. "We can wipe out the rest of the fleet en route."

"Blast our way out?" Hanna echoed incredulously.

Gerrard smiled, turning toward her. "You've said the ship's more powerful than ever. Let's see how much more. Battle stations, everyone." He spoke the command quietly, but the sound of it carried even above thrumming engines.

"Yes, Commander," Captain Sisay said, saluting. With a grin, she turned and climbed the stairs toward the bridge.

Hanna followed this tongue-in-cheek salute with a similar kiss. Blushing a little, she said, "Sisay'll need her navigator to get through these caves."

"Just so," Gerrard said through a gentle smile.

As Hanna passed between them, Fewsteem and Dabis grinned. "Must we kiss you as well, Commander?"

"Not if you'd like to live long enough to reach your battle stations," Gerrard replied.

Dabis rolled a seaman's cap nervously in his hands. "Sorry

to say, Commander, but our battle station was the galley, locking down pots and pans. We never were highly ranked."

"Come with me, then," Gerrard said, motioning over his bandaged shoulder. "You too, Tahngarth. We'll need the four of us to operate the forward guns. Acquit yourselves there, and you'll get a promotion." He strode up the stairs from the engine room, through the hatch, and out onto the deck.

"Forward guns! Possible promotion!" Dabis enthused to Fewsteem. "Better than pots and pans!" Across the deck, they scrambled to the guns.

In her centuries of existence, *Weatherlight* had been fitted out with numerous defensive measures—dimension disrupters, glasspitters, bombards, lantern-guns, acid atomizers. . . . All of these weapons, though, had been genteel compared to the massive Phyrexian ray cannons now mounted along the rail. Each consisted of a man-sized barrel above a muscular engine manifold. Conduits ran between the two as if they were networks of pumping veins. A pair of foot wells and a torso harness allowed the gunner to brace against the manifold while gripping the dual fire controls. The pivot that joined barrel to manifold was a ball-and-socket operation, permitting movement about two axes. Speaking tubes built right into the pivot formed an open channel of communication to the bridge. Pneumatic arms aided in smooth tracking. A targeting chamber mounted atop the gun allowed pinpoint acquisition.

Two such guns were poised on the upper deck, and Gerrard and Tahngarth climbed the stairs to these. They strapped themselves in. Man and minotaur gripped their separate fire controls, moving the barrels experimentally through their full arcs. Both of the guns could shoot forty-five degrees past the prow on the opposite side, allowing dual coverage of the whole forward quadrant. They each could also sweep back one hundred twenty degrees on their own sides. Their field of fire overlapped with the guns stationed to port and starboard amidships. There, Fewsteem and Dabis readied themselves. A fifth such gun perched on the tail of the ship, and even now, a certain green fellow climbed stiffly to the controls. Squee had overheard the call to battle stations, and he longed to fire the weapon he stared down at for agonizing hours. A sixth gun was mounted to swivel vertically down from the ship's belly, and a seventh to fire vertically upward from the center of the main deck.

"Whatever their other faults," Gerrard called over his shoulder to Tahngarth on the upper deck, "Phyrexians certainly know their weaponry."

Checking his range finder, Tahngarth replied in impressive deadpan. "I've never before seen a machine so worthy of my . . . adoration."

Fewsteem and Dabis, amidships, were similarly delighted.

"Strap in, boys," came the voice of Sisay from the speaking tubes. Gerrard glanced toward the bridge's windows to see her standing at the ship's helm. She waved. Through the tube came her voice. "Hanna's plotting our course. As soon as she's got it—"

The ship rumbled eagerly, surging higher up from the smoldering floor of the hangar. Intakes on either side dragged in long draughts of air. Steady and humming, the ship released a blast of fire.

Laughter filled the tubes. Then came Hanna's voice. "Sorry about that. We've got lots more power—" She too was interrupted as the prow of the ship swung suddenly about, pivoting on its central axis. *Weatherlight* swung in line with the caved-in passage.

"And she's more maneuverable," Sisay explained. "Everybody, hang on until we've got the feel of the ship."

"Hang on, strap in, and draw a bead on that rockslide," Gerrard ordered.

"Right, Commander," came Fewsteem's and Dabis's unison reply in the tubes.

"Take us in steady, Captain, a hundred yards from the cave-in," Gerrard said. "Karn, shunt all auxiliary power to the forward guns."

Though there came no response from the engine room, sudden heat filled the footwells. Fire crawled within the manifold conduits.

Weatherlight lifted smoothly above a ruined goblin skiff and then coursed down a corridor among smoldering hulks. She slid easily into place before the landslide and shivered to a gentle halt.

"Train guns. Prepare fire."

The guns locked in on two axes. Lenses shifted within targeting sights, bringing the rubble wall into precise focus. Within the barrels, mirror arrays aligned for optimal-range targeting. *Weatherlight* held so steady, the crosshairs did not shift a single stone. One by one, indicators flashed, showing synchronous alignment among two . . . three . . . four guns. Manifolds blazed underfoot.

"Fire!"

Four crimson beams awoke within four barrels. They stabbed out and struck rubble. Stone melted to magma, sand to boiling glass. Liquid rock gushed downward. A hole opened in the side of the rockslide. Its edges were fused together by stellar heat.

"Cut deeper!" Gerrard ordered.

Beams shifted, stabbing farther into the mound. More rock melted and poured away. Stone seemed wax before the beaming eyes of *Weatherlight*. A red river flowed down from the base of the glowing corridor. Steam and smoke rolled up along the ceiling of the cavern. The red walls of the cave dripped killing drops of lava.

"Wait till the walls cool before edging in there," Gerrard shouted above the keen of the guns.

Again, range finders shifted the guns. The final stones melted away. A wave of blue smoke from the main cavern rolled inward, hissing as it passed through the glowing cave.

"Cease fire!" Gerrard ordered.

The four guns sputtered a moment and went dark, streaming their own acrid smoke. The crew gave a cheer.

The passage was wide enough to allow *Weatherlight* through, and the ceiling was cool enough not to drip molten rock on the deck. Through the thick haze of the passage, ship fires were visible in the cavern beyond. Fissures in the ceiling of the main hangar streamed rainwater.

"Take us through, Sisay," Gerrard called. The ship's captain could steer through the tightest spaces. Gerrard smiled ruefully, remembering how at the start of this ordeal, he had steered into the only tree on the horizon. "Once we enter the main cavern, lay in a spiral strafing run around the chamber. Let's finish off this fleet and get a little gunnery practice."

As *Weatherlight* edged into the hot corridor, another cheer went up, echoing from glassy walls.

*   *   *   *   *

Volrath heard that sound. Where he lay, his torso cloven from collarbone to right nipple, he heard. It was a taunting, exultant sound. It meant Gerrard had broken out of the hangar. It also meant that Volrath could safely move.

His rent flesh slowly knitted itself back together.

In truth, Gerrard had not wounded Volrath as horribly as he had seemed to. It was a maiming strike, yes, but not a killing one. Desperate for time to heal that wound, Volrath had used his shape-changing ability to accentuate its appearance. That same ability allowed Volrath rapidly to heal wounds that would kill other men. This laceration would take him an agonizing hour to heal, but at least it wouldn't prove fatal. Volrath had been incapacitated by this cut, and the next stroke would have killed him certainly . . . except that Gerrard had not delivered a next stroke.

Even now, as Volrath realigned ribs and muscles, Gerrard's scorn echoed in his mind. *Hiding in someone else's skin . . . afraid to face me . . . coward . . .*

Volrath struggled to sit up. He couldn't yet. It was just as well. His blood was still crawling back into his veins. Soon he would be able to sit, to walk, to reach his own ship. Gerrard might destroy most of the fleet, but he wouldn't find Volrath's battleship *Recreant*. Volrath would scrape together a crew and reach his ship and fight again.

It was not cowardly to shrink from a battle that could not be won in order to wait for one that could. That was the better part of valor . . . *valor!*

Cowardice? No—valor!

Even in his own mind, the words rang false.

Gerrard had killed him. Gerrard had stolen everything from Volrath. It was only because of cowardice that Volrath had survived. Gerrard had killed him once again.

Gerrard!

Hatred gave Volrath a spine. He formed himself up around it. He needn't worry about cowardice and valor, only about hatred. Hatred would raise him again, and hatred would make Gerrard fall.

CHAPTER 24

All morning, the storm
poured its dark and vengeful
heart on the city. Rain fell in
sheets and aerial rivers. It pounded
paving stones loose and ripped
mortar from walls. It saturated
thatch and shoved the cold, wet
stuff down into rooms below. It
washed away whatever old encrustations once held stone to
stone. In the grip of its fury, Mercadia came to pieces.

The revolution below performed a similar function. Tides of
Ramosans flooded the streets, dragging down Mercadian
guards. Merfolk tangled pearly tridents with metal ones.
Rishadans sent whaling harpoons into the shoulders of raving
giants. A deluge of farmers aback jhovalls poured across mar-

kets, downing cateran enforcers and carrying off the extortion boxes they guarded. Slaves spilled from their pits and sent slavers cascading down into them. Every dry and ancient institution of Mercadian oppression washed away. The masses, who had been mortared together into vast structures that served the state, tumbled apart. No person was preeminent. All were made equal. The society of oppression was razed.

By late morning, though, the storm above and the revolution below had spent their fury. Curtains of rain thinned to misty veils. Swords ceased their slashing. Bodies ceased their bleeding. Dead Kyren littered the ground and live ones went to ground. Dead giants formed disheveled lines, laid out by kindred who had joined the revolution.

Was this justice, though? In the waning moments of the battle, it seemed the revolutionaries had only reversed the hierarchy of oppression, exalting the lowly and humbling the exalted. Such impulses initially feel like justice, but they are only vengeance. Over time, vengeance hardens into vendetta, and vendetta into tyranny.

It was a dangerous moment for the revolution. Everyone sensed it. The old vicious monster was dead, slain by a new monster who could prove twice as bad.

Heroes rose to cage the beast. Atalla rode his bounding jhovall to the rubbish wall to stop a mass execution of Mercadian guards. Lahaime marched his rebels to the upper market to quell rampant looting. Cho-Manno sent his water wizards to save merfolk from fires that ate away block after block. Orim tended citizens beaten by their own families and friends and neighbors, who sought to settle old scores by turning revolution to riot.

In destroying their ancient oppressors, the oppressed people had ceased to be. They lost their single defining characteristic and turned upon each other. So vicious and voracious was this new monster that it ate itself away from the inside out.

Hatred is no fit spine for heroes or nations.

"Cho-Manno! We have to do something!" Orim shouted desperately where she knelt beside a dying man. The white-haired fellow had been stabbed by his own grandson, the one he had willed everything to. Orim had done her best to cleanse and close the wound, but the old man's guts had been multiply severed. Death by sepsis was inevitable. "The people are killing each other! You must speak to them!"

The leader of the Cho-Arrim stood silhouetted against cloudy skies. His coin-braided hair dripped rainwater on strong brown shoulders, and his once-grand robe hung bedraggled. He stared down from a rise in the tower garden. He had established his command center here amid slender trees. Skyscouts and warriors came and went below, dispatched on missions of mercy.

"My people already do all they can to save the city," Cho-Manno said with quiet helplessness.

"Speak to the rest of them!" Orim said as the old man breathed his last. Giving a ragged sigh, she sat back on her heels. "Not just the Cho-Arrim. Speak to the Mercadians, the Rishadans, the Saprazzans—all these people must be your people now."

"I do not even speak their languages. You speak to them."

Orim shook her head. "They will not listen to me. I am not even from this world." She blinked blearily, thoughts retreating inward. "But were you to truth-speak with me, you would know all their languages. You could speak your thoughts in my words."

Cho-Manno heaved a sad breath. "It brings you such pain."

"This is worse," she said, flinging her hands out toward the rioting city. "This is worse."

The leader of the Cho-Arrim caught her hand in his strong grip and lifted Orim to her feet. He brought her to stand before him and released her fingers.

"Are you sure of this?" he asked gravely.

Orim's eyes were rimmed with tears as she said, "If there is no Uniter, perhaps you and I must become the Uniter. We must be united to bring the people together."

Cho-Manno nodded. He gazed deeply into her eyes. A gentle chant began on his lips. It tangled with the sharp air of the dissipating storm.

The song entered Orim's ears and washed away all else. She had been braced for agony, but it did not come. There was no stark violation, no bursting open of hidden memories. The true-speaking chant flowed into Orim like a healing stream. When last Cho-Manno had suffused her, he had sought scenes of murder and treachery. Now he sought only peace and beauty, truth and life. His thoughts didn't rifle through hers, stripping away barriers, but caught hers up in a glad dance. Together their minds mingled and turned and stepped and turned. . . .

Cho-Manno's entire life poured into Orim's consciousness. She felt his joy at seeing her again. She knew his resolve in riding the storm clouds to the city. Her heart was swelled with his courage as the revolution began, and was quelled with his regret as the victorious people turned to slaying each other. He felt no more than that, defeat and despair.

Orim felt more, though. Into Cho-Manno's aching emptiness flowed her warm, bright hope. It changed him. It renewed him, and with it came the Mercadian words he needed to convey hope to the hopeless city. The lovers' minds remained entwined in dance as Cho-Manno spoke. A simple spell carried the words out into the mists and clouds above, filling the whole of Mercadia with Cho-Manno's voice.

"My people, let the killing be done. The lambs have slain the wolves. Let us not become the wolves ourselves. Let the killing be done. . . ."

His words echoed prophetically through the city. Riots and executions and atrocities paused, if only in amazement.

He repeated the words in the tongue of the Saprazzans and the Cho-Arrim, and then went on.

"We came here to fight for justice, and we have won it. Let us fight no longer, or we will win back injustice."

Those thoughts echoed not only in streets, but in minds. Blades ceased cutting the air, lest they sever the words that lingered there.

"We came here seeking more than justice. We came seeking a Uniter. Old myths mixed with new hopes to make us believe that Ramos soared in fire across the sky, that he brought new children among the old. These new children gathered his soul and mind and body together, his spirit and heart and bones to resurrect him, to raise the Uniter. We flocked here to rally behind Ramos, to throw out evil, and be borne into a new world. We came here seeking a Uniter, but we found none."

A new strain of doubt had entered Cho-Manno's hopeful words. A lesser man would have feared to speak such words to mobs on the verge of riot, but Cho-Manno did not plant doubt in their minds. He merely expressed what already lurked there. His words struck all the deeper for it.

"Perhaps we can blame our ancient foes—nobles, Kyren, Phyrexians. Perhaps they have prevented the Uniter from rising. Rumors tell they captured Ramos—soul, mind, and body—to enslave or destroy him. Perhaps they have, and we fight each other in despair, believing we can never be one."

Trident hafts grew sweaty in the hands that held them. Rebels and farmers, pirates and merfolk stared up toward the tower in wonder that a man could so honestly speak the doubts that plagued them all.

"Or perhaps we should blame the old myths and the new hopes. They had the power to raise us and bring us here, but they did not have the power to raise the Uniter. There is a word for stories that tickle the heart of truth without ever grasping it. Lies. Perhaps we should blame the old myths and new hopes and brand them lies. After all, we must lay the blame somewhere—in foes, in lies . . . or in ourselves—"

Darkness came over every face. Sword tips grounded themselves in the soil—not in hope for peace but in the hopelessness of war.

"—Unless there is no blame to lay. We say the Uniter has not risen, but here we are, united. We say Ramos has not driven evil from Mercadia, but evil is driven out. We say the old stories have not come true, but they have come true. Ramos the Uniter has risen, and brought us together, and driven out evil, and set us on the threshold of a brighter world. We need only recognize that all this has happened. We need only gratefully, reverently step across that threshold."

Tears stood in many eyes. Tears of hope and despair. Cho-Manno's words were true—they all felt it—but truth was insufficient.

Truth is never as quick and sure as tyranny, and the tyranny of the mob is the surest and quickest of all.

A cool hand touched Orim's forehead. She opened her eyes. Cho-Manno spoke. "They will not listen. We cannot save them."

Tears streamed down Orim's cheeks. She embraced him. "Then we all are doomed—"

A sudden, shrieking thunder interrupted her words. She looked up. The sky split in two. A god shot through the air—a fiery body with angel wings and a throat that sang as loudly and gloriously as a heavenly choir.

All Mercadia fell to its knees. Even Cho-Manno dropped down.

Orim would have too, except that she had ridden in the belly of that god and knew it to be merely a ship. "*Weatherlight!*"

She seemed the only one to recognize the ship.

"Ramos . . . Ramos . . . Ramos . . . !" Every last creature—

Mercadian, Cho-Arrim, Saprazzan, Rishadan; giant, boar-man, griffin, goblin—knelt where they were and chanted the name of their god. ". . . Ramos . . . Ramos . . . Ramos . . . !"

Orim only stood, shaking her head in wonder. *Weatherlight* was beautiful and powerful in flight, grander than she had ever been, but she was only a ship. She was no god. Still, what did it matter? People needed gods. Better that they find them in old legends and flying machines than in tyrants and Phyrexians.

The chants suddenly ceased. An audible cry of dread came from the city streets. It formed itself into a new word—the name of a very old god. "Orhop!"

"Orhop?" Orim muttered in wonder. It was the name of Ramos's evil brother god—Ramos and Orhop, Urza and Mishra, Gerrard and . . .

Orim hissed as she saw the second ship—a Phyrexian ship, and she realized the one man who could be at its helm. "Volrath!"

At last, Orim went to her knees.

The Phyrexian ship, hoary in its huge magnificence, vaulted in the wake of *Weatherlight*. Atop the scream of its engines came the crackling sound of ray cannons unloading on the craft.

"Volrath . . ."

* * * * *

"We can't shake it!" Sisay's voice echoed urgently through the speaking tube. "The ship's just as fast as *Weatherlight*, twice as big, and has three times the firepower!"

"Outmaneuver!" Gerrard shouted back, clinging to the barrel of his ray cannon as wind ripped past him. "Turn broadside so we can draw a bead!"

"Hang on!"

Weatherlight sloughed suddenly sideways, air spilling across the deck. The Phyrexian ship came into view, just fore of *Weatherlight*'s port wing.

Beneath a breaking wrack of cloud, the ship seemed a soaring dragon skull. Its bridge was a sloping brainpan, its pilot a sinus bone between gaping eye sockets. From jutting tusks along what would have been the jaw of the thing, twin bolts of power emerged. They raked across the main deck of *Weatherlight*, vaporizing a section of rail.

Gerrard squeezed off a pair of blasts. The shots bounded past *Weatherlight*'s wing and cracked through the hull of the Phyrexian ship. Black smoke belched out, and debris fell, but the ship came on, heedless. It hurtled through the skies, intent on ramming *Weatherlight* broadside.

"Get us out of here!" Gerrard shouted.

Weatherlight leaped, surging from the space just as the larger ship soared through it. Glancing aft, Gerrard made out the ship's name—*Recreant*—and glimpsed a very familiar face at the helm.

"He's alive? Volrath's alive?"

Bolts lashed out from *Recreant* toward *Weatherlight*'s unprotected stern.

Almost unprotected. The stern ray cannon surged with sudden life. A certain green fellow flung ravening rounds aft. With the percussion of great hammers, blasts struck the Phyrexian beams. Energy tangled and riled and exploded in midair. A few of the goblin's charges even won through, striking *Recreant*'s center sail and ripping a wide hole in it.

Gerrard let out a whoop. "Nice shooting, Squee!"

Weatherlight surged out away from its attacker.

Recreant's batteries followed where its hull could not. Cannon fire ripped the air all around.

"It's no good!" Gerrard shouted. "They've got multiple guns on every side. As long as they're aft, only Squee can return fire."

Worse, *Recreant* was damnably agile. It banked violently and quickly closed the space, cannons blazing all the while.

"Fast, agile, deadly," Sisay shouted through the tubes. "What now, Commander?"

"Climb!" Gerrard replied. "Make Volrath haul that extra weight into the sky."

No sooner were the words spoken than *Weatherlight*'s prow swooped up toward the raveling clouds. Her stern swung down toward the muddy desert below. Engines surged. Intakes roared. Fire shot in twin columns out the rear of the ship. Squee gave his own whoop, watching the blaze. *Weatherlight* vaulted into the sky with the eager speed of a heaven-bound soul. Her wings flung clouds away from the lemon sky and the beaming sun.

Recreant followed. It clung tenaciously to its prey, losing little ground despite its vast bulk. At least the furious ascent weakened the blasts from its cannons. Auxiliary power was diverted to the engines. The cannon rays still blistered paint and flash burned fabric, but no longer did they vaporize wood. Doggedly, the Phyrexian ship climbed.

Gerrard gazed back, seeing his brother's mutilated figure, gripping the helm in rage. In ancient days, Mishra had been similarly mutilated, warped into a Phyrexian. Urza destroyed his brother in revulsion. It was strange how history repeated itself. Would this day end like that day? No. Gerrard's anger was gone. He no longer hated his brother. He felt only sadness. He would kill Volrath not in fury but in mercy.

"Divert all power to Squee's gun. Cut engines," Gerrard ordered.

"What?" came the incredulous response through the tube.

"Divert all power to Squee's gun and cut engines."

"We'll fall from the sky. He'll ram us."

"No. We'll ram him."

Reluctantly—"Aye, Commander."

There was sudden silence. The roar of *Weatherlight*'s

power plant ceased. Air stilled in the intakes. Even the wind that had raged over the bow grew calm.

Weatherlight hung for an instant in air, a pickax hovering before it falls.

In the hush, only Squee's gun spoke. It unloaded bolts so hot they shot clear through *Recreant*.

Then *Weatherlight* fell. Its long, strong stern pierced the bridge, shattering glass and helm. Volrath shrieked and dodged aside before it could slay him. The stern drove deeper into the ship and might have gotten mired but for Squee's cannon fire. Bolts of white-hot energy ripped away wood, metal, crystal—all. Nothing remained to foul *Weatherlight*'s stern.

In moments, the aft of *Recreant* was completely vaporized and with it a hundred tons of engine. Only the prow of the ship survived. It tumbled away, with Volrath clutching its severed hull.

"Engage engine!" Gerrard shouted. "Full power!"

Gerrard's command was ended by the roar of *Weatherlight*'s power core. The great ship pulled from its listing dive and rose again. Intakes filled with air, and foils hoisted the vessel toward the sun.

"Where to, Commander?" Sisay said happily.

"Take her up higher," Gerrard replied, staring over the rail at the plummeting wreckage that held his brother. "There's another ship approaching the city. Prepare a diving attack!"

*　　*　　*　　*　　*

Gerrard had done it, again. Gerrard had killed him again. Volrath knew he should die this time. It would be cowardly not to. He was utterly defeated. To live on now would be to live on as a worm. That would be a miserable life.

It would be a life, though—a life Volrath could endure.

Even as the prow of his battleship plunged in smoky ruin, Volrath clawed his way into his personal quarters. All was in disarray, tumbling loose in a deadly hail—but not the portal mechanism. It was fastened to the wall, behind a locked hatch.

Despite the chaos all around, despite the plunging death below and the utter defeat above, Volrath calmly worked the lock and opened the hatch.

Afraid to face me . . . coward . . .

They were no longer his brothers' words. Now they were Volrath's own.

He stepped into the portal device. That single simple movement took him out of death, out of Mercadia. He returned, a whipped dog, to his throne on Rath.

* * * * *

Orim had watched the two ships climb into the sun. Gerrard and Volrath . . . Urza and Mishra . . . Ramos and Orhop—all were overlaid in her mind as the vessels disappeared in the radiant sun.

The Separi story had told it all—two brothers battling each other, tearing down hunks of the sky to slay each other. . . . But that story had ended in devastation and death. How would this one end?

Cho-Manno pointed to a tiny meteor that streamed smoke as it tumbled down across the eastern sky. It was too small to have been even one of the ships, let alone both. "What is it? Do you suppose your friends—?"

"No," Orim said with a finality she did not feel. She struggled to see some sign of *Weatherlight* against the beaming sun. "No, it can't be."

All this while Orim had resented the intrusion of Gerrard and the crew in her new life. Now, faced with the possibility they were gone, she was staggered. As much as she loved Cho-Manno, as much as the Cho-Arrim had changed her life, her life still lay aboard *Weatherlight*.

"I don't know what that smoking thing is, but it's not them." She watched the spinning wreckage impact on the distant plains and then peered back toward the sun, where the warring gods had disappeared. "It wasn't them."

"What is that?" Cho-Manno wondered, pointing out another form behind them. It was much larger than the smoking wreck, and it approached from the west. "A ship?"

"That's them," Orim said hopefully even before she caught sight of the object. As soon as she saw it—metallic wings of gold shimmering with each vast stroke—she knew the thing was not *Weatherlight*. "No . . . that's not them. It must be another . . . another Phyrexian ship. . . ."

It was huge, and it grew larger every moment. Its metal frame was undeniable, its power and speed inescapable. Even from this distance, its Phyrexian design shone clear. Where was *Weatherlight*? What defense could the city have except *Weatherlight*? Everything the rebels had accomplished today would be undone by that singular ship.

Except that it wasn't a ship—too lithe, too living. The thing flew with surges of its metal wings. Before it, a slender neck coiled, and behind it, a lashing tail.

"A dragon engine!" Orim said, astonished.

Cho-Manno stared up in wonder. A smile spread beautifully across his face. "The metallic serpent! Ramos and Orhop fought once again in the sky, though this time, they were united into this creature—into the Uniter! For eons, this metal serpent has filled the dreams of my people!"

Orim stared upward, nodding absently.

It could not have been true. Gerrard and Volrath could never have been united, just as Dominaria and Phyrexia could never become a whole. One would destroy the other. For these people, though, it was true. For them, the evil unleashed by Urza and Mishra was at last ended. Ramos and

Orhop had been reconciled, and the dragon engine—the Uniter—was the symbol of that reunion. Evil had been driven out and the people of Mercadia brought together. It was all true. Cho-Manno's myth had no fact but all truth.

"Yes, Cho-Manno. The Uniter has come," Orim said in joy.

The enormous, beautiful, ancient dragon engine circled the city once, looking for a place to land. It spread its wings and settled lightly in the garden beside the tower. It folded metal mesh and stared down. Before it bowed Saprazzan merfolk, Rishadan pirates, Cho-Arrim warriors . . .

In a voice as ancient as the races, in a dialect as old as Urza and Mishra, the dragon engine spoke, "Children of Ramos, your protector has returned."

* * * * *

Two days hence, Gerrard and Orim stood on the distant plains and gazed up at the looming mountain.

Once Gerrard had realized it was the dragon engine, Ramos, below and not another Phyrexian ship, he had called off the diving attack. Instead, *Weatherlight* had risen high into the sky to slip away unnoticed. Better that the folk of Mercadia think their deliverer a dragon engine rather than *Weatherlight*. Gerrard had just gotten his ship back, and he wasn't about to sacrifice it again. Once *Weatherlight* had landed in the distant plains, Gerrard had sent Fewsteem and Dabis to the city to gather Orim and the rest of the crew and buy provisions for the ship. Meanwhile, Gerrard, Hanna, Tahngarth, Karn, and Squee repaired the battle-scarred vessel. Fewsteem and Dabis had returned from Mercadia with every surviving member of the crew, three cartloads of supplies, and a pair of dignitaries.

Beside Gerrard and Orim this morning stood Cho-Manno of the Cho-Arrim and Atalla, the newly elected Warden of Plains Farmers. Though *Weatherlight* hovered to one side, ready to depart, none of the four watched it. All gazed toward the strange, inverted mountain of Mercadia.

At length, Gerrard asked Cho-Manno, "What will you do now?"

Orim translated the question and the reply.

"We will work to join forest, mountain, plains, and sea—to make them allies instead of enemies. Perhaps in time we can find a way to unite all the peoples of this world. Until then, I'm content to heal the wounds the Mercadian nobles and their Kyren masters inflicted."

"What have you done with the goblins?"

"Most of them perished in the uprising. Some few were captured. We will take them far from here to where another ridge of mountains rises in the west. There, perhaps they can make a home for themselves. But we will not allow them near Mercadia for a long time." Cho-Manno smiled. "Some things about Mercadia we will not change, I think. It will always be a place of buying and selling. But we will buy and sell goods, not souls, and with coin, not treachery."

He looked at the ship hovering above them and sighed. When he spoke next, the words were for Orim alone.

"I understand that you must leave, chavala. Your place is among these fine people, on this ship that has brought the Uniter to our world. This ship has battles yet to fight in defense of your own world, battles that you must aid in. Even so, I wish you would stay. I love you. Every day, I will think of you. When the battles for your world are done—when your Ramos and Orhop are united and the evil is driven out—return here to me. I will be waiting."

She nodded, a tear forming in her eye. "Of course I will, Cho-Manno. I love you."

Gerrard asked, "What did he say?"

Smiling through her sadness, Orim replied, "He said that my destiny lies with *Weatherlight* for a time, but that I will return to him. This he has foreseen."

When she translated the question, Cho-Manno drew from his robe a small vial. He dripped a few drops of clear water onto his palm. Then he lifted his hand and touched Gerrard's forehead.

The Benalian felt a small, cold shock.

Cho-Manno withdrew his hand. "This," he said, and Orim relayed the words, "is water from the Navel of the World. Of this, Orim may have spoken to you. I do not know your destiny, Gerrard. Your future stands at a place where many paths cross, and I cannot see which way you will take. But in dark moments, think of the Navel of the World, and you will find comfort."

"I will. Thank you," Gerrard said. He turned toward Atalla. "And what of you? I understand your courage has earned you enough money for your own flying ship."

Atalla flashed a ready smile, and he shrugged. "I'd rather use the money to help the farm. With the coming reforms, we should be able to bring back the forest and reintroduce water to the plains. With money, hard work, and courage, we can turn these dust flats into rich farmland."

Gerrard laughed. "And I thought you were so much like me—an adventurer at heart."

"I am," Atalla replied without guile. "I just choose to find my adventure here."

"Excellent," Gerrard said, extending his hand.

Atalla looked puzzled for a moment, and then took his hand. Cho-Manno added his grip, and Orim hers. For a moment they stood still and silent.

Gerrard broke away. He turned and grasped a rope that dangled from *Weatherlight*'s rail. With an easy, hand-over-hand motion, he drew himself up onto the deck of *Weatherlight*.

Orim lifted her hand as well. With a single, lingering kiss, she bid farewell to Cho-Manno. Turning, she grasped the rope and rose with the same rapid ease as Gerrard. She climbed to the deck next to him. Side by side, they lifted their hands in a gesture of farewell to the two figures standing below.

"Well, I had best get to the sickbay," Orim said, her voice heavy with regret. "Squee is still not fully recovered from his ordeal."

"Or perhaps he's milking it for all it's worth." Gerrard chuckled. He noticed Orim's tears. "Ah, well, he's earned it."

She gave a sad smile and said nothing, only staring down toward Cho-Manno.

"You will return," Gerrard said seriously. "I have foreseen it."

Orim nodded. "Thanks." With a last look, she strode toward sickbay.

Gerrard meanwhile made his way to the bridge. As he entered, Hanna smiled from her place at the navigation desk. At the helm, Sisay gave a brief nod. Tahngarth lurked nearby.

Gerrard nodded. "Let's go."

Sisay spoke into the tube, "Full ahead, Karn. Stand by to planeshift."

"Take us home, Sisay," Gerrard said. "Take us to Dominaria."

*   *   *   *   *

Atalla watched the great ship slowly lift away from the hillside. It shrank as it accelerated. The air before it seemed to shimmer and bend. Then, as smoothly as a fish gliding through a still pool, *Weatherlight* disappeared into the clear heavens, which closed behind it with a boom.

Atalla smiled and remembered the night when he first saw the ship that flew.

Get the story behind the world's best-selling game.

The Brothers' War

Artifacts Cycle Book I

Jeff Grubb

It is a time of conflict. Titanic dragon engines scar and twist the very landscape of the planet. The final battle will sink continents and shake the skies, as two brothers struggle for supremacy on the continent of Terisiare.
And one alone survives.

Planeswalker

Artifacts Cycle Book II

Lynn Abbey

Urza, survivor of the Brothers' War, feels the spark of a planeswalker ignite within him. But as he strides across the planes of Dominia™, a loyal companion seeks to free him from an obsession that threatens to turn to madness. Only she can rescue him from despair and guilt.
Only she can help him fulfill his destiny.

Time Streams

Artifacts Cycle Book III

J. Robert King

From a remote island in Dominaria thousands of years after the Brothers' War, Urza tries to right the wrongs he and his brother perpetrated against their homeland. His task is immense, and his enemies are strong. Only a mighty weapon can turn the balance of history.

Bloodlines

Artifacts Cycle Book IV

Loren L. Coleman

Urza's weapon lacks but one component: a human hand to guide it. As the centuries slowly pass, he patiently perfects his plans, waiting for the right moment—
and the right heir.
The heir to his legacy.

Lost Empires

In nooks and crannies of the FORGOTTEN REALMS® setting, explorers search out hidden secrets of long-dead civilizations, secrets that bear promises and perils for present-day Faerûn.

The Lost Library of Cormanthyr
Mel Odom

Is it just a myth? Or does it still stand somewhere in the most ancient corners of Faerûn? An intrepid human explorer sets out to find the truth and encounters an undying avenger, determined to protect the secrets of the ancient elven empire of Cormanthyr.

Faces of Deception
Troy Denning

Hidden from his powerful family's enemies behind the hideous mask of his own face, Atreus of Erlkazar seeks his salvation on an impossible mission. Driven by the goddess of beauty to find a way past his own flesh, he must travel to the ancient valleys of the enigmatic Utter East.

Star of Cursrah
Clayton Emery

The Protector crawls forth, the shade of a dead city whose rulers refuse to die, and young companions in two distant epochs learn of a dreadful destiny they cannot escape.

From the pen of *Ed Greenwood* . . .

Stories of the Seven Sisters

Widespread and many-tentacled is the evil that threatens Faerûn. Before its heart can be found, all of the Seven Sisters, Chosen of the goddess Mystra, will play a part . . . and all too much blood will be spilled.

The Temptation of Elminster

The third book in the epic history of the greatest mage in the history of Faerûn.

The young Elminster finds himself apprentice to a new, human mistress—a mistress with her own plans for her young student. Tempted by power, magic, and arcane knowledge, Elminster fights wizard duels and a battle with his own conscience.

Elminster in Myth Drannor

It is the time of the great elven city of Cormanthor, and the mage Elminster enters where no mortal has gone. Among the elves of this great settlement, he learns magic, and when peril threatens, he helps spin the mythal that transforms Cormanthor into . . . Myth Drannor.

Elminster: The Making of a Mage

From his lowly origins, Elminster rises to become the foremost mage in Faerûn, one who will walk the centuries with elf and dwarf, mage and sorceress alike.